Mia Dolan is the star of ITV's *Haunted Homes* and the bestselling author of *The Gift*, *Mia's World* and *Haunted Homes* as well as two other novels: *Rock a Bye Baby* and *Anyone Who Had a Heart*. Her work spans from live shows in front of hundreds of people to helping the police. She also runs a psychic school which helps others develop their own gifts. Mia also won the paranormal celebrity edition of *The Weakest Link*.

She lives on the Isle of Sheppey.

D1078688

Wishing And Hoping

MIA DOLAN

EBURY
PRESS

1 3 5 7 9 10 8 6 4 2

Published in 2010 by Ebury Press, an imprint of Ebury Publishing
A Random House Group Company

Copyright © 2010 by Mia Dolan

Mia Dolan has asserted her right to be identified as the author of this
Work in accordance with the Copyright, Designs and Patents Act 1988

The Random House Group Limited Reg. No. 954009

Addresses for companies within the Random House Group can be found at
www.randomhouse.co.uk

A CIP catalogue record for this book is available from the British Library

The Random House Group Limited supports The Forest Stewardship Council
(FSC®), the leading international forest certification organisation. Our books
carrying the FSC label are printed on FSC® certified paper. FSC is the only forest
certification scheme endorsed by the leading environmental organisations, including
Greenpeace. Our paper procurement policy can be found at
www.randomhouse.co.uk/environment

Typeset in Goudy by Palimpsest Book Production Limited,
Grangemouth, Stirlingshire

Printed and bound by CPI Group (UK) Ltd, Croydon, CR0 4YY

ISBN 9780091948405

To buy books by your favourite authors and register for offers visit
www.randomhouse.co.uk

Acknowledgements

I can't quite believe this is my third novel and, I shouldn't say this myself, but it's my favourite so far.

Of course, a lot of people have been involved in this book, and it takes a team to make a successful series and I would like to thank the following:

Hannah Telfer and Anna Derkacz from sales.

Alex Young and Di Riley from Marketing, Sarah Bennie, Ed Griffiths and Hannah Robinson from publicity.

My Editor, Gillian Green, who never seems put out with working with someone strange like myself.

A special thanks to my family who continue to always put family first, and support me without ever questioning me.

I could never have finished these books without Jeannie Johnson, so big thanks and hugs to you.

And, finally, my biggest thanks to the special man in my life: Craig Darroch. It's so nice to be loved and never judged, and to be picked up no matter how many times I fall down.

I dedicate this book to Francesca Dolan, the golden gift that Peter left us.

Chapter One

1969

There were sparks and lightning and Michael was in trouble. She smelled something burning. She saw someone blind and, worst of all, she found herself parted from her husband.

'No!'

Marcie Jones sat bolt upright in bed gasping for breath and drenched in sweat.

Her husband lay beside her and he stirred himself awake, his voice groggy and confused at being disturbed.

'Marcie? What is it? Were you having a nightmare?'

Resting her hand on her chest she felt her racing heart. 'I thought I heard Aran crying,' she lied, unwilling to admit to him that he was right, that she had indeed been dreaming and the dream had seemed so real.

Aran was their son and only a few months old, a brother for Joanna, who wasn't Michael's child though he had raised her as his own. When Joanna had been born Marcie was a single mum, Marcie Brooks rather than the respectable Mrs Michael Jones. Joanna's father had been Marcie's first love, Johnnie, who had been killed in a road accident before he could make good on his promise to marry her.

Raising himself on one elbow, her husband strained to hear their son. There was no crying, no sound at all. There never had been.

'No,' he said, shaking his head. 'I can't hear anything.'

Marcie gave a short, light laugh. 'I must be hearing things. He's such a good kid,' she said as she snuggled herself back beneath the bedclothes and hugged her husband's warm body.

'Takes after his dad,' said Michael.

If Michael could have seen her expression he would have realised that Marcie had been lying about having heard the baby crying.

Marcie laughed again, though more relaxed, the dream behind her.

'Get some sleep,' he murmured sleepily, stroking her arm as he closed his eyes. 'We've got a long day tomorrow.'

She lay there listening to his breathing as it softened into sleep, half afraid to go back to sleep herself in case the dream returned. For four nights now she'd had that same dream and was convinced it was some kind of warning, a foretaste of things to come. Up until now she'd never admitted – even to herself – that she may have inherited her grandmother's gift for seeing things other people could not see. Michael might think she was a little touched if she did. In time things might change, but for now . . .

She looked at her husband, so peacefully asleep. She loved him and was very proud of him.

Tomorrow night would see the official opening of Michael's first nightclub, the Blue Genie. Marcie was to flick the switch that would turn on the neon light above the door. The neon depicted a blue genie rising out of a brass lamp. Like moths to a flame, the customers would be drawn by its bright blue gleam and the female – and very sexy – genie.

Marcie had suggested that it was slightly lurid, but Michael had persisted.

'They're not coming to a church bazaar after all,' he'd said. 'We're not selling apple pies and cups of tea. We're selling a dream, a few hours of fantasy.'

She'd had to agree with him. There would be drinking, gambling and scantily clad hostesses. It was all a little worrying. Her husband would sometimes be there without her, though he insisted they didn't interest him. She trusted him because she had to; they had a family in common. Besides, they really loved each other, didn't they?

'I've only got eyes for you, Marcie. Surely you should know that.'

His words and the look in his eyes had been re-assuring. The concerns were buried at the back of her mind. It wasn't easy to compartmentalise family life and business, but the older she got the more pragmatic she was. Business was business and Michael Jones had done very well for himself. He'd started his business buying up, tidying up and renting out commercial property. To his and everyone else's surprise, he'd found little competition in the commercial property marketplace. Then he'd come across the disused warehouse in Limehouse not far from the river. At one time it had been used to store tea and the old place still smelled of it – or had done until he'd done it up.

Marcie didn't know who'd suggested that he should turn it into a nightclub but suspected her father might have had a hand in it.

'It's a challenge,' Michael had said to her, his eyes shining with excitement.

She'd immediately understood what he meant and kept her mouth tightly closed against the protest that she'd wanted to voice. What Michael was saying was that he was challenging his father and his half-brother, Roberto. He wanted to prove that he was as good as them, even as hard as them. The latter especially troubled her. Michael's father was Victor Camilleri, the notorious gangland boss. Being the bastard son of one of Victor's many mistresses,

Michael had always considered himself second best. It was Roberto who got all the praise, all the affection. Michael always felt like the also-ran, hence this effort to be just as good as they were in their chosen field of operation. Nightclubs!

Her eyes closed despite trying to stay awake. The sleep would be welcome, but returning to the dream would not.

In the dream the sign above the new nightclub had developed a devilish beard, a broad male chest and a cruel expression. In effect the female form had changed into a male one – not a very nice male one.

It also spoke to her. Now what had it said?

The genie in Joanna's favourite storybook always said, 'Your wish is my command.' But in Marcie's dream it was twisted into something else. *Hoping is real. Wishing is fantasy.*

It made her think. She was hoping that Michael's nightclub would be a huge success – just like his commercial properties. She'd told him how proud she was of him. It seemed like he couldn't put a step wrong. They would be the envy of everyone, she'd said to him.

A shadow had crossed his face then and she fancied there was something he wasn't telling her.

'Is anything wrong?'

'Nothing for you to worry about,' he'd said and kissed the tip of her nose.

So she'd pushed the concern to the back of her mind. Michael was capable, and, although he knew some pretty tough characters, he could handle himself. As for wishing – well – she sometimes wished things could have been different in her life: that her mother had never left home, that her father was respectable and that Johnnie, her first love, had never died . . . But then if Johnnie hadn't died, she would never have met Michael. She wouldn't have her precious baby son.

The dream didn't return, though at one point it did seem as though someone whispered something in her ear.

'Face things head on and your wishes could be fulfilled.'

There was also a smell – a hint of engine oil – and a feel of leather. It made her feel better. She slept.

At number ten Endeavour Terrace, in Sheerness on the Isle of Sheppey, Rosa Brooks couldn't sleep. She'd been dreaming about an electrical explosion and someone she loved was close to it.

Having no telephone and the nearest public phone box being at the end of the street, she could not convey her fears to her granddaughter immediately. On the other hand she couldn't just lie there in the darkness mulling her fears over in her mind, so she did what she always did at a time like this.

Swinging her old legs out of bed, she felt with her toes for her slippers, found them and put them on.

Turning the light on might disturb Garth, her 'adopted' nephew. There was another reason for not turning the light on: it would do nothing much to aid her descent. Her eyes were getting bad – very bad.

Luckily she'd lived in the old cottage for many years. She knew its nooks and crannies, which stairs squeaked and how many there were between the top and the bottom.

Familiarity had trained her to know where the kettle was and, by their radiated heat, how hot the coals were in the old iron range.

Out of habit she went to the right hook on the dresser for her cup and the shelf for her saucer.

Once the kettle had boiled and the tea had brewed, she felt for her favourite chair and sat in it, her cup and saucer balanced in one hand.

The tea cooled. She hadn't taken a sip. Vestiges of the dream were still in her mind. They troubled her.

She sighed deeply and heard it echoing from the matching armchair on the other side of the fireplace. There was a sound as though someone heavy was making himself comfortable. Her husband Cyril had always sighed and the springs of the old armchair had always sagged and sang beneath his weight after a hard day at the docks.

'I had a dream,' she said softly. 'I think Marcie is about to have some trouble.'

'And you want to warn her.'

The words her deceased husband spoke were not heard in the usual sense; she *felt* them.

She sat there thinking for a moment. 'I suppose I do, and yet . . .'

'You think that p'rhaps you don't need to. You think she'll know herself?'

Rosa Brooks nodded. 'I think the time has come.'

Someone had tied a huge red bow around the switch that would turn on the neon light of the Blue Genie.

'Your very own nightclub,' Marcie whispered to her husband proudly. He deserved his success – he worked so hard.

Michael smiled back at her. '*Our* nightclub. Just remember that, babe. Everything that's mine is yours too – yours and the kids.'

When he kissed her, his lips were soft and warm on hers. Neither of them cared that everyone was watching them, though if they'd been in private they would have done much more than kissing. That's how it was between them still even after almost two years of marriage; they couldn't get enough of each other.

However, when she looked at the sign, the image from the dream came back intermittently, sending a cold chill down her spine.

She did her best to shake it off, revelling in the moment with more exuberance than she would normally show. She wouldn't let anything spoil this. She wanted everything to go perfectly for Michael's launch.

The staff and invited guests clapped as Marcie stepped forwards to turn on the switch. Her father was standing with them looking on proudly as though his little Marcie had done this all by herself – which wasn't true of course. Michael had already been in the throes of branching out into business when he'd met her. But this one, as he kept telling her, was special. He was going to be a thorn in his father's side and prove that he was a better man than his brother who was presently detained at Her Majesty's pleasure for causing actual bodily harm.

'I'm as good as the Camilleris,' he whispered to her.

'Better,' she whispered back.

Once again shaking off a shiver, Marcie flicked the switch. Everyone looked up as the neon flickered like a gas flame reluctant to ignite. But suddenly there it was; bright blue against the dark red brick of what had been an old tea warehouse. The sharp blue of the neon was reflected in the pavement beneath it, which was still wet from an earlier downpour of rain.

Everything happened so fast. Suddenly the sign sputtered and fizzed, sparks flaring and falling to the pavement.

A cry of alarm rose from the crowd.

Marcie was standing to the side of the sign looking up at it. Michael pulled her back as the sparks showered down on her and a second gasp of amazement went round the crowd.

'You OK?' It was her dad, Tony Brooks, who asked.

Michael answered for her. 'Yeah. She's fine.'

Marcie said nothing and was far from fine. She was looking up at the sign. Earlier the nubile and very female genie had sparkled with erotic cheeriness. Now what looked down at her was dark and slightly charred, similar to the image in her dream.

'It's a bad omen,' somebody said and sparked a rumble of amazed conversation.

Michael turned on them. 'Cut the gossip! It's an electrical fault, that's all.'

The smell of charged electricity hung acrid in the air. Only the more sensitive would have noticed it. Marcie was one of them.

The electrician who had installed the sign shook his head and looked dumbfounded. 'That shouldn't have happened,' he said.

'Accident or deliberate?' growled Michael through clenched teeth.

The electrician shrugged. 'I don't know. It shouldn't have happened.'

Chapter Two

'Hey, Tony. I wanna word with you, me boy.'

Tony Brooks had just come out of the bookies having had a decent win in the 2.15 at Kempton. His intention had been to make his way to his new girlfriend's place and give her a share.

Having a girlfriend had become something of a habit with him. OK, so he had a wife and three kids at home on the Isle of Sheppey. But he worked in London and in London he had a different life. In London he could be Jack the Lad and had the money to get away with it.

Things had gone all right since his daughter Marcie had married Michael Jones, a London lad with the nous and connections to go places.

Marcie was the daughter of his first marriage to Mary. Mary had been the love of his life but he'd always believed that she'd run off with another man when Marcie was only small. Eventually he'd divorced her on the grounds of desertion and married Babs, his second wife and mother of his three youngest kids.

But it had always been Marcie who had been the

apple of his eye and especially so now, seeing as her old man Michael had had the good grace to employ his father-in-law in his blossoming business enterprise and at his brand-new nightclub. Things would continue to go all right – or so he'd thought. That was until he saw Paddy Rafferty sitting in the back of the shiny black Rover. He instantly knew there'd be aggro.

Paddy Rafferty had started his career stealing cars and trading imported goods direct from the docks – literally stuff that had fallen off the back of a lorry or a convenient ship. From there he'd gone into the building trade. Not that he actually built anything himself. He was into importing building labourers from Ireland on the system referred to as 'the lump'. The labourers paid him a portion of their wages – the portion that the taxman never got to see. That was what the lump was: a semi self-employed system contracted to one company, one building firm, via the likes of Paddy Rafferty. Legal thanks to a loophole in the law, it gave Rafferty his basic income. Everything else he did was not nearly so legit and it suited him fine. However, money had failed to make him a better man. He'd been born rough – and rough he would remain.

Paddy curled his finger and beckoned Tony over. Paddy Rafferty was wearing suede gloves. He always wore gloves, even in the summer. It was said that he'd scalded his hands as a child and the skin had never healed. Some said his skin was as smooth as a snake – and purple.

Tony grinned as though he were truly pleased to see the man, when in fact it couldn't be further from the truth. Paddy Rafferty was bad news. Very bad news.

But still, if you run with the hounds . . .

Tony's mouth cracked into a smile. 'Paddy! How are you?' He sauntered over as though he were a man of importance. Inside he was wary. Paddy was not to be trusted.

Leaning on the car door as though he and Paddy were the greatest of chums, he got out his packet of Woodbines. 'Care for a fag?'

Paddy shook his head. He had a thick mane of hair. His complexion was totally at odds with the rumours regarding his hands, pitted as it was like a pink-skinned orange. 'I don't indulge in the habit, Tony. It isn't good for the health so I'm led to understand.'

'Is that so?' Tony was doing his best to sound nonchalant. Inside he was wondering what the fuck Paddy was after. A favour, he supposed. Everybody wanted a favour of good old Tony Brooks, especially now that his daughter was married to one of the Camilleris, albeit Victor's bastard son. The Camilleris were a big noise on the local manor.

Victor Camilleri was trouble, though nothing

compared to the likes of Roderico Parkhouse or the real big fish, Leo Kendal. Kendal was *numero uno* – him and his missus that is. Apparently Leo Kendal's wife was a bit of a looker with a sharp mind and a ruthless streak. Tony had heard all this by hearsay; he'd never met either of them, so he took it on trust.

In the meantime it was Paddy Rafferty who was demanding his attention.

'I wanted to have a little talk with you, me boy,' said Paddy. It wasn't often he adopted such an obviously Irish catchphrase. Despite the flash outfits and rough demeanour, Rafferty could talk upper-crust English with the best of them, depending on what he was likely to make out of it. He could also talk bullshit. Tony decided it was some of the latter he was about to hear.

'I hear your son-in-law's doing very well for himself. That's a nice nightclub he's got going down in Limehouse, though I doubt that the Chinks welcomed him with open arms. It's their territory after all. Has been for years.'

It was true that Limehouse had long been peopled by the Chinese, as a direct result of the opium wars. There were a lot of gambling houses around there, set up in cellars beneath old sugar refineries, and a few opium dens too, but basically there was little trouble. The Chinese did not wish to attract the presence of the police. They preferred to pay them to keep off their backs, and as long as there was no trouble in Limehouse, they got no aggro.

'They don't bother Michael,' said Tony smiling confidently and shaking his head. 'My son-in-law's got a good name round and about,' he added, purposely reminding Rafferty of the fact that they were family. He only just stopped himself from drumming his fingers nervously on the car roof. What was it to Rafferty how Michael was doing?

'That's good to hear, Tony, though I have to say that as the boy's only young he may be in need of some more mature guidance. I have to ask myself, has he really got the experience to be running that nightclub as he is? There are times when a young man is in need of a helping hand, you know, Tony, and, seeing as Victor Camilleri isn't around to guide him, I thought I might offer my services. All legal, of course. It's not so much the nightclub itself, Tony. It's the building. It's an old building and bound to be due for demolition before long. Then what's he going to do? You might like to mention to him that I know some blokes on the local council. If they see that I'm involved with the property there won't be a problem when it comes to redevelopment, know what I mean?'

'I don't know about that,' said Tony slowly, wondering where the hell all this was leading.

He knew nothing about redevelopment, though quite a bit about collecting the rents with menaces from the tenants of rotting Victorian tenements in the East End of London. He used to work collecting rents for Camilleri. The tenants, mostly immigrants, had paid dearly for the privilege of living in the squalor of the overcrowded London slums they'd rented from Camilleri.

Rafferty was putting him in the picture. The more he heard, the more misgivings he had.

'The boy needs a partner with some experience in the building, demolition and development game and I'm his man. Now you tell him from me,' he said, one gloved finger tapping at Tony's shoulder, 'that if he doesn't give me a ring about this, I'll be round to see him and explain what I'm offering in more detail. You got that then, Tony, my boy? You got that?'

Tony felt the tap of Paddy's finger turn to a stab hard enough to bruise him.

Straightening, he watched as Paddy's big black Rover drove off.

He was now in no doubt of where Paddy Rafferty was coming from. The partnership he'd suggested would only be legal as far as the paperwork was concerned. No money would actually change hands – or at least not from Paddy to Michael. Paddy wanted a cut of Michael's Limehouse property but he had no intention of paying for it. It was a glorified protection racket – extortion with menace.

* * *

Down in Sheerness, Rosa Brooks was giving the range a prod with a brass-handled poker.

Suddenly she stood up sharply.

'Anything wrong, Auntie Rosa?'

Garth was sitting at the table layering jam on top of a well-buttered doorstep of bread cut straight from the loaf.

'Nothing,' she said, but it wasn't true. The truth was that the blinder she became the greater her inner sight. She was seeing things more clearly than she ever had and to her mind there could be only one reason for that, a reason she would not voice to anyone, even to Garth who understood so well.

Chapter Three

The neon sign had been mended though it didn't shine as brightly as it had done. Every so often the light shivered as though it had seen a ghost. Despite this the nightclub was a great success from the very first night.

Marcie did not often go there but Michael had to. Running the club was mainly a night-time business so Marcie spent a lot of time with just the kids. Michael offered to hire a nanny so she could go there with him, but Marcie refused, preferring to look after them herself.

So most nights she spent alone, waiting for him to come home. Once the children were in bed she passed time doing chores around the house or watching the brand-new colour television Michael had bought her.

'Funny to see things in colour rather than in black and white; it doesn't seem natural,' she'd remarked.

He'd laughed and pointed out to her that real life was in colour so a colour television was bound to be more natural.

Sally, one of her best friends, had thought her mad

that she hadn't taken up the offer of a nanny. 'You're a fool to let a good-looking bloke like Michael out of your sight. Aren't you afraid that some little tart will get her hooks in him?'

Marcie replied that she was not worried. 'I trust him.'

It didn't mean to say that she didn't sometimes wonder whether he really was where he said he was and doing what he should be doing. But it wasn't often.

The hours until midnight seemed to drag. The hours between her getting into bed and falling asleep went more quickly. Instinctively she always woke up just before he put the key in the lock.

Just as she usually did, Marcie woke up aware that he was home. The room was dark, and when she looked at the illuminated figures on the bedside alarm, she saw that it was three o'clock.

Adjusting her eyes to the darkness and her ears to the silence, she waited for the light to come on in the hallway below or the soft tread of his foot on the first stair.

The house was a bay-windowed semi-detached built in the 1930s that had survived the war and offered them a proper family home away from his business and the more crowded tenements of London's East End. He'd been trying to get her to move to a more palatial house in Richmond, but she'd argued that the kids were settled and that their present home was cosy. A big house in Richmond would be less so, though at times she wondered whether they should make the move. They certainly had the money to do so.

Their neighbours treated them with courtesy rather than friendliness. Warily they eyed the sleek Jaguar parked in the drive and whispered guardedly about the fact that this couple was terribly young to be able to afford such a lovely home.

Michael had already set himself up before Marcie had met him. With a keen mind and the vigour of youth he'd driven himself ever onwards to do better for himself – and to do better than his father, Victor Camilleri.

Just because he owned property and a nightclub didn't mean that Michael was out to all hours all the time. The club had a manager and an agent and a lawyer handled the property portfolio, but still he went out of his way to check them all now and again. Tonight he had gone to the club with some business associates.

The light in the hallway downstairs eventually came on and she heard that first stair creak beneath his weight. The house felt different when he was home. It was as though the very walls themselves were sending her some telepathic message that they'd warmed up. She felt warmer herself once she knew that Michael was back.

She knew that out of habit he'd look in on Aran and Joanna first before coming to bed.

Marcie lay back on her pillow, eyes wide open. This was the best bit of the day – him coming home.

Some women couldn't live with the knowledge that their husband spent three nights a week at a nightclub where hostesses tripped around on four-inch stilettos and strippers danced naked on a floodlit stage. But she loved Michael and, what's more, she trusted him.

Marcie switched on the bedside light as Michael came into the bedroom.

Blinking, he held one hand in front of his face to deflect the sudden glow. 'Do me a favour, turn it off.'

His tie was already loosened and he looked tired. There were dark circles beneath his eyes. His face looked puffy – not as firm as it usually was.

Lying on her side, her head supported on her hand, Marcie eyed him quizzically. Even at this time in the morning, he wasn't usually like this. It was something that had always amused her about him; the time on the clock was of no consequence. If the work was there, then the work got done.

'You look tired. Is something wrong?'

'Nothing that I can't handle.'

He managed a smile, but Marcie wasn't fooled. She'd fallen in love with the gentleness she'd seen in this man and for the fact that he was so different to most of the men she'd known. He didn't smoke and wasn't a great drinker. Neither was he a braggart, which her father could sometimes be. He was a 'steady Eddie' as her father would say. Sometimes she knew very well that what he really meant was boring. But she didn't think Michael was dull. She loved him and hoped it would always be so.

Most times when he came home tired he was still happy. There were always business worries, but he was usually able to put them to one side until the morning. Tonight the concerned look was more weighty, as though he didn't know what to do about it.

She reached out for him. 'Michael? What's wrong?'

Shaking his head, he sat down on the edge of the bed and covered his face with both hands. 'Nothing you can do anything about,' he murmured through his fingers.

Her hand stroked his shoulder. 'Michael, we're married. Your problems are my problems.'

It came as a complete surprise when he shrugged away her gentle touch, a touch meant to reassure and to soothe.

'For Christ's sake, stop fucking nagging me!'

Shocked, Marcie drew back her hand, clenching her fingers into a fist. Her heart beat wildly, its thudding echoing inside her head.

Michael had never spoken to her like this before. OK, they hadn't known each other for much more than three years, but it was long enough so she could say with her hand on her heart that he'd never lost his temper.

'I wasn't nagging you,' she responded, unable to stop the hurt from filtering into her voice. 'I care when you're unhappy or worried.'

'Well don't,' he shouted, flinging himself up from the edge of the bed.

The sound of Aran crying filtered through from the other room.

Now it was Marcie's turn to be angry. 'Well that was bloody clever of you, wasn't it?'

She flung the bedclothes back, got out of bed and stormed out, mad at him for being angry with her and at herself for feeling so hurt, for needing him so much.

It angered her even more to see Aran's little face screwed up and red. Clasping his warm body against hers, she cooed sweet words against the side of his head. 'Never mind, my little precious. Never mind. It was just that nasty old Daddy shouting at Mummy.'

Reassured, the tautness left the baby's body and the softness of sleep and being secure returned.

She suddenly became aware that she was not alone. Michael was standing in the doorway, one arm resting against the frame, the back of his hand against his forehead. His expression was one of remorse.

'I'm sorry.'

'You're working too hard,' she whispered while returning the baby to his cot.

He raked his hand over his chin. The slight stubble that wouldn't now get shaved off until the morning made a rasping sound.

Not for the first time she thought how handsome he was and how lucky she was to be married to him. Heads turned when Michael entered the room. She sometimes wondered whatever he'd seen in her, a small town girl, when he could have had any girl in London or anywhere else for that matter.

His arms pulled her to him so that her head rested against his chest. She wound her arms around him, smelling and feeling the warmth of his body, the slight sweat of a man who was tired and wanted only to sleep.

'I'm sorry,' he said again. 'It's been a hard day.'

'Or even a hard day's night?' she said, hoping to lighten his mood.

'The Beatles have a lot to answer for,' he said immediately understanding that she was trying to cheer him up.

'I wasn't really nagging, was I?' she asked earnestly.

'No. Of course not. You're right. I'm tired. I need a break. We both need a break. How about we take the kids and nip down to see your gran at the weekend? How would that be?'

'Great if the weather holds.'

He hugged her tighter. 'Then that's what we'll do.'

They didn't make love that night, and Marcie had not expected to. She was content to stay in his arms and feel his warmth. In time, once she'd told him how her day had been – which wasn't terribly exciting, being about the kids mostly and the things they'd done – she fell asleep. Michael was home and all was well with her world.

Tired as he was, Michael lay wide awake, the events of the evening going round and round in his head. Nothing could have been worse than that his business should attract the attention of Paddy Rafferty. Marcie's dad had been the first to bring the news.

'What are you gonna do?' he'd asked.

'Tell him to sod off. What the hell do you think I'm going to do?'

Basically that was exactly what he'd done, though in retrospect it didn't seem such a good idea. Playing for time might have made more sense, but Rafferty had brought out the worst in him.

Tony had given Rafferty the message. 'But he won't like it,' he'd warned.

Michael had been unrepentant. 'I don't care. This place is mine and if it does ever get redeveloped, it's my sweat that's gone into the place and my money. I'm certainly not sharing it with the likes of Paddy Rafferty!'

Michael had specifically stayed away from the

places where his father owned clubs and branched out on his own. Now he'd attracted a different problem. Paddy Rafferty had a bad reputation. A day or so later, the ugly man with the pitted complexion who always wore gloves had stood in his office and told him – not asked him, *told* him – that he wanted half of the building housing the nightclub, though not right away.

'With a view to future potential,' he'd said to him, his eyes raking the bare brick walls of Michael's very modern office.

'No chance.'

Paddy had smiled coldly. 'You're in my territory, Mickey, my boy. When the time comes for this place to be redeveloped – which it will do – then you need a partner who knows the ropes. I've got friends in high places . . . the planning department at London City Council, even some politicians. Mark my words, Michael. This place will get redeveloped one day and when it does you'll have earned a fortune. And old Paddy Rafferty will be there to help you. Trust me, Mickey. You'll be in need of a friend – to smooth the way, so to speak.'

Michael's face had darkened and he been barely able to control his anger.

'My name's Michael, not Mickey. And this is London, not a bog in Ireland.' His tone was as uncompromising as his body stance.

Reading him correctly, Paddy's pale watery eyes had seemed to ice over.

'Insults about meself I'll forgive. Insults about Ireland I will not.'

'Stuff you and stuff Ireland! Get out.'

Rafferty glowered, his bottom lip quivering as though in the first stage of rabies and considering what or who to bite.

He pointed a hooked finger. 'I'll give you a few days to make up your mind, Mickey,' Paddy went on, attempting to bring his flaccid lips back into a smile, his eyes glassy and cold. 'By the way, did you know that I knew your mother? That was before Victor got her up the spout with you, of course. I was never that careless as to let any slapper get her hooks into me. But fair dos to the old broad, she was a good lay . . .'

Michael had been sitting behind his desk, Paddy standing in front of it. A steeplechaser couldn't have jumped the desk better. Ordinarily he would have gone round the desk, but Michael was so incensed he leaped up onto the desk top; the second leap took him down on the floor facing Paddy who looked dumbfounded.

The left hook to Paddy's chin was followed by a right. Paddy went down with blood pouring from his mouth and a chip of tooth hanging on his chin.

Paddy's shock was so great that he lay there for a moment as though trying to take it all in. Once it hit, his scowl was deep and the finger that pointed at Michael was like a sword aching for the blood of retribution.

'I'll have you for this, Jones. Damn you, I'll have you for this!'

Pumped up with adrenalin, Michael stood over him. There was no way he was going to take any lip about his mother. No way at all. His attitude towards Rafferty was one of total contempt.

'Oh, yeah,' he'd said, so filled with anger that he totally ignored Tony Brooks shaking his head in warning. 'So how about the gloves come off, hey, Paddy? How about it?'

There was only Tony, Michael, Paddy and one of Paddy's henchmen in the room. All the same there was a stunned silence as Michael whipped off Paddy Rafferty's gloves and they all surveyed the horror beneath.

The skin on Paddy's hands was pink and white and his fingernails were non-existent. The fire that had destroyed his hands had also damaged his ligaments so that his fingers curled in on themselves, like talons and not like hands at all.

Paddy was a legend for protecting his hands, for not allowing anyone to see them. It was rumoured that he even wore his gloves in bed – even to the bathroom.

'Two days, that's all I'm giving you,' Paddy snarled as the man with him helped him to his feet. 'Just two days. After that I'll destroy you.'

After he'd gone, Marcie's father glanced over his shoulder before closing the door. If the circumstances weren't so serious, Michael would have laughed. Tony was acting like James bloody Bond not some small-time crook from the Isle of Sheppey. He was less than cool though. Sweat had broken out over his forehead. James Bond never did that.

'He'll do you,' Tony gasped. 'Not just a bit of a going over, he'll do you personally good and proper. He plays for high stakes, that bloke.'

Michael still hadn't been perturbed – not until he'd been informed that two of their dancers had been cut up, their blood used to write a message on the mirror of their dressing room.

'Two Days.'

Michael had been shocked. OK, he'd expected himself or the club to be a target, but not two of his employees. The girls were – or had been – pretty. He felt responsible. His main worry then was that if he didn't give in Marcie and the kids could be targeted next. He'd told himself not to be foolish, that they lived in a safe suburb where people went to work in the City. Things like that didn't happen in such areas – and Rafferty wouldn't be able to find out their address. Then he'd found a dead cat tied to their front gate. There was no note. There didn't need to be. Paddy Rafferty knew where he lived.

Chapter Four

Rosa Brooks stood at the front door of her cottage. The sun had taken the opportunity to peer out from behind a cloud. The red bricks of her home sparkled with sea salt when the sun was brightest.

Rosa's face was turned in the direction of where her granddaughter Marcie and her husband were unloading their children and baggage for a weekend stay. She hadn't told anyone about her encroaching blindness and she wouldn't tell them now. She'd also sworn Garth to secrecy, treating the event like some kind of game.

'It's a secret,' he'd said.

'Not to be told,' Rosa had warned him. 'Not until it's your birthday.'

As Garth had no idea when his birthday was, it didn't seem much of a problem.

Her old heart had leaped with joy when Father Martin, a likeable young man who had replaced Father Justin O'Flanagan, had come with the news.

'Your granddaughter phoned me,' the young priest had explained.

She'd thanked him accordingly and then engaged

Garth to help her get things ready: the old cot out for the baby, the blankets and sheets to be aired, the bedrooms swept and the old range working flat out to warm the house and cook the roast dinner she intended serving.

Garth had been making paper chains from painted newspaper for Christmas. Tongue hanging from his mouth, he'd concentrated on snipping the pieces of newspaper into the right size strips, then gluing each piece together with glue made from self-raising flour and water. He'd done all the preparations himself and Rosa had left him to it. He'd seen how to do it on a children's TV programme called *Blue Peter*. Rosa hadn't had the heart to tell him that Christmas was still nearly four months away. It kept Garth occupied and happy.

He'd moved in with Rosa shortly after his mother died. It was either that or he would have been institutionalised. Rosa wouldn't countenance that. Although a grown man, Garth was a bit below par, but he didn't deserve to be cut off from the world. He was harmless and sometimes – just sometimes – he was a lot more than that.

Like Rosa Brooks, Garth had something of the psychic about him; not that he was aware of it. Having the mind of an eight-year-old, Garth was unaware that his frequent insights into the future were out of the ordinary for most folk. He accepted everything that happened in his small world.

Rosa had told him that Marcie was coming to stay for the weekend with the children.

'You'll have to help me make the beds and do the shopping,' she'd said to him.

'I'll help. I can do everything. I can be your eyes!'

Rosa carefully composed her face so that her surprise did not show. She'd never given Garth any reason for asking him to go shopping with her, or helping her out around the house. She'd never admitted that she was losing her sight. She'd come to the conclusion that God might have given men reason so they could work things out for themselves, but like the creatures he'd created, God had given Garth instinct, a finely attuned instinct.

The fact that she was losing her sight angered her. What had she done to deserve it? In consolation her insight – her gift – had become more pronounced. But at least she could hear her granddaughter talking to her children and she could still cuddle them.

She heard Marcie speaking to Joanna.

'Go on, Jojo. Go and give your great-gran a hug.'

She heard the four-year-old laughing and her tiny feet tip-tapping up the garden path. Fuzzy and indistinct, the child was a blur of pink face and yellow dress. A pair of hazy arms rose to hug her.

She bent down and hugged the child close. 'Joanna, you are the prettiest little girl in the world.' She closed her eyes and, not for the first time in this past year, she wondered how long she had to enjoy these little things, the simple things that are so taken for granted in day-to-day life. She was growing old and knew her time was near.

'How are you, Gran?'

Her granddaughter hugged her too. She welcomed the feel and warmth of her arms around her and attempted to puff herself out in order that Marcie wouldn't notice just how fragile she'd become, like a small bird that was getting ever smaller.

'Gran, how many cardigans have you got on?' Marcie exclaimed with a laugh.

'You people up in London do not feel the winds blowing in from the North Sea. It is colder here than it is up there. So we wrap up.'

Marcie laughed and said that she'd forgotten, though she wasn't feeling cold at the moment.

Rosa laughed too, confident that her ploy had worked. There was plenty of time to be honest about what was happening to her. But not yet, not until Marcie had got through the ordeal to come and Rosa had to be here for that. She had to help her through it.

Marcie suggested a walk to the pub once they'd eaten and put the kids to bed. She was still worrying that Michael was working too hard, that he needed more leisure time. After all it wasn't as though he was a one-man band. At the last count he employed thirty people including her father.

Getting him away from London and from work was becoming more and more difficult. Even though he trusted his manager, Kevin McGregor, to run things, and even trusted her father, business was never far from his mind.

'Don't even think about it,' she said as they passed the bright red telephone box at the end of the road.

'Ouch,' he said as though she'd kicked him on the shin. But he smiled all the same.

'Dad said something about the police being called in,' she said suddenly.

Michael turned up his coat collar and shrugged himself down into it before answering.

'Did he?'

'What was it about?'

'Oh, just some argument over two of the girls. They decided to leave but were afraid of some blokes hanging around outside.'

'Stage Door Johnnies? Isn't that what they're called?'

'Something like that,' he replied.

She sensed there was something he was not telling her, but that was Michael's way. He tried to protect her from the bad things in life. He still bristled at the fact that he hadn't been there to stop his half-brother,

Roberto, from brutally assaulting her when Marcie had first moved to London. Since their marriage he'd taken it upon himself to wrap her in cotton wool. At first it was nice, but now sometimes it jarred. She didn't need protecting, not now that Roberto was languishing in prison.

Banishing the negative thoughts, she clutched her husband's arm close to her side, glad he was there. The thoughts didn't go away that easily but like a rubber ball kept bouncing around inside her head.

A stiff breeze was keeping the rain at bay, chasing the clouds across the sky and sending sea spray travelling yards through the air.

Marcie's long blonde hair was being whipped round her face. Sometimes she pulled it back, holding it close against her cheek. Sometimes she let it fly because it helped to hide her expression.

What was Michael hiding from her?

It didn't help that Sally had phoned that morning. Marcie had mentioned Michael being a bit distant, a bit too wrapped up in the nightclub. She didn't mention what her father had said about the police.

'As long as he's not wrapped up in the arms of another woman,' Sally had responded chirpily.

Marcie's throat had gone dry. Another woman? She thought of the exotic dancers that used to come to her sewing room. The sewing room had remained closed for the last two years because she'd been busy

with her new husband, the pregnancy and the birth
of her son. The girls were gorgeous. Even the drag
acts were gorgeous once they were dressed in silver
lamé and diamanté.

'Oh, shit,' said Sally suddenly cottoning on to what
she'd just said. 'I didn't really mean that. Not Michael.
He thinks the bloody world of you. Oh no! He won't
stray. You can bet your bottom dollar on that.'

It was never going to be easy to trust someone who
worked in an environment surrounded by scantily
clad beauties and other women who at some stage in
the evening wore nothing at all. But she'd come to
terms with it and Michael had assured her that he
only had eyes for her.

Besides that he had a son and he had great plans
for his son. Nothing could come between him and
his ambitions for Aran.

'Did you hear what happened to Sandra and Polly?'
Sally asked suddenly.

'No. What?'

Marcie listened in silence.

'Don't know who did it,' said Sally. 'But there are
rumours. Might even have been that nutcase, Roberto
Camilleri. Do you know if he's out yet?'

Marcie had turned cold. Now here she was walking
along beside her husband. He wasn't being himself
and she wanted to know why.

'Penny for your thoughts?' she queried softly. He'd

hardly said a word since they'd left her grandmother's cottage except to comment on the sea, the sky and the smell of fish and chips still drifting in from the beach.

'Do you think we're putting her out at all – your grandmother I mean?'

'No. Of course not,' Marcie replied. 'She's always glad to see us. She'll move heaven and earth to fit her family in. That's the way she is. That's the way we all are come to that.'

He surprised her by kissing the top of her head. He was just tall enough to do that when her head was resting on his shoulder.

'She's never brought her bed down into the front room before.'

'Oh, no,' Marcie said breezily. 'She's sleeping on the sofa in there. She told me it was firmer and better for her legs nowadays. She is getting on a bit you know.'

Michael shook his head. 'I went in there by mistake. Her bed's in there.'

Marcie frowned, her thoughts about tackling him about the police coming to the club put behind her. Her grandmother was more important than a night-club any day of the week. 'Are you sure?'

He nodded. 'A double bed with walnut head and footboard. That's her bed, isn't it?'

This was too perplexing for words. Marcie frowned

against her flying hair and the wind blowing it across her face.

'She didn't tell me she'd done that. Garth's up in the attic. We've got my old room and the kids are in the other. That still leaves her room which means . . .'

'That she's sleeping in the front room all the time.'

'And that she's a lot more fragile than I thought,' Marcie murmured.

She might have given it more thought if she hadn't spotted two young lads leaning against the wall outside the pub. They appeared to be arguing over a cigarette.

'Tear it fairly. Half for you, half for me.' The voice was brusque and instantly recognisable.

'Arnold? Archie?'

Their hair tousled, their faces dirty, her two half-brothers were growing up. Their faces beamed when they saw her.

'Hey, Marcie,' said Arnold. 'Got a light?'

Grinning cheekily the two boys stuck the halves of the cigarette into the corners of their mouths.

She asked them what they were doing there

Arnold did a sidelong nod towards the pub door. 'Waitin' for our mam to bring us out two shandies and two packets of crisps. We ain't had no tea. She did promise us.'

It was no secret that her father's second wife was

far from being mother of the year, but things had gone from bad to worse.

'And where's your sister?' Marcie couldn't stop the alarm from rising in her voice. Annie was only a little older than her own Joanna. She'd taken care of the child when she was younger, mainly because Babs had been working in Woolworths.

'With Ethel next door. She plays with her kids then goes to bed with them.'

'You kids had no tea yet? Well, we can't have that, can we?' Michael was already rooting in his trouser pocket. 'Here. Take this. Half a crown each. Get yourself some cod and chips. OK?'

'OK!' said Arnold. His shrill response was accompanied with a loud rumble from his belly.

Archie turned towards the pub door.

'Where do you think you're going,' said Michael getting a good grip on the lad's coat collar.

'In to get a pint,' Archie responded.

Michael jerked him back out onto the pavement. 'You're not old enough.'

'I'll soon be fourteen,' Archie protested.

'That's still not old enough. Come back when you're eighteen. Besides, I gave you that money to you to buy fish and chips not beer. Get on with you. Off with your brother.'

Archie swaggered away, resigned to doing what he was told – though only for now – until Michael's back was turned – until he nipped into the off-licence and got what he wanted there. Or another pub. Archie told himself that he wasn't a kid any more and Marcie had no business ordering him about. He was almost grown up and reckoned he could look after himself.

Marcie was immediately reminded of her father and was saddened. He should be here with them, then perhaps they wouldn't go in the same direction as he had done – a lifetime of petty crime and imprisonment.

'Right,' she exclaimed rolling up her sleeves and swinging her handbag. 'I'm going to have it out with her.'

Michael caught her arm before she had a chance to yank the door to the public bar open. 'Stay cool, Marcie. It's not worth it.'

Marcie could not contain her anger. Michael's intervention wasn't entirely welcome. She cared for her brothers. She cared for her dad too.

'That bitch is in there knocking them back while the kids are farmed out with empty bellies. My dad sends her money for their welfare not so she can knock the booze back.'

It wasn't often she didn't listen to Michael's advice but on this occasion her blood was running fast and hot. She'd never been that close to her stepmother, though things had calmed a while back. But a leopard

never changes its spots, she decided, and in Babs'
case she was spotted all over.

The brass door handle to the public bar was in
need of a polish and sticky beneath her fingers. The
bar smelled of stale beer, men's sweat and the air was
filled with cigarette smoke and the sound of darts
thudding into the board.

If she hadn't spotted the boys, she and Michael
would have gone into the saloon bar for a drink. But
Babs preferred the public bar where the men gathered, and Marcie wanted a word with her.

Babs' raucous laugh could be heard above the
murmur of male conversation so she was easy to find.

Marcie grimaced. Her stepmother was sitting on
a stool at the bar, one leg crossed over the other.
Her skirt was a sliver of a thing, more suited to a
teenager than a thirty-something housewife with
three kids. Her hair was back-combed into a beehive
and her face was rendered pale by virtue of an ample
application of panstick. She was obviously enjoying
herself, with a glass in one hand and a cigarette in
the other. The smoke from the lighted cigarette was
mixing with the beehive. It wasn't impossible to
believe that a swarm of bees might evacuate it at
any moment.

Babs was in her favourite environment, surrounded
by men who were buying her drinks and offering her
cigarettes. In Marcie's opinion it was obvious what

they were after: get her drunk enough and it would be payback time. One of the men was already resting his hand on her thigh. Another was leering at the ample bosoms spilling over the neckline of her low-cut sweater.

Eyes thickly outlined with shiny black liner turned in Marcie's direction. Babs had seen her. The laughter was silenced and crack lines began to appear in the thickly applied make-up.

'Marcie,' she said, attempting to resurrect some semblance of a smile while hitting away the hand creeping up her thigh. On seeing Marcie with her long blonde hair and fresh-faced complexion, the two men leered suggestively. The leers soon disappeared once they saw the look on Michael's face. Seeing their plans were on hold for the moment, they moved further along the bar.

Babs sniffed and pouted as though she were still eighteen years old. She uncrossed her legs and clamped them tightly together.

'I wasn't expecting you this weekend,' Babs said tartly. 'Your dad didn't say you were coming down – but then he wouldn't – I don't get to see much of him at all nowadays. Thought Rosa might have said though.'

Mention of her grandmother pulled Marcie up short from the accusations she'd been going to throw. After all, she was feeling a little guilty that she hadn't visited too much of late.

'Oh. Have you been round to see her?'

Sensing a bout of female sarcasm was about to erupt, Michael murmured that he would get in the drinks.

Babs heard him. 'Port and lemon for me, Michael darling,' she said, swigging back what remained of her drink and handing him the empty glass.

Eyes blazing, Marcie intercepted it and placed it firmly onto the bar with a resounding thump. Luckily the glass was thick enough to stand it. 'Never mind having another port and lemon; why are the boys sitting outside waiting for a packet of crisps? Dad sends you money to look after the kids not to come down here boozing. And who's this woman you've left our Annie with?'

Other people besides Babs looked taken aback by the anger in Marcie's voice. Even her stance was far from being that of a young woman who at one time wouldn't have said boo to a goose. She was livid. Babs had always been free with her favours and too fond of a good time. In times past Marcie had not offered criticism, but she was older now and had kids of her own. Her opinions and reactions had hardened up.

Babs' jaw dropped and she adopted her gravely affronted look. 'That's none of your bloody business. They're my kids, not yours.'

'They're my brothers and sister. I have every right

to know how they're being treated and, anyway, Dad will want to know.'

Babs gave one look before guffawing with loud laughter. 'Your dad will want to know? Well, if he's so bloody concerned about his kids, maybe he should come down and see them a bit more often!'

'He sends you the money,' Marcie pointed out, already smarting at the truth of what Babs had just said. 'He is working up there you know, not seeing the sights!'

'Huh!' Babs exclaimed tossing her head. 'Don't make me laugh. My old man likes his bit of the other and he ain't coming down here to get it from me. And that means only one thing! He's getting it elsewhere.'

Marcie was momentarily taken aback. Tony Brooks was still her father and as a daughter it was hard to believe anything bad of him. She'd thought he'd learned his lesson after he'd almost come a cropper over the last girlfriend Babs had found out about.

Still, she had to put up some kind of defence for her dad's actions.

'That's no excuse for neglecting the kids,' She could feel her face growing hot. OK, her father was no saint, but then neither was Babs.

'Ooow! Lovely,' said Babs, reaching for the drink Michael had paid for and the barman had pushed in her direction.

Marcie grabbed the hand that reached for the drink. 'Answer my question. When was the last time you saw my grandmother?'

Babs gave a small shrug of her shoulders. 'Ooow, I suppose two or three weeks ago.'

'Two or three weeks since you've been round there?'

Marcie could barely control the urge to slap the panstick off her stepmother's face.

Babs blinked like they say rabbits do when they're caught in the headlights of a car. But she pulled herself together.

'Come off it, Marcie. You know how it is between me and Rosa. We're chalk and cheese. Never did like each other very much now did we, girl? She don't like me and I don't like her. Never going to be any different is it? Likely to start bloody World War Three me and 'er. So it's best I stays away. Right?'

'You said you saw her.'

'I did. She was out shopping with the spastic kid – Garth. He always goes out shopping with her.'

'I suppose the boys go round there for a good meal if they want one,' said Marcie.

Babs winced at the same time as smiling, trying to make it seem as though everything was sweetness and light. 'Yeah. They like it round with their gran.'

'And it suits you,' said Marcie accusingly, her fingers tightening over her stepmother's wrist. 'It

suits you to have an old woman look after your kids
so you can pretend to be single again.'

'I might just as well be,' Babs retorted hotly. 'What's
sauce for the goose is sauce for the gander. My old
man's shacked up with some tart up in London and
thinks that I'll be the good little wife and look after
his kids for him. Well, I've got news for him. I've
still got a life to lead and he's not the only fish in
the sea!'

The two blokes who'd been feeling her up were
listening and cheered her on at that.

Marcie scowled in their direction before turning
her temper back to Babs. 'You're not a fresh fish,
Babs. You're an old trout and them two there are
both married old men with faces that look as though
they've been slapped with a frying pan. Prince
Charming they are not! Just look at them, Babs, and
then when you get home tonight take another look
at yourself in the mirror!'

Her stepmother's countenance fell. She hated
being reminded of her age, hated the thought of no
longer being one of the prettiest girls on the island.
Those years were long past, but she hated being
reminded of it.

There had never been any love lost between Marcie
and her stepmother. Marcie could never quite work
out why her father had ever married her – except for
the fact that she was pregnant of course. Tony, being

of the old-fashioned type, had married her. It helped that Babs had resembled a rather overblown version of Brigitte Bardot at the time – all blonde hair, pouting lips and checked gingham dress. Babs was to Sheerness what Elsie Tanner was to Coronation Street; only in her case she was the tart with no heart – none discernible that is. The men came and went – even when she was married.

Babs was not the sort to remain deflated for long. Colour flooded into the pansticked cheeks like cheap rouge. The pouting mouth turned into a snarl.

'Now just you listen 'ere, you little bitch,' shrieked Babs. 'Don't you come in here as though you're bleedin' snowy white and throw the dirt at me! Your old man's left me high and bloody dry and thinks that money is enough to keep me tied to the bleedin' kitchen sink. Well, it's not! I deserve a good time. I deserve to be able to go out and enjoy meself just like he's doin' up in London!'

Sensing some unscheduled entertainment, the customers of the public bar fell to silence. All eyes were on the plump blonde wearing the tight skirt too short for her age and the gorgeous-looking girl with the cool-looking dude with London written all over him.

Marcie felt Michael gently touch her shoulder; he suggested they leave.

'She's not worth the aggro, Marcie. Leave it be.'

Rarely, if ever, had Marcie rounded on him and told him to stay out of it. But she did now. This wasn't about her and her stepmother's mutual dislike; it wasn't even about her father's honour or her grandmother's quality of life. It was about the kids. Marcie loved her own kids and couldn't understand why Babs could so easily neglect her brothers and Annie, seemingly without an ounce of guilt.

Marcie shrugged Michael's hand from her shoulder. She couldn't leave this be. She had to have it out with Babs here and now, but if direct confrontation and a reminder about her duties weren't going to do anything, perhaps a few home truths in front of an audience might help.

'This is my stepmother,' said Marcie playing to the crowd with a sweeping gesture of her arm. 'She has three kids, none of whom have been fed tonight. One of them, the youngest, has been left with a neighbour and the others have been left to fend for themselves. And here she is, in here boozing and acting as though she's love's young dream. And as for you,' she yelled, glaring in the direction of the two men who'd been fawning all over her, 'just imagine if it were your wife and kids. How would you like it, eh? How would you like it?'

Babs' eyes were blazing. 'You bitch! Running me down. At least I had all my kids after I was married. Not like you, you fucking bitch! Not like you!'

Marcie leaped at her, her fingers clawing at the beehive hairdo. It was like grappling with the candyfloss she used to sell to punters on the beach when she'd just left school – only harsher – like wire wool.

Strong hands pulled them apart.

'We're going,' growled Michael.

'No!'

Although she struggled there was no escaping Michael's firm grip. A couple of the blokes in the bar got Babs to her feet after she'd fallen off the stool – partly as a result of Marcie's attack, and partly because she was half cut anyway.

Once they were out on the pavement and the fresh air hit her, Marcie covered her face with her hands and muttered, 'Bitch, bitch, bitch!'

When she uncovered her face, she saw Michael looking up at the sliver of sky that showed between the buildings. He was shaking his head and looking exasperated.

'Let's go away for a peaceful weekend, she says. Let's get away from it all.'

Marcie was immediately overcome with a great sense of regret. This wasn't how things were meant to be at all.

'I'm sorry.' She hung her head and bit her bottom lip, seeking out the right words for a more fitting apology.

Then she hugged Michael's arm and lay her cheek against his shoulder. 'I'm sorry, Michael. It got out of hand, but the boys – Dad will be mortified.'

He looked down at her. 'Then he should be down here looking after them, shouldn't he? I would if they were mine.'

Marcie made no comment. He was right. Without her dad around, Babs fell to pieces. Without her dad around, the kids would run riot. There was no getting away from the fact that a great deal of fault lay with her father. He should be with his wife and family. Something had to be done about it and it would fall to her to tackle him about it. He wouldn't like it. It wouldn't be easy, but sod it! It had to be done.

Paddy Rafferty had slipped Tony Brooks a pony when they'd met up at a West End nightclub, a haunt of high-class whores and low-class politicians.

Normally Tony wouldn't have touched it, but loyalty to his son-in-law flew out of the window after a few bevvies. It was hard to say no when a gorgeous woman was hanging on to his arm asking him what he was going to buy her.

The woman sleeping beside him was called Desdemona. She was as dark as his previous girlfriend, Ella, had been and just as curvaceous.

Dark women were the exact opposite of his wife Babs with her peroxide-blonde hair and ghost-white face. Babs had put him off blondes. It was always dark girls nowadays.

Still, it was Rafferty's money that was on his mind today. His head throbbed just thinking about it, or was that partly due to the amount he'd consumed last night?

Creeping quietly across the cold cracked lino so as not to wake Desdemona, he slid his trousers from the back of the chair and delved in the pockets.

The wad of notes he brought out was thinner than when it had gone in.

After licking his thumb and forefinger, he began to count. What had been five hundred was now only three. Where the hell had the other two hundred gone?

He vaguely remembered having something of a party, buying drinks for friends and strangers alike. He might also have stuffed a few quid down the front of Desdemona's dress; on the other hand it could have been the waitress's dress or even the barmaid's.

He stared at the money, half afraid it might burst into flames in his hand. Rafferty was out to make him his man, but he didn't want that. Was it too late to turn back?

He picked up the phone and dialled Rafferty's number.

A woman answered. 'Yes.'

'Is Paddy there?'

'Who's calling?'

'Tony Brooks.'

The line went dead.

'Tony! To what do I owe the pleasure, me boy?' Rafferty sounded full of himself.

'I can't accept your money, Paddy. I'll send someone over with it.'

'All five hundred pounds? Now why's that, Tony? Were you offended?'

'No. Not at all.' Tony felt confused. His head ached. Desdemona was stirring and so was his guilt. 'I can't accept it,' he said more forcefully this time.

There was a pause, as though Paddy Rafferty was taking a very deep breath.

'All right,' he said at last. 'Send the money round – all five hundred of it mind – plus interest. I did say there was interest on repayment, didn't I?'

'I've only got three hundred,' Tony blurted. He realised immediately that he'd made a big mistake. He'd told Rafferty exactly what he wanted to hear.

'Sorry, son. I can't accept partial repayments. It's the whole McCoy or nothing at all – not until you've got the full amount. In the meantime, you owe me. I'll expect you to work it off.'

The line went dead. Tony stood starting at it. He'd got himself into a tight corner. He had to pay Paddy back somehow. What he couldn't afford to happen was for Marcie and Michael to find out what he'd done. Michael would likely fire him and would probably never trust him again. On the other hand how was he supposed to work it off? Deep down he knew. Rafferty wanted him to report back on his son-in-law's movements. Sod Rafferty. He wouldn't do it.

Chapter Five

'Why have you moved your bed into the front room, Gran?'

Marcie watched as her grandmother laid out the breakfast things on the table. 'It is warmer down here and my legs are old. I am finding it difficult to climb the stairs.'

Marcie's eyes met Michael's over the tops of the children's heads. Rosa Brooks was keeping her head down, busying herself over a job that didn't necessarily need to be that busy.

'I hope you didn't bring the bed down by yourself,' said Michael.

'Of course not. Garth got Arnold and Archie to give him a hand. Garth is very strong.'

Marcie had expressed her fears regarding her grandmother the night before.

'She's stubborn. What's the betting that something is wrong but she's not admitting it? Did you notice how many cardigans she's wearing? Three! Three thick cardigans.'

'What are you going to do?'

'See if she's been to the doctor – get him to keep

me informed. I'll try and get it out of her in the morning, but I doubt she'll tell me anything.'

Her prediction had turned out absolutely right.

'Did you sleep well?' her grandmother asked her.

'Yes, I did.'

Although realising that her grandmother was attempting to divert the conversation, Marcie had answered truthfully. She'd had no dreams about exploding signs whilst asleep here. Back in London was a different matter. She'd been having dreams about a man in a white suit sitting on a wall, his face shaded by his hat. She'd not seen his face but instinctively knew that he was looking for someone. In her dream she looked to the same stone archway he was looking at, but saw no one.

Just a dream, she'd told herself in the mornings after, but she couldn't help wondering at the identity of the man and whoever he was waiting for.

She would have gone on there and then to describe the dream and ask what her grandmother made of it. But more important things were on her mind. She was worried about her grandmother, worried that she wasn't taking good care of herself and that she might not be quite as well as she made out.

'Would you like us to walk with you to church today?' she asked.

'Could you take me in the car?'

For an uncertain moment Marcie felt as though

she'd walked into a trap. If her grandmother was going to church in the car it stood to reason that they'd all have to go.

Marcie considered declining. It had been a long time since she'd attended either mass or confession.

'OK. We'll go with you.'

'No. You stay with the children. There will not be room for all of us. Michael can drive and Garth will sit in the back with me.'

Marcie shook her head. 'If that's the way you want it.'

Whilst her grandmother was gone Marcie did the chores around the house, preparing dinner, making the beds and dusting in corners where spiders wouldn't have dared to spin webs in days gone by. There was no getting away from it; her grandmother was growing old.

'How was she?' she asked Michael when lunch was over and they were on their way back to London.

'Fine. A bit confused as to the whereabouts of the door handle in the car, but once she was on the pavement she was fine. In fact I've never seen anyone walk such a straight line into church. Garth took care of her. I followed on.'

'She's very independent,' Marcie muttered. 'She always will be.'

'There's nothing wrong in that.'

Marcie sighed. 'I just wish that Babs would pop round to see her more often. It wouldn't hurt her to do that. But no, that's my stepmother for you. Selfish through and through.'

Michael laughed.

Marcie eyed him accusingly. 'What's that for?'

'The concept of your stepmother being under the same roof as your grandmother. Have you ever seen that old Chinese sign for war?'

'No.'

'The sign for peace, so I'm given to understand, is one woman under one roof. The sign for war is two women under one roof.'

Marcie laughed too. 'Point taken.'

She dozed on the way back and, as she dozed, she dreamed. In her dream this time she saw her grandmother and stepmother living under the same roof. The air was electric, explosions happening all around.

When she woke up they were in the middle of a thunderstorm. A roll of thunder sounded overhead.

Michael glanced at her before turning back to the windscreen wipers lashing across the screen. 'Sweet dreams?'

'No. I dreamed that my grandmother and stepmother were living in the same house.'

Michael laughed and pretended to shudder all at

the same time. 'That's not a dream. That's a nightmare!'

She had to agree with him.

The next day was Monday and Marcie took the children into the sewing room with her.

Sally and Allegra were there.

'Kids!' Sally cried, her usual exuberant self.

Allegra was more subdued. Even the way she dressed was far less glamorous than in the past. Marcie put it down to the fact that she was merely adjusting to a life without Victor Camilleri. A few other men had offered to take her out – not surprising, of course. Allegra was stunningly beautiful. Few invitations had been accepted and those that had seemed promising in Marcie's eyes had petered out into nothing.

Reopening the sewing room had been a tough decision. Having two children now, Marcie had wondered if she would be able to manage work and looking after them. There had also been Michael's opinion to consider. She'd been afraid of him taking the old-fashioned view and not wanting her to work now she had children. A lot of husbands preferred their wives to stay at home despite all this bra burning by women who considered they were as good as men and could have home, husband, kids and career.

As it turned out, Michael had encouraged her to continue with designing and making stage costumes for the exotic dancers and female impersonators who performed in nightclubs all over London and further afield. He assured her that having an outside interest would do her good.

'Exotic dancers are the jam on our bread and butter,' he'd said to her. 'Someone has to make their costumes, so why shouldn't it be you?'

'Not quite my colour,' he'd added on holding a sequinned brassiere to his ample and very masculine chest.

She'd laughed and whipped his arm with it.

She was happy in her marriage and in her work. If anyone had told her a few years back what she'd be doing she would never have believed them. It had always been her ambition to design and make fashionable dresses, but getting into that scene had proved more difficult in London than she could have imagined. Fashion houses would only take on girls with some kind of design or art school qualification. Marcie had neither and although Mrs Camilleri, the wife of Victor Camilleri, Michael's father, had given her a start, it didn't last. It couldn't last once Marcie had found out the real reason she was there. Thinking her a virgin and a good Catholic, they determined she would be a good and uncomplaining wife for their legitimate son. It had all gone well at first; Roberto Camilleri had been enamoured of her and she'd been attracted to him.

As big a criminal as his father, he'd seemed at first to be a charming rogue, a ladies' man, but he really had wanted a wife with an unblemished reputation. Unfortunately when he found out that she had a kid out of wedlock his attitude had changed.

Marcie still shivered at the thought of the day he took her for a drive in the country. She'd never told him about Joanna, safely at home on the Isle of Sheppey with her grandmother. Thanks to a bitter ex-friend, Roberto had found out her secret. Not a word was said about it on that drive until she saw the walls of the home for unmarried mothers looming up in front of them. She'd denied nothing, and after that his mood had become violent. He'd raped her. How could anyone say they loved somebody if they could do that? And then he'd acted as if they could still carry on. He'd wanted her to give up Joanna. She'd refused, but he'd kept on at her, insistent that she would change her mind. Roberto Camilleri was used to having his own way.

It was Michael who had sorted things out; Michael who had caused his half-brother and his father to be arrested. Roberto had ended up in prison. Victor was out and, although he hadn't exactly vowed revenge on his son, Michael was wary and keeping his distance.

If it hadn't been for friends like Sally and Allegra – both of whom had been with her at Pilemarsh, the Salvation Army home for unmarried mothers – she didn't know what she would have done, gone back to Sheppey probably. And then there was Michael. For his sake as much as for her thriving little business, she'd stayed in London. Marriage to him had seemed a natural progression. She was happy with him and happier still when Aran had come along. Perhaps it was her own happiness with her life and family that made her so angry with her father.

'I think my father's got a fancy woman. Have you heard anything?'

She directed her question at Allegra who shook her head. 'I am no longer part of the nightclub scene, Marcie, so in all honesty, I wouldn't know. What makes you think that?'

Marcie began unwrapping some material samples sent to her by an East End fabric merchant.

'Oh. Just something my stepmother said. He's not going home much. The kids are missing him.'

She had no intention of describing her stepmother's outburst. Much as she disliked Babs, her words had not fallen on deaf ears. She knew her father too well.

'Perhaps he has just been working too hard,' said Allegra.

Her beautiful dark eyes looked trusting, as though no man could possibly behave like that. Since when had she changed, and why haven't I noticed before? thought Marcie.

Sally looked up and laughed. 'Rubbish. That's the way he is. He's that sort of bloke. A lot of blokes are like that. It's the chase that matters and as long as the wife is at home playing mother bleedin' hen, they consider it all right for them to be out chasing spring chickens – even though they ain't one themselves. And being involved in nightclubs don't help. Think of it as a playground for men or the kid in the sweet-shop. They're surrounded with the stuff of their dreams, only in their case it isn't chocolate or pear drops, it's sexy girls taking their clothes off. It's bound to get to them sooner or later.'

Sally said all this whilst playing horsey with Joanna. The voluptuous blonde who stripped off for a living was on all fours while Joanna sat astride her back shouting, 'Giddy-up, Auntie Sally.'

Allegra had picked up Aran and was humming a lullaby while smiling down into his sleeping face. Looking at her now, it was hard to believe that Allegra had once been Victor Camilleri's mistress. She'd left him following Marcie getting raped by Roberto. He'd beat her after finding out that she'd tried to warn Marcie that Roberto was looking for her.

Nowadays Allegra was trying to build a more respectable life for herself. At the same time she was also repairing the links with her parents, who had been appalled at her shacking up with Camilleri. All this had happened after her sojourn at Pilemarsh where she'd given birth. She'd never admitted who the father of the child was but swore that it wasn't Victor Camilleri.

At present she was studying for a law degree, though she admitted she hadn't quite made up her mind whether that was the way she wanted to go.

'The right path will come to me in a flash,' she said to her friends.

Allegra had a precise way of speaking which was laced with a Spanish accent. Her parents hailed from Jerez and were something to do with the sherry trade. She'd not been her old self since parting from Victor Camilleri, though her clothes were still designer and, thanks to her wealthy – though largely absent – family she was not short of cash. All the same, Marcie detected a change in her, a more deep-thinking Allegra had replaced the elegant confidence she'd known before.

'So do you reckon your dad is still knocking around with that black girl, Ella?' Sally asked.

Marcie shrugged. 'You tell me.'

'How would I know?' Sally said casually.

Marcie was not fooled. She could tell by the way Sally immersed herself in playing with Joanna, not meeting her eyes, that she knew more than she was letting on.

'I didn't know that her name was Ella,' said Marcie.

'I know that she had two kids and her old man does a runner every now and again, depending on whether the police are looking for him. I've not heard that she's around. So p'rhaps your dad is on the straight and narrow and it's all a mistake.'

'I'm not stupid, Sally.'

Sally had a way of sighing when she knew the game was up. She did that now. 'OK,' she said, tipping Joanna gently off her back. 'I did hear there's a new bird on the scene. But I don't know her name. That's all I know. I would have thought he would have told you more. I'm only repeating gossip – you know how it is in the club scene – everybody is always shagging somebody, the most unlikely people too, blokes who you'd always understood were happily married, but, as I said, that's the club-land scene for you. All blokes are the same – all of them, without exception –'

She stopped abruptly, suddenly aware of what she'd just said. 'Not Michael, of course. Michael I would swear by. Honest I would. He's the only bloke I know who I'd lay my life on being faithful. One hundred per cent.' She laughed lightly.

'I know he is,' said Marcie with undisguised confidence. 'I know he is. He's the best thing that ever happened to me – besides my kids that is. Absolutely the best.'

But the barb had hit home and that night, as she lay in bed waiting for him to come home, she wondered if he hadn't been with someone else.

Chapter Six

Paddy Rafferty lived in a palatial drum behind wrought-iron gates as far away from his centre of business as it was possible to get without being totally out of touch. London was still in his blood and the loot he made from his varied business interests flowed from the East End and North London into his bank account. From Tottenham to Whitechapel he had his fingers on the pulse of the less salubrious side of life. Prostitution, drugs, protection and property: they were all part of his book as he put it.

The brick detached bungalow he called home had its own swimming pool and an acre of garden. Little stone lions sat either side of the gates and there were gnomes in the garden. Both he and his wife had a thing about gnomes out of nostalgia for an Ireland they'd never even visited but had seen in films starring Mickey Rooney.

They didn't refer to their gnomes as gnomes; as a nod to their Irish roots, they called them leprechauns.

Paddy had just done his customary twelve lengths of the pool and was towelling himself down. Contrary to popular belief, it was one of the few occasions when he did not wear his gloves. One of his employees, a bloke named Charlie Baxter, with a square chin and hands like shovels, handed him his robe and a pair of soft suede gloves.

It was after midday so he ordered a double whiskey without offering one to his visitor. His visitor was Timothy Hampson-Smythe, his personal brief, who took care of the more paper-orientated legal matters, like contracts and deeds.

Timothy was over six feet tall, had mousy-coloured hair and practically no chin to speak of; the term 'chinless wonder' was made for him.

Of impeccable breeding and education, he used to work for one of the most prestigious law firms in London. Unfortunately he got caught making erotic overtures with a broom handle. He was 'let go' without notice. The broom handle was consigned to a bonfire.

Knees held tightly together, Timothy Hampson-Smythe was sitting on a plastic chair at the side of the pool, his briefcase clasped like a shield against his chest.

Paddy could tell by the ex-Cambridge, ex-guardsman's lack of eye contact that he was not the bearer of good news.

Paddy took a sip from his glass of Bushmills best Irish. 'Well, Timmy, will you tell me what our friend Mickey Jones has to say for himself?'

Timmy pursed his lips. He hated being referred to

as Timmy and had told Paddy so on many occasions. However, on the last occasion, he'd received a back-hander for his trouble and was told in no uncertain terms that Paddy Rafferty was paying the bill so Paddy Rafferty would call him anything he damn well liked!

His eyes, as black as crude oil and as shifty as wind-blown sand, flickered nervously between his client and his own clasped hands. On doing so he noted that his knuckles were turning white. Relaxing wasn't easy in the presence of Paddy Rafferty.

Timothy had just returned from a visit to the Blue Genie nightclub. Michael Jones had unknowingly bought a batch of rundown real estate that had been earmarked for Rafferty. Rafferty had friends in local politics so knew where the likely development opportunities happened to be. He held off offering until the very last moment, and that, as Timothy knew only too well, was his downfall. Now he was aiming to become a business partner of the man who had bought it. The problem was that Paddy wanted to pay no more than he'd had in mind to offer the original owner. He would have made a killing if he'd paid the right price at the right time. But Michael Jones had got in there first and getting on board as a partner – a sleeping partner in fact – was proving to be difficult.

Timothy cleared his throat before saying what he had to say. 'I'm afraid he again refused your offer, Mr Rafferty.'

Timothy Hampson-Smythe had not been keen to go along with the offer in the first place, offering as it did basically nothing. The contract was just a partnership, a system whereby Patrick Rafferty would cream off a portion of the profits until such time as the place came up for redevelopment. He had it on good authority that the place would become the subject of a compulsory purchase order of which he would take a portion when the time came. He would also get in on the development package and on top of that would provide cheap Irish labour for the job. In turn the Irish labour, who out of the goodness of his heart he would bring over from Ireland, would pay him that portion of their wages which was rightly due to the Inland Revenue.

'Heads I win, tails I win,' he'd said gleefully to his wife.

She'd barely looked up from the magazine she was reading, but did say, 'Yes dear.' As though she'd been listening!

To all intents and purposes it was a protection racket, though unlike most protection rackets, Patrick was in it for the long haul. Not that he didn't have a few straightforward 'pay up or get beat up' types of arrangement which were based on a weekly or monthly collection of funds.

Michael Jones' operation was more upmarket and bound to last for the long term and was therefore special. Paddy viewed future development prospects as something of a pension plan for himself and Millicent when they were old and grey and fancied the sun on their bones. They were considering the South of France though Spain was a possibility once Generalissimo Franco was dead and buried. A pound went a long way when exchanged for pesetas. In the meantime they were setting down the seeds of a very nice pension plan.

Paddy's nose twitched and his lower lip sagged. Having someone upset his best-laid plans was tantamount to throwing a dog's turd in his face. Paddy was not pleased. His watery eyes seemed to solidify behind his crisp golden lashes. His lips pursed once he'd gulped back the rest of his drink and he immediately ordered another.

'A double,' he said to Baxter, shoving the glass against the big man's chest. His eyes narrowed. His face froze. He whipped round to face Hampson-Smythe.

'What reason did the bastard give?'

'Well, basically, what he said was that he couldn't really see his way to taking you on as a partner. He didn't need one. It wasn't until I was examining the paperwork that I found out that he was lying and he already has a partner.'

'Partner?' Paddy's bushy eyebrows shot upwards like a pair of flying caterpillars.

This was the first time Paddy had heard anything about a partner. He'd done his research, or rather he'd had someone do the research for him. It always paid to have someone on the inside and Tony Brooks had a big mouth once there was plenty of booze flowing over his tongue. Tony had a bad habit of telling people things that to his mind seemed totally innocent. Most of the time he was boasting about how successful the club was; the schmuck even divulged how much the takings shot up on a Friday or Saturday night. Was the man mad? But even he hadn't mentioned a partner.

No. Not mad. Just drunk. A bit of a loose cannon that Michael Jones would do well to watch. Not that Paddy wanted Michael to watch his father-in-law too closely.

Tony had told him a lot, such as that Michael Jones had parted on bad terms with his father and set up on his own. If Camilleri were behind the clubs then he wouldn't touch him. He dare not.

'What partner?' he asked, his expression reflecting the consternation he was feeling.

Hampson-Smythe licked his bottom lip again before continuing. 'Well,' he began.

'Well, what?' Paddy couldn't resist the urge to hurry his lawyer along. It was obvious the man was scared of him. Paddy was pleased about that; he liked people to be scared of him.

Hampson-Smythe explained. 'I've heard nothing word of mouth. It wasn't until I examined the legal documentation that it came to me. It seems that his wife is his business partner, besides being his marriage partner, of course, though he keeps it quiet. I understand they're very close, inseparable in fact.'

Paddy frowned and began pacing up and down like a man possessed. 'His wife? What sort of outfit is he running?'

'I tried to reason with him, Mr Rafferty, but I am afraid he showed me the door and was quite belligerent . . .'

The pacing stopped. Paddy flung the whiskey glass over his shoulder and grabbed his brief by the throat.

'Belligerent? Speak fucking English, man! Does that mean he was taking the piss?'

'Not . . . quite . . . Mr Rafferty.' The words were choked out between struggles for breath. 'Aggressive. After that he was more, as you say, mocking in his reference to you.'

'Mocking?' Rafferty's eyes were glaring into those of Timothy Hampson-Smythe. 'What did he say?' he asked, his voice sinking into a low growl. 'What did he say about me?'

Timothy was gagging for air. 'I . . . can't . . . breathe . . .'

Paddy, seeing the other man turning red in the

face loosened his grip. 'Tell me,' he yelled, shaking the lawyer like a terrier might shake a rat, despite the fact that Hampson-Smythe towered above him.

The lawyer drew in a deep breath before he could answer. 'He said that his wife rated above a pseudo Irishman with poxy hands and a taste for garden gnomes.'

Paddy's face had turned bright red. His eyes were like ping-pong balls on which someone had crayoned in a pair of staring pupils.

Hampson-Smythe regarded him fearfully. He'd seen his client explode before, sending a chair crashing through a window. Rafferty was always the smouldering volcano waiting to erupt, beating up on anyone within hitting distance even if they were in no way responsible for his ire. He was almost tempted to sigh with relief when nothing immediately happened. His relief was short-lived.

'Bastard!' bellowed Rafferty.

Poor Timothy Hampson-Smythe found himself lifted into the air. His feet left the ground and he was flying straight from Paddy Rafferty's hands and up into the air.

The ledge running around the pool was narrow. The pool was fairly large. Hampson-Smythe, complete with his trusty briefcase, made a big splash.

While Baxter found the net they used to clean debris from the water to scoop him out, Paddy Rafferty went back to pacing the pool from one end to the other. With each pace he pondered on how best to pay Michael Jones back for his insults – and his refusal to enter a partnership.

He focused on the fact that Michael had chosen to have his wife as his business partner. What a crap idea that was! No woman could cope with that type of business. It was a man's world. He certainly wouldn't have his wife as a business partner – even a sleeping partner. Millicent wouldn't have a bloody clue. Bed and kitchen and shopping: that was all wives were fit for plus wheeling out when in respectable and legit company. But this! How smug could a man get? They were close! Fucking close!

Men like him didn't take insults lying down. Getting even niggled in his mind. What could he do to get back at Michael Jones and his perfect marriage? And was it perfect? Was it really perfect?

He stopped in his pacing as a wicked thought came to him. So Michael presumed his marriage was strong enough for business. His wife trusted him to be out night after night taking care of things. What if he sowed doubt in her mind? They were obviously close, but what if events could be orchestrated so that a few cracks might appear?

Smiling to himself, he shouted at Baxter to fetch him another whiskey. Leaving Hampson-Smythe dripping like a piece of garbage on the edge of the pool, Baxter went to the corner bar to pour his boss another Bushmills.

Paddy was feeling pleased with himself. Sorting Jones out might still not get him a partnership – though it might. On the other hand it would give him great satisfaction to pay back the little upstart for being so outspoken and for preferring his wife as a partner. Well, the pair of them wouldn't be so close by the time Paddy Rafferty had finished with them. Too bloody right they wouldn't! In fact, he thought, if he had a mind to, he'd separate them for good. Now how bloody clever was that?

Chapter Seven

Barry Masters – stage name Latoya La Monde – was being fitted for a sparkling backless number. Pink ostrich feathers floated out around his ankles fishtail style and he was preening himself in front of the full-length mirror.

'You look a hoot!' remarked Sally.

'I look good! Soooo gooood!'

Barry had a voice like a foghorn. On stage he wore a blonde wig and did a Marlene Dietrich kind of act. Today he'd left the wig at home and he looked strange standing there in a pink dress, his bald head catching the light and rivalling the sequins for brightness.

Barry was a regular customer, possibly the busiest drag queen in London nightclubs, though he kept a low profile outside the profession. It didn't do to betray any kind of inclination to dress in women's clothes, the cops and the 'queer laws' being what they were.

Besides making this dress, Marcie had copied the original *Blue Angel* outfit Dietrich had worn when she'd sang 'Falling in Love Again'. It had to be admitted that Barry certainly had the voice for it. He had the figure too – slinky and slim from the bosom down with a square shoulderline up top, just like Dietrich.

Marcie was on her hands and knees with Renee, her seamstress, pinning the feathers in such a way as to hide Barry's rather large feet. Most drag queens and transvestites had to have their shoes made for them. Shoes made for women might, if he was lucky, just about go up to his size but were usually a killer on width.

'So how's your love life, Barry?' asked Sally, who did a bit around the place during the day, which mostly consisted of making the tea and looking after the kids when Marcie was busy.

'You know how it is in our game, sweetie,' he replied in a smooth voice. 'We work unsociable hours so loving consists of snatched moments between shows and taking in the milk bottles.'

Both Marcie and Sally made sympathetic noises; they both knew that the hard-working nightclub turns usually got home at the same time as the milkman was trundling around in his electric milk float. When they got home they picked up the freshly delivered milk and went to bed.

Due to the nature of the items made in the sewing room, there was no shop window display and prospective clients made an appointment to come along and

discuss their requirements. Marcie's clients appreciated how discreet everything was.

Each costume she made was a one-off. The only
time she made more than one of any outfit was for the
Taylor Twins – two fat women who were something of
a legend on the burlesque circuit – and the odd chorus
line, which didn't happen that much anyway. Most of
the girls – or would-be girls – were solo artistes.

A sudden loud knocking at the door took them
by surprise. It was Sally who went to answer it. She
came back looking worried.

She addressed Marcie. 'There's someone to see you.
I've put them in your office.'

Marcie frowned. 'I wasn't expecting anyone.'

Sally said nothing, but Marcie could see by the
pallor of her face that something had unnerved her.

Her first concern was for her husband. 'Oh no. It's
not Michael is it? He is all right?'

'Is it the landlord? P'rhaps she's got behind with
the rent,' quipped Barry once Marcie had left the
room.

Sally looked at him askance then blurted, 'Of
course it's not the landlord. The rent's been paid and
all's in order, you silly sod. Would you be standing
here in the altogether if she hadn't?'

He gave a so-so shake of his head as though he
couldn't quite make up his mind. 'You just looked
shocked,' he added.

'Hmm,' she muttered and began helping Barry out of his outfit.

The truth was she was poleaxed by the woman she'd shown into the office. She knew her name, knew she used to work for the Camilleris and more recently for Michael at the Blue Genie.

She'd thought about asking the woman – Linda, if she remembered rightly – what it was all about, but had known by the look on her face that questions would not be welcome.

After placing the ostrich-feather outfit to one side, she looked the drag queen up and down. 'Barry, you need new underwear.'

Barry looked down at the salmon-pink corset he was wearing. 'I know it's a bit old-fashioned, but it was all I could get to fit.'

'It looks like it once belonged to a horse.'

Barry looked hurt. 'It was my mother's.'

'Sorry,' said Sally. 'My mind's elsewhere.'

The office was small. It contained a wooden filing cabinet of pre-war vintage, where Marcie kept all the paperwork and records she needed to run her business, and a desk on which sat a telephone and a rubber plant streaking upwards from a red plastic pot. There was a swivel chair behind the desk and a hard chair in the little space that was left. Tan-coloured carpet tiles covered the floor. The office had just one window overlooking the street above the shop selling darts and snooker trophies to local pubs and sports associations.

The face of the woman waiting there was very white. She was sitting in the hard chair, staring out of the window, though she didn't really seem to be seeing the buses, the cabs and the few remaining costermongers pushing their barrows away from their pitches on the other side of the road. The latter didn't linger much beyond three o'clock. Whatever they were going to sell that day had already been sold.

It was purely premonition, that sickly butterfly feeling that makes you think that something bad is about to happen. That's what Marcie was experiencing now, though in actual fact she had no real reason to feel that way. She didn't know this woman. She didn't know what she wanted.

Marcie took a deep breath and told herself to be calm. There was nothing to fear. Nevertheless, her heart hammered in her chest.

Marcie adopted an aura of calm and told herself not to be stupid. She greeted the woman and then asked, 'Would you like a coffee? A cup of tea perhaps?'

The woman shook her tawny bob. Her eyes were green. Her nose was pert and her lips glimmered with pink pearlised lipstick.

Marcie sat down and smiled across the desk at the woman who'd introduced herself as Linda Bell.

'I used to work for your husband,' she began, her

eyes downcast, her fingers smoothing at the hem of her coat which really did not need smoothing at all.

Lashes heavy with black mascara fluttered as furiously as the butterflies in Marcie's stomach.

'You worked at the Blue Genie?'

The woman nodded. At the same time she crossed one long leg over the other. Her tights were of a common colour – American Tan – probably by Pretty Polly.

'I only recently became a dancer . . .'

Although she could feel her stomach muscles tightening with nerves, Marcie nodded. 'I see.' Even to her own ears she sounded calm. 'So you were an exotic dancer,' she prompted, though striptease artiste would have been nearer the mark.

Linda Bell certainly had the legs for it. And the face. Everything come to that.

'I've been a hostess as well, but I really wanted to dance. Michael gave me my first break.'

'That was the first time you stripped?'

'Yes.'

Linda's glossy bob nodded with her head. 'I was very grateful to him for giving me the break. Nobody else would. But there, that's Michael for you – a lovely man. All the girls adore him.'

It felt to Marcie that her stomach muscles were in danger of cleaving to her spine. This girl was going to tell her something she didn't want to hear.

'Get to the point.'

The lashes fluttered again. There was the down-wards look, the nervous intermingling of fingers.

'We were always good friends. I never thought it would be anything more than that – though I hoped,' she said, her green eyes flashing up to face Marcie before they lowered again.

'What are you trying to say?'

A voice screamed in Marcie's head. *You don't need her to say anything because you know what she's going to say!*

When Linda Bell took a deep breath her breasts pushed against her coat so that the buttons strained and one came undone.

Marcie couldn't take her eyes off that button, prob-ably because she didn't want to look the woman in the eyes; she did not want to see the woman's face as she recounted the terrible news.

'Michael and I . . . well . . . we had a one-night stand. We never meant it to happen. Please believe that. But it did.' She shrugged her shoulders. As she did so another button came undone. Marcie's atten-tion dropped to that one in preference to the other – for no reason other than she wanted to claw the woman's eyes out.

In order to stop herself doing that, she stood up and crossed to the window, turning her back on the room.

The traffic on the street outside seemed to roll silently past. If there was any noise she wasn't really noticing it. She wasn't really seeing the traffic at all.

She was aware of Linda shifting in her chair, which creaked as she changed position.

'I'm not here to cause you any trouble. I just thought you should know.' She sounded breathless, like an excited child, and certainly not as though she was sorry for what she had done.

She had had a one-night stand with Michael.

'I see,' said Marcie, her voice as icy as the rest of her body. 'I take it you mean sex when you say it was a one-night stand. You had sex with my husband.'

She turned round to face the woman. She had a knowing, forthright look. Such a look probably suited a nightclub hostess, which this woman claimed to be. She'd been employed at one of the nightclubs owned by the Camilleris. The hostesses had a reputation for being pretty free and easy with their favours. But she'd wanted to be an exotic dancer and Michael, her kind-hearted husband, had given her the chance. Now how kind was that?

'So what do you want me to do about it? What are you here for?'

The slightly raised voice took Linda Bell by surprise. Her mouth opened but nothing came out.

'Well,' she said at last. 'As a mother I thought you should know that I'm pregnant.'

The chill intensified. Marcie felt as though the whole room had turned cold and that her body had turned to ice.

'I don't believe you.'

'I can assure you it's true!'

'No.'

Nothing, nothing on earth could have knocked the wind out of Marcie more so than this. All the same, she was wary. Women could lie for money. That was their job, stroking the egos of middle-aged men so that they would throw caution to the wind and spend more. Lies were their stock-in-trade.

'How do I know you're telling the truth?'

When the girl pouted Marcie was reminded of her stepmother. Despite the difference in colouring, this girl – Linda Bell – had the same brazen attraction that Babs had once had. Given half a chance, men were all over her.

But this woman was here for a reason, a reason that could tear her apart if she didn't keep her cool and so far she *was* keeping cool.

'You could ask him,' said Linda. 'I'd go round there myself but he'd only show me the door. He gave me a few quid and told me he didn't want to know.'

'So why are you telling me?'

The woman shrugged. 'I thought I should do the right thing.'

More like you wanted some kind of revenge, Marcie thought to herself, if what you're saying is true.

Marcie folded her arms and turned back to the scene in the street outside. Narrowing her eyes, she forced herself to analyse what she was feeling and her impression of this woman. On the one hand, she was feeling gutted. On the other, she couldn't believe that Michael had been unfaithful. He was different from other blokes she'd met. It was Michael who had saved her from Roberto Camilleri. Roberto was in Pentonville at present on a charge of actual bodily harm. It's what he'd got for being heavy-handed with some of the tenants of the crumbling buildings his father owned.

So how was she going to deal with this?

Follow your instincts.

She spun round. 'Right!'

The woman jumped.

Marcie picked up her handbag. 'Right. I think a taxi cab is in order.'

She called out to Sally that she was going out and for her to look after the kids while she was gone.

If she'd jumped before, Linda Bell looked quite startled now. 'Where are we going?'

Marcie grabbed her by the arm. 'To see my old man. Let's see what he's got to say about it shall we?'

'With you?'

Linda Bell looked astounded that a wronged wife

should wish to accompany her on such a mission. After all, this was all about wrecking a marriage wasn't it?

'I've got an appointment elsewhere,' said Linda who, if she was pregnant, certainly didn't have a bump just yet.

Marcie made the decision to treat this whole thing with contempt. She couldn't believe Michael was cheating on her. This woman was just an employee who'd been sacked and was now out to make trouble. Yes! That's it, she told herself.

Consumed with rage, she grabbed the woman's arm and flung her towards the door. 'Get out of here. There's nothing for you here. Get out of here now and don't ever darken my door again.'

The woman kind of hung there on the edge of the half-open door trying to catch her breath. 'You'll be sorry,' she growled raising her finger and pointing it like a gun at the spot between Marcie's eyes. 'I didn't come here for money. I only thought I was doing the right thing.'

'Fuck off!'

Marcie slammed the door. For what seemed like an age but could only have been a minute, she stared at it.

It was a while before she fully came to and got her thoughts into some kind of order.

Her first instinct was to phone Michael and call

him all the names under the sun. Her second was to play it cool in an effort to preserve her marriage. Their marriage was strong and they were happy. Best to forget that Linda Bell existed rather than rock the boat. Best to pretend that nothing had happened – just in case it had.

Chapter Eight

Linda Bell had never run so fast from a place in her life. The last thing she'd wanted was to have to face Michael Jones in the presence of his wife. One at a time she could cope with, but not both together.

She asked herself why the hell had she let herself get talked into this? The answer was swift in coming: money. Wasn't money the source of all evils? Bugger that! Money bought her all the things she wanted. New shoes. New clothes. And drugs.

She didn't stop running until she found a telephone box, which she nipped into and immediately dialled Paddy's office number.

'Paddy? It's me.'

Gasping for breath, she outlined to him what had happened.

'I did what you told me and sowed the seeds of suspicion to his old lady,' she said, 'but then the silly bitch wanted to take me along to face Michael. I don't mind stirring things up with one of them, but I don't know that I can carry it off with both of them there – especially if she started crying or something. That would be worse than them arguing in my book.

So I thought I'd better tell you. Did I do well, Paddy? Did I?'

On the other end of the phone Paddy Rafferty was close to blowing a fuse. Linda Bell was a good-looking bird but a bit lacking in the brains department. Besides having a drug problem, she fancied herself as a bit of an actress, which was why he'd offered her this part in the first place – with a prize at the end of it, of course. He'd told her that he knew a television producer who was looking for someone to replace one of the lead stars in *Coronation Street*. The truth was that the only bloke in television he knew was the bloke who'd come to plug in his new colour television set. But Linda was gullible and hungry for fame. On a day-to-day basis she was always hungry for drugs. He'd promised her an instant supply from some black geezer he knew down in Bermondsey.

Paddy ground his teeth, an annoying habit that even his wife complained about. None of the girls he slept with ever did. They wouldn't dare. They knew from his lovemaking that he got off on violence. Giving him an excuse to lash out was tantamount to earning a week or two in hospital.

In all honesty, he wasn't really angry with Linda. It was Marcie Jones that got his goat. The fact that Michael's wife had rebounded with the challenge that they both go and see Michael annoyed him. How dare she throw a spanner in the works? The bitch!

Another plan hatched in his mind.

'Now listen here, Linda. This is what you are going to do. You've seen the wife, now see the husband. I fully take on board what you're saying. You don't want to face the two of them. Well, my lovely, you're quite right I think. Divide and rule. Get them separately and you'll have played your part. Now this is what I want you to do . . .'

Linda Bell held her breath as Paddy outlined his plan. She was to go along to the Blue Genie. Michael was running all his businesses from a new office in the same building. She was to make a scene, to let everybody know what a louse he was both to her and his wife.

'Being unfaithful to his lovely and very loyal wife, getting a talented dancer pregnant and fobbing her off with a few quid. That's the line you're to play, me girl,' he said to her.

Linda exhaled all that breath she'd been holding in. 'You can trust me, Paddy. It'll be like the last scene from *Gone With the* bleedin' *Wind* when Rhett Butler bows out of Scarlett's life for ever.'

Paddy Rafferty smiled. 'That's right, my little pigeon. Make it that good and you'll be up on the silver screen along with that bloke Stewart Granger in no time.'

'Elvis Presley!'

'Him too.'

On the other end of the phone, Linda's attitude was changing. Should she really trust the roly-poly Irishman?

'Don't you let me down, Paddy. If you do I'll tell – you know I will.'

Paddy couldn't help his mind moving on to violent thoughts. The fact was he enjoyed violence and manipulation. There was a certain pleasure in destroying peoples' lives. It made him feel so good, so powerful.

He imagined how he could better destroy that bastard Michael Jones, a bloke who had *dared* to say no to him.

Both Jones and Linda deserved to be punished, and he was just the man to do it.

'Trust me, Linda. You'll make front page news by the time I've finished with you.'

His man Baxter watched as he smiled into the phone. He knew that look and where Paddy's plans were going. If he was a softer bloke he might have shivered. But he didn't. He was Paddy's man and would do his bidding.

Paddy Rafferty was still smiling when he put the phone down. 'Stupid bitch.'

Baxter waited for orders. He was standing in front of him, his big hands folded one on top of the other.

Paddy's chill blue eyes were unblinking as he looked at the man in front of him.

'Baxter, I have a job for you to do. You are going to be my version of Rhett Butler, only instead of you bowing out, it's my version and I'll tell you now, son, in my story it's Scarlett who'll be gone for ever.'

Chapter Nine

The last thing Michael Jones expected to see when he opened his desk drawer was a gun.

Perhaps he might not have picked it up if it hadn't been resting on his diary. He was into the habit of checking his schedule every morning before doing anything else. The urge to maintain his daily routine was too strong to ignore. He picked up the gun and looked at it, then rang for Kevin.

Kevin McGregor was a thick-set Scotsman with a reddish beard and piercing blue eyes beneath reddish, arched eyebrows. In the habit of a man used to wearing a kilt and being proud of it, he stood with legs slightly apart, hands clasped behind his back.

Ex-army, it was rumoured that he'd killed a lot of Mau Mau in the rebellion for independence in Kenya. The broad Scotsman had never disclosed whether the rumours were true or false. Kevin McGregor, like a lot of ex-army types, never spoke of it.

Michael held the gun up. 'You could have put it in the safe.'

Kevin frowned then shook his head. 'Sorry, boss. Not sure what you mean?'

'I presume that you or one of your team took it off a customer. Is that right?'

Kevin shook his head. 'Not me, boss, and none of the others mentioned it either.'

'Then ask them.'

Kevin nodded. 'I will.'

Michael locked the gun in the safe but not before he'd sniffed the muzzle and detected the undeniable odour of spent cordite. He knew enough about guns to know it had been fired, a fact that unnerved him, that and its appearance in his desk drawer. Somebody had put it there and not told anyone. It should have been reported. Someone had been lax and he aimed to find out who it was.

Because of the gun and his security staff not knowing about it, Michael Jones was not best pleased when he walked out into the narrow vestibule that formed the reception. The fact that his doorman was sitting on his backside reading a copy of the *Daily Mirror* didn't usually get up his nose, but it did today.

'I don't pay you to improve your reading standard, Jimmy. Put it away. It don't look good. Right?'

Jimmy folded the newspaper up and shoved it under the counter. Not minding that he'd been caught out, he grinned affably. Michael was a good bloke to work for, easy-going for the most part unless someone had upset him. He looked upset now with that dark glower on his face. Jimmy Watkins surmised that the little Jewish guy – Michael's lawyer – who'd come in with a briefcase full of paperwork had had something to do with it. Yesterday it had been a different lawyer, one representing that Irish git, Rafferty. The bloke had been as tall as a lamp-post and sounded as though his mouth was stuffed with plums. What a prick!

'Has Kevin had a word with you about what I found in my desk?'

'He did. Somebody must have fallen down on the job. But it wasn't me,' he added swiftly.

Michael nodded. Nobody would own up to it. Nobody wanted to face the consequences, i.e. getting a roasting by the boss because they'd failed to report it.

But, newspaper aside, Jimmy was a reliable sort and Michael had other problems.

'Have the electricians phoned back?' Michael asked him.

'Yeah. They said they'll be here in the morning but not to worry. It was only a short and nothing's likely to burn down until they get here.'

Michael's glower was no less deep. Jimmy winced beneath his glare.

'That bloody sign shorting out was no laughing matter. My wife could have been hurt the first time it happened. It should have been fixed properly then.'

He hadn't told Marcie that the sign kept shorting just like on that first occasion. He didn't know why he hadn't told her. It was a bit like tempting fate; it felt as though it might be unlucky to bring up the subject.

'Get back on to them again. I want this sorted out in daylight not tonight when we're full of punters.'

'I thought they might be still on their tea break or something.'

'I don't care if they're having a three-course meal with the Queen, ring them and get them round here. And stop thinking. Leave the thinking to me.'

Michael didn't usually snap at his employees. Jimmy looked suitably contrite. 'Sorry, boss.'

He liked Michael. He still seemed to be in love with his wife so he could understand him being nervous about that blasted sign. Why the hell the thing kept blowing he didn't know, but there was something funny about it. The electrician kept coming, kept scratching his head when it happened again and again.

'A spanner in the works,' Jimmy had said to him.

'Something queer that's for bloody sure,' said the electrician.

Jimmy sighed. He hadn't taken offence at Michael's sharpness. He seemed like a decent bloke. He never played around like a lot of other nightclub owners who thought it their God given right to sample the goods they sold – the booze and the birds. Michael didn't do that. Sure the bloke liked a drink, but not to excess; he'd never seen him drunk. As for the girls, well, they were willing enough to give the boss anything he wanted, but he had never seen it or heard any rumours that he sampled the goods on offer. His wife seemed to be the only woman he desired – not surprising really. Jimmy sighed. If he had a wife like that he wouldn't stray either. But he didn't have a wife – not any more. She'd run off with a farmer from Lincolnshire. A farmer for Christ's sake! He'd never understand that, but still, he was OK. The girls employed at the club liked big muscles – and he had them aplenty. He could take comfort in their arms if nothing else.

Michael came back out of his office just as he was putting down the phone from the electrician.

'Well?'

'He's on his way. Reckons he should be here in about an hour.'

'Good.' Michael looked at his watch. 'I'm off for a coffee.'

It was Michael's habit to pop out midway through the afternoon for a coffee at the trattoria opposite. It was a small respite but gave him time to take a breather and think things through.

He weaved through the traffic and waved to the portly figure on the other side of the window, who was already pulling out a chair and smoothing down the chequered tablecloth.

The Italian owner always kept a seat free for Michael by the window. Most people – the café owner and his employees included – assumed that Michael liked to sit by the window so he could keep tags on the comings and goings across at the club. During the day, the comings and goings were restricted to employees and deliverymen.

The truth was otherwise. Michael did a lot of his thinking just sitting and looking out at the road. He also heard the gossip regarding his half-brother, Roberto and his father, Victor Camilleri. Roberto was still in jail. His father was carrying on running his many business interests, which stretched from rent scams to racketeering to nightclubs to the rag trade. It was Gabriella Camilleri who provided the legitimate front to the rag-trade side of the business, running up or buying dresses for selling on in her King's Road shop, the Daisy Chain. The shop hid a more sinister aspect to the business; unknown to any of the assistants in the shop there was more than a single sewing room providing the dresses. Victor had sweatshops in the East End where girls newly arrived from Asia worked for long hours and meagre wages. The shop also provided pretty girls who wanted to work in London at any price. They also coveted the latest fashion to hit the swinging capital then found out it took more than the wages they earned serving in a shop. It was Victor who suggested they take jobs in his nightclubs as hostesses, only they ended up being much more than just pleasant to the customers. They ended up as high-class call girls – at least they were high class for a while. In time, once their innocence and their youth began to fade, they ended up on the slippery slope to street walking.

Michael had badly wanted his natural father to be proud of him. There was still a residue of that in his psyche. His brother he had merely tolerated and the feeling was mutual.

He sighed, glad to be away from them all and, although it was hard work, he was pleased with his life. Everything was going well. Rafferty was the only fly in the ointment. The man knew that Michael and his father had parted on bad terms and thus he was out from beneath Camilleri protection. He was vulnerable and Rafferty knew it.

Of course he could go back to his father and ask him to intervene with Rafferty, to persuade him to lay off or else risk gang warfare between the Sicilians and the Irish. Sucking in his lips, he thought about it. It would be so easy to run back with his tail between his legs, but his pride wouldn't let him do it. Besides, there was also the fact of what his brother had done to Marcie. He could forgive his dad perhaps but Roberto was another matter. And his father would always take Roberto's side. There was nothing else for it but to stand up to Rafferty or place himself under the protection of somebody who was more powerful and more dangerous. He needed time to think.

Aldo's Trattoria was an oasis of calm in his busy life. The atmosphere was unmistakably Italian, the windows steamy and the coffee hot and frothy. Aldo and his team spoke loudly and used their hands a lot. It was the in joke that if anyone ever cut off their arms, they wouldn't be able to speak.

Wearing a massive white apron that covered him from his chest and past his knees, Aldo came over full of welcoming bonhomie.

'You not look happy today, Michael. Your wife not love you any more?'

Aldo's question broke into his moroseness. He had to smile. 'My wife loves me very much – and very often,' he added with a salacious wink.

Marcie was the one thing in his life that always made him feel good. He deeply regretted losing his rag with her the other night, but he had a lot on his mind.

'Lucky man,' said Aldo, returning the wink with the salaciousness only a true-born Italian could show. 'I wish I had a wife like yours, but mine . . .' He laughed loudly. 'She prefer to be with her mother than with me. That is why I am in London and she is in Naples.'

'That's sad.'

Aldo laughed. 'No, my friend! It makes me very happy that she is there and I am here. We get on very well when we are miles apart. When we are together we fight like – how you say – the cats and the dogs. She is the cat and I am the dirty dog – that is what she says to me.'

Laughing loudly, he landed a heavy slap on Michael's back before returning behind his counter and his steaming espresso machine. Aldo and his relatives – because that was mostly who he employed – exchanged loud conversation in Italian which was interlaced with much laughter, much slapping of tea towels at each other and waving of hands in the air. It was pure theatre and the customers loved it.

Michael mustered a smile. Usually he would have laughed with them, but today his thoughts were elsewhere. Rubbing a circle in the steamed-up window, he looked out on the street. He wasn't feeling happy, though not unhappy either. It was imperative he kept positive and didn't let Marcie know how worried he was. All the same, it was difficult not to feel apprehensive.

He had been unable to shake off the feeling of foreboding he'd had since Paddy Rafferty had first tried to muscle in on his business. He realised now that hoping Rafferty would take no for an answer on that first meeting had been incredibly naive.

The tall streak of upmarket crap that was Rafferty's lawyer was proof of that. He'd told him to shove off with a flea in his ear too, but he was less hopeful that would be the end of things. This lunchtime his own lawyer had arrived wearing a worried frown and carrying a briefcase that contained just one item – a contract that basically made Paddy Rafferty a partner.

'That man has a bad reputation,' Jacob Solomon had said. He'd raised one bushy black eyebrow as he'd said it, which made him seem as though he only had one eye, the other eye was habitually hidden behind an unruly fringe. Solomon always looked as if he needed a haircut and as if he were wearing someone else's suit. But despite his casual appearance, Jacob Solomon was an excellent lawyer and he rarely missed a trick.

'I'm not letting him muscle in.'

Jacob had nodded sagely. 'Very noble.'

'You don't approve?'

'Of course I do. But I fear that our friend Mr Rafferty is not noble. I fear he will use ignoble means to get your compliance – or more specifically, your property.'

Michael nodded. 'I hear he's a man who bears grudges.'

Jacob Solomon had pursed his lips and fallen silent.

Michael took that to mean that he too had heard the rumour that the wife and children of the last man to refuse a 'business partnership' had died in a house fire. Person or persons unknown had poured petrol through their letterbox and set it ablaze. The police had failed to find the perpetrators and there was no evidence that Rafferty was involved. Paddy Rafferty had ended up with the property after the owner had committed suicide. A spurious contract of agreement had turned up from somewhere.

Jacob Solomon had left quietly after warning Michael to be careful.

Sitting in his favourite seat by the window, he considered what Rafferty's next move might be. He'd insulted the man as well as turning down his approach and no matter what he would still do it again. He'd worked hard to get his business up and running and nobody – absolutely nobody – was going to take a quarter, let alone a half, away from him.

He watched the action across the road. People came and went into the club – men and women. They didn't really register; he was that absorbed in his thoughts.

He didn't jerk out of them until the door opened and Jimmy was there. He'd been so preoccupied, he hadn't seen him cross the road.

'Boss. There's some woman wants to see you. She says it's personal.'

Michael looked up in time to see a tall brunette wearing a pink chiffon headscarf and matching lipstick pushing through the door.

'I told her to wait in your office, boss . . .' Jimmy protested.

The woman pushed past him. A cloud of what seemed to be expensive perfume fell over him along with the smell of face powder and hair lacquer.

'You bastard,' she screamed, pointing her finger at Michael. 'You got me up the duff and now you don't want to know me. Had your fun and now don't want to take the responsibility.'

Aldo came out from behind the counter. Everyone, customers and waiters alike, stared open-mouthed, drawn by the sight and sound of the woman.

Michael's face drained of colour as he half rose from the table. 'What the hell . . .?'

Linda Bell was enjoying this and well into her stride. She'd always been a drama queen, and now she had her sights on an acting career. She was playing the part for all it was worth.

'Don't you give me that, Mickey bloody Jones. You was always coming on to me at the Red Devil. Said I turned you on and persisted even when I kept turning you down. Well, now look at me,' she said, patting the faint rise in her belly where she'd had the foresight this time to tape a small cushion. 'You'll pay for this, Michael Jones. It's your kid and you're going to pay for it.'

Michael got to his feet. 'You lying cow!'

'So what's this, bleedin' Scotch mist?' she yelled, pointing a painted fingernail at her stomach.

Michael grabbed her. 'You lying bitch!'

'Oh yeah! I was a lying cow just now and now I'm a lying bitch. That's what they all say. Had yer fun and now you don't want to know.'

She tried to wriggle free, but Michael was having none of it. He held her chin so she had to look up into his face.

'I know who put you up to this, Linda. Tell Rafferty it isn't going to work. Like you he's nothing but a fucking amateur.' He threw her away from him.

Linda Bell looked frightened. Few people ever saw Michael angry, but he was certainly angry now.

She rallied for a moment. 'Well, just you wait until your wife finds out. We'll see what she's got to say about it Michael bloody Jones, you smug sod . . .'

Michael grabbed her again and dragged her to the door.

'Get out! Get out and stay away from me and mine. And tell that Irish idiot, Rafferty, to do the same.'

'Let go of me,' she shouted, her arms flailing and her handbag socking him on the chin. 'Let go of me, you vicious bastard. Wait till your wife hears about this. I'll tell her. You bet that I'll tell her!'

With one determined effort, Michael grabbed hold of her right wrist then her left. His eyes bored into hers. He was aware that Aldo and the other customers in the trattoria had fallen to silence and were watching him with spellbound anticipation but he couldn't help himself.

'Get this straight. If you dare go with your lying tales to my wife, I'll kill you! I'll fucking kill you!'

Chapter Ten

Marcie Brooks sat numbly following Linda Bell's visit. For all her bravado about facing Michael while that tart had been there, after Linda had left she hadn't had the energy or the courage to make a move.

'How do I play it?' she asked Allegra.

Allegra was nibbling at her thumb. At the same time she was eyeing Marcie worriedly. 'I don't know what to say.'

'I'm not asking you whether it's true or not. All I'm asking is how do I play it? Do I face him out or do I ignore the whole thing? Is it worth getting into a row about something that might have happened or might not?'

Allegra stopped nibbling her thumb. She was surprised that Marcie could be so forgiving – if indeed there was anything to forgive.

'I would say nothing. To err is human,' said Allegra. 'Michael is basically a good man and you two have a good marriage. Marriage may be a union sanctioned by God and His Holy Church, but that doesn't make it perfect. And humans are not perfect.'

Marcie watched her children playing on the floor.

Aran was so like his father. So was Joanna, if it came to that. She wondered briefly how marriage to Johnnie might have been. But the thought was fleeting and no longer caused her the pain it had once. Michael was her main concern. He was the man she loved.

She sighed. 'It hurts, but I don't want to split up over this.'

'Then don't mention it unless he does.'

'You don't think he might confess?'

'He might, but to a priest not to you.'

Allegra's words were surprisingly calming. Marcie decided not to mention anything to Sally who might be more belligerent about it. Sally had many lovers but no husband. All the same she took a dim view of men who cheated on their wives.

Marcie found the whole thing hard to accept. Why was it she couldn't find it in her heart to hate her husband for what he'd allegedly done?

Because at heart you don't believe it, she told herself. At heart you still believe that he's the man you married, loyal and loving.

The moment she came across an empty telephone box, Linda Bell reported back to Paddy Rafferty as agreed. 'That's my girl,' he said, sounding as though he were smiling at the phone.

Linda glowed with gratitude as though she were taking an encore on a West End stage not standing in a phone box which smelled of urine and cigarette ends and was littered with postcards advertising various services: 'French Polishing – reasonable rates'; 'School Mistress. Disciplined lessons.'

No more of that for me, thought Linda. She was on the up and nothing could stop her now.

'How did Jones take it?'

She hesitated, thought about gilding the lily a bit by lying, then decided to tell the truth. Rafferty might be grateful for that.

'He gave me a message. He said tell that bog Irish idiot Rafferty that I'll kill him if he ever comes near me and mine.'

She could almost hear the rumble of his anger down the phone.

'Did he now,' Rafferty growled.

She imagined his face turning red, just like it did when he was putting it into her. He always got hot and red in the face when he was in bed with a girl or two.

'He said he'd kill me too if I went to his wife and told her.'

'Where did he say this?'

'In a café. In front of everybody.'

'So there were a lot of witnesses?'

'Yes,' she said. 'There were.' She frowned. The pips would go soon if she didn't get to the point and she didn't have any more pennies to put into the slot. There was only one question on her mind.

'So! When do I get paid?' she asked, as she slipped the cushion out from beneath her clothes and let it drop to the grubby floor.

Paddy's response came surprisingly quickly. 'Corner of Cobden Street, down by the gas works, tonight round about eleven. I'll send Baxter along with it.'

Linda frowned. The time and location weren't exactly to her liking. Besides the gas works, the only other places of note down there were a couple of scrapyards surrounded by a fence of corrugated tin. Populated it was not. Deserted in fact at that time of night. Meeting anyone there was unnerving. She decided to check that she'd heard right.

'Cobden Street? It's a bit late to be down there at that time of night.'

'Well, we don't want anyone knowing you were putting on a show, do we, girl? Don't want any shady dealings affecting your prospects, do we?'

Linda had been fired from the last club she'd worked at for lifting the wallet of a drunken client. She hadn't taken it seriously when the club manager, an elegant black guy named Leroy, had told her that things were run pretty straight as per the boss's instructions. She'd disbelieved him and paid the price. Now she was getting her own back. Victor Camilleri had owned that club. As far as she was concerned, Michael Jones was his son and therefore as deserving of her revenge as his father was. Linda had a warped view of justice.

'I suppose it'll be all right,' she said, while thinking of how she was going to spend the money. One hundred pounds! A shopping trip along Oxford Street was most definitely on the cards. She might even venture up west and go in Harrods. A hundred pounds could buy her something really classy.

Paddy put down the phone and gritted his teeth over the Churchill-size cigar he favoured, rolling it over his tongue to the corner of his mouth.

'Stupid cow.' He looked up at Baxter. 'That bastard Jones threatened to kill me and then threatened to kill her. A bad mistake.'

'How's that, boss?' said Baxter.

Rafferty grinned like a snake about to swallow its dinner. 'He said it in front of witnesses.'

Baxter didn't need his boss to explain things further. He knew where this was going. Paddy Rafferty was only cool up to a point. Once somebody insulted, crossed him or turned him down on a deal – a deal that was in his favour – they were dead meat. Michael Jones had done all three. Paddy Rafferty was out for a sudden and very cruel revenge.

Their eyes met in mutual understanding. Baxter was as cold as Rafferty but like a bullet he had to be aimed at his target.

'She'll be there at eleven tonight. You know what to do?'

Baxter nodded. Of stocky build, Baxter had an inconspicuous air about him. He wasn't handsome, he wasn't huge and neither was he that imposing. In short he was the sort of bloke people didn't really notice. In the past he had been a freelance contractor known to every high-flying criminal in London. If any of them had wanted to get rid of someone, he was the man they hired. Nobody knew for certain how many people he'd killed in his time, and no one was counting. He was a convenience who'd never been found out – not for murder anyway.

Charlie Baxter had been working for Paddy since coming out from his last term in the 'Scrubs'. Paddy had been the only bloke to give him a chance even though he knew what he'd gone in for. Baxter hung about in lavatories waiting for willing men. Something about that turned the stomachs of some, but Paddy had given him a chance, providing he kept on the straight and narrow, went along to the counselling sessions and took the tablets – bromide mostly – same as Paddy himself had taken in his National Service days. He sometimes thought it was the best thing he'd ever got from the army. The rest of it was all bullshit as far as he was concerned. He still had contacts there; handy if he ever wanted a gun, which sometimes – just sometimes – he did.

*   *   *

The smell of grilled steak with all the trimmings filled Marcie's kitchen. She loved cooking for Michael when it was just the two of them. He'd even brought home a bottle of wine.

Together they'd put the kids to bed. Marcie loved that too. It wasn't often they got to do it what with him working some nights making sure the club staff were doing their jobs properly.

Friday night was usually a busy night so it had come as a complete surprise that he'd rang earlier and said he fancied a quiet night in.

'It's Friday. You're not usually home on a Friday.'

'I felt like a change. I fancy spending some time with my missus. Is that OK?'

His tone was a little sharp, but she didn't react. There was no point in looking for trouble or indeed a gift horse in the mouth. She'd love to have him home. If he was here he wasn't seeing the Linda Bells of this world was he?

The feeling that she'd been stabbed in the heart was still there, but she'd determined the subject would not be mentioned. Like a lot of bad things in her life, it would be brushed from her memory – at least she hoped it would.

Allegra's serenity had helped her come to terms with the shock. It was early days but she was sure she would get over it. She *had* to get over it for her children's sake.

She smiled at him brightly when he came into the room after reading a bedtime story to Joanna and taking a look in on Aran.

'Is she asleep?' she asked as she stirred the boiling peas – as if they needed any stirring.

'Both of them are dead to the world up there,' he said with a smile, moving in to give her a hug. Lifting her hair to one side, he kissed the nape of her neck as he'd done a hundred times before. This time it almost hurt. Had he done the same to Linda Bell?

Stop it! Stop it now!

The small voice in her head took her by surprise. It seemed a long time since she'd last heard it. But the voice – she liked to think it was Johnnie's – had always been right. She forced herself to fight back the feeling of betrayal.

She managed a light laugh into the steam from the peas. 'I wish you wouldn't do that,' she said to him.

'Why?' He continued to nuzzle her neck.

'Because if you carry on like it I won't want to eat steak – I'll want to eat you.'

She turned round to face him entwining her arms around his neck. He smelled good and looked even better. Little creases appeared at the corners of his eyes when he smiled. She closed her eyes when he kissed her, tried to forget their recent troubles and focus on how lucky they were to have each other.

Even so, the confrontation with Linda Bell was still at the back of her mind. And there it is staying, she thought to herself. The girl was a liar. She felt it somehow. Michael was the best thing that had ever happened to her and she wasn't going to let a vindictive ex-employee get to her. Besides, she'd run away once Marcie had offered that they go together to see her husband and have it out. Surely that meant something?

She must have tensed while her thoughts ran riot, because Michael noticed.

'Is something wrong?' he asked.

She shook her head. At the same time she pressed her hands against the nape of his neck so he could kiss her again.

'I'm going to die in your arms,' she said suddenly.

The comment came unbidden and without warning. She'd surprised herself by saying it. Michael looked surprised too.

'Where did that come from?' he asked her as she leaned against his hands, which were supporting the small of her back.

She shrugged. 'I don't know. I just felt I had to say it. I just felt it mattered.'

The peas chose that moment to boil over and curtail further kisses and the possibility that they might forego dinner altogether and make for the bedroom.

'Oh no! What a bloody mess!'

She turned the gas off immediately and dished out the steak, the chips, the salad and the peas as Michael poured the wine and lit a candle.

'Here's to my lovely wife,' he said in the softly seductive voice he'd used on their wedding night.

'And on a Friday night,' said Marcie. 'And it's not even our wedding anniversary. Do you have any other reason for doing this?'

A look she had trouble reading flashed into his eyes and then was swiftly gone. His smile was wide and reassuring.

'One year, six months and twenty-three days, six hours and forty-three minutes?' He closed one eye as though he really had calculated it to the very day, the very hour and the very second.

Marcie laughed. One year, six months maybe, but she'd need to put her thinking cap on with the rest of it. 'And don't think for one moment that I believe you've worked it out that precisely,' she said, still laughing, still entering into the spirit of his behaviour. 'How come?'

'How come?' He looked taken aback, pretending to be found out and not wanting to admit to anything.

Marcie flipped a finger at his nose. 'What brought on this sudden calculation of how long we've been together – and the fact that you're home on a Friday night?'

His expression changed in an instant. 'Does there have to be a reason?'

She didn't want his mood to change and instantly regretted what she'd said. 'No. Of course not. It's lovely having you here. The kids loved it too.'

She realised she was gushing, but if that's what it took to see him smile again, that's what she would do.

'I'm glad,' he said.

Just as he reached across the table to take her hand and kiss her wrist, the phone rang.

'Saved by the bell,' said Marcie.

Michael got up from the table. 'I'll be right back. And then I'm going to take it off the hook and ignore it. Tonight is for us!'

She laughed and this time felt happy.

The phone was on a half-moon table with wrought-iron legs out in the hallway. Marcie sat with her hands folded beneath her chin listening to Michael's murmuring voice and knowing – absolutely knowing – what he was going to come in and say.

'That was one of the waiters from Aldo's Trattoria phoning to tell me there's been trouble at the club. The poor bloke sounded so hysterical I could barely hear him.'

He moved smartly, grabbing his coat and his car keys, pausing only to peck at her cheek. Like a hurricane he whizzed down the hallway. At the door he stopped to call out that he would be back as soon as he could. 'And phone your dad. Tell him to get round there ASAP. OK?'

Marcie phoned her father as ordered. Knowing her father well, she phoned him at his favourite pub, the Black Dog in Lambeth. There was much raucous noise on the other end. Above it all she heard the barman shout for her father. When he came to the phone he sounded drunk.

'It's my night off and I'm here with friends.'

'Well, it isn't now. Michael said he needs you there.'

Her father wasn't happy about leaving the pub and grunted something about being ordered around like a dog before putting the phone down.

Not entirely convinced he'd do as requested, she sat down and finished her glass of wine before starting on the dishes.

'Well, that's that,' she said to herself.

If things had gone according to plan – that is dinner then bed – she wondered whether she would have had the courage to mention Linda Bell to Michael. She couldn't make up her mind about that one. There was no doubting that the girls at the club fancied Michael; nobody in their right mind *wouldn't* fancy him. When she'd first met him she'd never really noticed how attractive he was. He'd been overshadowed by his more obviously handsome half-brother. Michael's good looks were more subtle. She never doubted that she'd ended up with the better man, but discovering women found him very attractive had surprised her and she counted herself lucky that he was her husband.

The corners of her mouth turned down as her thoughts darkened. Linda Bell. What was she to Michael? And what was Michael to her? Perhaps they had meant something to each other in the past. Perhaps she was purely out for revenge. Was she really pregnant? And if so, was it Michael's?

She shivered. It wouldn't do any good to go there. The girl had been lying. That's all there was to it.

Tony Brooks was drunk and enjoying the company.

'My daughter,' he said to the four men he was drinking with. 'She's ordering me around like a bleedin' dog. I told her that you know. I told her that.'

'Why don't you have another drink,' said the man he knew as Sean.

'Your wish is my command,' Tony replied.

'We'll put one behind the bar for you.'

His four new friends made ready to depart.

'You're leaving already?'

They hadn't been his friends for too long. His mind was a bit addled as to when they'd actually met, but he did recall having one hell of a binge with them the night before. They'd trawled a few pubs before making their way to the Blue Genie in the early hours of the morning.

'Thanks for taking us to your club. You're a lucky man, Tony,' Gerry, one of the other Irishmen, said to him.

Tony didn't correct them as to the ownership of the Blue Genie. He boasted to a lot of people that he owned a nightclub. To his mind it wasn't that far from the truth. His daughter owned it, right? By being married to Michael Jones.

His smile was broad and fuelled with alcohol. 'No problem at all. Any time you want, just mention my name.'

The four Irishmen left him standing there at the bar. He lifted his hand in a desultory wave and made it seem that he had no intention of leaving the pub just yet. Who did Marcie think she was ordering him around anyway? All the same, he wasn't as drunk as last night. His daughter had been urging and it wouldn't hurt to go along and see what the matter was.

Outside on the pavement the four Irishmen began the long walk back to their digs. The woman they were lodging with kept a tin bath in an outhouse where they were required to bathe one night per week. She also had an indoor bath in which she kept the coal. The coal cellar itself was let out to a family of Jamaicans. Everyone wanted somewhere to stay and what did it matter if you piled them in?

'Make hay while the sun shines, that's my motto,' she told them when they'd asked why she kept her coal in the bath.

They'd carped on to one of Rafferty's men about the conditions they were required to live in.

'Nothing will come of our moans and groans,' Gerry had said, but he'd been wrong.

'Lads, in exchange for a little job . . .'

Rafferty had given them an option. New lodgings or cash in hand. They'd gone for the cash and done the little job he'd asked them to do.

Chapter Eleven

Marcie waited until gone three in the morning before she phoned the Blue Genie. There was no reply.

Following that she phoned her father. A woman's voice, which she presumed belonged to her father's latest girlfriend, answered.

'Hello.'

'Is Tony Brooks there? It's his daughter, Marcie.'

'He's here, but out of it. Drunk as a skunk. No good to man nor beast – and certainly no good to woman.'

'Who are you?'

'Desdemona.' She gave a little laugh.

Marcie persisted. 'I'm trying to find out where my husband, Michael is. No one's answering the phone at his club. Can you ask my father if he's seen him?'

'Sure.'

She heard Desdemona ask and heard her father's grumbled reply.

'He said to tell you that they were drinking half the night. He's probably out of it on that settee at the back of his office.'

Marcie paused. Michael did indeed have a studio couch-style settee in the small alcove at the back of his office. He dossed down there when he was too tired to come home. It wouldn't be the first time her father had led him astray, though it was only very occasionally and usually the drink was aided by weariness.

'Is that what my father said?' Marcie asked.

'He grunted something about drinking. I'm assuming the bit about the settee, honey child,' said Desdemona.

It occurred to Marcie that Desdemona had personal knowledge of the settee. Nobody would know it was there unless they'd made use of it. An empty feeling as heavy as molten lead seemed to swirl in her stomach. Either Desdemona had heard gossip from other girls about the couch, or she'd knowledge of it herself – possibly introduced to it by her father. It wasn't entirely unknown that he took advantage of the club's facilities when it suited him.

'OK. I'll leave it until the morning. You don't know what trouble happened last night do you?'

'No idea.'

'My dad never mentioned anything?'

'Nothing at all.'

Marcie concluded that there was nothing to worry about seeing as her father was sleeping like a baby. Michael would be in touch once he'd slept it off. All the same she cursed her father for curtailing what could have been a very romantic evening and passionate night.

Resisting the inclination to phone her husband was difficult, but Marcie was determined not to appear too needy. Michael might get suspicious that she was hiding something. She'd resolved not to make a fuss about the Linda Bell incident, and she would stick to her guns.

Even though he had not been in contact by the next morning, she went along to the sewing room as usual, taking the kids with her. Although she'd told herself she wasn't worried, the cracks were beginning to show.

The baby fell asleep and Joanna was playing with some buttons in a cardboard box.

Sally was telling her otherwise and kept asking her what was wrong.

'Nothing,' snapped Marcie.

The cotton on the sewing machine snapped as she tugged a snakeskin gaiter too quickly and roughly.

'From where I'm sitting it don't look like nothing,' said Sally. She turned to Allegra. 'How about you?'

Allegra was sitting in a chair by the window facing the street. The light from the window cast odd shadows across her face. She didn't hear what Sally had said.

Sally raised her voice. 'Allegra? Please come down to Planet Earth.'

Allegra looked round. 'Did you say something?'

Sally rolled her eyes. 'I said that Marcie seems to have something on her mind and should share it with us. One look at you and I see that she's not the only one with something on her mind. What the hell is this? Something contagious?'

Allegra apologised. 'I'm sorry. My mind was elsewhere. What were you saying?'

Allegra Montillado was a different person than the one who'd been in love with Victor Camilleri. He'd seen her at church with her parents, had seduced her and made her his mistress. Things had gone wrong when Marcie had appeared. Torn between her friend and her lover, Allegra had found Victor out for the brute he could be.

'Are you still mooning about Victor?' Tact never being her style, Sally was the one asking.

Allegra shook her head. 'No. Not any more. I've decided that there are more important things in life than men.'

Sally's eyes opened wide and her hands went to her hips. She was the picture of shocked amazement. 'I did not know that!' she exclaimed. 'What have you found that's better?'

Seeing that she was being mocked, Allegra smiled gently and shook her head. 'You wouldn't understand.'

'Try me.'

Dwelling as she was on her own problems, Marcie couldn't bring herself to make comment or to intervene. The only thing she did notice was that Allegra no longer wore make-up or jewellery and yet she owned the very best. Victor had been generous to his mistress. Perhaps, thought Marcie, she'd wanted more than that. But Victor was married. Just as Michael was married to her. She still couldn't believe that he'd been involved with a girl like Linda Bell, but hadn't had it out with him. Fear got you like that, she decided. Fear of the truth. Fear that her happy life was nothing but a sham.

Allegra seemed to come to a considered decision. She took a deep breath. 'I just feel that we sometimes pursue the same things other people pursue without really wanting them. Once they're gone we see them for what they were – just passing fancies . . .'

'Like Victor?' asked Sally.

Allegra glanced at her as though her intervention was predictable and not worth commenting on. 'If you like. It was an experience, and one I will not be repeating.'

'We've all said that,' laughed Sally. 'You'll fall in love more than once in your life. We all do. Isn't that right, Marcie?'

Marcie's fingers tightened over the piece of material. Johnnie would always have a place in her heart because of her daughter, but the feeling she'd had for him was slowly evaporating. Michael had replaced him and when they'd married she'd told herself that she would never want anyone else. He'd told her that he would love her forever. She'd believed him. And now there was Linda Bell . . .

Chapter Twelve

Michael stared across the table, unable to believe that he was being accused of murdering Linda Bell.

'No,' he said shaking his head. 'No way!'

'Witnesses say you threatened to kill her. Come on, Michael. You might call yourself Jones, but we all know who your old man is, don't we? Victor Camilleri. Catholic he might be, me old mate, but saintly he is not. Like father, like son, in my opinion.'

They were in an interview room at the local nick. The smell of industrial-strength cleaner failed to mask the lingering scent of stale sweat. The copper on the other side of the table was chewing a matchstick at the side of his mouth. He looked confident, cocky even.

His sidekick – introduced as Detective Sergeant Bill Floyd – was sitting next to him. A uniformed constable was doing doorman duty. He stood like a stone pillar against a white-tiled wall. Michael guessed that the same white tiles were used in the cells below, a foretaste to the accused of things to come.

Although he tried desperately to hold on to it,

Michael felt his confidence sinking fast, not that he'd let them know that.

'You have to be fucking joking!' he exclaimed.

The bloke chewing the matchstick shook his head slowly. 'Murder is no joke. You had a set-to with Linda Bell. You were heard threatening to kill her. Are you denying knowing her?'

'No. I knew her.'

'Witnesses said she claimed to be pregnant. Was it yours?'

Michael glowered. 'Fuck off!'

'Less of the bad language,' said the copper doing the interviewing, who had introduced himself as Detective Inspector David Daniels. He had a sandy-coloured moustache that shielded his upper lip from view. His eyes were a murky shade of hazel and his hair was like a sandy thatch sitting at a lopsided angle on his head.

Despite the circumstances, Michael couldn't help a wry grin. The bloke was definitely sporting a wig.

'What's so funny, Camilleri?'

Michael felt his facial muscles tighten and his smile disintegrate. 'My name's Jones, Michael Jones.'

He'd learned how to handle the police from his father. He knew that Victor had a few high-up members of the constabulary in his pocket, bundles of loot handed over in exchange for them looking the other way. But he knew that things had floundered a bit of late. The coppers he was now dealing with weren't the same ones who had got hold of details of Victor's very illicit business deals. They had Michael to thank for that. It was Michael who had passed over the accounts books and the lists of clients paying protection money. Michael had presumed that nobody would come asking *him* for protection money simply because he was Victor Camilleri's son. But they had. Now all he had to decide was which one of the bastards had set him up for this: his own father or Paddy Rafferty. The former had been really pissed off at being put inside on fraud charges on account of his own son. The other he had insulted and made clear to him that he was not going to get the partnership he'd pushed for.

Michael had been unaware that the building he'd bought was up for redevelopment. Not that it mattered much. Both his father and Rafferty possessed a similar brand of revenge mentality. He was in the firing line no matter who had loaded the gun.

David Daniels was not amused. He raised his voice. 'Wipe that smirk off your face! I think we've already made it plain that murder is no laughing matter!'

'I totally agree with you. Sorry. I was just thinking.'

'Thinking what?'

One corner of Michael's mouth lifted into a half-smile. 'How some men lose their hair quicker than others.'

Perhaps Daniels might not have lost his rag if Michael hadn't ran his fingers through his thick head of dark brown – almost black – hair. The policeman's face went bright red before he flung himself across the table, his hands groping for Michael's throat.

Michael kicked the chair back and stood up before he could reach him. The officer by the door came to life, catching the chair and stepping forwards ready to restrain the prisoner.

'Dave!'

Detective Sergeant Bill Floyd was a bull of a man. Although getting on in years, he was strong and had no trouble in getting his superior to sit back down.

'Got to keep to the rule book, Dave,' he said.

It was obvious from his tone and his words that Bill Floyd was a stickler for doing things by the book. That was probably why he was still only a Detective Sergeant, promotion having passed him by in favour of younger and more flexible operators. Michael recognised the steadiness in him and was thankful he was there. He adjusted his tie by way of fingering his throat. He looked at Daniels with a face full of swagger, even if inside he was reeling.

'Charge me or let me go,' he said to them grimly and with confidence.

Daniels pointed a warning finger. 'You did it, you

bastard! You arranged to meet her with the aim of killing her. She turned up hoping that you'd do the right thing by her and instead you shot her.'

Michael sat back down as directed by Detective Sergeant Floyd. 'This is ridiculous. I can't – couldn't – do the right thing by her. I'm married. I'm sorry she's dead but, like I said, I never had the pleasure.'

Actually saying that he was married filled him with fear. What was Marcie going to say? Surely she wouldn't believe that he'd been having a relationship with Linda Bell? He had to make her believe that it wasn't true. His life might depend on it.

He decided to say nothing until he had to. He didn't want to upset Marcie unnecessarily and he was so sure that the police would let him go that he hadn't even asked for a brief.

Then Daniels dropped the bombshell.

'We've got the gun. Your prints are all over it.'

Michael felt the blood draining from his face. The gun he'd found in the club the other night! Further enquiries of his employees had shed no light on where the gun had come from.

Michael had placed it in the safe until he decided what to do with it. Unfortunately it meant his prints were all over it. It was reasonable to assume that someone had been paid to plant it in the drawer. Up until now the thought had never entered his head. Now here he was, jumping to conclusions that this was some kind of a set-up. All the same, he had to bluff it out.

'I don't have a gun.'

'Not a legal one,' snarled Daniels with a hint of glee in his eyes. 'We checked our records. You hold no gun licence – but that doesn't mean you don't own one. Blokes like you operating outside the law don't go in for gun licences. Only blokes that shoot pheasants and rats do that. But then you are a rat, Michael Camilleri . . .'

'My name's Jones,' Michael repeated with an edge to his voice. 'Michael Jones!'

Daniels grinned. His eyes glittered. 'Whatever! Michael Jones, I am arresting you for the murder of Linda Georgina Bell. You don't have to say anything but whatever you do say may be taken down and given in evidence against you.'

Jacob Solomon had arrived in England as a refugee from Nazi Germany just before the Second World War and had immediately set up home and his legal practice in the East End of London amongst other members of the tribe of Israel. Having fled brutal oppression he'd been very relieved and happy to find such a safe and friendly haven, so much so in fact, that he rarely left the East End of London for anyone. But Michael Jones was one of his best clients and he liked him, recognising something of the son he'd once had who he had left behind with his wife in Germany. He'd hoped to make arrangements for them to follow him to London but he'd never seen either of them again.

Michael was a gentile and only a substitute for his dead son, but it gave him comfort. Jacob took pride in Michael's achievements as though he were his real son. He liked the fact that the boy had rebelled against the Camilleris. He'd heard what brutes they were, violent landlords of Victorian tenements that had survived the Blitz. He abhorred all violence. It was in his blood to do so.

Marcie was totally taken aback to see him standing on her doorstep. Her day at the sewing room had not been without its problems. Number one, Renee hadn't turned up. A note had finally arrived saying she'd tripped over a neighbour's cat and twisted her ankle. Normally she would have phoned but the shop phone was out of action. Following numerous calls from the public phone box, the Post Office people had eventually turned up and informed her that the fault was with the telephone receiver in the shop below with whom she happened to share a party line. Oddly enough the broken telephone connection made her feel better. Michael was obviously trying to ring her, but couldn't get through. It gave her some solace and even the hope that he could drop by the sewing room if he couldn't get through.

The problems of the day had been unexpected. Jacob turning up at their home was even more so.

'Jacob! What a surprise.'

At first she smiled, but on seeing that his solemn expression remained dark, her smile faded.

'May I come in?'

Joanna was gazing at *Muffin the Mule* on the television in the front room and Aran was asleep in his cot. Marcie took Jacob into the dining room and asked him if he would like a cup of tea.

He shook his head and sucked in his lips. His eyes flickered nervously behind his horn-rimmed spectacles.

His manner said it all. Marcie felt her face drain of colour because she knew, she knew beyond doubt, that something was terribly wrong.

'Are the police coming here?'

It sounded mad. Nobody had given her a reason that the police were coming.

Jacob nodded. 'They may very well do so. Michael has been arrested.'

She collapsed into a chair, the breath knocked out of her, her jaw slack, her mouth open. No words came.

Jacob sat down opposite her, set his briefcase down and rubbed his bony white hands together.

'I want you to be calm before I tell you this. Michael is convinced that he's been set up. I'm sure he has, but my belief in him is nothing compared to yours. You have to believe that Michael is telling the truth. A girl came to the club and accused him of getting her pregnant . . .'

'Linda Bell!'

Jacob's eyes opened wide. 'You knew?'

'She came to me and told me. I threw her out. I didn't believe her. I'll say it to her face too.'

The eyes behind the spectacles looked away from her. 'I'm afraid that will not be possible.'

It wasn't easy to subdue the shiver that ran down her spine like ice-cold water.

Seeing that she said nothing, Jacob came right out with the problem.

'Linda Bell's dead. Michael has been charged with her murder.'

Chapter Thirteen

'Let me take your arm, Garth.'

'All right, Auntie Rosa.'

With a feeling of great relief, Rosa Brooks slipped her hand through Garth's arm. 'The butcher's next,' she said to him. 'But not too fast. My legs are older than yours.'

'Right you are, Auntie Rosa.'

The truth of the matter was that her legs were not really the problem. The fact was that she could no longer clearly see where she was going.

A passer-by said good morning, addressing her by name as they went by.

'Good morning. How are you?' she replied while quickening her pace. She dare not stop in case the other person took her question literally and began telling her exactly how they were. She couldn't stand that. Not any more, the plain fact being that she hadn't a clue of the person's identity because she couldn't see them.

Rosa Brooks was becoming more and more aware that the darkness of the night was infiltrating her daylight hours. The doctor had told her this would happen. He called it glaucoma and said that it was as a direct result of her diabetes. He'd prescribed insulin tablets but told her she might have to have injections when the tablets no longer did their job. He could do nothing about her eyes.

'Four lamb chops, Mrs Brooks?'

'That's right. English lamb, please. And can I have an extra piece of white paper around it. I wouldn't want the blood to run into my bag.'

'And then I can draw on it!' Garth exclaimed.

Rosa dug her elbow into his ribs. 'Never mind that.'

The butcher didn't seem to mind going by what he said. 'Here. Have a folded sheet without any bloodstains. And all for the princely sum of three shillings and sixpence,' he said.

She could hear the amusement in his voice. If she'd been younger she might have blushed. The extra paper was indeed for Garth to draw on. He drew on any piece of scrap paper. She'd bought him a sketch pad but he'd used it up in no time. The pieces of white paper helped supplement the sketch pad and the odd roll of wallpaper. Garth was drawing all the time.

After shopping, they returned to the cosy cottage kitchen where familiar items meant Rosa could more easily find her way around. From the hook beside the range she took a saucepan and a frying pan. From the stiff drawer of the old painted dresser she took the sharp knife she used to peel vegetables. The saucepan was filled with water and put on the range. A knob of lard was added to the frying pan together with a handful of chopped herbs, which she grew in pots outside the back door. It pained her that she couldn't buy olive oil in Sheerness. Everyone cooked in lard or beef suet; shopkeepers had eyed her querulously when she'd first come to this country and asked for such an exotic item. On the odd shopping trip off the island she had managed to buy it and sometimes her son brought her a bottle back from London – when he remembered to.

She sighed as she placed the lamb chops in the sizzling pan. Her son was not as dependable as he'd once been. He'd seemed closer to her when Mary was around, almost as though he needed some form of support against such a powerful woman. Mary had not merely been attractive. She'd run rings around her son and Rosa had insisted that no good would come of their marriage. Girls in the old country had been subservient to their husbands and Mary Brooks had been far from that.

With hindsight she realised that she'd been wrong about Mary. Marcie had come along and Mary, for all her strong-mindedness, had been an angel compared to Babs. There was no doubt about it: Babs was brass to Mary's golden.

She sighed. It was not easy admitting to being wrong. Nearing the end of her days, she turned over her life in her mind. It was like turning the pages of a book; some chapters were more enjoyable than others.

Engrossed in her thoughts, it was a minute or two before she realised that Garth was saying something. It sounded like singing.

'What was that you said?' she asked.

'I wasn't speaking to you, Auntie Rosa. I was speaking to Arthur. He was telling me things.'

A light humming of the 'Londonderry Air' drifted like gossamer around the cosy but cramped kitchen.

Ah, yes. Arthur! Arthur was Garth's imaginary friend who she'd first heard humming the same tune at the mental hospital. According to Garth, Arthur had been a builder back in the nineteenth century when the hospital was built. He'd been killed on site before the building was finished, a fact that still plagued him in eternity. For some odd reason he'd attached himself to Garth and upped sticks to number ten Endeavour Terrace.

'So what was Arthur telling you?' asked Rosa, amusement quivering around her lips.

'He said there's been a murder. In London.'

Rosa froze. Garth had the gift of sometimes drawing things that would happen in the future. Of late Arthur had been feeding him information that he'd passed verbally on to her.

Her first thought was that her son, Antonio Brooks, had got himself into trouble again. It wouldn't be the first time, but he'd never killed anyone.

'Please God, no,' she murmured, mostly to herself.

Garth heard her. 'He said it was her own fault.'

Rosa heard. 'She?'

'A woman.'

To Rosa it felt as though a pair of hands were tightening around her jugular.

'Is it Marcie?' she whispered hoarsely.

Garth shook his head, seemingly engrossed in his drawing. 'She's got dark hair. It's not Marcie.'

Rosa closed her eyes. 'Mother of God,' she whispered. 'Thank you for that.'

An excited hammering on the back door jolted her back to her senses. There was no need for her to open it. The latch was on; it always was.

'Gran, we're starving.'

Archie and Arnold came tumbling into the kitchen, their noses upturned, their eyes already checking out the table, the bubbling saucepan of vegetables and the sizzling lamb chops.

'Are they for us?' asked Arnold.

'For you, your brother and Garth.'

'Ain't you having any?' asked Archie.

'No. I've already eaten. Divide the spare one between you.'

It was untrue, of course, but she couldn't see the

two boys go without. But never mind. She told herself that she'd have a cheese sandwich later when they'd gone and Garth was asleep.

I wish I was there to look after you, Rosa Brooks.

'Go away,' she said irritably.

The two boys looked at her. 'What?'

She smiled. 'Not you. I was talking to your grandfather.'

They both tossed their heads knowingly and rolled their eyes as though they considered her slightly touched. Grandma Brooks had a habit of talking to her dead husband, their grandfather. They'd got used to it over the years and besides they were here to eat. Their stomachs were rumbling.

'Where's your sister?' Rosa asked.

'A woman took her away,' they explained as they chewed.

Rosa raised her eyes to heaven. She had no doubt who the woman was. Someone had reported her daughter-in-law for neglecting her child. The poor mite had been taken into care.

She immediately whipped off her apron. 'God save us! Where's your mother now?'

'Gone to the pub.'

'Take me there.'

Archie screwed up his face in protest. Much as he loved his sister, his stomach was rumbling something chronic even though he'd eaten half his food already.

'Do I have to go?' he groaned.

Rosa grabbed his shoulder. 'Yes. You do. Now get me my coat. And get yours too, Garth.'

'What's he coming for?' said Archie, his face screwed up even tighter.

'I need him to lean on,' she said. 'My legs are not so good.'

'No. I'm your eyes,' murmured Garth.

Rosa clenched her jaw. The boys were too young and too wrapped up in their own world to realise the significance of what Garth had said. When it had become obvious that her eyesight was getting worse and blindness was just around the corner, she'd somehow thought she would ride it, as though her second sight – her great gift – would see her through. It seemed it was not to be. The fact pained her.

They left the house and made their way towards the pub.

It was strange to be sightless and suddenly to have happening what happened next. 'Garth! Stop!'

Garth did as he was told though not as abruptly as she would have liked.

'You all right, Auntie Rosa?' His voice was high and squeaky, but the sentiments were genuine. His watery blue eyes regarded her with concern.

'No, Garth. I am not all right. I'm seeing things more clearly than I have ever done.'

Her voice fell away into quietness. Her breath was

tight in her chest. Holding her hand against her chest, she tried to put into perspective what she was feeling – no! Not what she was feeling. What she was *seeing*!

'We have to go back,' she said to Garth, wheeling him around as though he were her partner around a maypole. 'Marcie may be trying to phone us and we need to be there.'

'Good,' said Arnold. 'Can I take some cake back for our Annie?'

'You said a woman had taken her away?'

'Yeah, but me and Archie got her back again. We bought her some fish and chips and she's sat at home in front of the telly. It's only a black and white one, but she doesn't mind. Are you going to get a colour telly, Gran?'

The last thing Rosa Brooks had a use for was one of the new-fangled colour televisions. She'd seen most of the greatest films ever made in black and white and was sure that anything in colour wouldn't be a patch on them.

'Right now, Auntie Rosa?' Garth asked her.

'Right now,' she replied.

For once her aching old legs found a sudden burst of speed, which threw Garth off guard.

They headed back to Endeavour Terrace, Rosa spurred on by the sudden fear that had come upon her. This only happened when a member of her family was threatened.

The phone in the public phone box at the end of the terrace was ringing just as she'd known it would be.

Without being told to, Garth heaved the door open. He did not attempt to answer it but stood back as though instinctively knowing that it was Rosa who must answer it.

Rosa stumbled against him in her haste to pick it up.

'It's me,' said the male voice on the other end.

'Antonio!'

He sounded grim. 'Ma, I need to come home this weekend. I'm going to get Marcie and the kids to come with me. Something terrible has happened.'

'Michael.'

The name was not posed as a question. Something bad had happened to Michael. This was what she had suddenly felt on the way to find Babs.

'You will be welcome,' she said, forcing her fear to stay in its place until she could effectively deal with it, until she knew all the details.

She did not mention that she'd expected him to phone. It didn't matter. All that mattered was that her son and her granddaughter needed her.

Chapter Fourteen

Tony Brooks sat watching his daughter. She'd been cradling the same cup of tea for twenty minutes now without saying a word. It was difficult to tell what she was thinking or what she was staring at.

She's like one of them bloody zombies, he thought. He'd seen a horror film about zombies at the pictures recently. He'd never heard of the word before that.

The silence was getting on his nerves and he began wondering what he could say to break it. Nothing he could think of seemed right. But then, how could it be? Michael had been arrested for murder. He couldn't believe it. Michael was meek and mild; OK, he had a shrewd business head and an average amount of nous, but Tony didn't regard him as a hard man, certainly not hard enough to commit murder.

The word on the streets was that the bird had been pregnant and had accused Michael of being the father. Tony wasn't sure what to believe. After all, the bloke was married to his daughter and it grieved him that his son-in-law could have treated her like that. His first reaction had been anger until he'd countered that with the conviction that they weren't that much different. Men were different to women. They had needs. It didn't mean they didn't love their wife and kids. They were just different.

The silence was overpowering. He found himself wishing that Sally hadn't taken the kids out for an hour. Any noise was better than this.

In the absence of anything useful to say, he studied his daughter. She looked distraught, still beautiful though, even if her eyes were so sad. A pang of regret stabbed at his heart. With her lovely blonde hair, Marcie was a lot like Mary, her mother, his first wife. The only woman Tony had truly loved beside his mum, if truth be told. If only things had been different. Still, he thought, water under the bridge.

There was nothing for it. He had to make a stab at conversation.

'He'll get off. Course he will. Everyone knows old Michael wouldn't hurt a fly.'

'His prints were on the gun,' Marcie stated, her voice hollow, her stance unchanged.

'That don't mean anything,' her father replied, with more conviction than the facts allowed. 'The girl was put up for it. We all know that.'

'And the blood-spattered shirt?'

There was no answer to that. The shirt had been a complete surprise. It was definitely Michael's shirt. The police had found it behind a bush at the bottom of the garden where they claimed Michael had hidden it with a view to disposing of it later without her or anyone else seeing.

'Planted,' said Tony.

'Beneath a rose bush,' said Marcie with a humourless grin. 'That was what was planted there.'

Tony gave a nervous laugh. 'Oh yeah! Planted. Funny – kind of.'

The silence descended again. This time Tony was determined not to let it continue. He put his arm around her. 'Look, love. It's doing no good you sitting there brooding on it. Life goes on and all that. Besides, you've got the kids to think of. How about we all go down and stay with your gran for the weekend? We could all do with a breather. It'll give us time to think. What do you say?'

The sweet faces of Joanna and Aran smiled in Marcie's thoughts. It occurred to her that she'd been neglecting her kids. Seeing Michael in the company of Jacob, his solicitor, and the police had been a terrible experience.

'I didn't do anything,' he'd said to her, his eyes full of fear and pleading. 'Honestly.'

She'd believed him. She still did.

Letting out a single, mournful groan, she hung her head. 'Dad, what the hell am I going to do if he's found guilty?'

Relieved the silence was broken, though his daughter was despairing, Tony patted her hand.

'Don't you worry, love. Old Jacob Solomon is on the case. If he can't get your man out of jail, nobody can.'

Marcie steepled her fingers in front of her face and frowned. 'The legal fees are going to be huge. I might have to mortgage everything to pay them – or at least the house. I don't want to, but there it is.'

The house – the family home – meant a lot to both of them. Michael had been really proud that he'd been able to buy their semi-detached outright. They had no mortgage. A second thought occurred. 'Best still that I sell the house and move back into the flat. It'll be handy for my sewing room. I don't like the kids living in the East End, but there it is.' She paused as a thought occurred to her. 'It'll also be handy for visiting the prison.'

Her voice came to an abrupt halt over the last word. Prison! She'd never considered her husband might end up there. Not like her father. She caught the look in her father's eyes and guessed he was reading her thoughts.

'You won't need to sell your nice house,' he said as though he had some control over events.

'Yes,' she said resolutely. 'I think I'll have to. In the meantime, I'll rent it out.' She got to her feet. 'I'm going to move back into the flat. I need to be on the job. I need to be there to keep an eye on what's going on.'

'So how about this weekend?' asked her father. 'How about we head home to Sheppey?'

Home. The word seemed to echo in Marcie's head before curling itself around her like a warm blanket.

She nodded. 'I think I'd like that.'

Marcie had a smart new Mini Cooper, which was great for ferrying herself and the kids around. Her father had acquired some middle-aged spread and tended to overfill the front passenger seat so they went down to the Isle of Sheppey in his car, a dark-green Ford Zodiac with pointed tailfins and chrome hubcaps.

The car was part of the flash image he'd lately adopted and went along with the Elvis Presley hairdo, bushy sideburns framing his face.

Marcie knew that he groomed himself to suit the women in his life. If she was honest she suspected there'd always been other women. Normally it would anger her, but nowadays she didn't want to think about it – just in case her husband Michael was tarred with the same brush.

There were whispers, of course; there always were in the shady world they lived in. Men working at night in close proximity to semi-naked girls were bound to attract gossip. That didn't mean the rumours were true.

She looked out at scenery, so familiar to her from a childhood where things had been cosier than it seemed at the time. Michael had taken her away from all this. Was she a fool to believe he was innocent?

Her grandmother seemed to be bustling around in the kitchen as usual, her face wreathed in smiles at the arrival of her granddaughter and her great-grandchildren. If she was any slower, it didn't really register with Marcie, though nothing much did at the moment. Michael filled her waking hours and haunted her sleep.

Garth was drawing pictures for Joanna. At the same time he sang a very off-key version of 'Old MacDonald Had a Farm' and encouraged Joanna to mimic the animal noises that he did so well.

Although aware of all that was going on, Marcie sat stiffly. Her body felt so cold, so empty. She'd expected her grandmother to look her over in that shrewd way of hers and immediately ask what was wrong. But Rosa hadn't once looked her over and the twinkling dark eyes didn't seem half as bright as she remembered them.

Strange that I want her to notice, to ask what's wrong. Surely she can see it in my face, she thought.

That's selfish!

The voice in her head brought her up short. Of course it was selfish. Her grandmother had raised her, cared for her when she was small and left without a mother. Now she was old.

The realisation left her feeling guilty and needing to apologise.

'I shouldn't have come,' she whispered to her father.

'Of course you should,' he whispered back.

If Rosa heard or saw, she said nothing. Absorbed in providing for a family she didn't see so much of nowadays, she looked happy in her work.

Abundant smells of cooking and all things warm and heartening filled the air. Saucepans on the old range gurgled and steamed. A plum pudding was fetched out of the oven.

Rosa set a cup of tea and a slice of home-made fruitcake on a plate in front of her granddaughter. 'There have been problems. Tell me about them.'

Father and daughter exchanged glances.

'I'll take the kids out into the garden,' said her father. 'We can play football. You coming, Garth?'

'Just one kid, Dad. Aran doesn't play football yet and he's currently asleep.'

Her dad nodded sheepishly. Garth was all chuckles and enthusiasm.

Grandmother and granddaughter were left alone.

Marcie looked into her grandmother's face. The steam from the cooking pots had plastered her hair to her head. It was her eyes that drew her greatest attention. To Marcie's eyes, it seemed as though a thin net curtain hid the dark lustre that used to be. Her eyes didn't seem so black. Her movements were less confident as though she was carefully considering what she was doing.

She's getting old. That's all, she told herself, and yet again rebuked herself for not noticing before.

Her grandmother pummelled a cushion on the hard oak chair and sat herself down.

'I dreamed of something bad,' she said.

Marcie's breath caught in her throat. 'Michael's been arrested.'

She went on to tell her grandmother the rest of it. 'He didn't do it, Gran. Michael's not like that.'

Even though her dark eyes seemed less lustrous, Marcie flinched beneath her grandmother's gaze.

'Are you sure?'

'Absolutely.'

Marcie filled in the rest of the details about the gun and the blood-stained shirt found beneath a rose bush at the end of the garden.

'They're checking to make sure that it's her blood.' Marcie shook her head. 'It can't be. He wouldn't kill someone. He wouldn't!'

Rosa took the news incredibly well, neither condemning nor sympathising. She nodded her head sagely, but her countenance remained unchanged and incredibly calm. How could she be so? thought Marcie.

She herself had been devastated, unable to move, even to speak.

'You must be strong. You must believe in him.'

She nodded. 'Yes.' Inside she was reliving the way she had felt when the shirt had been found. Michael had insisted that he'd ripped it at the club and had put on a clean one; he always kept spare shirts at the club. Was she naive in believing him?

'It isn't because of lipstick on the collar, or the smell of someone else's perfume,' she blurted. 'He always kept a spare shirt in his office.'

'Listen to the advice people give you, then make up your own mind. You know a person's truthfulness by listening with your mind, your stomach and your heart.'

Rosa Brooks indicated each body part as it was mentioned. Something about her doing that, plus the quiet way she was saying things, washed over Marcie like a wave coming in from the sea. She felt calmer and also refreshed.

'If you believe in him, then things will come right.' Rosa's eyes flickered. 'I recall a time when I had to believe in your grandfather. We were parted because of a misunderstanding. A silly thing. Just because I was Maltese Catholic and he was not. I listened to everyone's advice and then I made up my own mind.'

Marcie knew she was referring to the time when her grandparents had met each other just after the Great War in Malta.

'Tell me,' she said.

Her grandmother smiled. Marcie had never seen

her smile that way before. Suddenly the years seemed to fall from her face. The lines were gone, filled out with a shining happiness that was equally reflected in her old, tired eyes.

'It was like this,' she began.

Marcie listened to the story of her grandmother and grandfather.

Her Maltese great-grandmother had placed a potted plant – a pink geranium – on the first-floor window ledge of their narrow terraced house in the old quarter of Birgu, one of the old cities of the island. The potted plant advertised the fact that there was an unmarried virgin in the house. Unfortunately nobody knew that Rosa had already met the love of her life – a less than upright Naval rating with twinkling eyes and a way with words.

'They would not countenance me marrying him. He was English and not of the faith. He was also ten years older than me. I sat through many lectures when they told me that such a marriage would never work. The priest was brought in to lecture me on the error of my ways. For a time they threatened to have me put away. They even enrolled me in a convent for a whole week! The nuns were strict, but no matter what they did I refused to give in. They called me wild and even mad and told me that I would be put away for good if I did not obey my parents. I calmed down at that and eventually was allowed to go home. And then I ran away. We were married eventually, though it was never an easy path. I was a fiery young woman. My husband, your grandfather, was always chasing some crazy money-making dream. Not that he ever made much money. But it didn't matter. We loved each other and sometimes we hated; there is a thin line,' she said on seeing the look of disbelief on her granddaughter's face. 'We parted once. My mother had been ill. I felt guilty I had been in England. But we got back together and enjoyed making up.' Her smile widened. 'We always did.'

It was a moment before Marcie could speak. Listening to her grandmother was like reading a romance novel, but real.

'You love your husband.'

Marcie nodded.

'Do you believe in him in your heart, in your head and in your stomach?'

Perhaps buoyed up by her grandmother's life story, Marcie nodded. 'Yes.'

Then she shook her head. 'I can't believe it. Not of him.'

'Then don't,' said her grandmother.

They might have gone on talking about the problem, but were rudely interrupted.

The front door of number ten Endeavour Terrace was usually left unlocked so family and friends could come and go as they pleased. The sound of it slamming against the wall made Rosa and Marcie turn their heads. The door to the kitchen flew open too, bouncing against the wall and springing back on its hinges.

'Well! Where is the fucking bastard?'

Babs, Marcie's stepmother, came flying into the kitchen, her breasts bouncing against the top of a low-cut sweater. A safety pin glinted from a broken bra strap and a roll of fat sagged over the waistband of her skirt.

Everything about Mrs Barbara Brooks was looking shoddy and tired. Dark roots showed greasy against straw-dry blonde. There were dark rings beneath her eyes and she smelled stale, as though neither her clothes nor her body had been dipped in water for weeks.

In the past Rosa Brooks would have glared at her daughter-in-law and warned her to watch her tongue, either that or order her from the house. Instead she sank into a chair with a low moan, her forehead resting on her hand.

Marcie was appalled. 'Any chance of you being a bit more considerate?'

Babs snorted. At the same time she got out a packet of Woodbines from a white plastic handbag.

'Huh,' she snorted again as she attempted to light up. 'Look who it is! Miss High and Bloody Mighty. What do you want down here? Doing a bit of slum-

ming are you or looking for old flames? Well you
won't find your mate's old man that's for sure,' she
said with a snigger. 'Alan Taylor's body is a mouldering in his grave,' she sang to the tune of 'John
Brown's Body', then added, 'Rita Taylor's body is a
mouldering in her grave . . .'

Marcie felt her face turning red. She didn't need
Babs to tell her that Alan Taylor was dead. She'd seen
him die. She'd struggled and he'd fallen and hit his
head. Not that she'd ever told anyone what had
happened. She'd been scared. She'd run away.
Sometimes at night she woke up fearing the police had
arrested her and were taking her to prison. That was
bad enough. It was when they told her that she would
never see her children again, that was the worst.

'Anyway,' Babs went on, heading for the back door,
'I don't want to speak to you. It's my old man I want.
The bastard's leaving me short of cash. The kids are
starving. Bread and dripping. That's all I've been able
to give them. So! Where is me other half?'

The sound of laughter came in from the back
garden bringing Babs to her feet. Her expression darkened. 'Right!' she said, gathering her coat around her
and straightening so that the safety pin holding her
bra together pinged off into space.

Marcie stepped in between her stepmother and the
back door. 'Oh no you don't!'

'Get out of my way,' shouted Babs.

'I'll do no such thing. You are such a liar, Barbara Brooks. Not only that, you're a drunk and a slut. Just look at you! Hardly love's young dream!'

Bottom lip curling in disgust, she eyed her father's second wife from top to toe. The four-inch court shoes were scuffed and dirty. Her stockings were laddered and the hem of her skirt was sagging on one side, a loose thread trailing down to her ankle. She'd once been regarded as quite a looker. Now she looked a mess.

'Let her go.'

The voice of Rosa Brooks was tired and measured. 'Let her go,' she repeated. 'It is not for us to keep husband and wife apart.'

Marcie felt stung. Not for being taken to task. That wasn't what her grandmother was doing. It was as though she were seeing the whole situation more clearly. Husband and wife needed to confront each other. Each needed to be confronted with the problems they'd caused themselves.

'Ta!' snapped Babs and went out the back door.

Garth, instantly recognising an angry woman when he saw one, came in with Joanna hanging on to the hem of his pullover.

'I'm scared,' whined Joanna. 'There's a nasty witch out there.'

Marcie picked her up. 'Nothing to be scared of. You're with Mummy now.'

'Is she a witch?' asked Joanna, not looking entirely sure her mother could protect her.

'Not quite,' replied Marcie, mindful that she might give the child nightmares. 'But even if she was, your mummy's the good fairy and will wave her away with her magic wand. Isn't that right?' she giggled, tickling the little girl's tummy so that she giggled too.

'Old MacDonald had a farm . . .'

Garth was singing and drawing again. Joanna joined him, laughing as he made piggy noises or mooed like a cow.

The grunts and moos distracted the child, but Marcie and her grandmother were still aware of the noise beyond the back door. The pine planks it was made of were incapable of keeping out the sound of Babs shrieking obscenities at Marcie's father.

Marcie blinked at the confrontation she could see through the back window. All the pain and confusion of a young child left without her mother flooded over her. Her father had married this woman in place of her mother. Why her?

'He wanted somebody who was weaker than him,' said her grandmother as though reading her thoughts. 'Your mother was stronger than him. Much stronger. At the time I wished it hadn't been so. I was brought up in an age when women were supposed to be subservient to their husbands. Your mother was not that. She was never that.'

Marcie looked into the wrinkled old face, not sure exactly what her grandmother was saying. 'You encouraged him to marry Babs?'

She heard her own voice and knew she sounded shocked and amazed.

Her grandmother nodded. 'She was a silly, pretty girl who made it very obvious that she wanted him badly. I was foolish enough to think that he could manage her and that that would be enough. I was even foolish enough to think that he would settle down at last and not desire other women. I even thought that she would be of a mild disposition and prefer her children and home to anything else. I was wrong. They should never have married. Your father tired of her. I know now that he prefers stronger women, women who can stand up for themselves.'

'Like my mother,' Marcie whispered as she picked Aran up from his carrycot. Closing her eyes, she rested her chin on her baby son's head. 'Not that it matters much now.'

The sound of raised voices continued from outside.

'You bitch!'

'You bastard!'

'Slut! You deserve a bloody good hiding.'

Marcie winced at the words, wondering if her father had ever hit her mother. Somehow she didn't think so.

'Your father was in awe of your mother.'

Her grandmother's voice suddenly intruded into her thoughts.

'Did she used to sit under the apple tree – like Garth told me?'

Rosa Brooks nodded. 'Your father used to stand at the kitchen window looking at her in silence. He was amazed that she'd ever agreed to marry him. Because of that he used to treat her as though she were made of china. She always had her own way. She was the boss in her house.'

Marcie nodded silently. Her heart was racing. Her grandmother and her father rarely mentioned her mother. It was as though her memory had been erased from the house and their memories.

In time she would meet up with her mother again, but not yet, not until all was well in her own world and Michael was home again.

'I'm selling my house. Under the circumstances I think it's the best thing to do. I need to be in the heart of London so I'm moving back into the flat.'

'Your friend was living there?'

'Yes. But Allegra has other plans so is OK about moving out.'

It was true. Allegra had told her that she needed to be somewhere else for a particular reason. To Marcie's surprise she would not be drawn on the details. Marcie guessed she had another man in her life. She hoped so. Allegra seemed such a lonely soul at present.

'I sometimes wish I was back here,' said Marcie. 'Things seemed so much simpler when I lived here with you.'

Her grandmother handed her the tea towel whilst shaking her head. 'That time is passed. You have to go back to London. That is where you have problems and that is where you will solve them.'

'Just wishful thinking,' said Marcie. She had already made up her mind about that. There was no point in hiding away on the Isle of Sheppey whilst her husband was locked up. To her shame she found herself actually wondering if Michael really had killed that girl. Had he really got her pregnant? Did anyone know anybody that well? Really?

The back gate at the end of the garden closed with a bang. Looking out of the tiny kitchen window Marcie could see that the garden was empty. Her father and stepmother had either gone to see the kids or one was chasing the other with a view to continuing the fight.

Marcie sighed. It had occurred to her to leave her own children with her grandmother whilst she returned to London. Michael's business could not be left to run itself. Someone had to be there. She decided it wouldn't be a good idea, not with Babs flying in and out with her bad language. Joanna and Aran weren't used to that and, besides, Rosa was getting too old and tired to be bothered with children.

It was only half an hour later when her father returned, his face flushed and a bruise turning swiftly from red to black and yellow around his eye. Babs had caught him one.

His eyes were bright. 'Marcie!'

'I'll get a wet cloth.'

'Don't bother with that. The phone was ringing when I came past the box. It was Jacob Solomon.'

Marcie's spirits rose instantly. 'What did he say?' Her heart thudded like a steam train against her ribcage.

'Linda Bell wasn't pregnant.'

'That's wonderful news, isn't it?'

Tony Brooks blustered a bit. 'I think so.'

'There's no motive! Right?'

'Right! Except that . . .'

'She was lying! ' Marcie exclaimed with feverish excitement. 'He'll be released. They can't hold him, surely. He'll be coming home!'

The look on her father's face failed to reflect her excitement. He looked pensive as he thought through the possibilities and found them wanting.

Marcie shook her head as the truth hit her. 'But it doesn't matter if she was lying, does it? He thought she was telling the truth and that was why he shot her – that's what the police will say. His fingerprints were all over the gun.'

*   *   *

Number ten returned to its slumbering silence once the family had left and gone back to London.

Rosa was pleased with herself. Marcie had not noticed that she wasn't quite her old self. She had not noticed her failing sight or questioned the lack of sparkle in her eyes.

She lowered herself into her favourite chair, one of a pair of old armchairs placed either side of the old iron range.

The cottage kitchen was quiet except for the occasional sparking of the coals glowing bright red in their cast-iron nest. The smell of fresh baking hung on the warm air.

Rosa dozed, her thoughts wandering off into dreams of the past and hopes for the future. Not for her future, of course. She was too old to have much of a future. In her mind she was asking Cyril what kind of future he thought lay ahead for their granddaughter.

You always were a worrier. Always was upset easily, but I guarantee the worst of the past is behind you. Do you remember that night in 1942? What could have been worse than that?

The deepness of her sigh was such that her body sagged like an old sack leaking grain. Of course she remembered. She would never forget. She recalled it as if it were only yesterday, the pictures alive in her mind.

*   *   *

A dive-bomber screamed overhead, and a series of staccato firing from an accompanying fighter ripped into the dirt out in the street. The planes flew past towards Marsa at the end of the creek, where they would make a turn and come back for a second run.

Another sound: a low droning, instantly recognisable. Despite being alone she'd cheered out loud. Hurricanes – too few and too slow to be truly effective, but better than the old biplanes they'd depended on such a short time ago. They were just about holding their own against faster, more numerous planes. Flattening herself more securely between the buildings, she steeled herself for the bombers' return. Too many people had taken a lull in bombing as a sign that it was all over. It rarely was.

Returning planes droned overhead. Dock workers and others who had chanced coming out to inspect damage and retrieve bodies scampered for cover.

Dark greyish figures appeared in the fog of debris some way along the quay running towards her. For a moment it looked like a surreal vision of washing flapping and flying. The grey solidified to the black habits of fully committed nuns and the grey of a few novices shepherding a crocodile of small children.

The children were dressed in white and probably going to church for their first communion – if they got there. They'd got caught in the raid.

With fear clutching at her heart, she looked up at the sky; looked back at them.

The droning was getting louder. She imagined the spinning blades of the propellor, the bomb aimer, thumb ready on the button.

'No!' Stepping out from her hiding place, she waved her arms and ran towards them. 'Go back!'

The force of the blast blew her straight back into her hiding place, jammed there like a bundle of damp rags.

The earth, the buildings, the very air reverberated with aftershock. She didn't know how long it was before she emerged, staggering as though sun-blinded into bright sunlight, except that the sunlight wasn't blinding but clouded with dust.

For what could only be seconds, the silence was so intense that she thought she'd gone deaf. Even when all hell erupted around her, people running, shouting, screaming and crying, she did not – *could not* – move.

Just yards away lay what remained of the nuns and the children. Earlier they had been running along hand in hand. The worse thing was seeing two small arms ripped from children's bodies, the hands still clasped in death as they had been in life . . .

'I didn't tell them, Auntie Rosa.'

Garth's voice brought her back to the present.

'Garth?'

No longer sitting at the table, he'd made her a cup of tea and brought it to her with a mismatched saucer.

'What didn't you tell them, Garth?'

'That you can't see very well. But you'll see better soon, won't you, Auntie Rosa?'

Rosa smiled as she took the proffered cup and saucer. 'Yes,' said Rosa and thought of Cyril and of seeing him again – though not of course in this world.

Chapter Fifteen

Marcie hated the prison. She hated the high walls, the dense red of the Victorian bricks and the sound of the main gate closing behind her.

The prison prided itself on being modern; there was no mesh grille between the visitors and prisoners. Instead inmates and visitors slouched over the tables meant to keep them apart, as though slouching would bring them an extra inch closer.

Prison officers – whom everyone referred to as 'screws' – stood like dark pillars at strategic points around the walls. The windows were high above their heads.

The institutional smell of packed bodies and boiled potatoes permeated the air along with something else that Marcie could only interpret as desperation.

Just one look and Marcie could tell that Michael hadn't eaten. The rings beneath his eyes looked as though they'd been etched in with graphite. He was eyeing her pleadingly.

They said hello but were not allowed to touch – not even their fingertips.

Marcie swallowed her concern. It would do no

good to ask him how he was or question why he looked so awful. He needed hope, though she had precious little of that to give him. But there was one thing, of course.

'I suppose Jacob told you that Linda Bell wasn't pregnant.'

Michael nodded. 'He did. Not that it makes that much difference. It's the gun that's causing the problem – that and the shirt. How did the gun get in my office? How did the shirt get where it was found?'

She shook her head. 'Someone wanted you out of the way.'

'Rafferty is known to be harsh in repaying slights or insults. He'll try and get round you, get you to sign over the club. That's why I want you to sell it. Quickly.'

'To him?'

He sighed and hung his head. 'If you have to.'

'I won't!'

He looked surprised at her outburst.

'I'm determined to hold on to it.'

'Marcie, you don't know who you're dealing with. Without me there . . .'

'But you're not there, are you? You're in here. I have to do what I think fit. If this hadn't have happened you might even have been setting up another club by now.'

'Are you accusing me?' He sounded hurt.

Marcie sighed. It was difficult to take on board how even the silliest comment could upset a prisoner with nothing to do but dwell on his reason for being there. She'd reminded herself before coming to be careful what she said, but it wasn't easy.

'I didn't mean that. If you hadn't gone back in that night . . .'

'A passer-by phoned and said there was a fight outside . . .'

Now it was Marcie who was surprised. 'Isn't that why you employ bouncers? Why did you have to go in? Why?'

'I thought they were slacking.'

'And were they?'

Hanging his head, he ran his fingers through his hair and groaned. 'No. It was a hoax.'

'So why didn't you come home right away?'

'OK, I went into my office and fell asleep. Honestly.'

'Oh, Michael. Why did you do that? You should have come home.'

'I didn't do anything, Marcie. Honestly I didn't. I didn't get that tart pregnant and I didn't kill her.'

She glanced around her, making sure the screws weren't listening too closely before whispering, 'Linda Bell came to see me.'

He looked surprised. 'When?'

She told him.

He frowned. 'Why didn't you tell me before?'

She shrugged. 'I saw no need to tell you. I didn't believe her. I told her to clear off.'

His frown deepened. 'Christ, Marcie, you should have told me. I could have sorted it out right away.'

'Could you?'

She couldn't help the disbelief in her voice. The sharpness of his rebuke hurt. What he said next hurt even more.

'I barely knew the girl. She worked at one of Victor's clubs as a hostess. She was always on at Victor, at Roberto and at me to let her dance on stage. Victor and Roberto never did, though they promised – in return for her favours, of course.'

'And you? Did you give her a chance?' She recalled Linda saying he had.

'She danced at the Blue Genie, but only once. I said we'd give her a chance, but the punters didn't like her much.'

'You didn't date her?'

'Christ, Marcie!'

'I'm only asking!'

She watched his fingers course through his hair again, her heart aching to touch him and to hear the truth.

'I may have had a drink with her about a year or so ago, when she was auditioning. That was all.'

'You did? Then why didn't you tell me?'

She couldn't help the sudden anger in her voice. He'd denied knowing the girl. Now he was saying he had known her and that in fact he'd been out for a drink with her. It brought home one very obvious fact: it was all very well loving someone and depending on them, but did she really know the man she had married? Was he telling the whole truth and nothing but the truth as they said on *Perry Mason*?

Resting his head in his hands, Michael sighed deeply.

'I can't believe this is happening. Everything was going along so well. We had a great future you and me.' He looked up suddenly as though startled from a deep sleep and even deeper thoughts and fears. 'I need you to believe in me, Marcie. I need you to be my eyes and ears on the outside. I've got enemies, Marcie. You above all people should know that. My father for a start; he's never forgiven me for getting him and Roberto put in stir. As for Rafferty . . .'

Marcie looked at him. This man, her husband, had pleading in his eyes and sincerity in his voice. She'd come here uncertain whether he was telling the truth but she couldn't help believing him. He looked so desperate, so totally dependent on her. Besides that he was the father of her son and had officially adopted Joanna and given her his name. Would a deceitful man do something like that?

Making her mind up was pretty straightforward. Children needed two parents and this marriage had to work. She sat back resignedly.

'So what do you want me to do?'

His sudden surge forwards was met with a warning hand on the shoulder from one of the screws.

'Not too close, Jones. No touching.'

Michael retreated only as far as he had to and took a deep breath. His eyes held hers.

'I won't pretend it's going to be easy for you, so I've worked out what will be best. I'm hoping Jacob can get me off, but it could take some time. If I hadn't fallen asleep and stayed in the club in full view of everybody, there would be no case to answer. However –' he shrugged '– that's water under the bridge. Until I'm released I've got to protect you and the kids. So this is what I've decided. Keep the commercial properties, but sell the club. Speak to Jacob about likely purchasers. He's got his ear to the ground. Try and avoid selling it to Rafferty. I hate the bastard. I wouldn't be surprised . . .' His voice trailed away. She didn't need him to finish the sentence. She knew what he was insinuating.

'Should I go along and ask him outright?'

He looked alarmed. 'No! On no account do that.'

'And your father? I hear he's out of prison. Should I ask . . .?'

'No!'

Again his loud response attracted the attention of the screws.

Marcie shook her head, not at all happy with what he was telling her to do. 'But you love the club the best. You said it was just the beginning of an empire that we were to share.'

She hadn't exactly been keen about him getting involved in nightclubs just like his natural father. She herself had been considering getting rid of the sewing room where she made costumes for exotic dancers. It was still her dream to design and make fashionable dresses, but that was all it was, a dream. She was just a girl from Sheerness who had left school and got a job selling candyfloss on the seafront. What chance did she have?

Michael's look turned pensive as though he were mulling something over, debating with himself whether to confide in her. To some extent the thought of him having to decide whether to entrust her with whatever it was made her bristle. She told herself to calm down, after all he was under pressure and worried.

Marcie swallowed her doubts and agreed to do as he said. 'I wouldn't be able to handle the club and my own business anyway,' she added, though knew she was lying. Keeping the club for him was her way of believing in him. When he came out everything would be as it was. Very shortly he would be released from prison. She had to believe that. There was no point in jumping from the bridge until she had to.

Michael did not detect the fact that she intended disobeying him. He was nodding thoughtfully.

'Keep making your theatrical costumes. You're good at what you do, and, besides, I think everyone should have their own little bit of independence.'

His smile was fleeting but did not fool her. His eyes were heavy with worry.

Her heart went out to him.

'Michael, are you getting enough to eat?'

Her question pulled him up with a start. If it were possible, he looked even more alarmed than he had when she'd argued to keep the nightclub.

'I'm fine.' His eyes flickered. His jaw snapped shut.

'You look . . .'

'I'm just tired.'

She hadn't expected him to snap like that. There was something he wasn't telling her. The opportunity to ask him what was wrong was drawing to a close. She wasn't quick enough to ask what the problem was.

Visiting time was short, sweet and soon over. Responding to command, the visitors – mostly women, some there with young children – turned away from the men they'd come to visit. For their part the prisoners rose reluctantly. Even when their bodies were making for the door that led back to the cells, they glanced over their shoulders until there was nothing left to see; until the door had slammed shut between them, their loved ones and the outside world.

Only the sound of excitable children accompanied the visitors as they made their way back towards the prison gate. The women said little though one or two stole sideways glances at the clothes she was wearing.

She'd taken special care with her appearance. Her coat was navy blue, the collar, cuffs and belt bordered in yellow braid. It was a very chic outfit – very fashionable.

The coat had been plain. She'd added the braid herself.

Being admired was of no interest to her. Feeling empty and sick inside, she filed out with the others.

'Never mind, love. It'll all come out in the wash.'

She jerked up her head. The speaker was one of the prison officers, one who was senior to the others. He winked as he said it.

'I hope so.'

'I'll see he comes to no harm,' he added.

She didn't meet the look in his eyes. She didn't see the meaning there. Despite the fact that her father had been in prison, she wasn't familiar with what went on. Her grandmother had shielded her from that. She'd never visited and her father had never talked about it. Besides, all she had in her head was getting Michael out of there.

'He's innocent,' she said.

'They all are.' There was an undeniable smirk on his face when he said it.

Marcie didn't like his comment, but was too pre-occupied to react.

Although tinged with traffic fumes, the air outside the prison smelled far sweeter than it did inside. Even so it was hard to banish the stench of it from her nostrils. She promised herself a hot bath perfumed by her favourite bath salts when she got home. Her car being in the garage for new brakes, she'd come here by taxi and would go home the same way.

Nearing the edge of the pavement, she looked around for one.

'Excuse me.'

The last thing she'd expected on stepping out from the prison was to be hailed by a big man dressed in a badly cut suit. He was chewing gum.

'Mrs Jones? Michael's wife?'

She stopped and looked at the speaker. He had shoulder-length hair and was wearing a kipper-sized tie. She decided that she didn't know him.

'Yes. I am. Who are you?'

'That don't matter, love. It's my boss that wants a word with you.' It was hardly an invitation – more like an order.

Taken unawares, she looked beyond him to where sunlight bounced off a shiny black car. Quite a lot of cars were parked outside. She was vaguely aware of an equally ostentatious car pulling in somewhere behind this one. It must be a day for them, she thought. Perhaps a judge was visiting the prison. She turned back to the man.

'Who is your boss?'

'Mr Patrick Brian Rafferty, of course.' He proclaimed it as though everyone in London had heard of the name.

'I've never heard of him,' she responded loftily. Rafferty! The pompous little Irishman who was trying to take over her husband's club!

'But he knows you and wants to introduce himself.'

'Look, I've got to get home . . .'

'It won't take a minute. Mr Rafferty insists.'

Marcie was in no mood to conform to anyone's insistence unless she could turn it to her own advantage. If the circumstances hadn't been so dire, she would have quoted her father's favourite saying: *What's in it for me?* On the other hand and despite Michael's warning, it wouldn't hurt for her to have a word with him.

Holding her head high, she addressed the man chewing gum.

'I'll speak to him if he can give me a lift home.' She spoke firmly, not at all like the little girl she had been such a short time ago. The little girl she'd been was no more. The old Marcie had died around the time Joanna had been born. In this world she had to be strong for herself and those she loved.

The big man smirked. 'Play your cards right and you might be lucky.'

'I'll bet.'

Cupping her elbow, he eased her gently but firmly towards the shiny car. She let him do that, intrigued to meet this man who had tried to bully her husband into making him a partner.

The big man opened the door of the car.

'First I want your assurance that you'll drive me home after this. My kids are waiting for me.'

'Of course, my dear. Come along in. Sit yourself down and make yourself comfortable.'

She slid into the back seat. The interior smelled of new leather and old cigar ash. The man sitting in there was wide and took up most of the back seat. She was left sitting in roughly one third of it.

She looked at him, prepared to shudder, but holding it firmly at bay.

Paddy Rafferty's hair was sandy coloured and his eyes like chips of smeary glass, a dirty tan colour that could only loosely be described as hazel.

'My name's Rafferty. Patrick Brian Rafferty.' He offered her a meaty hand enclosed in a soft kid glove.

She kept her hands in her lap and looked him straight in the eye. 'What do you want from me, Mr Rafferty?'

His smile was crooked and as sincere as a rattlesnake about to strike.

'Well, first off I'm pleased to meet you at last. I heard you were quite an attractive woman, but on meeting you, I see the description is inadequate. You're quite a looker, Mrs Jones. Quite a looker indeed!'

His accent reminded her of Mickey Rooney in an old black and white Hollywood film, false and overdone.

'Are you a business associate of my husband's?' she asked.

His smile made her feel as though she was a meek and mild sparrow and he was a big cat about to pounce. Snake! Cat. He was a hunter that crept up on its prey.

Up close he smelled strongly of cologne; an attempt to cloak the smell of cigar ash, Marcie decided. She wondered about the gloves and didn't like his smile.

He hesitated before responding. She instinctively knew that the way he undressed her with his eyes was meant to unnerve her, to make her vulnerable. She steeled herself to ensure she gave no sign of fear.

Seeing her looking at him so defiantly, he finally took the cigar out of his mouth. 'You could say that. Mickey and me were about to become partners when this unfortunate incident occurred. Such a bloody shame, me darling! A terrible shame to leave a lovely girl like you burdened with business worries when all you really want to deal with is bringing up your darling little kids.'

'I can cope,' Marcie responded hotly. 'I'm not stupid.'

'Dear, dear, dear.' Rafferty shook his head in time with the words he uttered. 'A lovely young woman shouldn't have to cope. Business is a dirty game, Mrs Jones, a dirty game indeed. It certainly isn't for the likes of lovely ladies like you. No, no, no.' Again he shook his head in time with each word. 'Mrs Jones, me darlin', I think you should reconsider your position. Nightclubs attract danger and violence. It's also a place where women are exploited. Now would you really want to get involved with something like that?'

Sally being exploited crossed her mind and almost made her laugh out loud. Sally *loved* what she did. She was skilled at dancing and taking her clothes off. By her own admission she'd set out to be exactly what she was.

'You're pathetic, Mr Rafferty.'

His look hardened as he took in the insult. 'Careful, Mrs Jones. I have been courteous with you. Please pay me the same respect and be courteous with me.'

'I don't like being regarded as a silly little woman, Mr Rafferty. Please do me the honour of treating me with the same respect you would a man.'

He thought about it then nodded. 'You're right,

Mrs Jones. Of course you are right. I apologise,' he said with a curt nod. 'However, please consider what I'm offering here. Peace of mind, Mrs Jones; the chance to shelve business worries in exchange for enough money to see you and the little Joneses all right. Not a fortune, mind you, but a fair offer.'

'Fair to you, Mr Rafferty?'

'Fair to all concerned. As I said, Mrs Jones, night-clubs can be violent places and are full of sin. We all get tarnished with sin if we live day in and day out with it.'

'Is that why you're the way you are, Mr Rafferty?'

Although she smiled sweetly, she knew damned well that Rafferty was in no doubt with regard to her insinuation. The man was a gangster.

His smile remained fixed. 'No doubt you and me can come to some arrangement. A pretty girl by herself is going to need protection from the lounge lizards you find in seedy night spots.'

'Is that so?'

'Oh yes.' He paused whilst his eyes swept over her. 'I think you'll have to be very careful about who you trust, Mrs Jones. I think you'll have to be very careful who's watching you – both day and night.'

Her blood turned cold. Although the urge to shudder was very powerful, she managed to hold it at bay. 'Are you threatening me?'

'No, no, no.' He shook his head in time with each

word just as emphatically as he had nodded. 'Would I be so crass as to threaten Mickey's lovely wife? Of course not, me girl. Of course not! And I guarantee Mickey would be the first to agree with me. In fact he and I are of the same mind when it comes to women.'

Calling Michael 'Mickey' did not endear him to her. Nobody called Michael that. He hated it.

'I'm not sure I believe that, Mr Rafferty.'

Throwing back his head, he laughed uproariously. 'Ah, but you women are all the same. You want to know everything your men folk are up to and that's a fact. Come now. We men have to have a few little secrets, don't we?'

She felt his eyes boring into hers and didn't like it. The time for being pleasant was at an end.

'Now let's get this straight, Mr Rafferty. I have to get home to my kids. You promised to take me there. As regards the other matter, I'm afraid it will have to wait. Another time, another place. Better still contact our solicitor. He'll lay it on the line.'

He chuckled. 'No need for you to worry your pretty little head about getting back to your kiddies. I'll get you home in style. Claude? Let's get the little lady home.'

The driver in the cheap suit responded. They were already out in the traffic but had not proceeded with any great speed up till now. Claude pressed his foot on the pedal and blew the horn.

The car nudged its way through the traffic. It was late afternoon and the rush hour was just beginning.

'I live at . . .'

'I know where you live, Mrs Jones.'

If it was possible to turn colder, she did that now. Paddy Rafferty knew where she lived? The prospect was worrying. Determined to stay cool, Marcie swallowed her nervousness.

'I've driven past your place,' he said as though answering her unasked question. 'Nice little avenue. Nice little area. I noticed there was a school up the road. I take it your little ones will be going there?'

'I have no wish to discuss my domestic arrangements, Mr Rafferty.' She kept her voice even and businesslike.

'Call me Paddy,' he said, a mouthful of teeth exposed in a grin that was as wide as Chelsea Bridge. 'All my closest friends call me Paddy and I'm sure you're going to be one of them.'

Marcie was thinking that the last thing she wanted to be was close to Paddy Rafferty. 'What do you want, Mr Rafferty?'

'Paddy,' he said insistently.

'Paddy,' she returned, though curtly.

Despite her manner, his grin persisted. 'I thought I'd already said, me girl. It just goes to prove my point that the ladies have not the head for business. But never mind, me dear. I'm willing to be patient. I'll outline the details again for you and you alone. Now this is the deal. In the present circumstances it seems to me that the most sensible thing is for me to forego becoming a partner to your husband and instead buy the place lock, stock and barrel. Running a night-club isn't a job for a *colleen*. I will say it again and again, business is a man's world. A tough world.'

'I might be tougher than you think,' she said, thrusting her chin forwards.

Paddy Rafferty was making her feel like a silly little woman whose place was firmly in front of the kitchen sink – or in bed – his bed no doubt. The stupid man wouldn't know it, but he'd thrown down a challenge and she was picking it up. Back at the prison she'd been in two minds about disobeying Michael and keeping the Blue Genie going. Now this man, this terrible man, had made up her mind. Not that he would know it. His idea had been to scare her, not to put her on her mettle.

'Aye,' he said the grin more menacing and cruel. 'I'm thinking you look as though you might want to put up a fight, but think about it. You could get hurt. Your children could get hurt. Now we wouldn't that, would we?'

She was suddenly filled with the greatest revulsion for this man and wanted to be as far away from him as possible. He reeked of danger and destruction. Why hadn't she seen that earlier?

'You are quite right in guessing that I shall be running my husband's business whilst he is awaiting trial. But I'll still be running things past him. I trust my husband's judgement.'

'Your husband's judgement? This is the man who got a tart pregnant then topped her when she told him the good news. Aw come on!' Slapping his hand on his fat thigh, he guffawed as though she were the most foolish woman God had ever put on earth. 'He wouldn't be the first man to play the field and get caught out. We've all done that in our time. But he murdered the girl. The police found the gun and a blood-stained shirt half buried between a rose bush and a raspberry cane. There's no way he's coming out of that place in that much of a hurry, my sweet girl. And you're not capable of running a nightclub. You'll be eaten up alive and spat out in pieces. Mind you,' he said with added chuckles, 'I wouldn't mind being the one to eat you up any day of the week.' His gloved hand folded over hers. 'I could look after you in a number of ways until your old man gets out, Mrs Jones.'

Marcie snatched her hand back from him, her face hot with anger. 'The air in here is too oppressive, Mr Rafferty. In fact it stinks. Let me out. Let me out now. I'll get a taxi.'

She reached for the handle of the car door. The speed with which his hand recovered hers came as a surprise. For someone who was as wide as a door, he moved quickly. This time his hand landed with the impact of a shovel. His grin had become a tooth-filled snarl.

'Not so fast, Mrs Jones, me darling. Not until you've heard me out. I've got plans for that club and no little tart is going to stop me from getting my hands on it. I'll be getting my brief to send the paperwork to the little Jew in Whitechapel, that shrivelled little man who works for you. If he knows anything of my reputation he'll be getting you to sign on the dotted line. Now go if you must, but remember, old Paddy will be after you. Old Paddy always gets what he wants!'

Chapter Sixteen

After phoning Allegra to make sure the children were all right and that she didn't mind staying, Marcie made her way to Jacob Solomon's office in Whitechapel.

The entrance to his office was nothing more than a blank wooden door leading directly off the street. A brass name plaque to one side stated MESSRS JACOB SOLOMON, SOLICITORS. Although the plural form of title was used giving the impression that more than one lawyer worked on the premises, there was only Jacob and his assistant Fred Faraday who doubled as clerk, bookkeeper and secretary. Faraday was not Fred's real name. Like Jacob he'd survived a Nazi death camp. Keen to cut the past from his life, he'd altered his name to that of the man who'd invented laughing gas. A strange choice, but Fred had lived through strange times.

The sound of a clattering keyboard greeted Marcie as she entered. Ancient brown lino squeaked in response to each footstep. The place was old and smelled of linseed oil and dusty paper.

Oak-panelled walls and shelves lined with the gilt

spines of legal tomes gave a solid, trustworthy air to what might have been a depressing Victorian darkness. The window was large but only looked out on a blank wall opposite. An old enamel hoarding advertising Cherry Blossom shoe polish relieved the monotonous courses of brick along with the odd weed that had managed to gain a foothold.

Even in summer little light found its way through the old sash windows. At this time of year, eight weeks before Christmas, a number of one hundred watt bulbs fought bravely but failed to pierce the seasonal gloom.

Jacob Solomon and Fred Faraday shared the same office; it was no secret that the two of them also shared the flat above the office. It was possible that they also shared a bed, but neither Marcie nor her husband ever questioned their lawyer's domestic arrangements or personal life. His wife and child had died in Nazi Germany. He'd never remarried and he was obviously homosexual.

Jacob had a fantastic professional reputation and boasted a very worthy client list. His sharp mind and knowledge of the law overrode any prejudice his clients might have.

As far as Marcie and Michael were concerned it was easy to be both sympathetic and tolerant. The two men had lost everyone and everything they'd held dear in the war. All they had was each other.

The moment Jacob looked up and saw her face, he was on his feet offering a chair and bidding Fred to put the kettle on.

'Will do, Jacob. Will do,' said Fred, papers flying as he left his ancient typewriter with its clunking keyboard, making for the small kitchenette just off the office.

'Tell me all,' said Jacob, his face wise and his speech gentle. Perching himself on the corner of his desk, he looked intently down at her through his horn-rimmed spectacles. Marcie was reminded of a wise old owl.

She told him about Paddy Rafferty apprehending her outside the prison. He already knew what Rafferty had been up to from Michael.

'Do you fear him?'

'I find him threatening.'

Jacob nodded grimly. 'You are wise to do so. Hardly a man of letters and best avoided as all ignorant people should be.'

'He scared me, Jacob,' she said. 'He's not asking if I want to sell, he's insisting.'

'For a song. In effect he was offering your husband a partnership – on his terms of course. He thinks he can get away with purchasing the property off you for next to nothing, purely because you are a defenceless woman.' Jacob pronounced the last few words as though he were declaring a battle slogan.

'I am not defenceless.'

'He thinks so.'

'The man's a crook.'

Jacob made a chewing motion with his mouth. 'Mr Rafferty is not known for being honest in his business dealings. He runs the legitimate alongside the illegitimate. His main line of business is the exploitation of labour. He brings over labour from Ireland, charges them a fee and charges the building company one too. Needless to say the labour force work long hours and get little in return. Neither does the taxman for that matter.'

What he said was no less than Marcie had expected to hear. 'He said he's already sent you the paperwork. Is that true?'

Jacob pursed his lips, clasped his hands and nodded. 'He did. I told his messenger that I would take instructions from my client.'

Marcie eyed him warily. 'What did the messenger say to that?'

'Initially he said that he would break me if I did not comply. I told him the decision was not up to me. I also told him that more ruthless men than he had tried to break me.'

'And?'

Jacob pursed his lips and regarded her as though assessing whether she could take the truth. He decided he saw a strong woman who could cope with it. 'He said that my client would sign immediately if she knew what was good for her and her family. He also said that I should do my utmost to persuade her if I knew what was good for me.'

Marcie's knuckles turned white as she clasped the chair arms and leaned forwards. She was in no doubt that her face was as chillingly white as her knuckles. 'What do I do, Jacob?'

Fred Faraday laid his hand gently on her shoulder. 'Calm down, dear lady. Please. Drink your tea.'

She took the bone china cup and saucer that Fred Faraday handed to her. To her great relief the cup didn't rattle in the saucer. She didn't want that. She didn't want to be scared or at least she didn't want to give the impression of being scared.

'I will do whatever you want,' said Jacob, sitting upright on the corner of the desk, his arms folded. He nodded at Fred.

'I just need to take these to Messrs Coleman and Co.,' said Fred. He was being discreet, leaving Jacob to talk to her alone.

'Stay,' she said. 'Please. I would prefer you to.'

He nodded and sat back down behind the old black Imperial.

The tea was hot and sweet. She didn't usually take sugar, but Fred had doubtless decided she needed it. She did. Her nerves were on edge, but through it all a little voice seemed to be telling her to stay calm, to be strong. She didn't question whose voice it was. Her thoughts were confused. She needed to pull herself together.

'They frighten you?' asked Jacob.

She nodded. 'Of course they do. Did they frighten you? I know you said you've known worse, but . . .'

Jacob Solomon had shoulder-length hair, which had once been coal black but was now liberally laced with grey. When he threw back his head it landed like a cape on his shoulders. He laughed a deep throaty laugh that was mocking rather than humorous. The hand that clasped her shoulder was reassuring and kind. 'Let me show you something.'

The hand was removed. His expression turned sombre.

She watched as, methodically and thoughtfully, he unfastened his shirt cuff and rolled up his sleeve. The skin of his inner arm was abnormally white. Etched into it was a number. He tapped it with his finger.

'That is the number I was given at Belsen. My dear Marcie, I have been terrorised by experts. I have seen horrors you have never dreamed of.' His voice was now more measured, mournful with regard to the few years he'd spent when death was a daily occurrence. 'Let me tell you something else,' Jacob continued, nodding at the same time as pointing Fred to a specific file from the shelf behind his assistant's head. Fred handed him a buff-coloured folder. 'This is the matter of the Blue Genie premises. Michael did not know how valuable it was when he bought it for a song from the previous owner. He did not know that it was up for redevelopment. It seems only a few people knew that. Those few people were so arrogant, so certain that they had everything sewn up with regard to the property that they did not for one minute think that the owner would sell it to someone else before they had a chance to put in an offer. Michael got there first. Did he tell you that he was being approached to sell even before he opened the club?'

Marcie shook her head. The fact that Michael had kept things from her was surprising and got her wondering what other things he hadn't told her. She told herself that he was only trying to protect her, but at the same time she felt uncomfortable. She'd thought there were no secrets between them.

'I think we can get more than Rafferty is offering,' Jacob continued. 'Shall I begin making enquiries?'

Marcie sat staring into space. The nightclub had been Michael's dream, a challenge that would prove he was as capable of running such a business as his father and his half-brother. She understood what it meant to him. If this hadn't happened there would have been no question of him selling. But it made her think something else too. Why hadn't he taken her into his confidence? Like Rafferty, did he think that as a woman she wasn't capable of running a business?

Of standing up to the bully boys of London's East End?

She frowned at the power of her own thoughts. If she was her father's daughter, she would grab the money and run. She'd be the woman most men expected her to be. But she wasn't like that. She was her mother's daughter, the mother Rosa Brooks had described as 'strong', self-reliant. 'Can I have some time to think it over?'

She felt Jacob's eyes on her. 'You're thinking to run it yourself?'

He didn't sound surprised and for someone who had lived through so much violence, his voice was surprisingly sympathetic. He also had great insight. Strange as it seemed, it was almost as though she could feel his mind prying into hers.

'Am I mad?'

He shook his head. 'No. You are not mad. You are brave and you know the old English saying?'

She nodded. 'Fortune favours the brave.'

Chapter Seventeen

Carla Casey was on a mission and didn't continue with the window-shopping she'd set out to do that morning. If she hadn't bumped into Sally Saunders in Oxford Street she would have continued with what she was doing.

Sally was warmly wrapped up in a black and white checked coat and wearing a fashionable knitted 'pixie' hat that fastened beneath the chin. Her boots were black suede and trimmed around the top with tassels, a bit like the ones on a lampshade, thought Carla.

Sally was one of the most indomitable people she'd ever met and usually wore a beaming expression. Today she was looking gutted. She spotted Carla at once.

'Carla! Have you heard about Michael Jones? He's been arrested for murder. Marcie's almost out of her mind with worry. What the hell is likely to happen I don't know; 'course men being men, Linda Bell could very well have been pregnant by him, but Christ Almighty, I can't see that he'd top her. Not Michael. He's not like that.'

Carla feigned ignorance though she had of course read the papers and heard the rumours. Sam Kendal – formerly Mary Brooks, Marcie's mother – was hassling her about it, asking her to find out more. It made Carla wish for Sam's old man to die so Sam could go and do the business for herself. Old Leo should be made to understand that blood was thicker than water. But Sam was having none of it.

Carla had been friends with Sam for years. She knew about her memory loss, how she'd been married to Tony Brooks but couldn't remember anything about it. By the time her memory returned she was married to Leo Kendal and a different woman than the one she had been. Saving her from the streets was all down to Leo. She owed him everything and much as she wanted to be reunited with her daughter, she couldn't hurt him. Hard as she had become, she just couldn't do it.

'Of all the blokes I've ever met in my life, Leo is the one who's been good to me. The rest were a load of shits. He stood by me, so I'll stand by him.'

There was no arguing with Samantha Kendal when she'd made her mind up. The window-shopping was only a 'by the way' kind of thing. She was off to do Sam's will – not that she could tell Sally that.

She feigned innocence. 'Blimey, Sally. That's terrible. I don't watch the news much myself, but I did hear tell there was something awful happening.

Funnily enough I was just on me way over to see Marcie at the shop. I take it she'll be there?'

Sally confirmed that she would be – as if Carla needed any confirmation, which she did not. Someone was always keeping an eye on Marcie – if she but knew it.

Sally was rabbiting on. 'Marcie reckons that keeping busy helps her stop worrying so much. Me and Allegra are standing by her, of course, looking after the kids and that when she has to go off and see her old man. Christ knows what's going to happen to him. They've charged him with murder, all because of this bloody gun that he found in his desk drawer. It's got his prints all over it. He reckons somebody planted it there, but don't know who. Not many people get to go in his office. Mainly family and friends and the club manager, that bloke Kevin McGregor.'

'Poor girl.'

Sally carried on. 'Terrible state she's in. The police said the evidence was overwhelming. I said to Marcie that if that was the case then he'd be called to trial in no time and not to worry. Something would turn up.'

'Let's hope so.'

Carla Casey was a big woman with a penchant for big earrings and fur coats. She had ten fur coats – that's if you counted boleros and mink fur stoles.

She'd known a lot of rich geezers in her time and when they wanted to buy her a present she always opted for a fur coat. Some girls preferred diamonds like in the Marilyn Monroe song about diamonds being a girl's best friend. But not Carla. Carla preferred fur coats.

Carla wanted to see Marcie alone. Sally wasn't getting the message. Even though she was walking briskly, Sally kept pace with her, chatting nineteen to the dozen.

'It's good you're going to see Marcie. She needs her mates round her at a time like this.'

Carla grunted some kind of response. If Sally regarded her as Marcie's 'mate' at this moment in time, then all to the good. In a way she was, but being paid for it of course. Carla never did anything unless she was paid for it and her boss paid well. In return Sam Kendal received out and out loyalty. Carla believed in giving good service for good money.

It was pretty obvious to Carla that Sally wasn't going to be shaken off. She resigned herself to Sally Saunders tagging along.

'We'll get a taxi,' she said resignedly. 'I'll pay.'

She made the offer as though the money folded tightly in her purse was hers and hers alone. It wasn't. The boss had given her expenses – generous expenses.

When they got to the sewing room above the trophy shop in East London, a twin act was being fitted up with angel costumes. These particular angels wore very few clothes and their wings – cunningly contrived of ostrich feathers – were a vibrant shade of pink. The little triangle covering their privates was also made of feathers, cupping the area between their legs like a feathery hand.

Carla looked at the outfits and made her own judgement based on past experience. She'd taken her clothes off for princes and kings and knew what they liked. The punters would love that look. In their minds they would imagine that the feathery hands were theirs and very much of flesh and blood and that they were the ones doing the clutching.

Designing costumes for exotic dancers was an art, an art that Marcie was very good at. She'd go far, further than she ever would in the world of high fashion where qualifications and knowing the right people went a long way on the road to success.

Marcie looked up from stitching sequins onto the tips of the feathers and saw her.

Carla gushed bonhomie and girlish glee. 'Marcie! Love! Let me give you a big hug!'

She didn't wait for a reply. Marcie was smothered in a pair of big arms enclosed in a thick coat by a woman who stood over six feet tall in stiletto-heeled boots. For her part it was like being hugged by a bear.

'Nice to see you Carla. I suppose you've heard.' Marcie sounded more tired than nervous.

'You sound shattered, love. You're really up against it. That's why I'm here. And ain't that what friends are for?'

'Thanks.'

'Anything you want, you just have to say the word. How's the legal eagle? Is he doing his job? If he ain't and you need the best, the money's there for taking on someone better.'

'Jacob Solomon is on the case. He's a good bloke.'

'Ah,' said Carla with a jerk of her head. 'You couldn't be in better hands.'

She meant what she said. Everyone who was anyone knew Jacob Solomon. In a city lousy with lawyers, Jacob Solomon was held in high esteem.

Carla glanced to where Sally was fussing over the two kids and exchanging words with Marcie's other friend – Allegra – the classy bitch who had once been Victor Camilleri's bit on the side. None of the women in this room was to know that she too had once been Victor's mistress. It was a long time ago and she'd been a lot younger then. She'd also had a different name. People in her business – stripping/exotic dancing – changed their names with as much frequency as some people changed their underwear.

Nonetheless, she'd been jealous of every other woman Victor had had since. The fact was that he too had been younger then and, despite the gammy foot, he'd had presence and been a right stud between the sheets. She'd loved him. Always had. Always would.

Cruel, she thought, but it pleased her to see Allegra Montillado looking so pale and distant – almost as though she was on drugs, certainly not on this planet. The girl had changed since splitting with Camilleri. She didn't look glamorous. Beautiful, yes, but there were no adornments, no sparkling baubles dangling from her ears, just a single silver cross hanging around her neck.

Carla pulled herself back from old memories and glib observations. Her attention went back to Marcie.

'Look, love,' she said, lowering her voice and looping her arm into Marcie's. 'I think we need to have a little talk in private.'

Marcie frowned. Her head was aching and her eyes felt itchy, probably due to all the crying she'd done. 'Carla, there's nothing anyone can do unless you can conjure up the murderer and force him to confess.'

'That could be possible – with the right contacts.'

Marcie sighed. She was in no mood for people like Carla offering to use their weighty contacts to get her husband off the charge. It couldn't be done. The evidence, so she'd been told, was too damning.

'Look,' she said trying hard not to sound ungrateful or impatient. 'I've already told you, Jacob Solomon is taking care of things.'

Carla's blood-red talons traced lines through Marcie's hair, stroking it behind her ear on one side. At the same time she leaned forwards and whispered, 'We need to talk about Paddy Rafferty and what we can do about him.'

Marcie visibly started. Their eyes met in mutual understanding.

'I'm just taking Carla into the office to discuss a bit of new business,' Marcie called to Sally and Allegra. 'You all right with the kids?'

'You take your time, darlin'. Your kiddies are OK with us,' declared Sally.

Allegra smiled that same sad smile she'd had for some time now. 'It is always a pleasure.'

Her two friends who she'd first met at Pilemarsh Home for Unmarried mothers grabbed any opportunity to look after her children. She felt for them. She'd kept Joanna. Both Sally and Allegra had given their children up for adoption.

It suddenly struck Marcie that if she wasn't worrying about her husband, she would be worrying about Allegra and the change in her. Today Allegra was dressed in a simple navy-blue dress with a boat neckline, in line with the more subdued style she adopted nowadays. The brandy brown hair that had once bounced around at shoulder level was gone. The elfin style she now sported made her unmade-up face look paler, her dark eyes luminous. The only item of jewellery she wore was a simple silver crucifix. It had been like that for a while.

Marcie closed the door to the tiny office. Carla sat down on the hard chair in front of the desk, which was from an old set of dining chairs belonging to her grandmother. Although she could afford better, Marcie liked these old things because they reminded her of home, and sometimes, more frequently nowadays, she wished she were there.

Marcie sat in the swivel chair behind the desk, steepled her fingers and looked across at Carla. 'You mentioned Paddy Rafferty. What do you know about him?'

Carla was slightly taken aback by the fearless look on the face of the young woman opposite her. In the short time she'd known her, Marcie had grown up. In the past she'd listened to advice and acted on it without question. Now, Carla fancied, the young woman before her held her own views and did not necessarily act upon the views or the will of others. Marcie Brooks didn't just look like her mother, she was also beginning to act like her. It struck Carla that both Marcie and her mother – Sam Kendal – would do anything for the people they loved. It was sad that they'd been parted when Marcie was so young, but still, she reasoned, it was only a matter of time before they were reunited.

Carla went straight into the speech she'd rehearsed

on the way over. 'I've heard a rumour that Paddy Rafferty wants the Blue Genie premises and that he was pressing your old man to make him a partner.'

She could see from Marcie's expression that the fact that she knew had surprised her. The surprise was short-lived. The confidence returned.

'How do you know?'

Carla shook her head and waved her hand dismissively. 'It doesn't matter how I know, only that I know what a rotten bastard he is and that he'll stop at nothing to get what he wants. Has he made you an offer?'

Marcie seemed to reflect on whether she should answer before she actually did. 'Jacob Solomon has the details.'

'It makes sense for you to sell it. What does Michael think?'

Marcie swallowed. Mention of his name got to her badly. The world seemed empty without him, his name echoing against the emptiness. 'He wants me to sell it.'

'It makes sense.'

'But I won't.'

Carla's eyebrows shot up. They were thickly pencilled in black and presented an odd contrast to her peroxide blonde hair. She wasn't that surprised by Marcie's decision. Her mother would have reacted in a similar fashion. Neither of them were women who could be pushed around. Still, she had to pretend she was otherwise.

She looked at Marcie in shocked disbelief. 'You can't be telling me that you're going to keep it! How the hell would you manage? You've got this place to run. Besides that, you're a woman. Women don't do things like that.' She paused as though a sudden thought had struck her. 'Well. Not many women anyway.'

'I can do it. I can fight them. You see if I can't,' Marcie replied hotly.

Carla immediately regretted her comments and flinched at the prospect of having two of the same kind of women to deal with.

Sam Kendal had ordered her to find out the lay of the land and put a deal down on the table. Marcie must not be allowed to run a nightclub. It was better being run by other, more capable, hands. She hadn't expected Marcie to be so stubborn. On the other hand, she should have expected it given the similar traits of mother and daughter. Carla bit her bottom lip as she thought things through. What to say next?

Marcie was glaring at her, arms folded. 'You just wait and see! All of you! I can be as tough as any of you. I can cope with them all. You just see if I don't. And don't look at me like that. Don't think that just because I'm blonde and look OK that I'll let a bloke have his way. I won't. You just watch me, and remember this, Carla Casey, I am not a child!'

'Nobody said you were,' Carla said soothingly in an effort to regain control of the situation.

'Then why are you looking at me like that?'

Carla blinked.

Marcie dropped her arms. 'You're thinking I look like her, aren't you? You're comparing me to my mother!' Marcie heard a pounding in her ears and realised her heart was racing.

Carla nodded. This was a very delicate situation and she had to handle it right. On the one hand, Sam Kendal wanted to help her daughter. On the other hand, she wanted it handled discreetly – at least until Leo had passed on. She'd built herself a new life that was worlds away from the woman she'd once been and she didn't want to hurt Leo if she could possibly help it.

Marcie was as quick as her mother to pick up on peoples' body language. She read Carla now. 'She heard about Michael?'

Carla nodded again, though jerkily, as though reluctant to divulge the fact. She wasn't usually so hesitant about stating her reason for being there, but dealing with Marcie on behalf of her mother was always going to be awkward. 'Is the judge still alive?' Marcie asked.

The question took Carla by surprise. 'Yes,' she said

swiftly. The story she'd told Marcie was that following her mother's loss of memory, Mary Brooks had remarried an aged judge who was presently dying slowly of cancer. The judge knew nothing of his wife's past and finding out would kill him. That's why they could not meet – at least that was the excuse. The truth was a whole world away, but Carla could not divulge the details – not without the say so of Marcie's mother. She decided to lay it on the line from the other direction, warning her of what she was likely to be taking on.

'Look, love. Paddy Rafferty is a shit of the highest order. You don't want to mess with him. Honest you don't.'

'I won't let him have the Blue Genie,' Marcie responded defiantly.

'Of course you won't – not if you can help it. But he won't *ask* you, love. He'll threaten you and your kids if you don't play ball. How can you cope with that?'

'I will cope! Everyone treats me like a kid,' Marcie exclaimed. 'Even Michael. I can run that place. I know I can. And I will. It was Michael's dream and I'll keep it alive – even though he thinks that I can't,' she added.

'It's worth a try. If you really want to,' said Carla. 'But not alone. You can't do it alone.'

'Yes, I can!'

Carla laughed. 'A young woman all alone; the sharks will be around love and they'll eat you for breakfast. After meeting Paddy Rafferty you must know that.'

'I can handle him.'

'Can you? Do you have the muscle he's got – and I mean meat on the hoof, love? Can you get an army of over-muscled numbskulls around you, intent on doing your bidding – for a price of course; there's always a price.'

Marcie thought of her father. He'd drifted in and out of the criminal underworld all his life. He was bound to know the right people. But then there was the other side of the coin. Valuable property being considered for redevelopment usually drew the attention of local politicians and professional people like architects, bankers and lawyers. That's where Jacob Solomon would come in. He could help her cope with that side of things; she knew he could.

Her mind was working overtime, planning things out for herself, but she wouldn't let Carla know that. Or her mother for that matter. Why should she? Even if she concentrated really hard, she just couldn't bring her mother's face to mind. Neither could she remember her touch or anything they'd ever done together. Determined to sort this out to her own advantage, her expression hardened. Throw the ball back into Carla's court.

'So! What's the solution?'

Carla tugged at the dangling earring in her right ear and made a clicking sound out of the corner of her mouth. 'It takes fire to fight fire. My suggestion is that you team up with someone as tough as Paddy Rafferty. Someone who Rafferty respects. That's my suggestion.'

Marcie eyed her sidelong as though somehow that would clarify what Carla Casey was all about. 'And you know just the right criminal to fit the bill?'

Carla did a so-so motion with her head. 'Like I said, you have to fight fire with fire.'

It amazed Carla to see how calmly Marcie was taking all this. Some unfortunate wives would be hysterical, crying that they couldn't cope and horrified at the prospect of throwing in their lot with a gangland boss, a well-respected gangland boss who could deal with the likes of Paddy Rafferty. Marcie Brooks – or rather Jones as she was now – had a lot of guts. It should come as no surprise of course, bearing in mind who her mother was. And far from being married to a judge, Mary Brooks had married the most powerful gangland boss in London.

'I think you're right,' Marcie said thoughtfully, eyes downcast, then suddenly flashing wide. 'So who do you have in mind?'

Marcie's look was so strong and so confrontational that at first Carla was taken aback. Then she said,

'Leo Kendal. Rafferty wouldn't cross him. He's a right powerful bloke and guaranteed to scare the pants off scum like Paddy Rafferty.'

'Do I get to meet him?'

'No need. Leave it to me. I'll make all the arrangements and fill Jacob Solomon in on the details when the time comes. And don't worry, it'll be a loose partnership that can be settled once Michael is out of prison.'

'You think he will be out of prison?'

Carla almost sobbed at the sudden brightness of Marcie's face. All the girl wanted – at least at this moment in time – was her husband lying in bed beside her.

'Who knows? Don't worry,' she added on seeing the look of sudden alarm on Marcie's face, 'it'll be a fair partnership and will give you a breathing space while the court case is going on. You'll be safe. I suppose you'd prefer to tell Michael yourself that you're going to run things. I presume he doesn't know you're going to disobey his orders. Will he be OK about that?'

Marcie tossed her head defiantly. 'Of course he will be. He trusts me and knows I can handle myself.'

Carla nodded, though didn't look that convinced at how Michael would react. 'It might be best if you didn't – not yet anyway – until we've sorted things out.'

Marcie nodded. 'OK. We'll leave it at that. I won't tell him, not until there's some hope of him being freed.'

Deep down she'd been hoping for Carla to say that the old judge had died and her mother wanted to see her. If ever there was a mover and fixer in London, Carla was it. She moved in diverse circles and seemed to know everybody who was anybody. There was another thing preying on Marcie's mind that had made her wary of allowing Carla into her confidence.

'By the way, how did you know I'd met Paddy Rafferty?'

The statuesque blonde paused in the doorway. It was obvious from her expression that she'd been caught off guard. Her face froze then thawed quickly.

'You know how word gets round.'

Marcie wasn't fooled. She watched from the window as Carla left. At first the woman in the fur coat stood on the kerb and raised her hand as though hailing a cab. But it wasn't a cab that pulled up. It was the same black limousine she'd seen outside the prison. Mary Brooks was never far away. How long, Marcie wondered, before they met? How long before she could quell the bitter anger lurking in her heart?

Chapter Eighteen

It would be so easy to place a cushion over her husband's face and let him go, but Sam Kendal couldn't do that.

She watched him sleep, his breathing rasping like sandpaper over wood.

His lungs were shot away; their chronic condition a direct result of strong cigarettes and hard liquor.

Leo Kendal had lived life to the full and, until meeting her, had never married.

She'd been a lost soul when she'd met him, without a home, without a penny to her name – not that she'd known her real name. All she recalled was drifting into a life as a nightclub hostess where she'd attracted his attention. The nightclub was his and he'd started to take an interest in her.

Eventually he'd asked for her real name. By then her strong personality and good looks had got under his skin. She'd hesitated and dropped her eyes. That was when she'd admitted that she didn't know because she'd lost her memory.

'I don't know. I picked the name Samantha from a TV programme.'

'No name?'

He'd raised his eyebrows. It had been difficult to read the look on his face. She hadn't realised what she was seeing until much later when he'd offered to give her his name – in marriage. She realised then that she'd actually aroused the protective instinct in this grim, hard man. He liked her because she had a strong character as well as good looks. She'd told him the truth about herself – as far as she knew it. He told her the truth about himself, a cruel truth about a mother who had abandoned him, leaving him with a grandfather who'd taken a belt to his bare backside, had locked him in the cellar, had sent him out stealing, the money earned spent on beer and betting.

'My grandfather worked on the docks. He used to bring stuff home from there – mostly bags of sugar and salt which he divided up and sold off.'

'How long did that last?' she'd asked him.

'Until I grew bigger than him.'

He'd told her how he'd finally grown bigger both physically and by reputation. The leather belt had come out one last time. Leo had beaten his grandfather into an inch of his life.

'And then I picked up a sack of salt that he hadn't began dividing up and poured it over him. I rubbed it into the cuts. I took pleasure in doing that, the bastard. And then I left.'

From the very start he'd trusted her with his secrets

and with his business. As it turned out, he'd made a very wise move and had judged her well. She had a sharp business mind and was totally loyal to the man who'd given her his name even though he knew nothing about her.

He'd fallen ill just as her memory started to return. His lungs filled ever more with fluid and the cancer that was threatening his life. Still loyal to him, she had held back on telling him about her returning memory. By the same token, she had been unwilling to disclose the fact that she was still alive to her ex-husband, Tony. It had occurred to her to tell Tony, but facing her past was difficult. He wasn't the sort to believe in lost memories. From what she remembered of their past life, he would rant and rave and call her a liar. She couldn't face that. She didn't need to face that.

Only her daughter, Marcie, knew that she was alive, even if she didn't yet know the whole truth – and they hadn't yet met. That was another thing she couldn't bare to do just yet. The truth of the matter was that tough as she might appear to the outside world, when it came to facing her daughter, she was shit scared.

She had said to Carla, 'Tell her I'm married to an old judge who's been good to me and that if I tell him about my former life, he'll be a goner. I can't do that to him. Tell her that. And also tell her not to divulge my secret to a soul.'

Carla had done her bidding and Marcie had stuck to her word.

Sam looked at her husband. Sensing her presence, his eyes flickered open.

She smiled at him and covered his hand with hers. 'How are you, love?'

He gave her a weak smile. 'Finished.' His voice was fragile.

'Not yet,' she said softly.

'Soon,' he responded.

She didn't argue. They'd always been honest with each other and would be now. 'You know I'll take care of everything.'

His nod of assent was barely perceptible.

'I've got a problem with Paddy Rafferty. Any objection if I deal him a heavy hand?'

The shaking of his head was as weak as his nod had been. She'd wanted that agreement, before he went, before she could cross old bridges and rebuild her life.

Chapter Nineteen

The doctor removed his spectacles. Rosa Brooks could tell by the way he paused before delivering his verdict that he was loath to do so. Although her eyes could not detect him rubbing at the bridge of his nose with one finger and thumb, she knew that was what he was doing. It would be bad and only confirm what she already knew.

'Your eyes are getting worse. The pressure behind them is caused by the diabetes. It's quite common in older people. Unfortunately you are also developing a cataract problem. No matter how hard you stare at me, the situation will not get any better.'

She knew she was staring at him as though she could see through her foggy version and fancied he smiled. She gave the impression of being an indomitable lady who was not easily beaten. And she was not beaten, not entirely. She still had her second sight.

Her gift for seeing the unseen had lain dormant in her youth, a fancy rather than a factual thing. The gift had not manifested itself until she was married with a child.

As a naval reserve, Cyril had been recalled to active service. He had ended up in Malta, the place where they had first met. Having many relatives there, she had gone too, taking Antonio, their son, with her.

'You are a widow, Mrs Brooks?'

'Yes. For twenty years.'

She heard the scribbling of pen on paper. The sound of paper being shifted around his desk reminded her of the rustling of paper-thin garments that had once been good cloth, of dry skin that had once been supple.

'Do you have anyone to look after you?'

'Garth.'

'I see.'

She heard the rustle of paper again. His chair rumbled as he wheeled it around to face the fireplace.

'It's a little cold in here.'

There was a popping sound as the gas fire flared into life.

It did little to brighten the wintry afternoon. Her world was turning dark, though it could never be as dark as the true darkness she'd known during the siege of Malta.

In her sleep she often relived those terror-filled days, especially the one when she had got caught out and had to take cover in the catacombs. The shuddering of a bomb blast had found her even there.

The old tombs had collapsed on top of her. She had been buried beneath a mountain of ancient corpses, their skin and their clothes as crisp as paper, their bones as dry as dust.

The doctor's voice invaded her lapse into memories. 'We are all getting older.'

'Yes,' she said, knowing he was being kind and sympathetic to her, a woman nearing the end of her life.

The poor man was totally unaware that he was far more ill than she.

She couldn't see him that clearly; all she could see was a colour mutating around him into peaks and troughs, though sluggishly, as though the power to radiate energy was getting weaker.

Her intention had also been to mention her toe as well as her eyes. Weeks ago she'd dropped a pan on it and cracked a toenail. The resultant wound was not getting any better; in fact it was beginning to smell bad. But the colour around the doctor was not good. She had no wish to add to his woes – woes he didn't yet know he had.

'You are telling me that new glasses will do nothing for my vision. But that is all right. I can see the things that are most important to me.'

The good doctor, who had served in the Sheerness surgery she attended since she'd first arrived in England in the years between the First and Second

World Wars, shook his head and sighed. She didn't tell him about the light shining around him, a message that his own time on earth was coming to an end.

He cupped her elbow in his hand and escorted her to the door.

'Keep taking the insulin tablets. At least we can keep the diabetes under some sort of control.'

Garth sprang up from the chair in the waiting room as she came out on the doctor's arm.

'Have I got to go in and see the doctor as well?' he said anxiously.

Rosa shook her head. 'No. You are healthy, Garth.'

Outside the surgery, with its flat roof and modern façade of glass-framed teak, Rosa Brooks stopped to take a deep breath. The air was spiced with the saltiness of sea air mixed with the sweeter smells of candyfloss and fish and chips. It was always so when the wind was blowing directly up the beach and into the town. All the smells came with it.

She could also smell people passing by; small children smelled of milk and bubblegum. Some women smelled of cheap perfume and face powder, others smelled of weariness. Old men smelled of damp wool, mothballs and strong tobacco. Some people smelled bad, either because they did not wash too often or because of something else, something evil hanging around them in a slimy green aura.

Funny, thought Rosa, how other senses grow stronger when one sense is fading.

'Can we get some fish and chips, Auntie Rosa?' Garth asked.

He asked the question with all the gushing enthusiasm of an eight-year-old. Poor Garth. With one hand God had taken and with the other had put something back.

'Of course we can. Give me your arm and you can guide me there. What do you fancy? Cod or haddock?'

He opted for cod, just as she guessed he would.

The day was unseasonably sunny and a few day trippers were making the most of it. Children were running in and out of the crowds and retired people were sitting in sheltered areas, eating home-made sandwiches whilst staring out at a surprisingly tranquil sea.

Local girls in short skirts, the hems barely reaching halfway down their thighs pushed babies in pushchairs.

Some of the local boys pushed against Garth and laughed when he told them politely not to do that. The boys made faces and blew raspberries.

'They shouldn't do that, should they, Auntie Rosa?'

'No,' said Rosa. 'They should not. It is very rude.'

The fish and chip shop had a drop-down counter

so customers didn't need to go into the shop to choose what they wanted.

Rosa and Garth joined the queue. Rosa rummaged in her tapestry bag with beechwood handles for her purse. Once she'd found it, she struggled to get it open. The clasp was so stiff.

Concentrating on opening her purse, she wasn't immediately aware of the running boys who had been watching her. She wasn't aware at all what they were up to until they barged into her, knocking her backwards.

Her purse fell to the ground, pennies rolling out everywhere.

Rosa fell against Garth.

'My purse!'

Swooping like a bird of prey, one of the boys snatched her purse from the ground and ran on. The others went too, whooping and hollering with glee.

The woman serving the fish and chips came out from behind the counter and helped pick Rosa up from the ground along with what few coins were left there.

'Are you all right, love?' she asked earnestly.

With her free hand, Rosa patted the ground, feeling without seeing for her purse.

The more she searched, the more troubled she became.

'My purse!' she exclaimed. 'Someone has taken my purse.'

The woman who had come from behind the counter nodded to the owner who was still serving inside the shop.

'Mr Hancock! We need to get the police. Little tykes,' she muttered, glaring in the direction the boys had run. 'I'd belt the lot of them if I saw them again.'

Chapter Twenty

The den was made of old sheets of corrugated iron left over from the war. The supporting walls were made of concrete and had once protected gun emplacements. Inside smelled of cats' pee and musty old furniture mainly because the old sofa cushions that provided the seating had once belonged to an old woman who had kept a multitude of moggies.

The boy with the purse, who wore corduroy trousers, the hemline torn and saggy around his knees, took centre stage. The others gathered round.

'Come on. Let's have a look-see.'

'What you got in there? What you got in there?'

Grimy fingers that had avoided soap and water all week scrabbled like dirty claws for possession of the brown leather purse.

'It's mine!'

'No it ain't! You know the rules. Share and share alike.'

'I did the thieving.'

'That ain't got nothing to do with it. And anyway it's up to the General.'

'Someone talking about me?'

A flash of light came in from outside, by virtue of the tarpaulin, which formed the door, being pulled aside.

The three boys fell away from their squabbling. The lad in the corduroy pants held up the purse so that the gang leader could see what he had.

'I nobbled an old woman,' he exclaimed. His triumphant grin was wide enough to split his face in half. 'Share and share alike,' he said. Like the others he was wise enough to know when to fall in with gang rules.

'Give it here.'

The boy who'd done the thieving didn't argue. The purse was handed over to the boy they called the 'General'.

The tarpaulin was pulled back again. The three boys nodded at the new arrival.

'What you got there then Archie?' said Arnold, peering with interest over his brother's shoulder.

'The spoils of war,' his brother Archie exclaimed. He'd been going to the pictures a lot of late. Most of what he'd seen was war films or crime capers and so he'd picked up some of the lingo. 'Old Sandy here wasn't going to share it out,' said Archie.

The boy named Sandy winced at the fierceness of Archie's look. Arnold Brooks grinned. His brother Archie certainly knew how to handle the likes of Sandy. He guessed what was coming next.

Archie nodded at the other two boys. 'Sandy Harris was going to keep this for himself and be a bit of a greedy sod. Now what do we do to greedy sods?'

The two who had been in on the steal immediately began pummelling the unfortunate Sandy. The victimised boy wrapped his arms around his head and bent from the waist in an effort to escape the worst of the blows.

Archie stood with his arms folded – just as he'd once seen Bully Price do in the days when he'd been a schoolboy and Bully, real name Billy, had been calling the shots. Bully had moved on from that. Apparently he was presently doing time in borstal for stealing and selling on car tyres from his employer.

'That's enough!'

His order resulted in the immediate withdrawal of the pummelling assailants. The boy on the floor began to unravel himself from his protective position.

'That'll teach you to keep stuff to yourself,' stated Archie, his chin jutting out just like he'd seen the heroes do at the pictures. He nodded at Arnold. 'One for his cheek.'

Arnold obligingly went over and clipped Sandy around the ear.

'Ouch!' Sandy's face was red and snot was running down his nose, which he wiped off on the back of his sleeve. 'I'm sorry,' he said. A red flush spread over his face drowning his ginger freckles.

'So you should be, buster,' said Arnold in his best James Cagney voice.

Archie, being the gang's leader in fact as well as name, shared out the meagre proceeds from the brown leather purse. Once he'd done that he flung the purse into a corner where it sank behind one of the cushions. He didn't recognise it at all, nor did he notice the gold crucifix that fell out of it. Neither did he see the grainy black and white snapshot in the side pocket of himself and Arnold as babies, their cheery little faces grinning at the camera.

'Right,' he said rubbing his hands together. 'Let's go and buy some fags then some fish and chips.'

A big cheer went up.

Arnold wrinkled his nose. 'I don't like fags very much.'

He winced as Archie fetched him a cuff around the back of his head similar to the one he'd given Sandy.

'Chicken shit!' exclaimed his brother. 'I'm not having any brother of mine being chicken-shit scared.'

If there was one thing Archie prided himself on it was being as hard on his brother as he was on the rest of the gang. No favouritism crept into his dealings no matter whether they were related or not. That's what he told them and cuffing Arnold was proof of that. That's why they respected him.

'Are you having a fag then, Arnold?'

Although there was no doubting his distaste for cigarettes, Arnold agreed to go with them and do as the rest of them did. He'd probably be sick afterwards, but he couldn't lose face. Neither could his brother.

Off they all traipsed, first buying their cod and chips and then eating and smoking in an empty yard behind the sea wall where locals tipped all manner of old rubbish. Rusty buckets and broken car seats were utilised as temporary seating and an upturned bathtub did service as a table.

After finishing his supper, Archie screwed up the newspaper it had been wrapped in, threw it amongst the other rubbish then burped and patted his stomach.

'Right. I'm off.'

Arnold got up to go with him. Archie pushed him back down again. 'You stay 'ere. I've got a bit of business to attend to and it's private. Know what I mean?'

He slicked back his hair with a generous helping of saliva. The message was clear; their leader, the 'General' was going to meet a girl. Girls had only just started becoming interesting. Anyone who made any headway with a girl was viewed with the utmost respect. They were all looking up at him with their mouths open.

'I said, do you know what I mean?'

The boys looked up at him.

'Yes, sir.'

'Yes, sir.'

'Yes, sir.'

'OK,' added Arnold.

Archie let the tarpaulin door fall behind him. He'd not only left his gang and his brother in the den, he'd also left some money he'd saved over a period of time. Part of it was for purchasing a pair of jeans. He considered himself too old for short trousers and, although he did have a pair of long trousers, it was a pair of jeans he wanted. A pair of Lee Cooper for preference. Everyone wore Lee Cooper. Nobody who was cool would be seen in anything else.

The money was safe and not necessary for immediate use thanks to Sandy nicking the old woman's purse. Never in a million years would he admit to his gang and his brother what he was up to next. It was too vital. Too secret.

Back he went to the fish and chip shop, then towards home though he knew that wasn't where he would end up. His little sister Annie was sitting on the step outside the pub waiting for their mother. The kid should be in school. Even for a little girl her face was pinched and white; her limbs and body far thinner than they should be.

His heart leaped with joy when she looked up, saw him and smiled.

'Archie! Have you got something for me?'

He grinned and almost felt bashful. 'Of course I

have. Wouldn't leave my little sister without some decent grub, would I?'

She snatched the newspaper parcel from him as swiftly as one of his gang members might snatch an old lady's purse. For a little 'un she was certainly becoming streetwise. He found himself wondering what she would be like when she was fully grown.

'What you gonna be when you grow up, our Annie?'

The little girl chewed and swallowed before replying. 'A princess.'

'What's that supposed to mean? How can you be a princess? You ain't one now.'

'Yeah, I can,' she said with a bewitching smile. 'Cos when I grow up I'll be beautiful and then I can be whatever I want.'

'We'll see about that,' he said, uncomfortable with the little girl's innocent view of the world. 'Get on with yer supper.'

He watched her as she ate, cramming the hot food into her mouth as fast as she could.

'Steady on,' he said, placing a restraining though loving hand on her arm. 'Don't want to get a belly ache now do you.'

Hunching her shoulders, she giggled in the pleasant way she did, the way that made him feel like hugging her close and taking her away from their mother, the council house they lived in and the local pub.

'I'll take you to London one day,' he said suddenly.

'Oh, yeah.' She looked pleased about that.

'But in the meantime I'll look after you, Annie. You know that? I'll always be there to look after you.'

'Lovely,' she said, and in her smile he felt all the weight of the world on his young shoulders. At thirteen he'd become the man of the house in the absence of his father. It was a huge responsibility and he knew damned well that it was about putting a meal on the table and looking after the ones you loved – only his dad didn't seem to know that and neither did his mother.

He looked down at the little girl and felt a tightness in his chest. Whatever it took he would look after her, and if it meant stealing from old ladies then so be it. Annie came first and just behind that came the rest of his family. He'd steal for them. He'd even kill for them if he had to.

Chapter Twenty-one

Marcie was desperate to hear some good news, but it was certain she wouldn't be getting it from Michael's solicitor.

Michael had made a formal appearance in court. Bail had been refused.

Jacob was looking sombre. Outside the courtroom, he took hold of her shoulders and outlined his views on the matter. 'I won't tell you not to worry. You're an intelligent woman. You know how things stand. All I can tell you is that we'll go to trial then after that we'll appeal.'

'And if he's convicted? What will he get?'

Her voice sounded cold and strangely calm. Inside she was anything but. Her husband was being accused of murder for Christ's sake!

Jacob shrugged. 'I won't lie. It could be anything from twenty to thirty years – life.'

Marcie felt numb, hardly able to believe what she was hearing. Michael could be sentenced to thirty years. Thirty years!

The evidence had been overwhelming. The gun he stated he'd found in his desk drawer at the nightclub was covered in his fingerprints. He protested that it would be. He'd found it in his drawer and, after mentioning it to his manager, had locked it away in the safe.

Kevin McGregor's word was not enough to convince the police or anyone else that he was speaking the truth.

There were statements from other witnesses to consider. For a start, his old friend Aldo confirmed it was when Michael was partaking of his usual coffee break in his usual seat that Linda Bell had come into the café. He repeated word for word what she had said – heavily accented of course. He'd gone on to say, 'Mr Michael was very angry. He denied what she said.'

'What did Linda Bell say after that?' the prosecution had asked.

'That she would tell his wife.'

'And what did Mr Jones – Mr Michael – say then?'

Aldo had taken a deep breath then paused, his eyes frantically searching for some way out of what he could not avoid saying.

Seizing the advantage, the prosecution had pressed him further.

'What did he say Mr Benuzzi?'

Aldo looked at Michael. 'I'm sorry, Mr Michael.'

'Mr Benuzzi?'

The prosecution had scented blood.

Aldo sighed. 'He didn't mean it – it was just said . . .'

'Mr Benuzzi! Will you please answer the question! What did Mr Jones say – word for word?'

There was no escape. Aldo replied, 'He said that if she went to see his wife he would kill her.'

Other witnesses, Aldo's customers, also testified to Linda Bell visiting him and him threatening to kill her. Then there was the shirt covered in blood that the police had found buried beneath the rose bush.

They'd asked Marcie about it, questioned whether she'd found it in her laundry basket and, realising what had happened, buried it out there herself.

Jacob had cautioned her against lying or risk her children being left without father and mother. She'd had to tell the truth.

Jacob had managed to throw in some questions about intruders prowling around the place, about the dead cat being tied to the front gate, about the girls in the nightclub being attacked and some kind of gangland vendetta being fought. He suggested that Michael Jones was being framed because of this.

The judge refused to accept his argument, terming it as little more than conjecture.

'I could ask you not to worry, but I know it will do no good,' Jacob added before making his way back to Whitechapel.

Marcie bid him goodbye. Her mind was working

overtime. She refused to believe that Michael had done such a thing. Following Jacob's line of conjecture, she decided that everything emanated from the Blue Genie. Paddy Rafferty wanted to muscle in. He had to be a prime suspect. But she couldn't rule out Michael's father and his half-brother.

She made her way to their house, meaning to confront Gabriella.

Gabriella's reception was as cold as ice. 'What do you want?'

Marcie stood in the doorway. Gabriella was wearing a brown cap-sleeved dress with a tan, red and brown tartan waistband. She looked a little more tired than when Marcie had last seen her. The dark eyes were still fiery, but living without her son was wearing her down. No matter how cruel or unfaithful, Gabriella lived for the men in her life. She would be loyal to both of them until the day she, or they, died.

'I wanted to ask you whether Victor or Roberto had anything to do with framing my husband?'

'Michael!' Gabriella almost spat his name. It was obvious judging by the look in her eyes that she'd tolerated Michael for her husband's sake. Her jealousy was never well hidden at the best of times.

'Whatever your beef with him, Gabriella, he does not deserve to be framed for something he didn't do.'

Gabriella's eyes flashed with anger. 'What makes you think you know him so well? He is a man.

A red-blooded man needs more than a wife. Do you think him a saint? Do you think him better than my Roberto? Better than my Victor? Your husband betrayed his own father. Remember that.'

Gabriella attempted to close the door in Marcie's face. Marcie jammed her foot into the gap and held on to the door.

'Yes, Gabriella. And that says it all. They would frame him, wouldn't they? But this is a life sentence we're talking about, Gabriella. Not just a short sentence for running a protection racket.'

'My Roberto has been jailed for violence. My Roberto is not violent. His mother knows this.'

'Rubbish!'

Marcie couldn't help it. Gabriella deserved to know what her son was really like. Marcie told her as matter-of-factly as she could manage about Roberto attacking her and Victor's violence towards Allegra. She'd already presumed that Gabriella must know about Allegra.

She saw the older woman's expression change. Yes. She knew about Allegra all right, but it was Marcie's rape she focused on.

'No! No! No!' she said, shaking her head emphatically. 'My Roberto would not do such a thing. It is you,' she shrieked, pointing her finger into Marcie's face. 'You are a slut with a bastard child. He told me that you threw yourself at him. It was you who seduced him!'

Marcie could not believe what she was hearing. She felt her face reddening with anger as she gripped more firmly on the door that was threatening to close in her face.

'Your son is a psychopath. A head case who thinks he can have any woman he wants. Well, he couldn't have me! And do you know what, he couldn't cope with that. A woman had actually said "no" to his face. So what was not given he resolved to take. He attacked me, he raped me and he even wanted me to have my child adopted just so I could cater to him and him alone. I hope Roberto rots in jail.'

Gabriella's face froze then thawed swiftly. Her smile was cold and the look in her eyes was cruel.

'No. It is that bastard Michael who will rot in jail. My Roberto is coming home. He will be here tomorrow.'

Marcie came away feeling stunned and also fearful. Gabriella would report her visit to her son and to Victor. No doubt she would present herself as a mother standing up for her darling child.

She could imagine the vengeful look in Roberto's eyes. He would relish Michael languishing in prison. She only hoped that he wouldn't get in contact, but knew it was more than likely.

Her concern proved correct. Roberto Camilleri phoned. He'd been let out of prison.

'Sorry to hear about Michael. Dad's sorry too. He sends his love. I can do more than send it if you're willing. How about I come over and take you out on the town. Arrange for that old grandma of yours to take care of the kids and we can start up where we left off.'

She slammed the phone down, her eyes blazing and her face red with anger.

He phoned back again. 'I'll be watching you, Marcie. I'll be watching you all the time.'

Again she slammed the phone down. Although she half expected it, he didn't ring again that day. All the same, she couldn't help glancing out of the window now and again, suspecting she might see his car parked across the road.

The move from the house to the flat above the sewing room had gone relatively smoothly, mainly because she had rented the place out fully furnished.

Tonight was the next step in her plan. She was going to the nightclub, determined that she could cope whatever might happen.

Allegra arrived to look after the kids, looking almost dowdy in plain black and without make-up. It occurred to Marcie that the former mistress of Victor Camilleri was beginning to resemble something completely opposite to the woman she'd once been. The glamour and confidence had gone, replaced by a meditative demureness; she'd also admitted to attending confession much more often.

'Will you be OK, then?' Marcie asked before leaving for the club.

Allegra smiled. 'Of course I will. Will you?'

Marcie took a deep breath and pretended that straightening the hem of her dress was very important. 'Oh, I'm a big girl now.'

Yes. She was a grown woman, but usually she would have consulted Michael about doing this. She had not.

Trying to tell herself that she was up against some heavy problems had done no good. She likened herself to a tigress protecting its cubs, though in her case it wasn't just her cubs; it was her mate, her den, the things they'd both worked for.

'Be careful,' Allegra said before Marcie had buttoned her coat.

Marcie pretended she hadn't heard, but she had. She knew she had to be careful. Michael would be horrified if he knew, but she hadn't yet told him that she was intending to run the Blue Genie herself. So far the manager, Kevin McGregor, had taken care of things. But at the end of the day, it paid for the owner to keep their eye on things and Marcie intended doing just that. There was also the matter of keeping her ear to the ground. Any whispers from the underworld were bound to be picked up there, not sitting at home waiting for things to happen.

She drove her car to the club. The pavements were wet and icy. The night was cold.

The weather wouldn't make that much difference to the punters. Men liked to unwind and a nightclub was the place to do it in.

Olivia Oliver was dancing tonight. She was a great favourite with the crowds and had trained as a Bluebell Girl. Her legs were long, her figure looked as though she'd been poured into a perfect mould: full breasts, narrow waist and rounded hips.

There was also a singer tonight, a woman named Cressida Carter. She sang in bare feet like Sandie Shaw, though the dress she wore revealed more length of naked thigh than Miss Shaw had ever exposed.

After saying hello to Jimmy and Kevin, Marcie made for Michael's office.

Kevin had looked apprehensive that she was here at all. She'd had to explain to him that she was not here to spy on him.

'I'll be in the office. Can you come along once I've got myself settled?'

He said that he would.

Once in the office she took off her coat and hung it on the hook behind the door. Fighting off the urge to shiver, she ran her hands down her skirt, took a deep breath and looked around her.

Michael's office at the Blue Genie seemed cold and empty without him in it. It was swish all the same, a glass and chrome desk dominating the room, a six-foot tall rubber plant growing from a pot in the corner.

She contemplated what was on her mind. This was where someone had planted a gun. But who?

Everything seemed as it usually was. The desk and safe were firmly locked, but she had the keys.

Speculating about what had happened here was useless without concrete evidence. Nobody had a clue about the gun.

She opened the desk drawer, slowly pulling it out just in case something had been left behind, something that the police may have overlooked. There was nothing.

Closing the drawer, she eyed the desk itself and imagined his hands resting there, flicking through files or accounts books.

A pink blotting pad, a silver-plated inkstand and a writing pad drew her attention. She thought about sitting there and writing to him, telling him that she was not going to sell anything; telling him that she had every intention of taking his place.

Writing was so much easier than facing him. If she told him to his face he'd try to talk her out of it. On the other hand, she didn't want to be dishonest. Like he'd said to her, 'I want to be kept informed of what's going on. I want top dollar for the place. Just remember that.'

Jacob would act in that regard of course, but not until she'd given him leave to sell – if indeed she did sell.

For the moment she needed time so decided not to write to him. There was bound to be something she could learn here. She'd tell him face to face the next time she visited. Telling him wasn't so easy. She'd tried and failed on her last visit. The words never came. But at some point they had to, preferably before someone else told him. And what about Carla's contact? Carla had promised to get back to her but hadn't, not yet.

She pulled back the curtain behind Michael's desk and looked in on the studio couch on which he slept when he'd stayed here into the early hours of the morning. Had anyone else slept there with him?

A knock at the door roused her from pretty miserable thoughts.

'Come in.'

Kevin McGregor barely fitted across the width of the doorway. He fully accepted that she was overseeing things on her husband's behalf, but had no idea that any sale, partnership or takeover was imminent. That was the kind of information she kept to herself.

Kevin's expression was grim. It was never any different. 'How are things?'

She shrugged. 'As well as can be expected. I wanted to ask you about the gun. You saw Michael with it in his hand?'

'He took it from the desk drawer and asked if it was mine. I told him I'd never seen it before.'

'And then he put it in the safe.'

'Yes.'

'Did you see anyone else come into the office that night? Anyone who shouldn't be in here?'

He shook his head. 'No. I did not.'

Marcie sighed and hung her head. 'No man. No woman.'

'As I said, no. Everything was normal that night.'

'Normal?'

It was the way he said the word 'normal' that caught her attention.

'Aye. It was normal. Not like the night before when the police came by because of the fight outside. They suggested we close to avoid further trouble.'

Marcie frowned. This was the first she'd heard of any fight. 'So who were they?'

'Just blokes. Micks, I think.'

Marcie frowned. 'So you closed early.'

'As requested.'

'There was nobody here?'

'Only Jeff, the night watchman, though he was a bit late. Not that it mattered much. Everything had gone quiet. Old Jeff likes it quiet. He sets his alarm clock to do his rounds, but snoozes in between the times it goes off.'

Marcie nodded silently. She knew old Jeff's routine

as well as Kevin did. Michael often laughed at the old man's antics, the large enamel-plated alarm clock complete with a pair of bells that clattered like an express train every two hours. Two hours was thought to be enough of a time lapse. Up until now it had been. Now Marcie was wondering whether old Jeff had missed something very important.

Kevin spoke. 'Your father's in.'

Absentmindedly she checked the duty roster for the doormen and general security staff. Her father's name wasn't on the list. 'It's not his night to be in.'

'I think he's drowning his sorrows.'

'Think his latest girlfriend has chucked him out?'

'Probably.'

Marcie swore and rubbed her forehead with fingers that had become stiff with tension. 'I'll deal with it. I'll be right out.'

Tony Brooks ordered himself another double Irish then immediately changed his mind. 'Make it Scotch. Stuff the bloody Irish!'

The barman did as directed.

'And put it on the tab,' Tony added.

He downed the drink in one swift move, the taste in his mouth sour and his head throbbing with too many thoughts, every one of which was a problem.

First his son-in-law charged with murder, then Babs filing for divorce, swiftly followed by the news about his mother. Worst of all was the guilt he was carrying around with him. How the bloody hell would he explain what he'd done? How could he explain?

'Another. Make it a triple,' he said to the barman.

'No. You've had enough.'

Marcie's voice was crisp – just as her mother's used to be. Tony looked up at his daughter with blood-shot eyes.

'Babs wants a divorce.'

Marcie cocked one eyebrow as though surprised, which was far from the truth. Her father's visits to the Isle of Sheppey were becoming less frequent. Even when he did go back, he didn't stay long visiting his mother, seeing his kids and avoiding his second wife if at all possible.

'That's a surprise. I thought your latest girlfriend had thrown you out.'

'What girlfriend?'

Marcie grimaced. It was no big deal that her father was lying and she couldn't totally condemn his behaviour. Babs was hardly a saint.

'Dad. I'm all grown up.'

He chose to disregard her comment. 'I've got a lot of worries in my life. Like they say, it never rains but it pours.'

'Oh, yeah. Like what?' She couldn't help the mocking tone.

'Your gran's on her way out.'

Marcie felt her breath catch in her throat. Her father getting divorced she could cope with. Her grandmother being seriously ill was something else. Rosa Brooks had brought her up and was everything to her. She didn't know what to say. She didn't know what to think or how to cope with this. Being young it had never seemed to occur to her that something bad could ever happen to someone she loved. She wanted to ask for more details but couldn't. Why was that, she asked herself? The answer came swiftly: you're afraid of what you might hear.

She watched her father's finger circling the lip of the glass.

'What's wrong with her? She seemed OK when I last saw her and I've phoned her since. She didn't say anything.' To her own ears her voice sounded clipped and uncaring, but she knew that wasn't true. The fact was if she showed her emotion she would burst into tears. She wouldn't be able to cope.

If what her father said was true, why hadn't she noticed anything? She hated herself for being so wrapped up in her own life and taking her grandmother for granted.

'You've got enough on your plate,' her father said, glad that he'd cottoned on to something that made sense to his getting drunk. There was no way on earth that he could tell her the truth about what had happened with regard to her husband. She'd never have anything to do with him again. Michael will get off without your help, he'd said to himself. The truth was he wasn't sure of that at all. The booze had dulled his senses so that he didn't notice her tears or the trembling of her voice. But that was Tony Brooks. If he didn't want to notice something, he wouldn't.

'Want a drink?' he asked, lifting his own glass with hope in his eyes.

Marcie shook her head. 'I don't drink on duty.'

Her father looked as though she'd slapped his face. 'You sound like a copper.'

'Hardly likely at this moment in time,' she said with a glower. 'My husband's in prison, remember? Now come on, Dad. You'd better get off home. I've had enough of you for one night.' She gritted her teeth. There was so much more she could say and none of it good. She was hurting but he hadn't really noticed.

'Can't I stay here?' he asked hopefully.

She sighed. He could be as boyish and appealing as Arnold or Archie when he wanted.

Silently calling herself a sucker, she gave in. 'Get in the back room.' Anyway, what did she care where he was? Tonight she felt weighed down with worry. Tonight he could do what he wanted.

The back room she referred to was the small sitting area behind Michael's desk in the office and the studio couch she'd eyed with such trepidation earlier.

On her first night at the club following Michael's arrest, she'd lain down on the studio couch where he himself had admitted to grabbing forty winks when working to the wee hours became too much. On that particular night she'd stroked the rough red moquette wondering if he had lain there with Linda Bell. The thought of it had clamped around her heart like an iron fist. She could not believe that their marriage was a sham and his fidelity pure fiction. He'd told her that Linda Bell was a liar and she'd chosen to believe him. She had to believe him or she couldn't love him any more.

She gave her father the key to the office. 'I'll be along in a minute.'

'That's my girl,' he said blithely, relieved that she'd noticed nothing odd about his behaviour. You've given nothing away, Tony my boy, he thought to himself and breathed a deep sigh. With nervous fingers he held on to the bar counter for support.

The guilt suddenly crept up on him. Of course he had to say something! What sort of father would he be if he didn't?

'There was something . . .'

He started to think about doing the right thing, but Marcie was already checking the barman's stock receipts. Nobody got any booze from the cellar without a signed stock receipt. She didn't hear him.

If Tony Brooks was half the man he thought he

was, he would have interrupted and confessed there and then that he might very well have had something to do with the gun the police had found in Michael's office. The trouble was he couldn't be sure about it.

Again and again he'd gone over that night in his mind, the night when a fight had broken out outside.

He'd been well and truly smashed just like on that other occasion when Alan Taylor had tricked him into thinking he'd murdered somebody. This time he'd been in the company of a gang of Irish bricklayers and such like; rough men over from Ireland brought in to raise tower blocks on the cleared bombsites left over from the war. Tower blocks were springing up like mushrooms all over London. 'Cities in the Sky' they were calling them, modern living for a modern age.

He didn't rate them himself but much preferred a house with a garden front and rear – a bit like the one he'd grown up in. Still, if it gave some poor blokes a job . . .

The Irish had been talking tough and egging him on.

'Tony, you're just the broom that sweeps up the rubbish in the morning.'

That's what they'd said to him when he said that he worked in a nightclub – correction – that he'd actually *owned* a nightclub.

'And I'd slug any bloke who wants to tell me otherwise,' he added with his usual gusto.

The plain fact of the matter was that he couldn't bear anybody being tougher than he was. It was kind of like a right for him to be the toughest of all. In reality it wasn't strictly true, but he had a reputation to maintain. He'd told them he was Michael Jones' right-hand man because the owner of the Blue Genie was married to his daughter. In fact he told them that they were partners.

'Yer lying. We don't believe you, do we, boys?'

The others had chorused that they didn't believe him either.

He was being egged on but the booze had blunted his judgement. Unwilling to appear weak and watery, he'd said he would show them, that he would prove he was telling the truth.

He'd taken the keys from out of his pocket.

'Follow me,' he'd said to them. 'Come into my office for a nightcap.'

Nobody had challenged him. He'd heard about the fight and guessed things had shut down early on the insistence of the police. The fact was that some of the toffs who attended the club wouldn't go near it with a ten-foot barge pole if the police were hanging around. Business would be too slow to bother with so everyone had gone home – with the exception of the night watchman of course and he only came round every two hours. Tony decided that if he timed it right they would be gone before he came round, and so he asked his Irish friends if they'd like to come into Michael's office for a nightcap . . .

It had been Michael's night off and somehow or other he'd managed to sneak them in just as the doorman was otherwise engaged. Even when he did notice Tony he only threw a quick nod of recognition in his direction. Tony was a face, a member of the family, and therefore beyond reproach.

After a few more drinks he'd gone to the bathroom, leaving them knocking back a few more whiskies. Immediately on getting back they'd said their goodnights – well, it was two in the morning. He himself had fallen into a deep sleep on the studio couch in the little restroom behind Michael's office. That was where he'd woken up desperate to get out before he had to face Michael and apologise for drinking his whisky. Not that it would have been the first time. Michael kept good whiskies for visitors and business associates, though he knew Tony sampled a few.

Michael didn't mind that, of course. Tony was family and this was typical of the nightclub scene – family and friends – whoever they might be.

Chapter Twenty-two

Carla Casey blew out a cloud of cigarette smoke with such force that Sam Kendal half expected her to hoot like a steam train.

'I can't understand why you don't just up and tell her. For Christ's sake, Mary, she's your daughter.'

The woman she addressed threw her a warning look. 'Don't call me that. I'm Sam Kendal and don't you bloody forget it!'

'OK. Sam. Whatever. I know you're thinking about Leo, but is he likely to notice, the state he's in? Anyway, she's still your daughter. Are you going to help her out?'

Samantha Kendal was imposing, glamorous and as hard as nails. She threw Carla a warning glare. 'Leo has been good to me. I won't chance hurting him. Besides, it's only a matter of time.'

Carla had lied to Marcie about her mother's husband but felt no guilt. She'd failed to mention a lot of other stuff too – in fact she'd done a lot of lying on her boss's account.

Leo was a lot older than Sam when they met and married. After being raped by Alan Taylor, the new woman who'd merged from the carcase of the old was bereft not just of memory but of some of her basic characteristics. It was as if the kinder part of her had been overruled by her strength and the determination to overcome anything. The good fairy had turned into something darker, something she herself sometimes found difficult to live with and was almost surprised at.

Sam Kendal was taller than her daughter, still attractive, her figure upright and not prone to middle-aged spread like Carla.

Carla watched her as she stalked the room. She feared but also admired her. The way she paced made her look as though she were the commander of an army contemplating the strategy of battle. In a way she was. Leo was knocking eighty-five. Not having any sons to carry on in his criminal wake and being unwilling to share responsibility with any of his closest partners, he'd decided that Sam would be the conduit for his will. Sam had been running things for a long time.

As it turned out the arrangement worked well. Sam fitted easily into the groove he'd carved for her. Leo respected her and, on seeing that he did, the hard men that worked for him respected her too. She had the maturity and she had his backing. She was a woman, but not one to be messed with and nobody ever did.

Sam smoked through an ebony cigarette holder. As she did so her finely plucked eyebrows dipped into a gentle frown.

'Paddy Rafferty needs his claws clipped,' she murmured thoughtfully.

'Needs gelding from what I hear,' muttered Carla.

'That can be arranged.'

Carla knew she wasn't joking. Although Sam looked like an upper-crust model from a *Harpers and Queen* magazine, she would do what had to be done.

'And the Camilleris had better watch it,' Sam added.

Carla knew that the Kendal outfit was more than a match for the Sicilians. The former had a lot of clout in the East End; people looked to them to sort things out more so than they did the police. It was rumoured that women and kids could walk in safety wherever the Kendals ruled. And Sam was the head of the outfit.

Carla envied Sam her poise, her clothes and her power, but mostly her clothes. Not that she was dowdy herself. She wore a plain shift dress beneath her fur coat. It was of good quality and classy, but Sam outshone her.

Sam Kendal was dressed in a pink Chanel suit. The jacket had neat brass buttons, was boxy and edged with navy-blue braid. The skirt was short, though respectably so. Sam Kendal had taste and the money to pay for it. Her earrings and the gold choker she wore around her neck were by Christian Dior. Since marrying Leo Kendal she could afford the best. Her world was a galaxy away from the Isle of Sheppey, memories of which had only started returning a few years back and were fragmented. Memories about her daughter, Marcie, had been buried deepest of all, but little pieces were coming back.

No one, not even Carla, knew that she'd began returning to Sheppey a few years back. She'd found her way to the beach and, although she remembered the cottage in Endeavour Terrace, she had stayed away, afraid of being seen.

As it turned out, she'd seen her ex-husband, Tony, in the pub with his new wife. She'd also seen Marcie. Worse than that, she'd seen Alan Taylor fawning over her daughter just as he'd once fawned over her.

Seeing what he was doing had filled her with blind fury. She'd seen him accost her daughter on the beach. Marcie had pushed him. She'd seen him fall, seen Marcie run off.

The day had been dull, fast drifting into winter. There had been few people about. Even if there had been, nothing would have stopped her pressing him that bit more firmly onto the piece of rough wood sticking out of his head. He hadn't been moving but he had been breathing. But not once she'd done that. He'd breathed no more.

Worrying about Marcie and doing this balancing act between her and Leo gave her pins and needles in her head. She loved her husband and her daughter and was fiercely protective of both of them.

Thoughts of Marcie gentled her; so did knowing that she was now a grandmother – a very glamorous one at that.

Sam stopped and faced Carla. The light from the window behind her shone around her body.

Like the bloody Virgin Mary, thought Carla.

'I've considered a number of options,' said Sam. 'Number one, I did consider letting you be my agent but then I decided it wasn't a good idea. You worked in clubs but you never ran them – not like that. And how would I protect her? No,' she said shaking her head whilst blowing out a cloud of blue smoke, 'I have to use someone who will have no choice but to protect her.'

'She isn't too keen on having a partner.'

Sam pulled her mouth into a half-smile. 'I didn't think she would be. I bet she hasn't told her old man she intends to keep the club.'

'Bet your life she hasn't,' said Carla with a knowing laugh. 'Whether you like it or not, she's a chip off the old block, Sam. She's you to a T – or at least how you used to be.'

It pleased Carla to see Sam's smile broaden. She'd known Sam in the good old days when they were young, before she'd married Tony, and before she'd lost her memory.

Sam had been Mary, a pretty little girl with blonde hair and big blue eyes full of hope and innocence. Well that had certainly long gone thanks to the likes of Tony Brooks and then that bastard Alan Taylor. Both of them were small-time crooks and neither of them had treated the lithesome beauty that well. Only Leo had done that.

'So what have you got in mind?' asked Carla.

Sam tapped the stalk of the cigarette holder against her chin. As she did so, Carla admired the wrinkle-free complexion of a woman halfway through her forties. Sam would always be one of those women who aged well, unlike Carla who used too much make-up and dyed her hair mercilessly every month.

'The Blue Genie is in the market for fresh bouncers. I will ensure that the manager takes on a few of my own hand-picked team. Kevin McGregor is a good bloke. Trustworthy. Did you know he used to work for us?'

Carla shook her head. The Kendal family had very long tentacles; it was amazing who they knew and who they could use.

Carla carried on. 'You will suggest to my daughter that she have a bodyguard with her at all times; if not Kevin McGregor himself, then a member of staff.'

'Even at home?'

Sam looked contemplative. 'If I could do more I would. Paddy Rafferty is a wild card. I can give him a warning, but he's a greedy sod since he muscled in on the property game. He's also a male chauvinist pig. Never mind burning my bra, I'd like to bloody strangle him with it. He knows that Leo is weak and dying. Paddy has no respect for women and I can't let him know just yet that Marcie is my daughter, not until Leo is gone. I know for a fact that he's got a few city councillors in his pocket so I have to tread carefully. Leo expects me to take care of his business and, besides, he still doesn't know about Marcie. Worse still he doesn't know that I was married to Tony Brooks!'

Chapter Twenty-three

The smell of disinfectant and food boiled to mush was instantly oppressive. The kitchens couldn't have been close by, yet the smell crept over everything.

Marcie had finally owned up that she intended keeping the Blue Genie.

Michael was furious. 'I told you to sell it!'

Marcie met Michael's glittering eyes. 'Would you have preferred Paddy Rafferty owning it, or being my "partner" as he suggested. Though we both know what he meant by that!'

'Of course not!'

'You know what he was implying, don't you?' Marcie asked hotly feeling her cheeks turning red.

'The bastard! Of course I do. I'm not bloody stupid!' He sighed deeply. 'Don't torture me like this, Marcie.'

She only just stopped herself from reaching across the table. As it was the brushing of her fingertips against his earned her a barked order from one of the screws.

'No touching!'

Marcie curled her fingers into the palm of her hand and made a fist.

She apologised for being thoughtless. It must hurt him badly to think that she was attracting sexual overtures from Rafferty whilst he was in here, unable to help her.

All the same, she was convinced she was right to keep the club. She attempted to explain. 'I couldn't do it, Michael. The Blue Genie is your dream and I felt that as long as I can keep that dream going I can wish and hope that all of this is just a temporary nightmare. The two are combined somehow. Don't ask me how. I just know.'

'You're going to be working day and night, or are you thinking of closing your sewing room?'

'I'll see how it goes. I might have to.'

'I thought you loved designing and making the outfits?'

She nodded. 'I do, but . . .' Deep inside she was still unsure why she wanted to keep the club. It had something to do with the dream, the sparks flying from the sign and the cheery image of the half-naked genie turning into something more sinister. She wouldn't tell him that. 'I couldn't sell the club. Somehow it would be so final. The Blue Genie was supposed to be one of many stretching far into the future . . .'

'I might not have any future,' Michael snapped. 'You're my wife, Marcie. You're supposed to love, honour and obey!'

The loudness of his voice made her jump. A few other visitors and prisoners looked their way. A prison officer threw him a warning look, unfolding his big arms as though about to spring into action and exercise physical restraint.

Marcie had bravely hoped that Michael would see her point without her having to tell him about the dream.

She tried again. 'I've got everything under control. I've even sorted out your filing. You never were much good at that.'

She gave a little laugh, hoping it might lift his spirits. Instead he glared at her.

'You've been snooping in my drawers? You've got no right doing that. A bloke's got a right to some privacy. Bloody women! You suck the lifeblood out of us! All of you. You're all the same!'

Marcie stared at him. It was on the tip of her tongue to ask if the comment was as much for Linda Bell as for her, but she couldn't.

He wasn't bearing up well at all and her heart ached at the sight of him. His face had turned gaunt since he'd been inside and there was a nervous wariness about him. There was a fuzzy yellow-purplish place on his cheekbone and shadows beneath his eyes. The corners of his mouth were down-turned, plus there was a small cut. When had that happened? And why hadn't she noticed before?

'Michael, is everything all right?'

He glared at her. 'Are you kidding? I'm banged up in here! Of course I'm not all right.'

'It's just that you look . . .'

'Quit nagging,' he snapped.

She swallowed hard. Only once had he ever spoken to her that way before.

She looked at him as though seeing him for the very first time. Something was very wrong here.

He sat looking down at the table, seemingly far away. Again she was tempted to reach out and touch him, to tangle her fingers in his thick, dark hair.

She kept her fist clenched, staring at the top of his hung head.

It was a strange silence, both locked in their own thoughts.

Michael spoke first. 'How are the kids?'

Marcie took a deep breath. 'Fine, except that Joanna keeps asking for you.'

'What have you told her?'

'That you're away on important business and will be back as soon as you can.'

'Soon? Christ! That's pushing it. Perhaps you'd better tell her that I won't be able to give her away on her wedding day.'

The cynicism was not like him, but Marcie decided it was best not to comment on it.

'Jacob will get you out,' Marcie said as cheerfully as she could. 'If anyone can, he can.'

'That gun was not mine,' Michael said, his eyes holding hers. 'And that shirt, I didn't put it there, Marcie. Honest I didn't.'

Chapter Twenty-four

Paddy Rafferty lay in bed wearing a pair of cotton gloves that helped soothe his aching flesh as well as hiding its red rawness from curious eyes.

His wife was away visiting her sick mother and, as the old saying goes, when the cat's away the mice do play. Well, Paddy was playing and Sheila Ashton had made him hard, harder than his wife ever could.

At present the white-fleshed stripper – though like all of her kind she preferred to be called an exotic dancer – was bending over, her big buttocks exposed to his gaze.

She was in the process of putting on the tiny pair of bikini briefs that were supposed to cover her private bits. They were made of purple gauzy stuff and hid nothing from his view. The cheeks of her rear remained smiling through.

She made a show of putting on her brassiere just as she would when she was up on stage only then of course she would be taking it off. When putting it on, it would have been simpler to fasten it at the front before turning it, slipping her boobs into the cups and sliding the straps over her shoulders; but

Sheila had an audience, an audience of one and that was him: Patrick Brian Rafferty.

Sheila was an expert at taking her clothes off – and putting them on. She did private performances for Paddy at least four times a week and more when his old woman was away – like now.

He liked the way she squealed when he raked his gloved hands over her. He liked the way she slid up under the bedclothes from the foot of the bed and did delicious things to his body all the way up. Sometimes he bent her over his knees and slapped her with his gloved hands – the leather ones. She said she loved it, but then she would say that. She was a professional scrubber and he paid her well.

He noticed her struggling back into the schoolgirl outfit he'd taken her out of some two hours before. 'You're putting on a bit of weight, Sheila.'

'Cheeky sod,' she said, throwing him a glance over her shoulder.

She'd arrived with the uniform hidden beneath a belted trench coat. Her hair was still in bunches and tied with white ribbons.

'You're not up the spout, are you, girl?'

She blew him a raspberry. Sheila was a girl of few words.

'Your money's there,' he said, pointing to the dressing table.

He watched the way she picked it up and began

counting it slowly. It unnerved him. She'd never done that before. And she was dawdling, as though she had something she wanted to say before she left. He guessed it was to do with money. Everything Sheila did was to do with money, including the squeals when he slapped her with his gloved hands. He reckoned he was paying a ten bob note for each one.

She eyed him slyly, coquettishly even, as though she really were a silly little schoolgirl wanting something from him.

'That Michael Jones. Now he's out of the way, are you going to make a play for his missus?'

Paddy cocked an eyebrow. The Blue Genie was what he wanted, though in all honesty the thought of seducing Mrs Jones had occurred to him.

'What the hell is it to you might I ask?'

She shrugged her narrow shoulders and slammed her eyelids. 'I knew you wanted the club and wondered whether you wanted her as well. I expect she'll be a bit scrawny without her clothes on. You'll be disappointed.'

He grinned. 'You're jealous.'

She sniffed and turned up her cute little nose. 'She won't let you do the things to her that you do to me.'

'Of course not. She's not a scrubber like you. She's a respectable girl.'

Sheila bristled. 'Charmed I'm sure!'

Paddy laughed. 'Sheila, I bed you. I ain't likely to wed you, even if I didn't already have a missus.'

'Of course not! That's not what I'm saying.'

He saw her face go red.

He'd had it in mind to tell her to sod off and not cloud his door again, but Sheila had a point. She catered for the more kinky aspects of sexual practice, and she was right that he might not get the same service elsewhere.

He decided to level with her, as much as he was able. 'It's what she's got that I want.'

'The club?' Sheila's eyes opened wide. She almost sounded excited.

Paddy realised then that he'd walked into a trap. The girl was after something all right – too much something if his instinct served him right.

'Yes,' he said slowly. 'I'm interested in the club.'

'And her. That's why you got him put away, didn't you? Without him around the poor little wife is going to need somebody to take the club off her hands – or help her run it. And Michael wouldn't allow you to muscle in. But you think the wife might. Is that it?'

Paddy frowned. 'You ask too many questions.'

'Oh come on, Paddy,' she said, her breasts ballooning from her bra and the partially buttoned blouse as she went down on all fours crawling up the bed towards him. 'I didn't ask you hardly anything when you got me to nick one of his shirts. Did you dab it in Linda's blood? Is that what you did?'

Paddy glared. He moved swiftly, grabbing her jaw and twisting it as though he intended ripping off the lower half of her face.

'I suggest you take a well-earned rest at the seaside. Somewhere like Blackpool would be best. Somewhere far away. Do you get my drift, Sheila?'

His frown had intensified. Sheila was like a bloodhound when it came to money. Plenty was never enough. She always wanted to go the extra mile, sniffing out a wedge of tenners like a dog on heat. Only she was a bitch. A right bitch.

Give the bitch her due, she wasn't easily scared.

'You've only given me enough money to stay away for a couple of weeks, Paddy. And I don't fancy Blackpool. How about Spain? A lot of people are going on holiday to Spain nowadays . . .'

He tightened his grip. 'Don't push your luck, Sheila.' His voice was full of warning.

Sheila kept playing the innocent schoolgirl as though that would break some ice with him. 'I could do a lot with an extra five hundred pounds.'

His gloved hand slammed across the side of her face, sending her sprawling from the bed. The blow was so violent that her head jerked to one side before she landed on the floor.

Paddy glared at her. 'Five hundred? Fuck off, you silly cow!'

A surprised Sheila sat fingering her jaw, thrusting it from side to side, not sure whether it was broken.

Keen to maintain the advantage of surprise, Paddy leaned across the bed and grabbed a handful of her hair.

Sheila screamed.

'Now look here, you silly bitch! Cross me and I'll be giving you more than a spanked backside. I'll be raising a team to use your head as a football. Do you catch my drift, Sheila? Do you, Sheila? Do you?'

He called for Baxter after she'd gone.

'She knows too much. You know what to do.'

Chapter Twenty-five

Marcie took the children down to her grandmother's for the weekend. The pressures of London, of Michael in jail and of running his businesses as well as her own were getting to her. She was feeling rundown and listless, couldn't eat and generally didn't feel well. The fact that her grandmother was ill only added to her worries. She had no time to worry about herself.

'You didn't tell me,' Marcie said to her grandmother. 'What is it? What's wrong with you?'

Rosa Brooks smiled. 'I am getting old. There is nothing you can do about it. Anyway, the condition is only temporary. The doctor told me so.'

They were sitting across from each other in the two winged armchairs placed either side of the fireplace where the old range chugged and spluttered like an ailing donkey.

Rosa Brooks was using the poker to dislodge some clinker from the fire bed. All her attention appeared to be fixed on it, as though her illness was nothing at all to worry about. But Marcie knew better.

Reaching across, she touched the papery thin skin of her grandmother's hand.

'Gran, I know you're lying. Dad told me it's serious. He told me that you're going blind. He said the doctor called him and told him you have diabetes.'

Rosa stiffened in her chair. Old she might be, but she was still resolute.

'Your father does not come here often enough to know anything. He even thinks his wife is divorcing him. The fool! As long as he sends her money, she will do nothing of the sort. Besides, they had a Catholic wedding. They cannot divorce.'

Marcie shook her head. She did wonder if her father had been talking rubbish about Babs wanting a divorce. He always liked to play for sympathy with her. It helped counter the guilt he was feeling because he rarely came back to Sheppey and, when he did, all he and his wife Babs did was argue and fight. There was also the matter of his girlfriends, of course, though that was something Marcie made no mention of.

Sitting very still, she stared into her grandmother's face, seemingly without her knowing. The two dark eyes she'd known all her life were not nearly as bright as they had been. The film of a double cataract misted them both.

The sound of Joanna chuckling caused a smile to cross the old face.

'Joanna is growing fast,' said her grandmother, smiling in the general direction of where Marcie's daughter was sitting on the floor, drawing. 'See how pretty she looks in that pink dress.'

Marcie felt as though her heart would break. She'd overheard her grandmother asking Garth what colour dress Joanna was wearing and he'd told her.

At present Garth was sitting next to Joanna. Her grandmother could not possibly see her great-grand-daughter.

Marcie held back the tears. She'd cried enough of them of late, mostly when she was in bed alone at night, unable to sleep, unable to face the dreams that might come.

The fact was that she had to accept that things were much worse than her father had stated. Her grandmother was virtually blind, but was managing to find her way around the house and do all the things she had always done purely because she was familiar with her surroundings.

The family had never been the sort who touch and hug at the drop of a hat, but that was what Marcie did now. Reaching across she took the bony hand of her grandmother into her own then hugged her grandmother's head before cupping her cheek in her hand.

'Gran,' she said softly. 'That's Garth you can see. He's sitting between you and Joanna.'

It wasn't easy, but she effectively controlled the

trembling of her voice. If her grandmother was being strong then she had to be the same.

Rosa Brooks hesitated before jerking her chin in a short, swift nod. 'So you know. Then that is it. There is nothing to be done.'

'What did the doctor say?'

'He said that I am old.'

'Doctor Sangster must have said more than that.'

'Not Doctor Sangster. He is dead. He died last week from liver failure. A young West Indian doctor has taken his place. He's a good man but he says that there is nothing he can do.'

Marcie sat back in her chair not able to believe how helpless she felt. The feeling was short-lived. She refused to believe that there was nothing that could be done. The everlasting hope of youth took over.

'There must be something. Why don't you see another doctor? If this one is only young . . .'

Her grandmother shook her head. Again, her voice was very gentle. 'There is a time for all things, Marcie. I am not afraid. I have my faith. Besides, I know that your grandfather is waiting for me on the other side. We talk a lot more now and he visits me in my sleep. Do you know that when we meet we are young again? Is not that the most wonderful thing? Everything we were together we will be again.'

Her face shone. For one solitary moment it seemed

that the wrinkles were smoothed out and that her flesh was firm and young again.

Feeling as though she were choking on her tongue, Marcie swallowed a sob and brushed away a tear. What she marvelled at most of all was the look on her grandmother's face. Her face was glowing. She wanted to cherish the hope that her grandmother's condition was improving, but deep down she knew it was not so.

'My legs ache,' said Rosa Brooks. 'Can you dish up the dinner?'

Marcie said that she would. 'Can you manage Joanna and Aran?'

'I would love to. Joanna. Come here where I can see you.'

'I'll get Garth to dig up a few carrots while I cut a cabbage.'

'They'll be the last before the frost gets them,' her grandmother called after her.

Marcie told Garth that she was dealing with dinner and they went out to the garden together. 'My grandmother's legs are aching. The cold isn't good for her,' she explained.

Garth nodded stoically. 'Auntie Rosa doesn't like walking any more.'

'She's getting old, Garth,' Marcie said gently.

'And she hit her toe. That hurts a lot.'

'She stumbled, did she?' Marcie remarked. It was perfectly understandable. Her grandmother's failing eyesight meant that she was bound to be bumping into things.

'It bled,' said Garth.

'Oh dear. Did she put a plaster on it?' Marcie was always careful to speak to him as though he were a child so he could understand better.

Garth had no conception of lying so always told the truth regardless of the implications.

'Not a plaster,' he said with great vehemence. 'It wouldn't be big enough. A bandage! That's what she did. But it's not crusty yet. It stinks.'

Marcie frowned. What did he mean by crusty? 'It sounds horrible.'

'It's true,' he said and looked at her in a way that made her feel she'd misjudged him. 'It smells bad. And sometimes she gets dizzy and doesn't know where she is. And sometimes she's asleep for ages.'

The warmth of the kitchen welcomed them back in from the garden where a mist was rolling in from the sea and crisping the air.

Marcie thought about what Garth had said as she ran the tap water to swill off the vegetables. 'Does she sleep for long?' She said it quietly so that her grandmother wouldn't hear.

Garth nodded and dropped his voice to suit. 'Sometimes I can't wake her up.'

Marcie looked over her shoulder to see if her grandmother had heard what they were saying.

Apparently not. She was totally absorbed in entertaining the children.

Marcie listened to her grandmother telling some wonderful tale about castles, fairies and goblins. Joanna was all rapt attention. As she watched, Marcie came to an instant decision. Tomorrow, by hook or by crook, she was taking her grandmother to the doctor. Asking her what was wrong would achieve nothing. Her grandmother was beginning to subvert the truth. No. She had to persuade her to go to the doctor and to let her go too. It wouldn't be easy, but it had to be done. Marcie wanted the truth about her grandmother's health and knew she wouldn't get it from the woman herself.

The following day she offered to take her shopping.

Her grandmother protested at first. 'There is not much that I need.'

'Bread? Milk? Bear in mind that Aran and Joanna are going to want milk. Joanna can have cow's milk. Aran needs another tin of Cow and Gate.'

Seeing as it seemed she was the one in need of shopping, her grandmother gave in. The truth was that she'd brought a spare tin of Cow and Gate with her, but an extra tin wouldn't come amiss.

'You can push – if you don't mind that is.'

Of course her grandmother wouldn't mind!

With Aran and Joanna crammed into the pushchair, she allowed her grandmother to push whilst she walked to one side keeping a firm grip on the handle. Garth opted to stay at home and do some drawing.

It suited Marcie fine. She had a plan. Rosa Brooks was concentrating on pushing the pushchair so it wasn't too hard to alter course to the doctor's surgery. With a pang of foreboding, Marcie noticed her grandmother limping.

She was careful to go slowly, directing the pushchair away from the shops and towards the surgery.

'Are we changing direction?' her grandmother asked.

'No. We're going exactly where I intended to go,' quipped Marcie without really giving away that they were headed for the surgery.

'We're here,' said Marcie pushing open one of the wide double doors.

Her grandmother looked panic stricken. 'This is not the fishmonger! I wanted fish for Friday!'

Marcie managed to guide her into the reception area.

'The doctor promised he would see us the minute we got here.' Marcie clung tightly but gently to her grandmother's arm, knowing that given half the chance she'd dig in her heels and refuse to move.

Craning her neck whilst wrestling with the pushchair, door and grandmother, she caught the receptionist's attention. Old Doctor Sangster had never had a receptionist. Like most old-time doctors of his generation, he had let his own patients in and out. His more modern replacement had changed things a great deal.

'Oh! It's Mrs Brooks,' said the receptionist with a welcoming smile.

Rosa Brooks stopped in her tracks. 'Why have you brought me here?' she demanded of her grand-daughter.

The receptionist looked both amused and impressed that Marcie was attempting to do so many things at once. They exchanged a knowing look. Everyone knew that Rosa Brooks was of independent spirit.

'Let me help you,' said the pleasant-faced young woman, coming out from behind her high reception desk.

'I do not need to see the doctor,' Rosa protested. Her eyes might be bad, but Marcie could read what she was thinking. Her grandmother was angry – very angry.

'He's very keen to see you,' said the receptionist to Rosa Brooks as though totally unaware of her resist-ance. She turned to Marcie. 'Do go in, Mrs Jones. I'll take care of the children for you.'

'Gran. You have to see the doctor about your toe.'

'Toe?' she exclaimed accusingly. 'There is nothing the matter with my toe.'

This was never going to be easy, but Marcie was

determined. Even if it meant telling a lie, she was going to get something done here.

Cupping her hand over her mouth, she whispered in her grandmother's ear.

'Gran, it's not healing and because it's not healing it's beginning to smell.'

Marcie's grandmother took a backwards step and looked shocked. Recovering quickly she glared at her granddaughter accusingly. 'I do not need you to come in with me.'

'Well, I am.' Marcie was determined. 'You've taken care of me all my life, Gran. Now it's time for me to take care of you. So don't argue.'

In the past Rosa might have protested more vehemently, but she was weaker than she had been. Marcie winced on feeling the fragile arm beneath the black tweed coat her grandmother was wearing. It was as though there was no flesh, only bones barely covered by skin.

'Marcie. Please. You do not understand. I can take care of this myself. I do not wish to be pulled around like a piece of meat on a slab.'

'This is a doctor you're seeing, not a butcher.'

The weak pleading of her grandmother's voice tore at her heart, but she was determined to get to the bottom of this. There was some truth in her saying that her grandmother's injured toe was beginning to smell. What was wrong? She had to know.

The doctor had sad brown eyes and coffee-coloured skin. His smile was warm and so was his voice as he steered her grandmother to a comfortable chair. 'I am so very pleased to see you, Mrs Brooks. You should come in and see me more often.'

'I would not wish to waste your time,' Rosa responded indignantly. 'You would not be doing that, Mrs Brooks. I like to keep my eye on senior patients. I think that is only wise.'

Rosa Brooks was having none of it. 'I am not sure I agree.'

'Please, Mrs Brooks. Let me be the judge of that.' Placing his hand on her shoulder, he pressed her gently down onto the seat at the side of his desk.

'Now,' he said, still smiling and brimming with the professional confidence of a young man keen to do his stuff. 'Your granddaughter tells me that you hit your toe and it's not healing as it should. Is that right?'

'It is nothing,' said Rosa in a resolute manner, one hand waving at him as though he were a fly and should leave her alone. 'I used herbs but not the right ones. I can take care of it myself.'

'I think I can do better,' said the young doctor, his smile undimmed. At the same time his eyes met Marcie's over her grandmother's head. She saw the concern there and knew instantly that he was aware of the blindness and that the problem with her grandmother's toe was somehow attached to it.

The doctor placed a chair for Marcie beside that of her grandmother. 'Please. Take a seat, Mrs Jones.'

Marcie thanked him. Knowing her grandmother wasn't best pleased, she slid a sidelong look in her direction. The walnut-brown face had set like sun-dried clay, criss-crossed with cracks. Marcie was thankful that the jet-black eyes were staring straight ahead, the strong little chin trembling.

'Now,' he said, looking directly into Rosa's face. 'Will you let me take your shoe off?'

'You may if you wish, but, as I have already told you, I will heal it with herbs. It is just a deep cut that is taking a little longer than usual to heal. It is because of the cold weather.'

The doctor's amused expression turned slightly more serious. 'As I have already intimated, Mrs Brooks, I think you should let me be the best judge of that. That's what the National Health Service pays me for. Please allow me to earn my keep.' He said it with a light laugh, but it was obvious from her grand-mother's expression that she wasn't finding this funny at all.

Marcie marvelled at how secretive her grand-mother had been about her toe. If Garth had not told her about it, she would not have known.

The doctor cradled her grandmother's foot in one hand and began to undo the bandage with the other.

Marcie leaned forwards, her frown deepening and

her nose wrinkling as more and more of the bandage was undone. The smell was terrible – like rotting meat. She covered her nose and mouth with one hand, wincing on seeing the blackened, suppurating toe.

He looked at Marcie, then back at her grand-mother. His smile had disappeared completely. 'Can you smell it, Mrs Brooks?'

Her grandmother stared at him silently for a moment before answering. 'Yes.'

'It's badly infected.'

'Yes.'

Marcie had heard old men talking about terrible injuries during the Great War of 1914 to 1918 and of how legs and arms had had to be sawn off, the smell indicating that saving the limb was hopeless.

The young doctor put it into words. 'Gangrene,' said the doctor. 'That's what this is.'

'Is it serious?' Marcie asked.

His glance held a bucketful of sympathy. He nodded. 'In certain circumstances it is. Some people are susceptible to it and some people cannot fully recover from it without an amputation being carried out.'

'You can tell her,' Marcie's grandmother said suddenly.

'Seeing as I have your permission, then I will,' said the doctor. 'When an injury such as this occurs to people with diabetes, it rarely heals unless it is very minor indeed. I think you were already aware what it was, weren't you, Mrs Brooks?'

Rosa Brooks was surprisingly placid, apparently unmoved by what he was telling her. 'Yes, but it is of no consequence. I am dying day by day, doctor – as we all are. I am old. I have had my time, and please do not look at me as someone to be pitied. I may not be able to see but I can tell you are. I'm an old woman whose flesh is rotting and eyesight is failing. I was not always like this. I was a baby once, a child and a young woman – a beautiful young woman I might add.'

'I am sure you were,' the doctor replied, his manner polite and not at all condescending. 'Time levels us all, Mrs Brooks. I can't promise anything, but I will do my best. You're an intelligent woman and I will treat you with the respect you deserve. I will tell you the truth. The toe will have to come off.'

Rosa nodded.

Marcie sat silently shocked. Both the doctor and her grandmother were being so matter of fact about this. She was the one who didn't want to accept this.

'Just her toe?'

'Hopefully it will be only the toe that has to come off. I'm not sure we can do anything about your eyes,' the doctor added.

'What's affected my grandmother's sight?' Marcie asked him. 'Is that also to do with diabetes?'

He nodded.

'Stop fussing, Marcie. I can manage without them,' snapped her grandmother.

Marcie sighed. Rosa Brooks was strong-willed and even though her physical strength was ebbing away, her will was as strong as ever. And she was proud. She would always be proud.

The doctor seemed to be doing his best not to look sad. 'It's partly her diabetes but she also has cataracts. It won't be long before we can deal with them very effectively with modern medicine, but that's not your grandmother's problem. The vessels at the back of her eyes have been damaged by her diabetes; it's called glaucoma.'

Marcie's head was reeling. How could so many bad things be happening to her? First, Michael being arrested for murder, and now, her grandmother not only going blind but in need of an amputation. Only a toe, she reminded herself, and couldn't help saying it out loud.

She put her arm around her grandmother and hugged her tightly. 'Only a toe. Thank goodness for that. I suppose it could be a lot worse.'

There was something about the doctor's expression that made her think that the amputation of her grandmother's toe wouldn't be the end of things. She'd ignore that for now. Nothing else bad must happen. She didn't think she could cope with it.

The doctor rewrapped her grandmother's foot and told her that he would arrange for her to be admitted to hospital for the operation to remove the toe. Rosa Brooks looked less than pleased at the prospect. The doctor saw her expression.

'Mrs Brooks,' he said, taking hold of both her hands. 'Let me put this bluntly – if that toe doesn't come off we'll be looking at taking your foot off, perhaps even your leg. The poison has to be stopped from spreading. If I could avoid surgery, I would.'

Rosa didn't seem all that impressed. She shrugged her thin shoulders. 'I suppose it has to be.'

'I suppose we'd better get some shopping,' said Marcie once they were out in the fresh air.

Her grandmother limped along beside her. Marcie guessed that only the presence of the children prevented Rosa Brooks from tearing her off a strip.

'We'll go to the fishmonger's first,' said Marcie.

'You tricked me,' said her grandmother. Her voice was low. Her eyes were fixed on the two children though she couldn't really be seeing very much of them, just blurred shapes.

'I had to,' said Marcie. 'You weren't telling me the truth.'

'I was not telling you lies.'

'You weren't telling me anything.'

'You have enough concerns. You have two children,

a husband in jail and a business to run. None of it is easy. And you must listen to your inner voices and have a care for your dreams. Dreams can solve a lot of things.'

The comment about dreams made Marcie wonder. She hadn't conveyed any part of her dreams to her grandmother. In fact she hadn't admitted to having any dreams – vibrant or otherwise.

The dreams were of no real consequence. Marcie concentrated on shopping with a vengeance.

Buying fish, vegetables and fresh sliced bread did nothing to soften the blow of knowing just how ill her grandmother was. She did everything as though she were running on clockwork and had a huge key in her back that was turning fast but would wind to a halt later. It helped to keep the worries at bay.

By the time they arrived back at Endeavour Terrace, Aran was asleep in his pushchair and even Joanna's eyes were drooping. Marcie was also feeling tired. She'd told nobody, but running Michael's business and dealing with all the other family problems arising thick and fast was going to be doubly difficult.

She sighed when she reached the front gate of number ten, stopped, took a deep breath and closed her eyes. For a moment the world went away, yet she could *feel* her grandmother's eyes on her. She opened her own and met those of the woman who had had most influence on her life. Her grandmother's look was steady, almost as though she really could see Marcie very clearly, though obviously she could not.

'Does Michael know?'

She wanted to say, 'Does Michael know what?' but there was no point.

'You have been feeling tired lately. You have not been eating properly. The child will be born at Easter.'

Marcie's jaw dropped. 'Gran, I can't be . . .'

'Of course you are. You know it. It's just that you're not listening to your body. It's understandable. You have too much to think about at present. But there will be a child. I guarantee it.'

Marcie was stunned, but her eyes were open. For weeks she'd been denying the fact that she hadn't had a monthly period. No, she hadn't told Michael – mainly because she hadn't admitted the fact that she was pregnant to herself.

'I don't think I am,' she said, still unwilling to face the inconvenient truth. 'Not really. It's just that I'm rundown with all these problems I have to deal with.'

She felt herself blushing. Michael had been on remand just under three months. Was it really only that long? It felt so much longer. She was missing him badly.

'You must take better care of yourself,' remarked her grandmother.

Marcie was dismissive. 'Never mind me. It's your welfare that concerns me at present.'

'I will be fine.'

Marcie was no longer so sure about that. Someone had to call in on her grandmother now and again to make sure she was taking care of herself. Garth would be a help, of course, but he was hardly the most responsible person in the world, and certainly not the most intelligent. There was only one other person, besides the Catholic priest, who could find the time to call in on her.

There was only one relative of the right age though negligible responsibility who could call on her grandmother and that was her stepmother.

Before returning to London, Marcie went round to the scruffy council house where her stepmother and brothers and sister lived. The moment she turned into the street she heard raised voices. A crowd was gathered around the garden gate, shouting encouragement at the spectacle taking place on what passed for the front lawn. Barbara Brooks – Babs as she liked to be called – was wrestling with another woman. They were screaming at each other, grappling with each other's shoulders and collars; shoes flew off, stockings laddered and mud-spattered skirts were hoisted up exposing large nylon knickers.

'You cow! Keep away from my old man, you effing slag!'

Marcie groaned. The woman's insult wasn't far from the truth. Babs loved flattery. Loved attention and loved the men even more.

Babs screamed back. 'Who the bloody hell do you think you are, calling me that?'

The screeching was deafening and embarrassing. The fight, together with the exposed backsides and naked thighs, was drawing a lot of hilarity.

'Blimey, who'd want to go further with them big bums?'

Laughter and amused tittering ran through the gathered crowd.

Marcie was mortified.

'Right!' she shouted. 'Out of my way.' She barged through the people massed around the garden gate. 'Let me through.'

Heaving an elbow here and there proved the most efficient way of getting into the garden.

'Babs,' she shouted.

No joy. Her stepmother was busily screaming a torrent of obscenities at the other woman who in turn was hurling a few more back.

Marcie managed to get in between them, but she couldn't do it alone. 'Can someone help me?'

A woman with a harelip and wearing a sacking apron helped her prise the two women apart.

'What the fuck do you want?' shrieked Babs, her smudged mascara making her look like a panda.

Marcie held on to her. 'I was going to ask you to keep an eye on Gran. She's not well.'

Babs laughed mockingly, her uneven teeth stained yellow by nicotine. 'Get lost. I'm nothing to do with you lot any more. I'm getting a divorce. Didn't yer dad tell you that?'

Chapter Twenty-six

The mirrored back wall of the Rose and Crown reflected the smoke-filled bar and the old walls reverberated with the sound of raucous conversation and the tinkling of an out-of-tune piano.

Tony Brooks was in the thick of it, leaning against the bar and regaling anyone who would listen with his usual boasts of how important he was and that he owned one of the busiest nightclubs in the whole of London.

Regardless of the truth, Tony was well oiled with one too many drams of Irish whiskey and beyond what was the truth and what was not.

'Another drink for you, my boy?'

The fella who asked was called Gary as far as he could remember – or it might have been Patrick. Whatever. There were plenty round about who were hanging on to his every word. He presumed they were all friends and fully immersed himself in the party atmosphere.

The woman – a tasty piece who said she was a nightclub hostess – was all over him like a rash. She told him her name was Gloria.

Unfortunately for Tony they were far from being friends, but he didn't know that at the time, not until he came to, with no idea where he was.

He tried to open his eyes but found he couldn't. He also tried to move his arms but he couldn't do that either. His wrists were sore though not aching as much as his head and something sticky was running into his mouth.

Something – most likely a boot – thudded into his side.

'Wakey, wakey! Time for the sleeping beauty to open her eyes.'

He knew that voice. Paddy Rafferty!

Tony's mouth was as dry as the bottom of a bird cage so he said nothing, only groaned in response to the kick in the ribs.

'Get 'im into a chair.'

Two pairs of rough mitts dragged him to his feet and shoved him unceremoniously onto a hard chair.

'What . . .'

He couldn't say any more. Everything ached. His head was swimming. He guessed somebody had clonked him on the head. He tried to remember where he was when it happened. Gloria! He remembered the voluptuous girl with bosoms too big for one hand to cover and a ribald laugh. She'd made him feel good. They talked, laughed and got drunk together. So what if she was a nightclub hostess with a few years' experience under her corset, she was fun. That was the great thing about most of those hostesses; they were uncomplicated. Buy them a drink, have a laugh and that was it, they were putty in his hands. He vaguely remembered her suggesting that they went back to her place. He'd gone willingly.

He couldn't recall having heard her give the taxi driver the address. In fact he couldn't remember whether it was a taxi he'd got into. He only knew that Gloria was big and beautiful and warm to cuddle up to. Not that they ever got to her place. He remembered the car – not a taxi at all – coming to a halt down some ramshackle road lined on each side with sheets of corrugated iron. He recalled dogs barking and the smell of rusty cars.

'Out here,' she'd said.

She didn't get out with him. He'd been dragged out and hit over the head. He'd passed out and had now come to. Sticky tape kept his eyes closed. His hands were tied.

'Where am I?'

'It don't matter where you are, Tony, only the reason for you being here.'

That was Rafferty all right.

Tony concentrated on listening, trying to work out where he was. Once again he heard the barking of dogs. They had to be close to a scrapyard, though God knows where. There were tons of them around the East End, where whole streets had been flattened in the Blitz leaving vast expanses of cleared, rough ground. Nothing grew in these places except dusty weeds and piles of rusting cars and vans.

Tony was scared. He knew – or thought he knew – what they wanted. If only he hadn't drank so much. If only he hadn't got a conscience.

'I ain't said nothing.'

'About what, Tony?'

He curbed his first instinct to spout out about the gang of Irish labourers and the gun. Wasn't it wiser to let them state the reason? Just in case he got it all wrong.

'About you asking me to persuade our Marcie to flog you the club.'

Rafferty made a tutting sound like an old woman about to birch him for being cheeky. 'Come on, Tony boy. Don't take me for a bloody Mick straight from the bogs.'

'I don't know what you mean, Paddy. I swear I don't.'

'I want you out of London, Tony. I don't want anybody – including your daughter's old man – knowing that we've ever associated. Get it?'

Tony didn't take long to think about it. 'Of course not. If that's what you want, Mr Rafferty. Whatever you want.'

Even to his own ears he sounded scared. He *was*

scared. On the other hand he also thanked his lucky stars that he hadn't blabbed about the Irish blokes and the gun. He'd been drunk on that occasion too and hadn't twigged what they were up to. Only with hindsight had he seen that he'd been set up. And here he was, drunk again.

'All I want is for you to put a little pressure on that daughter of yours. She's too headstrong for her own good. The more she holds me off from what I want, the more I'm going to be beating the shit out of you, Brooks. Have you got that?'

He was about to protest that Marcie was more like her mother and wouldn't listen to a word he said. Just in time he realised that sort of comment would result in another beating. 'I'll do what I can.'

Paddy's gloved hand slugged him around the head so hard that he fell off the chair.

A pair of meaty hands dragged him up from the floor and sat him back on the chair.

'Now,' said Paddy. 'Run that by me again. What is it you're going to do for me, Tony?'

Tony Brooks licked at the blood trickling from the corner of his mouth. 'I'm going to have a word with my daughter. Get her to see things your way.'

'Good! Good, good, good!'

He flinched when Paddy patted his shoulder. A pat was the last thing he was expecting.

His mind was racing. There was no way he was

going to cross the likes of Paddy Rafferty. On the other hand, intimidating his daughter was out of the question. Number one, she wouldn't listen, and, number two her old man would give him what for if he did.

'I'll make sure you'll be reimbursed for your trouble once the building is in my hands. Just don't let me down, Tony,' Rafferty said, his fingers digging like claws into Tony's shoulders. 'Take the girl in hand. Show her who's boss. Right?'

'Right, Mr Rafferty.'

Right! Paddy Rafferty was out of his mind if he thought every woman in the whole wide world would cave in to a bloke's bidding – husband, father or whatever. Tony was already totally convinced that he didn't have a chance. The little girl he'd once bossed around was gone. He saw a girl who was very much like her mother had been.

'Go to it,' said Rafferty.

Well, he'd most certainly do that. He'd be off out of London as soon as he could. The obvious destination was already in his mind. He was going home. At least he'd get to see his old mum and the boys. He grimaced at the thought of seeing Babs and having to make amends, but he'd do it because he had to. It wouldn't take much to persuade her to drop the divorce proceedings; a bit of a kiss and a cuddle and that would be it.

Once he was staggering away from trouble, his mind went into overdrive with freshly laid plans. He was going home and he wasn't leaving Sheppey again until he was sure that the coast was clear.

At least if he was there he could think how he might be able to help his daughter – if at all. If he was safe he could think of something – he was sure he could.

Chapter Twenty-seven

To hear that her father was off to make it up with Babs came as something of a surprise to Marcie. He telephoned from a local call box in Tottenham Court Road saying he thought his place was back on Sheppey with his kids and his sick old mother. Marcie didn't argue with that but told him it was for the best and that he was doing the right thing by his family.

'Thank God someone will be there for Gran,' she said to him. 'Let me know when she's had the operation. Tell her I'm thinking of her.'

'You're not coming down yourself?'

'I can't. I have to keep an eye on things up here. She told me she understands. Then there's the kids . . .'

Feeling guilty as hell, she put the phone down. If she could have torn herself in half, she would gladly have done so. She needed to be here in London to keep things going. Her husband deserved that. On the other hand, she desperately wanted to go to Sheppey to support the woman who had brought her up.

Two of the most important people in her life needed her. Her grandmother was sick and her husband was in prison. The responsibilities were weighing heavily on her shoulders. Although she too would prefer to be back on the island, she couldn't possibly go – not yet, not until a few things had been settled.

'I'm sorry I can't be at the club,' her father had said before hanging up.

'I'll manage,' Marcie had responded.

The fact was that she could manage perfectly well without him. He was hardly the kingpin of the place.

She grinned at the thought of it as she checked through a pile of invoices Kevin had left on her desk.

When it came to managing the club, Kevin McGregor was the bee's knees. He treated her with the greatest respect and so did the other staff that worked there, especially the bouncers.

'I get the impression that if anybody dared upset me, one of you might bite him,' she had said to Kevin.

Kevin had grinned at that. 'The boss is away. We wouldn't want anyone taking advantage of that now, would we?'

So that was it. Even though her husband was inside, he was taking care of her. Kevin and the bouncers were just following orders.

McGregor brought her a cup of coffee. She thanked him.

'Rafferty wants this place. You know that don't you?'

She sipped at her coffee thoughtfully before putting the cup back on the saucer. 'Do you think I'm mad to hold out?'

'No. I think you're brave, though that's not surprising. All things considered. It's in the blood.'

She smiled at that. OK, sometimes her dad was brave but if there were an easy way out of something, he'd take it. Which made her think of him going back to Sheppey. What was that all about?

'Rafferty is a nasty piece of work. Me and the boys will come running if you need us. Just yell.'

'Or scream?'

Michael had been cagey about Paddy Rafferty and what he was capable of because he hadn't wanted to frighten her.

It was Jacob Solomon who had put her wise and told her a bit of his form. It wasn't good to listen to. Paddy had a history. People who had defied him were dealt with savagely. Places had been vandalised and even burned to the ground by his thugs.

'We're taking it in turns to stay here overnight,' Kevin said to her. 'The night watchman is not near enough.'

She thanked him. 'I much appreciate you and the boys taking care of me.'

Kevin smiled. 'Think nothing of it. We're just doing what we're paid for.'

She knew very well that it was much more than that and decided to mention it to Michael the next day when she went to see him. She loved him all the more for thinking of her with all that he had to contend with at present.

'Tomorrow I'll tell Michael how kind you've been,' she said.

Kevin's smile was hesitant. 'No need for that,' he said.

There was something about his smile that she couldn't put her finger on. It was as though he didn't really want her to mention it to Michael at all.

Kevin and his boys deserved to be mentioned, she decided. And tomorrow she would do just that.

Allegra, as loyal as ever and seemingly without any life of her own nowadays, had offered to look after Joanna and Aran.

'Do I look good?' Marcie asked her.

Her dress was white with crisp white daisies scattered all over it. Her coat was pillarbox red and she wore black pull-on boots.

'He'll fall in love with you all over again,' said Allegra.

Marcie took a deep breath and nodded. A host of butterflies were fluttering in her stomach. She hated the prison. It reminded her of Pilemarsh, though without the ribald comments and laughter of girls like Sally Saunders.

*   *   *

The day was grey and the sight of the prison made it seem greyer.

Marcie shivered the moment she entered the prison gate and, even when she was inside the building and out of the bitter cold of the December day, she didn't feel any warmer.

The high ceilings, the plain painted walls and solid floors only added to the cold atmosphere. Nobody could ever be warm in here, Marcie decided.

First, along with all the other visitors, she had to go through security.

'Here again then, Mrs Jones.'

The prison officer smiled into her face whilst searching her bag. It struck her that he was taking his time searching and standing far too close. Her suspicion was confirmed when, leaning close to her, he lowered his voice and said, 'You look right lonely, darling. What a dirty rotten shame. If you ever need a bit of company, just tip me the wink. I'll give you my address. I'm sure I can think of some way of keeping you entertained.'

She felt herself blushing. It wasn't something she did much nowadays, but in the presence of this man she couldn't help it. His intentions were obvious and far from honourable.

She hurried on, aching to see Michael, even though it was in a room full of complete strangers.

He was sitting as usual at a table, his hands folded before him. When he looked up she stifled a gasp.

'Michael?'

He nodded at her in acknowledgement. She spotted a bruise beneath one eye and reached out to touch it.

He pulled back from her. They weren't supposed to touch. 'It's OK.'

She noticed the nervousness with which he surveyed the watching prison officers.

'What happened?'

'I fell.'

She knew enough of her father's time in prison to recognise the age-old excuse for having been at the receiving end of some brutality, usually on the part of the uniformed staff.

'What's going on?'

He shook his head. 'Never mind me. What's happening with the club? Have you found a buyer yet? Jacob seems reluctant to tell me what's going on though he did tell me that Paddy Rafferty was putting the screws on. He went round to see him and Fred. He didn't stay long, but he made his point. I've told Jacob that we can get more than he wants to pay. It's ripe for redevelopment. You'll be OK then.'

She looked down at her hands, the wedding ring and engagement ring shining bright on her ring finger.

'It was always your ambition to have a nightclub.'
She said it sadly.

'Marcie, have you noticed this one small matter
that I'm not there to run it at present?'

'There's no need to be sarcastic.'

'Sod it! I'm stating a fact. The Blue Genie's going
to go right down the drain without me there to run
it.'

'I can run it,' she stated, looking him straight in
the face. 'I can do it. Honest I can.'

His face, white and pasty already, turned a whiter
shade of pale. 'You're a woman!'

'You've noticed.' She felt the anger welling up
inside her.

'Women don't get involved in that kind of thing
– not women like you.'

She tossed her head. 'So all women are fit for is
to take their clothes off in those places.'

He shook his head angrily. 'You can't do it. I won't
let you do it.'

'I can do it – I *am* doing it! And what sort of
woman am I supposed to be? I'm stronger than you
think, Michael. And I can't be the only woman out
there in a man's world. Besides, Kevin and the boys
are keeping an eye on me. They won't let me come
to any harm. You asked them to look after me and
they are.'

He blinked. 'That's good of them.'

He sounded genuinely surprised which wasn't at all what she'd expected.

'I think so.'

Sighing, he shook his head. 'Marcie, you have to understand that nightclubs attract a criminal fraternity. Tough men, Marcie. I only know of one woman . . .' His voice trailed away as though he were confronting the truth of the matter and didn't want to go there.

Marcie wasn't interested in female gangsters. Despite hating their surroundings, she'd been looking forward to seeing him.

'We shouldn't be arguing,' she said quietly. 'We have so little time together.'

He nodded in agreement. 'How are the kids?'

She told him that Aran was walking and Joanna was a right little chatterbox, following her around and asking questions all the time.

He didn't bother to ask whether Joanna enquired the whereabouts of her adoptive father. The answer would only cause pain.

'That bruise,' she said unable to take her eyes off it.

'Drop it.'

'Have you seen the doctor?'

'It's nothing. Don't fuss.'

Their conversation swung to the reason he was on remand. Michael told her the facts.

'Jacob reckons that everything hinges on the gun.

It isn't enough to prove it was planted. We need to find out who put it there. Someone has to know.'

Marcie nodded. 'You hear a lot in a nightclub.'

'Criminals admit nothing,' stated Michael.

Marcie raised her eyes to his. 'They do to their girlfriends. Some even admit things to their wives, but their girlfriends – the hostesses and strippers – for some crazy reason men think that the sex overshadows everything else. That somehow the secrets and boasts they divulge never leave the bedroom – or their lover's head.'

Michael looked taken aback.

Marcie's mind was buzzing with possibilities as she got up to leave, so much so that she didn't notice that she was being followed.

The same prison officer, who'd taken so much time searching her bag and making suggestions, collared her again.

She gritted her teeth. Bloody screws! Give a man a uniform and power over others, and they thought they could do as they liked. Well, she was going to give him a piece of her mind.

'Let go of my arm.'

He leered into her face with what passed for a smile. 'Shame about your old man's accident,' he said in a low voice. 'He deserves better service really. Mind you he could have better service. Could live the life of Riley, but of course, there's always a price to pay for special service.'

'I take it that bruise had nothing to do with an accident.'

He shook his head. 'These old places . . .' he said, waving at the cold Victorian walls with one meaty hand.

'You bastard.'

His leer was sickening and she wanted to spit in his face. But what he was saying sunk in and was far more sickening than that leer. He was telling her that Michael was being singled out for rough treatment by the screws. The price for Michael receiving better treatment depended on her.

The thought of 'being nice' to this man was totally repugnant and her first thought was to tell him to get lost. Michael's safety curbed her angry reaction. She had to be careful for his sake.

Before she had chance to respond, a more senior officer intervened. 'Morgan. I need to speak to you.'

'Let me know. Here's my telephone number,' Morgan said softly.

Marcie shuddered as she took the slip of paper he handed her. He'd come all prepared for her to agree to his demands.

At first she was tempted to screw it up and throw it away, but she stopped herself. This wasn't about her well-being; this was about Michael. Her blood ran cold.

She was still feeling icy cold when she regained the outside world. Responsibilities were tumbling onto her shoulders like raindrops, only heavier and far more deadly.

How would she get round this? Who could help her out of this one?

Chapter Twenty-eight

Allegra and Sally almost fought over the chance to look after Marcie's children whilst she went to the Blue Genie; their way of making up to themselves what they had lost. This evening, it was Allegra's turn.

Marcie outlined her plan to ask the girls at the club if any of their men friends had told them secrets or whispered in their sleep.

'It could be dangerous,' Allegra warned her, while cradling Aran in her arms. 'And the girls might be too frightened to talk. I know what Victor was like.'

Marcie conceded that she was right, but she was desperate. 'It's the only way I can think of getting to the truth. If only I can get to the bottom of how that gun got there.'

Marcie noted the thoughtful look in her friend's eyes and jumped to an instant conclusion as to what Allegra was thinking.

'I don't believe he was having an affair with that girl. Michael wouldn't do that.'

Allegra shook her head. 'I wasn't thinking that. I was thinking how lucky you are to have each other. The two of you were meant to be.'

Her smile was a little sad. She was sitting on the floor helping Joanna build a brick tower. Marcie knelt down so her face was level with that of her friend.

'I'm sorry about you splitting with Victor. But it isn't the end of the world, Allegra. You have to believe that. There's someone out there waiting for someone like you. You just wait and see. Who knows, this time next year you might have had a whirlwind romance and be getting engaged or even married.'

Allegra half turned her head away as though she didn't want Marcie to see the look in her eyes. 'I don't think that's what God has planned for me. I think he has other plans. I think he'd always had other plans for me. It's just that I haven't been listening to him.'

Even though her grandmother was Roman Catholic, Marcie couldn't get used to talking about religion as though it were a radio programme and God as though he were a next-door neighbour. Allegra had changed a lot. She knew her friend attended mass more frequently than she used to. But it wasn't just that. To Marcie's knowledge Allegra no longer went up West, clubbing, dancing and dining. She was always available for babysitting and when she wasn't doing that she stayed in reading, listening to the radio or watching television.

'I may do something none of you expect me to

do,' said Allegra. 'I hope you don't think me mad when I do it.'

'It's your life, love,' said Marcie, patting her friend's shoulder. 'Don't listen to me or anybody else. You follow your conscience.'

She straightened, feeling quite proud of herself. She'd given Allegra the best advice she could under the circumstances. Her own life was a mess at present. There were big hurdles to overcome and she was about to start jumping over them.

She'd opted to wear a trouser suit to the club. It was pin-striped and had a deep reefer collar and a hip-skimming jacket. The trousers were slightly flared – the very latest fashion from America. All the hippies were wearing them. She'd seen them on television and for one wistful moment had wished she didn't have the responsibilities that she did. She wished she was young and carefree and into flower power – whatever that was.

She'd bought a white blouse trimmed with broderie anglaise around the collar and cuffs and she wore her hair pinned into a French pleat. Her reflection confirmed that her intentions were fulfilled; she looked older and more businesslike. Michael's black briefcase completed the picture, though she still took her black velvet handbag, tucking it inside the more voluminous leather case.

She was tempted to take Michael's car but couldn't

bring herself to do it. The interior would smell of his presence and she'd break down. She took her own.

The queue outside the Blue Genie was more than satisfactory. The nightclub was doing well and attracting a broad church of people. Beautifully dressed people were queuing alongside the more flashily dressed to get in. Businessmen, bankers and barristers were jostling shoulders with county types up from the country and criminal types from the wrong side of the river.

Even without its freehold value, the Blue Genie was a very worthwhile proposition.

Marcie slid into the front of the queue.

'Excuse me,' someone said in a rather superior tone, 'but I think we were here first.'

'That's the boss,' explained the doorman, barring the man's way with an arm the size of a battering ram.

'Oh!' said the man who had spoken, his tone one of surprise that a good-looking blonde could possibly have any idea of how to run anything.

The subdued lighting of the nightclub was provided by the neon blue female genies coming out of typically Aladdin-style lamps. Crisp white tablecloths covered the tables. In the centre of each table was a small lamp with a blue shade. Like the blue genies on the wall, the lampshades were mounted on Aladdin-style lamps.

The club was breathtakingly atmospheric. Marcie couldn't help the lump that rose to her throat as her eyes roamed the special place he'd so lovingly created. Michael had been so proud of his achievement.

They would not lose this. Come hell or high water they would not let it go.

People wanting to buy drinks were pressed up against the bar. In amongst the crush she could just about see the tops of two heads that she knew very well. Sally was here. So was Carla, the latter making her way to the Ladies.

After putting her briefcase in the office and locking the door, she was aware of admiring glances following her as she made her way back into the bar. Her skirt was short and red, her top was black and her shoes fashionably flat with stacked soles.

Sally was perched on a particularly high bar stool.

'Well, you're looking the bee's knees! Quite sophisticated in fact.'

'I'm feeling businesslike.'

'How's Michael?'

She told her about his injuries and the attitude and demands of one particular screw in particular.

'Bastard!'

Marcie nodded. 'Of the highest order of bastards.'

'Are you really running this place yourself?'

She ordered a gin and orange from the bar before

answering. 'I'm determined, Sally, so don't try to talk me out of it.'

It was at that moment that Carla emerged from the ladies' cloakroom. She looked from Sally to Marcie. 'What's going on here?'

After taking a sip of her drink, Marcie said, 'I'm here for a reason, Carla. Well, two reasons really. Number one I refuse to let this club be sold. Michael was so proud of it. Number two is that this is where all our problems began. This is where the weapon that killed Linda Bell was found. Apparently the whole case against Michael depends on that gun and how it got into his desk drawer and I don't think he put it there. I thought that one of the girls might have heard something – you know how some men talk.'

'So this gun wasn't his?' said Carla, as though a man and his gun should never be parted.

Marcie took umbrage. 'He's never had a gun,' she snapped. 'He does bookkeeping, not guns!'

'Keep your shirt on,' muttered Carla, whilst shrugging in her low-cut gown and in serious danger of her boobs popping out.

'It might just work. So what did Michael have to say?' asked Sally, intent on cooling things down.

Marcie averted her blazing eyes from Carla's face, though she was far from being placated. Sally mentioning Michael had brought other problems to bear.

'As I've just been telling Sally, he's been getting some bad treatment.' She explained about his eye and the sullen look.

'Other prisoners can be bastards,' snarled Carla. 'But it can be sorted,' she added with a wink.

'Not necessarily other prisoners,' said Marcie after taking another large sip of her drink. She went on to explain about the prison officer and the deal he had offered her.

'If I'm nice to him he'll make sure that everyone is nice to Michael.'

'Something needs to be done about the bastard!' Sally exclaimed.

'What's his name?' asked Carla. Her eyes were narrowed as though she were thinking hard.

'David Morgan. He's slimy. It makes me shiver just to think of him.' Marcie shrugged. 'There's nothing to be done about it. I could report it, but if I do that they'll treat him even worse. I'm stuck!'

Carla's arched eyebrows beetled into a deep frown and she looked as though she were grinding her teeth. 'So where does he want you to be nice to him? Surely not at the prison?'

'At his home. He's given me his telephone number. I'm to phone him to arrange it.'

'Bastard!' Sally exclaimed again. Marcie had told her the details before Carla had joined them and she was still voicing her disgust. Sally was like that. Like a dog with a bone she wouldn't let it drop. When Sally disapproved of people – men, that is – it was the one word she used over and over again, like a record player needle stuck in the groove.

Carla wasn't saying anything. She was strangely quiet.

Carla gave Marcie the creeps when she did that. It was almost as if there were a different and more lethal Carla beneath the blousy dresses and the fox fur coats.

Marcie acted to divert the conversation. 'Let's not talk about that. I need everyone to keep their eyes and ears open. Kevin's asked the barmen and girls to keep their eyes and ears open.'

'Ladies and gentlemen!'

The master of ceremonies making the announcement was a chap called Bert Laidlaw. He had a mane of white hair, a chiselled pink face and was elegantly turned out in bow tie and tuxedo.

The light coming from the blue genie lights and the ones on the table dimmed a little as the stage brightened.

'And may I now present, the one and only Cathy Cooper!'

The audience clapped enthusiastically. Cathy Cooper was a popular singer who'd just had a big hit with an old Anne Shelton number.

Once she was leaning against the grand piano, the

familiar strains of 'I'll Be Seeing You' tinkled from the piano keys.

Marcie turned round to listen and to look, and not just because she admired Cathy Cooper. For a fleeting moment she could forget her troubles and relish the fact that the dress Cathy was wearing had been designed and made up in her own sewing room. It was tight fitting and black. Droplets of glittering jet dangled from all over it, the teardrop ends catching the light from the stage backlights.

Sally leaned across and told her how lovely it looked. 'A bit more work in it than the usual stuff,' Sally added.

She was right of course. The exotic numbers she made were tiny compared to a full-size gown. Although Cathy's dress was off the shoulder and plunged deeply to reveal an admirable décolletage, it was still a major project compared to the bras and wispy G-strings she made for the exotic dancers and chorus girls.

'She's considering asking me to design and make two or three more, though it all depends on a tour that's being planned and an appearance at the London Palladium. She's also hoping to get a television appearance.'

'Good for her,' Sally whispered.

Their faces lit by the light from the stage, they stopped talking for the duration of the performance.

Once it was all over and the clapping had died down, the lights came up again.

'Fancy another drink?' asked Sally.

'On the house. How about . . .?'

Marcie looked to where Carla had been sitting. The bar stool was empty. Carla was nowhere to be seen.

'Gone to the lav maybe,' said Sally.

'I didn't see her go.'

For the rest of the night she looked for Carla but didn't see her. It wasn't usual for Carla to leave without saying goodbye, but there was always a first time.

She mentioned it to Sally when they caught up with each other after both had circulated, asking questions and generally being sociable – though listening and watching all the time.

Sally laughed. 'It must have been something we said.'

'Of course it wasn't.'

It wasn't until later on that she realised Sally had hit the nail on the head. It was something *she'd* said, and Carla had gone off to act upon it.

Chapter Twenty-nine

Sam Kendal believed in striking while the iron was hot and if Paddy Rafferty didn't toe the line he was likely to get burned – badly! Paddy was in need of a warning and Sam Kendal was the person to do it.

She'd given the order for Paddy to be apprehended and brought to her and here he was.

'Enough!' Sam's voice.

Said goon took a breather and so did Paddy, though every breath was like swallowing razor blades, his back was that sore.

'What's this all about, Sam?' His voice creaked and blood trickled from the corner of his mouth.

Paddy Rafferty couldn't believe what was happening to him. His gloved hands were encapsulated in a vice and a goon with fists like steam shovels was pummelling his kidneys as though trying to beat them out of his belly.

'Look, Sam. Ask your old man. I made a promise years ago that I wouldn't tread on his toes. And I've never done that, Sam. Honest I have not.'

The Irishman rushed his words and was panting with exertion. Sweat was dripping off his forehead and onto the workbench on which the vice was situated. Why was she doing this? He just didn't get it.

Relaxing his arms a bit so they didn't ache so much, he moved his head so that his sweat dripped onto the floor, making penny-sized roundels on the dusty boards.

A pair of feet clad in black patent court shoes came into view. The stockings were a smoky-grey colour. He smelled her scent, all flowery and feminine just as female perfume should be.

The woman known as Sam Kendal ruled her husband's empire with an iron fist. By turning his head, he managed to look up at her with one fearful eye. She was standing with her arms folded. Her jaw was rock-solid firm and there was no smile on her face.

'You taking the piss, Paddy?'

'No!' he exclaimed, shaking his head vigorously. 'I wouldn't do that, Sam. Honest I wouldn't.'

She lowered her face so it was level with his. 'I'm angry with you, Paddy, but because you've been loyal in the past I'm going to let you off with a warning.'

'I've always been loyal, Sam. Always!'

'Until you decided to branch out on your own, Paddy.' She shook her head. Fine wrinkles creased the corners of her heavenly blue eyes, eyes that could be as bright as cornflowers or as cold as steel. 'Let's get this straight, Paddy. You're the bloke who brings the labour over from Ireland. OK, you can dabble in a bit of property yourself when the occasion arises and when I give permission, but nobody gave you leave to muscle in on the Blue Genie. That's our territory, Paddy. I was not consulted!'

The word 'I' was shouted into his ear thus leaving him in no doubt that she meant what she said.

'I'm sorry.'

'You will be!'

Paddy gritted his teeth. He thought he'd been so careful cultivating the friendship of certain city politicians. It was so easy really. Give them a good night out when the champagne flowed and the girls were willing and they were putty in his hands – or rather putty in the hands of Sam Kendal and the company she ran for her husband. Sam Kendal was right about that. He'd acted underhand, chancing his luck by himself instead of referring the takeover to the Kendals.

On paper the company was totally legitimate, but the Kendals were ruthless. The respectable veneer hid a multitude of more sinful sidelines. And Sam Kendal ran it all.

'What about the Blue Genie, Paddy?'

He fancied her tone of voice had changed and not for the better. There was a more incisive, icier tone to the rounded vowels. She always sounded a bit upper class, did Sam Kendal. Rumour had it she'd gone to public school – a bit like the one Princess Anne went to.

His sweat had begun to cool, but now it ran anew. 'I wasn't just doing it for myself,' he blurted.

'Liar!'

The fists pummelled into his back again. He groaned and spat blood on the floor.

Sam began pacing up and down and it unnerved him. 'You made one big mistake, Paddy. The Blue Genie is already ours.'

She proclaimed the fact in a husky voice close to his ear. To all intents and purposes such a voice would turn most men on. Sam Kendal was seductive in looks and speech. In action she was ruthless and he didn't want any more of Sam Kendal's action. He'd made a mistake, a mistake that could lead to his death if he didn't cover his tracks.

'I didn't know. Honest I didn't.'

He racked his brains as to why he hadn't been aware that the Kendals had an interest in the Blue Genie. He thought he'd done his research well. The joint was owned by Michael Jones. What connection did Sam Kendal have with him? He couldn't for the life of him work that one out.

The problem was that he'd set Michael up with that Linda Bell bird. It was the sort of thing the Kendals would do themselves, so no big deal. But, to have set up someone outside the Kendal circle was one thing; to set up one of their own was something else. He couldn't admit to what he'd done. He daren't admit what he'd done or heads – his head in particular – would roll.

The thing was he still couldn't work out the connection between Michael Jones and Sam Kendal. Were they lovers? It wouldn't surprise him, though Michael did have a lovely little wife.

'No more visits to the Blue Genie,' Sam Kendal was saying. 'If I hear you've been pushing your weight around down there I'll cut your balls off and stuff them in your gloves for you to fondle at your leisure. Have you got that?'

He nodded so vigorously that his head seemed in danger of falling off.

'Get out of here.' The husky voice had changed to a growl.

Paddy was all apologies and humility. If he were to stay alive he had to be. It seemed that Sam Kendal was unaware of him setting up Michael Jones for murder. Normally he might have boasted of what he'd done and the Kendals would have gained from it. But somehow he felt that she wouldn't be pleased and he didn't know why. It could be that when she did find out he would be mincemeat. It struck him that he had two options: either head for a faraway place where they couldn't reach him – Buenos Aires might be a good bet – or put somebody else in the frame. It would have to be Baxter.

For her part, Sam Kendal had another important matter to deal with. Carla had phoned outlining a problem Marcie was having to face and it was something she could do something about.

She called in the big bruiser who had stuffed Rafferty's head in the vice.

'How do you feel about uniforms, Neil?'

Neil had a slow, sexy smile that she liked a lot. 'Depends who's wearing it – if you get my drift.'

'Cheeky sod.'

She knew he fancied her and wasn't averse to coupling up with him once Leo was dead and buried. But not yet. She'd never been unfaithful to Leo and she wasn't about to start now.

'Not me or you,' she returned with a grin. 'A prison officer. A screw.'

Chapter Thirty

David Morgan knew that Marcie Jones would have to phone. He'd sensed her reluctance of course, but he'd laid it on the line: play ball with me and I'll ensure your old man's left alone.

With his eyes on the clock and a whisky or two inside him, he sat ruminating on the pleasure he'd got from her phone call.

'So when are you coming round?' he'd asked her, a smirk running from ear to ear.

'Tonight?'

He could barely hear her. 'Speak up.'

'Tonight,' she said again.

He glanced at his watch. It was reading seven o'clock. 'Tonight. Eight o'clock. On the dot.' He could barely control his smug satisfaction as he stipulated the time. He gave her the address.

He'd been inclined to say that she didn't have much to say for herself, but he guessed she was nervous. That's why she'd sounded so abrupt, more clipped in speech than when she visited the prison.

Smiling, he poured himself a drink, sat down and waited.

Car headlamps swept over the ceiling. The curtains were drawn and he resisted the urge to look out. He wanted to savour this moment, to open the door and feel her fear. She had no choice but to submit to him; not if she knew what was good for her and her old man.

The doorbell rang. Smiling again, he took his time tipping the last of the whisky down his throat and then padded over the dark-turquoise shag pile carpet into the hallway in his slippers. His long departed wife had always stipulated that he wore slippers. Although she was dead and buried he just couldn't get out of the habit.

The top half of the front door constituted a glass panel. Normally he could see the shadow of the person waiting there. At this moment in time he could not. He guessed she had stood down from the doorstep. Perhaps she was even stepping away from the door, halfway to changing her mind. Well, he'd certainly take care of that!

Smoothing back his thin fair hair, he reached for the catch and turned it. The door flew back, surprising him and hitting him off balance. Two bruisers who must have been three times the size of Marcie Jones crashed into him like two-ton bulldozers, pushing him back along the hallway and into the curtained room. A third bloke closed the door in an obscenely gentle fashion, as though they were there to have a church meeting. David Morgan's instinct told him that religion had sod all to do with what they were there for.

He was proved right.

By the time they'd finished with him his guts were aching and already he was pissing blood. He could smell himself, the fear sweating out of him.

The biggest of the three had huge hands. One of those hands was gripping him by the throat. A breathy voice said, 'Don't worry, old son. There won't be any bruises. Now then, a little word from our boss. Hands off Michael Jones and his missus. While our mate Michael is in your care we want him to have the best of service. You got that?'

David Morgan nodded; an action that immediately brought on a severe bout of coughing.

'Right, old son. You've got the point. Now. As for Michael's missus, it's obvious that your hormones are more than you can handle.'

He nodded to one of the others, a big black guy; a gold earring glinted in his left ear. Wasn't that the sign of a poof?

The black guy picked up the half-finished bottle of whisky. Glass shattered from its base as he hit it against the fireplace.

David Morgan's eyes opened wide in alarm as the jagged edges of what was left were brought to his face. He waited for the impact, the tearing of his cheeks, the gouging of an eye. As he did so he was aware of his flies being undone.

He cried out, 'No!'

His eyes fastened on the jagged glass and his now flaccid penis.

His cry became a whimper. He felt the glass cut his groin then lightly skim the stem of his John Thomas.

'Christ, no,' he whimpered.

The blood was matting his pubic hair. He fainted when he thought they were going to cut off his tool. When he came around again he still had it. Only his groin bore the marks of their visit, plus the aching in his guts and his ribs.

Trauma got the better of him. He retched up everything he'd ate that day, pissed some more and smelled the unmistakable stench of his own faeces as his bowels let go.

Chapter Thirty-one

Being December, the Isle of Sheppey was shrouded in a chill mist that cloaked buildings and people like a thick gauze veil.

It was far from cheerful and not a healthy climate, but that didn't bother Tony Brooks. London wasn't too healthy either, though it had to be said, London was far more exciting.

Babs had thrown a few things at first but had come round when he'd handed over a bundle of money and promised to take her out that night. Money and drink were definitely the way to his wife's heart – that and a good session in bed.

For a while things were fine. He'd liked indulging the kids at first but living with Babs was not to his taste. Tony Brooks could stand his wife for just so long. He would have stayed longer on Sheppey if his sons had been around more. For the most part he got lumbered with the little girl who made him feel awkward. He still wasn't entirely sure that she was his.

The boys appeared surprisingly independent, a little secretive, a little more grown up than when he'd last seen them. He fancied they were involved in things they shouldn't be, but counselled that they were still children and couldn't possibly be turning criminal just yet, conveniently forgetting that he'd been a tearaway at their age.

Regardless of the threat from Paddy Rafferty, he was seriously considering going back to the Smoke when someone knocked at the front door. On answering it he found himself face to face with a uniformed copper and a plainclothes bloke with shoulder-length hair and a fuzz on his upper lip that was pretending to be a moustache. Both looked surprised to see him.

'Mr Brooks? Tony Brooks?'

'What's it to you?'

'In a way. Can we come in?'

'Why?'

He couldn't help being surly. Up until now the police had never paid him social visits; they always meant business. He held the door tight against his chest, the opening too narrow for a man to get through.

'It's about your boys.' The plainclothes copper glanced at his notebook. 'Arnold and Archie.'

'Christ! Are they hurt?'

He flung the door wide open and the two men stepped inside. He took them into the living room, shoved a pile of ironing aside and bid them sit down.

'We'll stand.'

The plainclothes copper introduced himself as Lenny Oswald and his colleague as Constable Plaistow.

Tony felt his stomach heave into his mouth. He could cope with just about anything except something tragic happening to his kids.

'What is it?' His heart hammered. He stared unblinking.

'This is something of a social call.'

Tony stared. His fear plummeted. 'Well, that's a bit of a turn up,' he said scathingly.

'We picked up some boys breaking into a warehouse. They reckoned they were doing it on the orders of your son, a right little Fagin by the sound of it.'

Tony remembered enough of his schooldays – the few days he'd attended – to know that Fagin was the fence in a story called *Oliver Twist*. He even remembered who'd written it.

'Charles Dickens! That's the geezer who wrote that.' After he'd said it, he realised how much he sounded like someone in a TV quiz like *Take Your Pick*.

'Do you know where your son is?'

'Why?' His tone had turned surly. His stance was defiant.

'We've got no real evidence, but it wouldn't hurt

to have a word with him – with your permission of course.'

'Get stuffed!'

Detective Sergeant Lenny Oswald shrugged his shoulders. He had a leaning towards helping kids before they got into trouble too deeply. It was his belief that nipped in the bud early enough a youngster could be steered back onto the straight and narrow.

Implementing such a strategy hit the bumpers when confronted with an attitude such as that fostered by Tony Brooks. What chance did the boys have with a father like that? Lenny had heard rumours that the boys' father wasn't around much. Apparently he spent a lot of time up in London and was involved in God knows what.

He sighed. 'Well. At least you know your boys have acquired a name for themselves. I'll leave it up to you then.'

'Yeah. You do that.'

Shoulders back and fists clenched, Tony escorted the policemen to the door, holding his stomach in as though he was all tight muscle when in fact he was rapidly running to flab. One punch would have knocked the stuffing out of him.

Once they'd left, Tony grabbed his coat from the hook behind the door where everybody hung their coats. Luckily his was top of the pile. He vaguely wondered when Babs was going to have a clear out.

She just tossed stuff onto piles and never put things away properly.

It was beginning to rain, a fine spray windblown in from the sea. Turning up his coat collar he headed to where he'd had a 'robbers' lair' when he was a boy. It had been a good spot away from prying eyes and ideal for boys to hide in. It had always boasted a sign saying NO GIRLS. Later on, as the hormones had taken over, the sign had remained but the boys took their girlfriends there, safe in the knowledge that they wouldn't be disturbed.

He smiled when he came to the ramshackle construction half hidden behind old wartime concrete built to protect the island against an enemy who never got there. He suspected the corrugated-iron roof might be the very same that he and his pals had used years before.

'Oi!' he bellowed at the same time as hammering on the roof.

Mutterings and the sound of grunted orders came from inside before a freckled face appeared. 'Clear off!'

Tony grabbed the boy's hair before he had a chance to disappear. 'Arnold! Archie! Come out 'ere before I come in there and drag you out.'

Silence. Tony grinned. He could imagine the surprise on his boys' faces; the old man was waiting outside. They could be in for a clip around the ear if they didn't get their story straight.

The moment he saw their expressions, he knew he was right.

Shoving his hands in his pockets, he sauntered a little way from their hideout looking thoughtful and wearing a troubled frown.

'The coppers are looking for you two.'

'We ain't done nothing,' Archie blurted.

'Nothing much,' Arnold added more hesitantly.

Tony was tempted to smile, but he had a part to play. He was their dad after all and they were supposed to respect him – right?

'I don't want them coming round to see me again. Got it?'

The two boys nodded.

'You better had. What the other kids do is up to them. Here,' he said, after rummaging in his pocket. He gave them half a crown each. 'Don't spend it all at once.'

He went off whistling. By the time he was out of sight, Archie and Arnold were back inside their 'den', telling the others that their dad was a real hard case and had done time in prison.

'I wouldn't want to do time,' said the freckle-faced lad whose name was Sammy.

'That's 'cos you're a wimp,' said Archie, giving his shoulder a shove. 'Right. Now let's see what you got there.'

The boy handed over a bicycle lamp and a handful

of penny chews he'd snitched from another kid under threat of being pummelled into pulp.

Tony Brooks sauntered off along the seafront sniffing the air and looking at the view. He was feeling self-satisfied. His sons were sorted. No more police. It didn't really occur to him that he hadn't warned them to behave themselves, merely to avoid getting tangled up with the law.

The fact was that he was feeling restless. Sheerness just didn't have the buzz of London. It didn't have the women either. The fact of the matter was that he didn't fancy his wife any longer. Regardless of the threat from Rafferty, he had to get back there before he died of boredom. The only reason he would ever come back to Sheppey was to see his old mum.

His mood plummeted at the thought of her. He'd gone to the hospital with her. The doctor had taken him to one side and put it on the line.

'We can't do anything for her blindness, of course, and I have to warn you right now that we may have to take more than her toe off. It may be the whole of her foot. It all depends.'

People regarded Tony Brooks as a tough guy. When the doctor told him that he'd felt sick and totally helpless. He'd wanted to cry, him, the hard man of Sheerness and London.

'You can't!'

His voice had sounded faint and faraway. Obviously

the doctor didn't think so. He'd stepped back, looking quite alarmed. It came to him that he was shouting but hadn't realised.

The doctor regained his composure. 'It's a fine line between her living and dying. She's signed to give her consent for whatever has to be done.'

Tony couldn't get it out of his mind. Perhaps that was why he wasn't feeling so scared of Paddy and not purely because he was thinking of his mother. The truth was that he couldn't face seeing her suffering and the possibility that she might end up a cripple, walking with crutches or in a wheelchair.

When it came to sickness, Tony Brooks was an out and out coward and he knew it.

Chapter Thirty-two

The nightclub was buzzing, the neon Blue Genie lights bathing the customers in a chill blue glow.

Marcie looked for Sally who that week had been performing on stage with two pink feather fans and a trio of discreetly placed silver stars. Tonight was to have been her night off, her place taken by Slinky Salome and her twenty-foot python. All the same she had promised to call in, though when Marcie thought about it she realised Sally had only said 'might' which was really unusual. They always met up on her nights off. Sally gave sterling support to a woman who was missing her husband.

Still, Marcie told herself, there was no law that said Sally had to be there.

People had congratulated her on doing a good job of running the Blue Genie. Marcie had managed to charm most of the clientele and men's eyes lit up at the sight of her. Should any of them be accompanied by their wives or mistresses, she was charmingly polite. If they were alone the charm was laid on that much thicker.

The club had to be a success. She owed it to

Michael. But she was charming her way around gangsters, bankers and other rich and powerful men for a very good reason.

People were aware of the affairs of Paddy Rafferty. Rumour had it that although he was a past master at the exploitation of Irish labour on the building sites, he fancied his chances of taking a cut of the development action. He wanted to be bigger than he was.

The political animals who frequented the Blue Genie were the obvious starting point. What was Rafferty up to? How did he operate? Who did he employ to do his dirty work?

She wasn't rightly sure of finding out anything useful, but she had to try. Her husband and her family were depending on her and, even though it meant leaving the children with Allegra, she had to try. Allegra would look after them. She was one hundred per cent sure of that.

She was at the bar sipping at a cocktail. A local politician by the name of Randolph Cramer was playing her court. She allowed him to do so, safe in the knowledge that the bouncers were close at hand and the politician's mistress was sitting at a table, a fixed smile on her face and a furious look in her eyes.

There were reasons for Marcie allowing Randolph to think he was in with a chance. He was rumoured to be a close colleague of Paddy Rafferty and Marcie was sure that Paddy Rafferty had had something to do with Michael being arrested. It was also rumoured that Randolph had once been in a close relationship with Linda Bell.

His eyes roved over her body. Far from being handsome, Randolph had pale eyes, pale hair and a shiny pate. But of course he had wealth and power in spades, sure-fire compensation for his less than playboy looks.

Her instinctive reaction was to move away from him, but she forced herself to stay put and even to smile at him as though his attentions were appreciated.

She saw him glance over his shoulder. His girl-friend was no longer sitting at the table. It was a safe bet to assume that she'd gone off to powder her nose. She guessed what he'd say next.

His fingers stroked her arm. Mr Local Politician turned into Mr Seductive.

'How about you and me getting together sometime?'

Well, she could play the seductive game too, though there was more purpose to her being seductive.

Her smile was wide and her eyes flashed with hidden promise. 'You know I'm married?'

He nodded. 'Of course I do.'

She detected his attempt to adopt an upper-class accent, but his roots somewhere down Rotherhithe way shone through.

'What about Agnes?'

He shrugged and tipped his brandy glass, swallowing

the measure in one. 'She means nothing to me.' He signalled to the barman for another.

'And your wife?'

She'd done her homework well. Even though Randolph had never brought his wife to the club, she knew he had one. It had purely been a case of phoning his office and pretending to be his wife.

The telephonist had not hesitated. 'Christine? Darling. What do you want?'

She'd put the phone down without saying a word. Thank goodness there was no way for him to check who had called – except for asking his wife that is.

'My wife understands me,' he replied, his colder tone a direct result of his surprise that she knew he had a wife.

He slid his left hand into his pocket – as though not flashing his wedding ring would alter his station or improve his chances. The arrogance of the man!

'She would have to. I've seen you with other women besides Agnes.'

He drank more brandy. 'I like women. They never last, of course. One-night stands for the most part.'

Marcie smiled. Shaking her head, she wagged a finger at him. 'I think you're fibbing, Randolph. A little bird tells me that you have had more long-term relationships. Linda Bell for one.'

She caught him in the middle of another slug of brandy and thought he was going to choke.

'I had nothing to do with it, Marcie. I don't know anything about it.'

She caught the sudden change of mood, the nervous tic beneath his right eye, the sudden flaccidity of his jowls. She guessed he'd been holding his stomach muscles in. Like the rest of him they relaxed too and sent a button popping from his waistband.

Marcie fingered the rim of her glass. 'She was a good-time girl. Right?'

'You could say that. I wasn't the only one taking her out. Rafferty did for a start. In fact he even set her up in a flat for a while.'

Marcie nodded. What he was telling her was only what she'd expected. Rafferty had a lot to do with it, but without any evidence . . . She needed to know who had planted the gun.

It was a terrible rush, but the following day Marcie set off to see her grandmother. She would be coming out of hospital shortly and Babs had suggested she move in with her, which came as something of a surprise. The two women had tolerated each other for years and were better off apart.

Allegra had offered to go with Marcie and help with the children and her assistance was much appreciated. Joanna wanted to run around all over the place and Aran didn't care much for travelling. He was a baby who liked routine. He also loved Allegra and seemed resentful that his mother was in charge and carrying him in her arms.

Marcie drove them down in her beloved Mini, the children asleep in the back and Allegra sitting serenely at the front. The weather was turning cold. They passed one particular house that had put up their Christmas decorations weeks ahead of everyone else. Still, thought Marcie, everyone has to have something to look forward to. In her case it was a fragile hope that Michael would be released in time for Christmas, but it didn't look likely.

First stop was to drop the children and Allegra off at Endeavour Terrace. Garth was in the kitchen, pouring tea into three cups and a milkier version into a plastic tumbler for Joanna.

Marcie held her breath. Garth had even provided a saucepan of hot water in order to warm Aran's bottle.

'Did you hear us pull up?' she asked him.

'No. I just knew what time you'd get here,' he replied.

Of course he did. She should have known.

After sorting a few things out like the sleeping arrangements and whether there were clean sheets on the beds, Marcie left for the hospital.

At least the interior of the hospital didn't smell as bad as the prison had on the day before when she'd visited Michael. To her great relief he had looked a lot better than on her last visit and confided in her that he wasn't 'falling down stairs or walking into doors' any longer.

'You must have a guardian angel,' she'd said to him.

He'd smiled. 'I must do.'

'She's still asleep,' said the doctor.

Her grandmother's bed was at the very end of the ward. The curtains were pulled halfway and there was a metal cage beneath the bedding, keeping it away from her injury.

Marcie felt her eyes filling with tears. Rosa Brooks looked so tiny and frail in the hospital bed. The frame beneath the bedcovers looked like some kind of monster, eating her from the bottom up. She supposed in a way her grandmother was being eaten.

Swiping a tear from the corner of her eye, she asked the doctor when she was likely to be up on her feet again and had the toe been removed successfully.

'I'm afraid there were complications. We had to remove half her leg.'

To Marcie it was like being hit by a blast of cold air. She couldn't breathe. Surely she'd misheard.

'Are you all right?'

The doctor's voice pulled her back from the shock she was feeling. She nodded weakly.

'Will she live?'

'We're not sure. Her age goes against her, of course,

but she is strong-minded. We find having a strong will aids recovery no end.'

'How will she . . .?'

Marcie almost choked the words out. She wanted to say how will she get around, but somehow she already knew what he would say.

'We're pretty sure she'll need a wheelchair. Does your grandmother live in a bungalow?'

She shook her head. 'An old cottage.'

Visualising the rooms she'd known for most of her life, Marcie was painfully aware that a wheelchair and number ten Endeavour Terrace did not mix. The cottage had steps at the front door and stairs up to the first floor. Besides that, the hallway was narrow and the bathroom was out the back. Her mind was already darting around, trying to organise what had to be done. Her grandmother would have to move in with her and the children. There was no other alternative.

On her return to Endeavour Terrace, she discussed her plans with Allegra, who made her sit down, drink tea and eat a ham sandwich.

'You are getting so thin,' Allegra pointed out.

Marcie ran her hands through her hair. She was half inclined not to leave the Isle of Sheppey. Life had been so much simpler here, though poorer, of course: no nice clothes, house or nippy little car. She couldn't help snapping.

'And you're becoming so bloody sanctimonious!'

Allegra's classic countenance froze for barely a second, but enough to make Marcie feel guilty.

'I'm sorry,' said Marcie.

'No need to be,' said Allegra in that calm, collected way of hers. 'I suppose I must seem a bit that way of late. I know very well that I'm not at all the person I once was when I was with Victor. I've come to the conclusion that my life had lost its way when I was with him.'

Marcie didn't know why, but she felt slightly embarrassed. It was as though she'd probed too deeply into Allegra's personal life – though really what had she said? Only that she thought she had become sanctimonious and even then it was purely an outburst because she was worried about her grandmother.

Allegra's big brown eyes shone as she looked directly into Marcie's face. 'I don't believe that I will be around for you much longer, Marcie.'

Marcie was instantly filled with alarm, suddenly realising just how much she depended on Allegra. 'Where are you going? Back with your parents? Abroad maybe?'

Allegra shook her head. 'Not back with my parents, though I may very well end up being sent abroad.'

Sent? What was she talking about? Marcie stared, waiting to hear more.

'I've decided to join a religious order.'

Marcie still said nothing. The ball was very much in Allegra's court.

'I've decided to become a nun.'

Marcie sat there, not sure whether to congratulate or commiserate. She didn't say anything until she got her thoughts into order.

'Are you absolutely sure about this?'

Even after she'd said it, Marcie knew what the answer would be. Wrapped up in her own world with her own problems, she'd noticed the change in Allegra but hadn't enquired why it was so. She immediately felt quite selfish and also very, very surprised.

Lowering her eyes, Allegra nodded slowly. 'I've thought about it long and carefully. I don't pretend that the church is perfect – or rather the people serving it are not perfect; they're only human after all.' Her eyes flashed as she raised her eyelids. 'I've wrestled with my conscience and my sins and have decided that it's the perfect life for me. I was born into a wealthy family and Victor was wealthy too. Perhaps I had an overdose of wealth and luxurious living and now I yearn for something simpler.'

'But Victor was not the father of your child. You said it was a priest.'

Allegra nodded. 'I know you're finding it hard to understand, but the church is not to blame for the sins of one man. I know it's where I want to be.'

Marcie sat stunned though strangely enough she understood. 'I'll miss you. So will Joanna.'

Allegra smiled. The little girl, unwilling to be ignored, had climbed onto her mother's lap and was eating one of her sandwiches.

'I'll miss all of you – even Sally. By the way, how is she?'

The conversation had turned a corner. Marcie guessed Allegra was unwilling to discuss her decision further. When and where she decided to carry out her plan would be kept under wraps until she was ready. Marcie's mind turned to Sally.

Sally's child had been the result of a relationship with a married man. She'd had no choice but to give him up and was sure he was happy. To some extent Sally had got over the experience. Allegra, she decided, never had.

'I haven't seen her for a couple of days. She was performing over the weekend, but I haven't seen her since.'

'That's unusual, isn't it?'

'It is. It may be that she's got a new man in her life and is keeping him under wraps.'

A sudden thought struck her. What if Sally had a new lover, one she might commit herself to long term? Could it be possible that she was about to lose both of her best friends, one to the church to be celibate and one to the altar to become a wife? Sally had often said she'd like to be married.

Suddenly Marcie felt very alone and very worried about all those she loved.

Back in London, Leo Kendal had breathed his last. Sam dressed in black for the funeral. People from all walks of life came to pay their last respects. It was only to be expected. Leo and his business had touched many lives. Some were in his pay, some merely worked for him and some were close.

Sam was the closest.

The wake was held at the Café Royale.

'Leo would have loved this,' Sam said wistfully. She raised a glass of champagne to his memory. 'To Leo. May you rest in peace.'

After the toast, she found Carla and took her to one side. 'Tell my daughter I want to see her.'

Carla nodded. 'Whatever you say, boss.'

Chapter Thirty-three

Rosa Brooks was only vaguely aware that her grand-daughter had visited. It was as though she were floating above everything, as though she were seeing her life through a book and the characters in it.

Old memories had become as fresh as if they had happened yesterday, but in a strange way not just from her point of view, but from those who partici-pated in her life. She was dreaming, but not in the same way that she had ever dreamed before.

In her dreams, the sun was setting and she was sure he would be there. In her dreams, she was watching him, imagining how it had been for him nervously waiting for a wife who had sworn not to return to England.

She saw him as if in an old Noël Coward film or something by Hemingway. He was wearing a cream suit and matching hat, sitting on the wall outside the main gate to the city of Mdina, that the Maltese sometimes called Rabat.

Fortified to repel invaders, the great stones that formed the city walls changed colour as the day wore on. In the early morning and viewed from a distance, they were soft lavender, by midday pale gold, like undercooked biscuits, but now, bathed by a blood-red sun, they blushed like ripe peaches and were warm to the touch.

He had taken up position around three o'clock, a fact noted by a number of people about their normal business. A farmer passed pushing a handcart stacked with wooden cages containing rabbits, hens and pigeons, a squalling kid trailing behind, old enough to leave its mother and to provide meat rather than milk. A sharp knife hung from his belt.

The same man eyed him curiously on his way back, his load lighter now, the kid no longer trailing behind but sold, killed and skinned ready for the table. Despite the knife at his belt having been wiped on his trousers, a sticky film dimmed the blade.

Cyril narrowed his eyes, unheeding of passers-by or the ginger cat that had chosen to sit a few inches from his heel, perhaps unaware that this was a living man, so still was he, so intent on watching the gate.

If anyone had asked him how he was feeling, he would have found it hard to put so much apprehension, hope and emotion into words. It was rather like overeating, too much to digest. That was why he had arrived early. He couldn't bear to confront the prospect of no more waiting, no more sunsets. If she did not appear today then he would never return but respect her wishes.

A passer-by, more brazen than his fellow countrymen, eyed him carefully, noting the way he passed his cigarette between his fingers and back again, the oldness of lines marring a young man's face. Drawing the conclusion that he knew his type if not the man, he made his approach.

'Excuse me.'

Although he did not exactly welcome the intrusion, Cyril made the effort to look at him.

'Were you here during the war?'

Cyril nodded. 'Yes.'

The man jerked his chin in acknowledgement. 'Men flew through the air in France. Did you do that?'

'How did you guess?'

A warm smile crossed Rosa's face as the dream developed further. Cyril had always been prone to elaborate on the truth.

The man grinned. 'I looked at you and I knew.'

He was still grinning as he sauntered off, hands in his pockets, his eyes seeming to search the ground for old memories, old comrades.

Cyril knew what he meant about knowing with one look that he'd been in combat. They all looked the same: older beyond their years, a haunted look in their eyes as though they had lost their innocence along with their friends. It hadn't been any different for him and his comrades in the Royal Navy. Whatever the future brought, their lives would never be the same.

But they had to hope, and his greatest hope had kept him going. If she didn't come today the last chapter would have been written and read, and all his hopes would be dashed.

The sun was now a blood-red ball sinking into a coppery west and turning the flat-roofed houses into silky squares of mauve, blue and purple.

The burning intensity of colour made his eyes water. When he returned his anxious gaze to the city gate a great fear came upon him. He was truly afraid that in one moment of gazing he might have missed her.

Blots of blackness blurred his vision. The city on the other side of the archway appeared darker, more purple than usual; the light was fading fast. Panic stricken, he turned to look at the dying sun, not wanting to believe that with these last rays his waiting would be over. She would not come.

'No!' No one in all history could have expelled that tiny word with such despair as he did now. Sweeping his hat from his head, he stood staring, willing it not to set, not to dash his hopes.

The last slim crescent hung on.

Someone touched his arm. 'Cyril?'

He looked down into her face. In dreams of this moment he'd shot her all the most romantic lines he could think of. Now it had finally happened, he stared at her dumbly, too overcome with emotion to speak, to think, to do anything.

She was wearing a simple dress and carrying a brown suitcase. Her face was as fresh and warm as he remembered it. Her hair was short but glossy. He wanted to run his hand through it; he wanted to touch her cheek, even to kiss her, but he couldn't.

'Are you real?'

She nodded. 'Yes. Very.' She stood on tiptoe to kiss him.

He didn't ask why she'd changed her mind about going to England with him.

'This place hasn't changed too much,' he said as three sailors, obviously on leave, laughed at the antics of a colleague who was walking along the wall, balancing precariously, no doubt as a result of drink. 'It's still a boys' place.'

'No it isn't.'

'It isn't?'

She shook her head. 'It's a brave place. One day you'll see that.'

Her eyes shone. She wanted to laugh, she wanted to cry, but most of all she wanted to get to know him again but wasn't quite sure where to start.

'You were watching me.' It was Cyril's voice, though not back then in those years between the wars. It was now and he was waiting for her on the other side. 'Are you coming now?'

'Oh, yes.' Then she frowned. 'Except that I must

see Marcie one last time. I must tell her that she has inherited the gift.'

'I don't think you need to tell her,' he said. 'I think she already knows.'

Experiences had hardened Marcie Brooks into the Marcie Jones she was now and it hadn't been long coming about. The teenager who had fallen in love with a boy on a motorbike had been superseded in double-quick time by a determined young woman who had no intention of letting anybody – anybody at all – injure her family in any way.

It had happened at last. She was reunited with her mother but was unsure how to handle things.

They hadn't kissed. They hadn't embraced. It was as though neither of them could take the first step.

Marcie was sitting down, handbag on lap, fingers tapping it nervously.

Her mother broke the ice. 'Under the circumstances, I think it would be a very good idea if I became your partner in the nightclub. You can't possibly run it without Michael around.'

Marcie's eyes were drawn to the woman looking out of the window with her back to her. She looked and smelled expensive, but it cut no ice with Marcie.

'I don't want a business partner. I can manage by myself. I've done it before.' She said it proudly.

'I loaned the money to purchase the premises to

set up the sewing room,' said the woman, her voice seductively rich.

'I paid it back,' Marcie responded hotly. 'I can do the same again. I do not need a partner.'

'I know you did. That's why I'm offering to back you again.'

Marcie blinked. She'd always assumed that the money Allegra had leant her was her money to lend. Now her mother was implying otherwise. 'What do you mean?' she asked, surprised at the hoarseness of her own voice.

'I'm offering to back you again. Let's just say that I recognise when someone is in trouble. I've been there myself. Somebody was there for me. I'd like to be there for you.'

Marcie stared at the woman in the red silk dress who smelled of Chanel and was more elegant and classier even than Gabriella Camilleri, Victor Camilleri's wife.

This woman was her mother and it appeared she was also her guardian angel.

They hadn't hugged. She realised that wouldn't happen. Too many years had passed; too many differences had arisen between them.

'Carla said you were a judge's wife.'

'I had to protect my identity. I didn't want my husband hurt. He was very ill. I promised myself that nothing would touch him to hurt him, that I would hover in the background for you.' She sighed. 'It hurt that I could not acknowledge you, but I contented myself with providing you with protection and money.'

'So you set me up in my own sewing room. You didn't protect me from Roberto Camilleri though, did you?' She stated it sarcastically. It hurt that her mother had not acknowledged her and been there to comfort her.

Then Marcie stared at her mother as the realisation sunk in. 'You were there on the beach?'

She nodded. 'Alan wasn't quite dead – doubtless he would have lived but I made sure he didn't. I was there for you. I still am now. We have to get Michael out of prison. I'm making enquiries right now. I'm sure we'll find out exactly what happened.'

Charlie Baxter was found burned to a crisp in his car. A suicide note was found at his flat supposedly owning up to the killing of Linda Bell.

The possibility that he had murdered Linda Bell was believed; the probability of him committing suicide was not.

Chapter Thirty-four

Carefully, so as not to snag it with her long, lacquered fingernails, Sally slid her stocking over her painted toes. With slow deliberation, knowing he could see her reflection in the window, she pulled it up over her calf, her knee and then her lower thigh.

Every move she made was designed to tease. Even when she had finally fastened her suspender, she took time to straighten her seam, running her hands over stocking top and bare thigh and noting that nylon and skin were equally silky. She did the same with the second stocking. Her hair fell like a silky curtain hiding half of her face. She watched him without him noticing. Even if he did, he would probably think she was seeking warm appraisal, affection, or merely a faint echo of his earlier passion.

Lenny O'Neill was Paddy Rafferty's right-hand man. He was good-looking in a rough diamond kind of way and it hadn't been too sore a mission to lead him on, to get her hooks in him.

She was acting on Sam's orders. Despite her elegant appearance, Sam was as hard as nails, though with one exception. She was playing guardian angel to the daughter she'd abandoned as a child years before. Sally sensed it was a matter of pride as much as affection. Nobody was going to make her kid's life a misery if she could help it.

'We need to find out who planted that gun in Michael's desk,' Sam had said to her. 'Baxter is dead and Rafferty is playing dumb. Not surprising really considering that he'll do the time if Michael is cleared. We need to get close to someone likely to talk. I've heard that Lenny O'Neill is the weak link in the Rafferty outfit. His brain's located firmly behind his flies. I want you to make whoopee with him. Get close. Get personal and for Christ's sake, find something out.'

Sally hadn't been too keen on the idea. OK she used to turn a trick or two when she was short of dancing work and had no bloke in her life. But she didn't need to do that now. However, it was no good reminding Sam of that fact. She owed a lot to Sam. All the girls did.

'I'll do what I can.'

When Sam's jaw tightened and her eyes blazed, Sally was instantly reminded of her Marcie, the friend who didn't know that Sally had sometimes been paid money for her sexual favours.

Lenny O'Neill looked away from her reflection and took a cigarette from a packet lying on the window ledge. A flame shot from the ivory-cased lighter that he cupped in his hands.

He offered her the open packet. She took one, bending her head as he offered the flame from the lighter.

The fastenings on her dress weren't particularly difficult to do up, but she turned her bare back to him anyway. 'Can you do me up? There's a love.'

She tensed, waiting for his fingers to brush against her flesh as he buttoned her dress. It didn't happen. She was grateful for that. Earlier he had almost ripped her dress off in his impatience to get at her. Relieved, she clenched her jaw.

She turned so she was facing him and they were both blowing smoke into each other's faces.

'Nice lighter,' she said.

He glanced at it. 'Got it cheap, though when I say it was cheap it still cost a few quid, just not shop price – if you know what I mean.'

She knew exactly what he meant. The lighter was stolen. Burglary most likely.

She managed to stretch her lips into a smile. 'When are you free again, darling?'

Sally strolled to the mirror, slid her lipstick from her bag and reapplied it to her naked lips. Without him noticing, she eyed him via the mirror. She felt overcome with contempt when he looked at his watch and frowned.

'Damn! I'm late already. Cissy will be waiting for me.'

'Your wife. I didn't know you had one.'

'My sister. I live with my sister. She's the light of my life and thinks the sun shines out of my backside. Family matters a lot to us Irish.'

Sally hid her contempt beneath an impassive mask, slid her lipstick back into her handbag and scraped a smudge from the corner of her mouth. Inside she simmered.

He put his arms around her, his hands squeezing her breasts. She pretended it didn't hurt, but it did. This was only her second date with Lenny but already she'd sized him up; the longer their relationship lasted the more brutal he'd become. With a bit of luck she'd find out what she wanted before things got too bad – but there were no guarantees and she'd promised Sam and Sam was her lifeline.

After giving up her baby for adoption, Sally Saunders had fallen apart. She'd got into drink and drugs, her habits paid for by prostitution. Hired as an escort to the Swiss banker who had become her lover, she'd met Sam Kendal. At first she'd understood her to be the wife of a high court judge. Later she found out from her cop boyfriend that Sam was the wife of the most powerful crime godfather in London. It was Pete, the policeman, who had taken her to the party.

She'd seen Sam angry – really angry – and it was usually over kids. Sally had got drunk at the party. Sam had found her blubbing in the bathroom. Everything had come out about the home for unmarried mothers and giving her baby away. She hadn't realised why Sam had suddenly hugged her close. Even to this day she couldn't quite believe that she'd seen a tear squeeze from the corner of one of Sam's eyes. It was only later that she realised what she'd said. She'd told her about the good friends she'd met there: Allegra and Marcie Brooks, the gutsy little girl from the Isle of Sheppey. She hadn't realised she was talking about Sam's daughter.

Sam had been good to her, paying for dance lessons, kitting her out with her first costumes before she'd started earning well and getting her spots in some of the best nightclubs in town.

But there was always a darker side to Sam Kendal. 'One day it's gonna be payback time.'

Well, here it was. Get under Lenny O'Neill's skin to see what she could find out.

Lenny couldn't possibly know it, but her heart was in her mouth. She'd noted the details of the lighter in double-quick time; show too much interest and he'd be asking her why so bloody nosy.

They talked about his friends and the Irish workers that Paddy brought over from Ireland. 'They'll do anything for old Paddy Rafferty,' he said to her.

It wasn't unknown for Sam to have the truth beaten out of someone but she was pretty mellow at present what with Leo dying and being reunited with Marcie.

'I hear that Tony Brooks is back in London,' said Lenny. 'You know him don't you?'

'My mate's dad.'

Lenny laughed. 'An out-and-out boozer. He's been working for Paddy and didn't even know it.' He laughed at that.

'What you laughing at?' she asked him.

'I'm laughing at Charlie Baxter being dead. Couldn't stand the bloke.'

'Did he really kill Linda Bell?'

''Course he did.'

'But the gun . . . the police aren't going to be that convinced, what with Michael's prints all over it.'

'Ask the blokes who went partying at the Blue Genie, invited there by Michael Jones' father-in-law.'

This was the information she needed. On the whole it hadn't been a bad afternoon.

Sally let Lenny drop her home then dialled Sam Kendal's number.

The woman who was now named Samantha Kendal poured herself a gin from a cut-glass decanter then filled the glass up with tonic water and thought about the last days of her husband's life.

She didn't usually knock her drinks straight back, but she was remembering the doctor's last visit. His prognosis had not been good. Her husband was dying.

She wiped a tear from her eye. Leo Kendal had

had no idea that his wife had been married before. Neither had he known that she had a kid nor how she'd come to London in the first place.

Sometimes in her dreams she again found herself at Victoria train station. She recalled looking around her, wondering what she was doing there. She couldn't remember arriving, why she was there and where she was from.

A man she'd never seen before asked her if she was lost. She couldn't remember answering. All she could recall was him buying her a coffee and saying he would take care of her. He'd done that all right; what was more he remembered her from somewhere though couldn't recall where. Neither could she.

Needing a job, a place to stay and, most of all, a name, she'd gone with him. What did it matter if she found herself in his bed? She'd lain there like a block of wood as he'd done what he wanted.

Disappointed that she'd shown so little enthusiasm, he'd shaken her and told her to lighten up. She hadn't done so.

He'd decided that she was a junky and told her he was putting her out on the streets and she'd have to earn her keep. On seeing that she did nothing to attract the punters he decided to earn from her another way. He dressed her up and took her to a nightclub. That was where she'd brained him with a beer bottle when he'd got violent with her for being so unresponsive. The manager had noticed her and given her a job as a hostess. That was where Leo had met her.

It was the anger that had attracted Leo, that and her beauty. As for the sex, well, he was an old man. If it happened at all it wasn't very often. Besides he liked having a young beauty on his arm.

He'd told her his name: Leo Kendal. 'And what's yours?' he'd asked.

'Samantha. Samantha Kendal.'

He'd laughed at her instantly adopting his name and took it as a sign that he should marry her, so he had.

Sometimes he'd gone on endlessly about his first wife who he'd admitted cheating on but loving all the same. He'd put her up on a pedestal, missed her badly but only spoke about her in any great detail to Sam.

Sam had never once shown any sign that she was jealous of the other woman in his life. Why should she? Leo made her feel safe. He was more of a father to her than a husband and at that time being with someone who made her feel safe was better than anything.

She hadn't needed anyone else. She could not endure a man to approach her with passion. Eventually, she recalled that it was passion that had brought her to London. Alan Taylor, her first husband's friend, had raped her. The memories had taken a long time to return and by then her first husband had remarried, had more children and her own daughter, the little girl she'd sat with beneath an apple tree, had forgotten her or cursed her for abandoning her at such a young age.

Marcie turning up in London had come as something of a surprise and Sam finding out was all thanks to Sally Saunders. It was Sally who had told her about meeting her daughter at a home for unmarried mothers.

Sighing, she closed her eyes and rubbed at her brow. Samantha Kendal was a very different person to Mary Brooks. The old gentle Mary had died long ago when Alan Taylor had raped her. The only part of Mary left was the part that loved and wished to protect her daughter. On one occasion she'd gone back to Sheppey and followed her daughter. To her horror she'd seen Alan Taylor trying to do the same to Marcie as he'd done to her. Luckily, her daughter had pushed him away and ran. He'd fallen back and hit his head. He'd been near dead when she'd found him. She'd made certain of it before she left.

The phone call from Sally interrupted her moment of outright satisfaction, the best she'd felt all day. Sally told her about the ivory-cased lighter. 'It's Michael's cigarette lighter. I remember it. Marcie thought he'd lost it. I'm thinking it was nicked.'

'And he had it before the arrest?'

'It's too big a coincidence to lay it at the door of a member of staff. Rafferty has to have had something to do with it.'

Sam agreed with her.

'Did you want to see Pete?' Sally asked. Pete was Sally's long-term boyfriend – a copper.

Sam nodded thoughtfully. 'I think the time is ripe.'

'Oh, and Tony Brooks had something to do with the gun, though the poor sap didn't realise it,' Sally added.

'Why am I not surprised?' Sam muttered. Tony was part of her past. The only good thing about him as far as she was concerned was that he was the father of her child. Apart from that he was nothing to her.

'So how did the gun get there?' she asked, and Sally told her.

Chapter Thirty-five

The same group of Irish labourers that Tony Brooks had taken back to his son-in-law's club were about to set off for the crummy digs they presently called home, when a big sleek Bentley drew up.

The driver stayed in the car. Mr Rafferty, complete with his entourage of three lesser associates, headed their way. It was noted by the group that two of the big men who accompanied Paddy Rafferty were slipping their hands into some serious-looking knuckledusters.

'Fuck,' said one.

'Christ save us,' said another.

The four of them had come over to England in order to work, save a little to send home to their long-suffering spouses, and have a bloody good time. They didn't care that all four of them shared a room and that the bathroom was shared with another half a dozen occupants of the same seedy tenement. It was the money and the bright lights of London they were here for. They'd never had so much money in their lives and being away from the bosom of their family and the Catholic Church was an added bonus.

The biggest bonus of all was when Paddy Rafferty had employed them to take Tony Brooks on a drinking spree followed by a 'little private drinking party' at the Blue Genie. He'd specifically told them to suggest the Blue Genie to Marcie's father. They hadn't questioned his reasons; they didn't care where they drank.

Tony Brooks had taken little persuading. Drunk as a skunk, he didn't notice one of their number carrying out the other little job Rafferty had asked them to do. One of them had planted the gun, sliding it out of a plastic bag so that their prints wouldn't be on it.

'It's wiped clean,' they'd been told. 'And I want it to stay that way.'

They hadn't had a clue what the outcome was meant to be. Besides, Rafferty had given them ten pounds each to keep their mouths shut.

Unfortunately, Gerry Grogan, the man who had planted the gun, had read about the owner of the Blue Genie being banged up for murder and had put two and two together. He'd mentioned it to one of the others who had in turn mentioned it to one of Rafferty's associates, hence the visit.

There was nobody around on the building site except for the labourers and the enforcers who'd come to visit them.

Rafferty and his men stood like a human wall between the Irish and the gate, which the new arrivals had thought to close behind them.

Paddy Rafferty smiled. He took pleasure from watching the fleeting expressions on the labourers' faces. They knew what was coming and even though they could usually take care of themselves in a pub brawl, they weren't so fly in taking on the professionals. And that's what he and his boys were: professional enforcers through and through.

Paddy tutted disapprovingly and shook his head. He held his gloved hands behind his back as he did it.

'You know, boys, I have a great love for the old country and my countrymen. That's why I go out of my way to help out the likes of you, bringing you over here, setting you up with work and somewhere to stay. Come on, lads, you're rolling in it, but are you grateful?'

The four men exchanged nervous looks; the one who had shouted his mouth off to the wrong person in a crowded pub looked the most nervous of all.

One of the men, named O'Hare, nodded. 'Of course we are, Mr Rafferty. We're very grateful.'

Paddy's eyes were like sharp needles when he narrowed them, turning their full force on the broad-shouldered Irishman. 'That's not what I heard,' said Rafferty, with a cruel sneer. 'I heard that you've been abusing my generous nature by running me down in public – and to think I gave you extra money, cash in hand for you to go out and enjoy yourselves.'

Gerry Grogan gulped. 'I said nothing about the gun, Mr Rafferty. Nothing at all.'

The needle-sharp eyes that had been eyeing all of them now turned on Gerry Grogan. He was a young man with coal black hair and pale blue eyes. Though not as grossly broad as the others, it was easy to see that the beer and the fat-filled food would ultimately make him the same. For now he was relatively lithe and fleet on his feet. In fact he'd been quite an athlete at school, but that was years and a lot of boozing ago.

'So!' said Paddy Rafferty with a swift nod of his chin. 'You said nothing about the gun.'

Grogan nodded. 'I did not.'

He became aware of his friends bunching their fists, preparing themselves for what they all knew was bound to come. Their so-called benefactor, Paddy Rafferty, was going to give them a hammering.

Grogan wanted to run right now, but counselled himself that he didn't need to. His buddies would stand by him.

Paddy gave the order.

Grogan's three buddies pressed around, doing their best against the thudding metal cracking their cheek-bones and their jaws.

The Irish labourers were no match for the violence of the East End villains. Blood was flying everywhere along with bits of tooth, snot and drool.

Judging the fight was going against him, Grogan

took off, slipping and sliding over the uneven ground and building site gravel.

'Run, Gerry! Run!' shouted one of his mates.

They were doing their best to hold off Rafferty's men, but failed.

Gerry Grogan heard the thudding of running feet behind him. He went further into the site, climbing the scaffolding hand over hand although the blood from a cut forehead trickled into his eyes, blinding him to the course he was taking.

He hadn't thought that his pursuers would climb the scaffolding too, but they did.

He ran like the wind along a newly laid concrete floor, climbed more scaffolding onto the next floor where he ran yet again.

Glancing over his shoulder he saw the top of a head appearing at floor level, then a body and knew the others were not far behind.

The blood from his wound continued to blind him but he didn't stop running. Again he climbed to another floor, hoping that they'd get breathless and give up. Men on building sites were naturally agile and used to climbing scaffolding and ladders. He hadn't expected his pursuers to climb so well. Ultimately he came to the obvious conclusion: they too must have been brought over from Ireland as labourers. They too had once worked on these sites – thanks to Mr Paddy Rafferty.

On coming to the end of the building, he discovered there was no more scaffolding. Instead a stairway of ladders had been tied one to the other, zigzagging down between floors, first one way then the other.

With only a second's pause, Gerry was over. Choosing speed over safety, he shunned using the rungs, instead bracing his feet either side of the ladder and sliding swiftly downwards.

Off that ladder he came and slid down the second one sloping in the opposite direction.

On coming to the third he slid to the bottom, undid the ropes tying it in place and watched as it clattered downwards taking planking and pieces of protruding pipe work with it.

The blood clouding his vision, he looked upwards, just about making out three pale faces looking down at him.

He didn't hang around. Terrified out of his wits he had to seek safety. The police station was the obvious place to go, but he'd never trusted the police – not even back in Ireland. There were a few outstanding charges he had no wish to face. Oh no, he had no wish to go back to Ireland but he needed to be safe with people who would not betray him.

The streets were turning dark and the night was turning cold. Keeping to the shadows he made his way through the gloomy streets until he saw the lights of a church. The sign outside declared it to be dedicated to the Sacred Heart. It could only be a Catholic church with a name like that.

Exhausted and blinded by blood, he pushed open one half of the church door and staggered inside.

Chapter Thirty-six

It felt strange driving with Allegra in the car beside her. Tonight they were both having a night off: Marcie from going to the nightclub and Allegra from looking after the children, who were asleep in the back of the car. Carla had offered to look after them. All Marcie had to do was drop them off at Carla's place on the way.

Marcie couldn't help taking furtive glances at her friend who was sitting beside her dressed in a plain black dress. A white headband kept her hair back from her face and a large silver cross hung from her neck.

Marcie couldn't help stating the obvious. 'You already look like a nun.'

Allegra's smile was as enigmatic as that of a plaster saint, almost as though she knew a secret that nobody else was party to. 'I'm beginning to feel like one.'

Marcie was tempted to say that of course she was; she'd had little to do with men since parting with Victor. In fact it was becoming obvious that Allegra was loath to be left alone with male companions, as though not trusting herself or perhaps not trusting them.

'Little angels,' said Allegra, looking over her shoulder at the sleeping children. 'Kiss them good-night for me.'

Marcie watched as Allegra alighted from the car and made her way up the steps into the church. A shaft of amber light fell out into the darkness immediately reminding Marcie that Christmas was coming. After Christmas Allegra would be gone and, although it saddened her, she comforted herself with the knowledge that her friend was truly committed to the religious life. It had occurred to her that the action might be some form of repentance for falling into sin and giving the resultant child away. Whatever, if Allegra felt it was the right thing for her at this moment in time, then so be it.

Inside the church Allegra headed for the confessional. A red curtain covered the door halfway up. The bottom half of the door was made of shiny red mahogany. There wasn't really that much to confess, so little in fact that she was sure that Father Beretti, who was eighty years old if he was a day, had fallen asleep on the other side.

He needed a little prompting to wake him up. 'How many Hail Marys was that, Father?'

She quite often had to shout and more or less declare her own punishment for some very minor sins.

A gentle snore came from the other side of the fretwork screen.

Allegra sighed. It seemed such a shame to wake him. And what for? Because she'd been tempted to contact Victor, purely to ask for his help in fingering the people who had got Michael put in jail? Or being annoyed when she'd broken a fingernail when she'd been scrubbing the bathroom floor? She used to have a daily come in and clean for her. Now she did it herself, considering it fitting practice for the convent life to come.

As she sat there contemplating what to do next, the oak door to the church opened and shut rapidly. Hurrying footsteps tapped over the white marble floor.

Thinking that some other poor soul was in greater torment than she was, Allegra came out from beneath the red velvet curtain.

The person who had come in from the cold fell onto his knees. Blood from a gaping wound dripped onto the floor.

Allegra gasped. 'You poor man!'

His eyes were curtained behind a veil of blood. He tried to open them but could surely see little. 'Sister! Help me!'

His chest was heaving. His hands were dirty and, despite the wintry night, he was soaked in sweat.

She reached out her hands. He grabbed them with as much fervour as a drowning man.

'You're hurting.'

He apologised. 'I'm sorry! I'm sorry! But you have to help me.' He looked terrified.

'Do you wish to confess? The priest is . . .'

She was going to say that the priest was already in situ awaiting the next abject sinner in need of forgiveness. She didn't get the chance.

'I did something terrible and a man was arrested for murder. I did it for money and to impress my pals. Rafferty told me to do it. "Put the gun in the desk drawer," he said, and I did it. And then I got drunk and told a few people and Rafferty got to her. He'll kill me, he will that. Will you help me, sister? Will you help me?'

Allegra's first thought was to contact the police but the moment she mentioned doing that the man, who gave the name Gerry Grogan, went berserk.

'I can't go to the police, woman! I'm wanted meself back in Ireland. No way! No bloody way!'

On flicking the blood from his eyes, he seemed to come to and suspect that he wasn't speaking to a nun at all.

Allegra thought quickly. It was imperative that she heard what he had to say. Michael had been incarcerated unfairly, that much was for sure. Now here, within her grasp and in the Holy Mother Church, was the key to everything that had happened.

'Wait,' she said, glancing swiftly over her shoulder

to see if the din had awoken the old priest. 'Come on. I'll take you into the presbytery.'

Once they were alone together, she got him to sit down. She even found a drop of communion wine to loosen his tongue. It wasn't really meant for such occasions, but she prayed God would forgive her, seeing that it was all in a good cause.

He told her all about the night he and his mates went drinking with Tony Brooks, her best friend's father. He also told her about being paid by Paddy Rafferty to leave the incriminating weapon in the office of Michael Jones, the owner of the Blue Genie nightclub.

'But I don't want to speak to the police,' he repeated urgently.

'But we need to speak to someone,' Allegra countered.

Marcie was signing some papers Jacob had brought in when she received the telephone call from Allegra.

Her heartbeat went into overdrive as she listened to what her friend had to say.

'Oh my God!'

'I've promised him that we won't inform the police,' said Allegra.

'Of course we have to!'

'Marcie! I gave my word.'

'You're not a priest, Allegra,' Marcie snapped angrily.

'No. But I am about to join a devout order.'

'*You* promised him. I didn't.'

'Marcie! Surely there's someone else we can tell? Someone who can deal with Paddy Rafferty?'

Marcie held her breath. She had no wish to compromise Allegra's promise. On the other hand, she desperately wanted her husband home and, on hearing about the note Charlie Baxter had left, had thought the day was imminent. What a wonderful Christmas present that would be! However, there was still the matter of the gun and nobody – nobody at all – thought Baxter a likely suicide case.

'He might not admit to anything unless he feels safe. Then where would we be? Can we protect him, Marcie? Can we?'

Although not entirely willing to protect this man from the law, Marcie held her anger in check. Who else could she contact? She decided there was only one person who might know what to do.

First of all Marcie phoned Carla and asked her if she could come round and look after the kids. Carla asked her if there was a problem. Marcie had no choice but to tell her the truth. Time was of the utmost.

'OK,' said Carla and made a quick telephone call before rushing over.

* * *

Tony Brooks was making love to a very sexy nightclub hostess and exotic dancer named Coco Chocolate. If Desdemona who he lived with when in London was his full-time partner – not counting his wife of course – then Coco was his bit on the side. She reminded him of Ella, a married Jamaican woman whom he'd never quite dismissed from his mind.

He ignored the phone at first, but Coco grabbed it, reaching her long arm over him to take it from its cradle.

'Hello,' she said, in her usual gravely voice.

'I need to speak to my father. It's urgent.'

Coco waved the phone in front of Tony's face. 'One of your kids.'

Tony groaned. He was aching to have Coco under him, bucking like a bronco as he rode her to a top-flight orgasm.

'What's it about?' he groaned, his lips closing around the erect nipple that protruded upwards from Coco's shiny right breast.

She repeated the message to Marcie.

'Tell him it's about a bunch of drunks, a gun and the Blue Genie nightclub.'

Coco did as directed.

Tony immediately stopped what he was doing and grabbed the phone. 'Marcie? Who told you?' He raised himself up onto one hand and eased his body away from his latest hot bed partner.

'Never mind that.'

'Where are you?'

'At home. I'm going to ask Allegra to bring him here.'

Once the call was ended, Tony swung his legs out of bed. For a moment he just sat there, staring into space.

'Something wrong, honey?' asked Coco, a hand draped over his shoulder.

'Yes. Me,' he said, feeling like a heel.

Chapter Thirty-seven

At the beginning of the week Marcie had phoned the hospital to check on her grandmother's progress. The doctors weren't happy that the wound left open following surgery had failed to heal.

'Doctor would like to keep her a little longer and try a different approach,' explained the ward sister. 'I only hope we can keep her here. She keeps telling us that she wants to go home. We can't allow that. Not just yet.'

Marcie decided that she had no option but to accept whatever they advised. Some staff were off sick at the nightclub. There was no one to cover for her at short notice and it pained her deeply. She was desperate to get down and see her grandmother. Garth also concerned her. She wondered how he was coping at home alone.

When she next got down to Sheppey she would also be paying her stepmother a visit. Marcie bristled at the thought of Babs. Boozy, blousy and brash was the best way to describe her. Any woman worth their salt would have been round seeing that Rosa was all right. As far as Marcie knew, her stepmother hadn't been near the hospital.

It was now Friday night and Allegra was due to arrive with Gerry Grogan. The phone rang and she answered it, half expecting Allegra to say that Grogan had chickened out. But it wasn't him. It was Babs, her stepmother, calling with wonderful news.

'Rosa can come home next week. The doctors weren't too keen, but she said she'd walk out if they tried to keep her in. Then they said she could but only if the district nurse called in on a regular basis to change the dressing. I've said she can come and stay at our place, but she's being stubborn. But the doctors have insisted that she can't live alone – and Garth doesn't count,' she added as an afterthought.

Marcie felt as though she'd been hit in the face with a tennis racquet. Babs, offering to accommodate her grandmother? Well, that was certainly a first! Mother-in-law and daughter-in-law had never seen eye to eye.

Marcie fully understood why her grandmother had no wish to move in with Babs. Like Marcie she was perhaps questioning her intentions. The obvious one was that Rosa was not long for this world and the cottage would be sold. Babs would have no trouble spending the money.

'I don't think she's being stubborn,' said Marcie. 'She's lived in that cottage for years. It's her home. It was her and Granddad's home and she feels close to him when she's there.'

Babs sniffed. 'That's as may be, but I still think she'd be best here.'

'It could be for years, although she is ill. Her family are very long lived. You know what they say, a creaking gate can last for years and years.'

She could easily imagine the look on her step-mother's face. Babs had been banking on a short-term arrangement, probably a year at the most. What purgatory that would have been for Rosa – as well as for Babs.

'Anyway, I was going to make arrangements to have her here. There's also Garth to think about.'

'He's not family,' Babs retorted hotly.

'That's not the point. Gran is fond of him.'

Babs sounded deflated when she said goodbye, the fervour with which she'd presented her plan totally absent.

Marcie couldn't help it. She had to check with the hospital to make sure that Babs was telling the truth. It hurt in a way. She felt obligated to have her grandmother stay with her. A little voice in her head told her to be sensible. She had two kids, a husband in prison who she needed to visit in order to keep his spirits up, a nightclub and Michael's other business interests to attend to.

For the first time ever she wished that her husband hadn't been so successful. She wished they could be ordinary, just one big happy family.

But there was no turning the clocks back. What had to be had to be. Besides, Babs mightn't make too bad a job of looking after her grandmother and Rosa might even exert a positive influence over her step-mother's chaotic life.

One thing at a time said that little voice in her head.

She made herself a cup of coffee and sat down to await the arrival of Allegra and the man who had caused her husband to be accused of murder.

Tony Brooks staggered from a pub in Bermondsey feeling too cocky for his own good. He'd done a runner from Babs and everything seemed OK on the manor; nobody had apprehended him. Now he was off back to the crummy flat he shared with Desdemona, but something was troubling him. Grogan. Marcie his daughter was meeting him. Everything would come out and he couldn't cope with that sober. Not at all!

The road he was walking down was lined with red-brick terraced houses. Most of them were in darkness. Some had an upstairs bedroom light on. One or two showed one downstairs too.

Not a sound broke the silence except for the odd mangy cat fighting with its neighbour.

The first inkling he had of trouble was when he heard the sound of a car, which skidded to a halt beside him.

There was no time to protest. Strong hands threw him into the back seat.

Not exactly a stranger to being picked up and bundled into the back of a car, Tony braced himself for whatever might come.

The woman was a complete surprise. At first it didn't sink in. She was gorgeous and expensively dressed. He could smell her perfume, saw the sparkle of exquisite diamonds around her throat and in her ears. She was wearing black satin evening gloves and a severe black dress that did wonders for her figure. Diamonds glinted from a bracelet worn over her right glove, an expensive watch over the other. He knew little about furs but guessed the pale blonde stole she was wearing cost a pretty packet.

At first he wondered who it was – and then it hit him.

'Mary!' Her name caught in his throat. He couldn't believe what he was seeing. Was this really the woman who had deserted him all those years ago?

'I used to be Mary. My name is now Samantha Kendal.'

The words didn't really sink in. His anger was rising. Where the bloody hell had she been? He'd been through hell. He'd almost been arrested for murder.

His anger burst out. 'You bitch! You deserted me.'

'You deserved to be deserted. You're a waster, Tony

Brooks. You were a waster when I was married to you and you're still one now. I'm not going to go into our history at this moment in time. Marcie needs our help. Now! What do you intend doing about it?'

'Never mind about Marcie, Mary, where the fuck . . .?'

She slapped his face. 'Don't call me that. I'm Sam, remember? Sam Kendal!'

Suddenly it sunk in. In the past Tony would have lashed out and caught her a heavy slap across the chops. But the name she had uttered burned deep into his brain. Sam Kendal. He'd heard rumours about her but, of course, never met her. Now he knew why. He also knew that Leo Kendal's missus was someone you didn't mess with.

For her part Sam eyed the man who she'd fallen in love with as a teenager. The best thing he had ever done was fathering Marcie. The worst thing was entrusting his innocent young wife to a man like Alan Taylor. How come grown men got to hero-worshipping other men simply because they threw them a few crumbs from their tables?

Alan had given Tony a job when he was outside prison and was often the cause of Tony ending up in prison.

'You're frightened of Rafferty.'

He shook his head then paused. 'Well, I was.' He looked up at her. 'But what's Marcie going to say? It was my fault for getting drunk, but honestly Ma–' He stopped himself in time from saying her old name. 'Sam,' he corrected. 'I didn't realise what they were up to at the time. I didn't put two and two together.'

Marcie's mother crossed her slim arms. A trio of gold rings gleamed on the third finger of her left hand: wedding ring, engagement ring, eternity ring. None of them had been given to her by him. They were all from Leo Kendal.

'You never told Marcie I was still alive. It's likely she'll never forgive you for that either.'

'I didn't know for sure did I? Does Marcie know?'

Sam nodded. 'Only because Carla told her. Not you.'

Tony clenched his hands together and looked down at the floor. It was coming home to him that he was far from the best of fathers. He'd made a lot of mistakes in his life.

'You always were a selfish bastard.'

He looked up at her when she said that, surprised at the bitterness in her voice and how it affected him.

'I did love you,' he said. 'There was never anybody else when you were around.'

'If I'm meant to feel grateful in any way, forget it.' She heaved her shoulders in a deep sigh. 'No matter. You've come at the right time. It's time for me to be reunited with my child – *and* to sort out this mess.'

'You're going to tell her?'

It amused Marcie's mother to see the alarm on his face. 'Don't worry. You won't get slammed up for bigamy though Christ knows you deserve it. I understand we were divorced on the grounds of desertion – me doing the desertion – not that I knew sod all about it at the time.'

The car came to a halt and Sam gestured to Tony that he should get out. 'You can go.'

He looked her up and down before he did. 'You always did look good in black.'

A sardonic smile momentarily lifted the corners of her lips. 'That's what Leo would say if he could see me now. But he's gone and unfortunately you're still here.'

Chapter Thirty-eight

Paddy Rafferty had the distinct impression that the police were watching him. He'd tried to catch them at it – told his 'boys' to keep a lookout, but they hadn't come up with anything.

'Just yer age, mate,' he'd muttered to himself.

It was then that he'd decided to warn Grogan and Co. to keep their mouths shut. He'd been livid when he'd heard that Gerry Grogan had been overheard in the pub boasting about the night he got into the Blue Genie for free. Irish thicko!

The fact that he was of Irish descent himself didn't come into it. His family had had the good sense to leave the Emerald Isle years ago. Emerald? Shit tip as far as he was concerned.

Everything should have gone relatively smoothly on the building site. He'd made sure to bribe the site foreman to keep the four men he wanted to see on site far later than anyone else.

'I'll find something for them to do,' the foreman had said.

'Ten quid for your trouble,' Rafferty had said to

him. Everyone had a price and most of them were cheap – that was Paddy's opinion.

He'd decided that the four of them were up for a slapping; Grogan for a more severe one than the others, the big-mouthed Mick!

In his opinion everything had gone smoothly enough except that he hadn't expected Grogan to run like a hare on heat. Percy the Perv – so called on account of his sexual inclinations towards anything on four legs – had pursued him for a few streets then finally lost him.

Paddy asked Percy whereabouts he'd lost sight of him.

'Anywhere near a Catholic church?'

Percy thought about it.

Paddy had his doubts that Percy even knew what *any* church looked like. He very much doubted he'd ever been inside one. Percy was from Manchester not Ireland.

However, as it turned out his opinion was proved wrong.

'Yeah. It had big doors and windows.'

It wasn't difficult to work out which church it was. Paddy recalled there being a church dedicated to the Sacred Heart hereabouts.

'Let's go.'

Piling back into the car like a cartload of

overweight packages, they set off for the church, then parked outside to watch and to wait.

'He's got to be in there,' said Paddy.

'Shall we go in?' asked Percy.

Paddy shook his head. 'No. He can't stay in there all night. He's got to come out some time or another.'

Half an hour later a taxi pulled up. A young woman who looked like a novice nun came rushing out. The young man with her was dressed in black. At first glance he looked like a priest. On second glance – too late for them to stop him getting into the car – they recognised Gerry Grogan.

'Get after them! But quietly,' Paddy added. 'We don't want to attract attention.'

'But we want to catch him,' said his driver in a quizzical voice.

Paddy wanted to bash Brian, his driver, around the head. Instead he pointed out his biggest fear. 'Has it occurred to you that he might be heading for the cop shop?'

'Point taken, boss.'

Marcie was on an all-time high. She could barely breathe for excitement. Allegra was bringing Grogan here. All she had to do now was plan how to make the best use of his testimony. She'd thought of ringing the police but her father wouldn't like that. Although he had to bear some guilt in this, he was still her father. She still had affection for him.

He sounded drunk when he eventually phoned her to apologise. 'I did wrong, Marcie, but it wasn't me who put him up to it. That's what you need to find out.'

She agreed to follow his advice.

One after another she allowed cups of coffee to turn cold. How could she drink or eat at a time like this?

A soft knocking at the door preceded Allegra's entrance. 'This is Gerry,' she said.

A man with a face sticky with dried blood came in behind her. The black clothes he was wearing were too small for him and looked as though they had belonged to a priest.

Allegra saw her looking. 'Father Sullivan won't notice they're gone. He was snoring in the confessional when I left.'

The scene she painted was laughable and Marcie would have laughed if the occasion hadn't been so serious.

Gerry Grogan eyed her cautiously, his body from head to toe as stiff and unyielding as a rock. She guessed he was scared. From what she knew of Paddy Rafferty she too would be scared in his position. But deep down his fear was of no concern to her. All that mattered was proving Michael innocent.

'Would you like a drink?'

Her voice sounded far away. She didn't really want to make him a drink. She wanted him to get on with what he had to say.

He shook his head. 'No. Look. I don't want to hang around . . .' He looked over his shoulder at Allegra and the door behind her.

'I want to know about the gun,' Marcie blurted. 'Where did it come from?'

He eyed her warily like a wild animal caught in a car's headlights and about to leap for cover. 'You have to know that I won't testify.'

Marcie controlled her anger and the need to hit out, to strangle the truth out of him. 'Just tell me. Please. Tell me.'

The wary stare of a man afraid of his own shadow was how she would always remember Gerry Grogan.

'Rafferty gave us money to go drinking and to get into conversation with a bloke that worked at this nightclub. He wanted us to persuade the man to take us back to the nightclub; to needle him somehow – call him a chicken if he said he couldn't do it.'

Marcie knew what he was going to say, but she asked the question anyway. 'Who was this man?'

He described her father. 'Tony, he said his name was.'

'And the gun?'

'I slipped it into the desk drawer just like I was told to.'

'And you were paid to do this.'

He nodded. 'Yes. But I can't testify,' he repeated in a sudden rush. 'I have a few problems back in Ireland . . .'

The door through which Gerry Grogan had entered opened. This time it was Pete Henderson, Sally's policeman boyfriend, who entered.

'Did you hear everything?' Marcie asked him, aware that her voice sounded as flat as molten lead.

'Oh yes.'

It was all over so quickly. Grogan was arrested.

'We'll probably do a deal over his offences in Ireland,' he told her. 'We won't force him to go back as long as he co-operates.'

She thanked him.

Once they'd gone, Allegra eyed her worriedly. 'It's your father, isn't it?'

She nodded. 'There are times when I could quite happily kill him.'

Chapter Thirty-nine

Rafferty and his colleagues hadn't expected to be abducted. Keen to deal with Gerry Grogan and the knowledge he possessed, they hadn't noticed the sleek black limousine cruising behind them nor the one behind that.

'Rafferty. The boss wants a word.'

Paddy Rafferty couldn't help the smug smirk. Like anybody who was anybody in London's underworld, he knew that Leo Kendal had snuffed it and fully expected someone else to now be in charge of his outfit. He certainly didn't expect to hear Sam Kendal referred to as the boss even though she'd been her husband's mouthpiece for years. Being an out and out chauvinist, he couldn't handle the fact that she was more than capable of running her husband's crime empire or that she was as hard as any man. And now that good old Leo had died, the poor woman would be easy to deal with. At least, that was what he'd thought.

On getting into the back seat of the car, she smiled at him and he felt strangely privileged. Christ, he thought, but she's one hell of a looker even though she's the wrong side of forty.

For a fleeting moment he wondered what his chances were on the sexual front. The poor bird must have been without attention for years, Leo being so old.

He smiled back at her, certain that he could do her as much good as she could him. He decided to make the first move.

'Perhaps we could . . .'

She moved quickly. He felt a sharp pain in his arm.

'Talk,' she said.

The look on her beautiful face was frightening, either that or it was the effect of the stuff she'd stuck into his vein.

'What the hell . . .?' Raising his arm, he attempted to point to his car and the blokes who worked for him. They were still in his car. His arm felt like a ton weight.

She read his actions. 'They're being taken care of.'

She meant every word of it. Samantha Kendal knew exactly what her own men were doing. Rafferty's men were getting the same kind of treatment as Rafferty – except for the driver that is.

'Drive,' the gunman had said.

Rafferty's driver did exactly that, following behind the car in which his boss was seeing a world slowly spinning out of control. A third car followed behind that.

Streetlights flashed past in a blur of sodium orange and mercurial brightness.

The cars eventually came to a halt on a bombsite that had once been a dockyard warehouse. The whole place was covered in tumbled bricks and rampant weeds. The smell coming from the river was a mix of sewage and effluent from the old gasworks further along. Things rustled in the weeds and scuttled in the shadows: rats mostly and feral cats out to bag their supper.

Paddy Rafferty was doing his best to focus on what was happening, but it wasn't easy. He was being hauled from the car and was only vaguely aware of the alarmed faces of the members of his gang gazing out at him.

His legs being like jelly he fell onto the dusty ground, cutting his knee on a broken brick, breathing dust and feeling scared.

He looked up at Sam Kendal, trying his best to understand what was going on. His mouth was dry as a sandpit, but somehow he managed to speak. 'Why?' he gasped. 'What have I done?'

'The wrong thing,' Sam snarled.

He managed to get to his feet and, crazy as it seemed, staggered off into the darkness towards the river. Nobody bothered to follow.

Sam Kendal watched him staggering away. He wasn't likely to get far. The river mud was thick in that direction and would suck down a man unsteady on his feet.

Stanley, one of her best men, came up behind her. 'So what do you want me to do with them?' He jerked his head at Rafferty's men.

'Get what you can out of them, then go and see the Irishmen.'

Little Annie Brooks was making herself a jam sandwich. She was small for her age but agile and sharp as a weasel; the poor kid had to be. She had a mother who didn't look after her properly and two brothers who were busily embarking on a criminal career. Like their father, they wanted to be regarded as hard men in a world where gaining wealth by dishonest means was almost a virtue.

'Do you want a jam sandwich, Gran?'

Although Rosa couldn't see it, she knew the little girl was beaming at her with pleasure. The child had been left alone or with neighbours while Rosa had been in hospital, her daughter-in-law having a haphazard approach to motherhood. To have someone there with her all day was a luxury she very much enjoyed.

'I would love one,' said Rosa, though she knew that butter and jam would be plastered on the bread with gay abandon and thick as a doorstep.

Rosa was in a wheelchair and she was sharing a

bedroom with her granddaughter. She had no choice; the bathroom was on the same floor. The stairs to the ground floor were a barrier to her mixing properly with her son's second family. She wished fervently that Marcie were here, though more than that she wished she had the use of both her legs.

Blindness she could cope with, but being dependent on someone wheeling her where she wanted to go was hard. Sometimes it seemed as though she still had both her legs. Sometimes it seemed as though the leg they'd amputated was still there, jerking in phantom spasms as the nerves might have done when the flesh was cut and the bone sawed through.

The little girl was her only lifeline to the world downstairs. Babs rarely came up to see her except with a cup of tea and sausage and chips from the shop on the corner. Babs rarely cooked anything. Most of the time it was Annie or one of the boys who brought up her meals or anything she needed.

'Are you there, Gran?'

She recognised Archie's voice and the clomp, clomp, clomp of his feet climbing up the stairs. It sounded as though his brother was not far behind him. They always came home from school at lunchtime and made themselves toast or a sandwich.

'Have you seen Garth?' she asked him.

'Yeah. Fine.'

'You gave him the money for food?'

'Course I did.'

Rosa detected a hesitance in his voice. The cataracts may have taken her sight but in recompense she could hear when a person was lying. Archie was lying.

Her grandmother's heart sank. Without anyone needing to tell her she knew that the boys had probably taken a portion of the money for themselves. Worse still was Garth getting enough money to pay the bills and feed himself?

'See you later, Gran.'

'Boys! I wish to speak to you.'

She heard their feet clumping down the stairs. They hadn't even bothered to say goodbye.

Being confined to a wheelchair was the most frustrating thing that had ever happened to her. Not being able to get around was worse than not being able to see. The two together were unbearable. Nevertheless she had to get out from beneath her daughter-in-law's roof. She wanted to go home. But how?

'Annie?'

'Coming, Gran. I'm bringing your jam sandwich.'

Rosa smiled in the direction of Annie's voice. 'Annie. Where are the boys gone?'

Annie didn't answer. Rosa guessed the worst.

'They haven't gone to school, have they?' It was

a statement not a question. 'Tell me where they've gone.'

'They're at the den.'

Rosa clenched her jaw. Babs had got herself a job as a barmaid. After closing she did a bit of work as an usherette at the matinee at the Roxy. Then it was back behind the bar of an evening. The woman was rarely home; hence the house smelled dirty and the children were being left to fend for themselves. Rosa feared it wouldn't be long before a social worker was nosing around. The district nurse who came round to change her dressings and give her an injection had begun asking questions about the children. Despite her infirmities it was down to her to do something.

'Will you go to them and get them to phone Marcie? Tell her I have decided to go home.'

'OK.'

'Take some pennies from my purse.'

'How many pennies, Gran?'

'Take six plus a shilling.'

She heard Annie count out the coins. 'Is this a shilling, Gran?' Not being too sure, she placed the shilling piece into her grandmother's palm.

Rosa fingered the coin. 'Yes. That is a shilling, Annie.'

The fact that Annie had asked her to confirm the identity of the coin made her smile wistfully. The two boys who she knew for sure were fathered by her son were taking her money. Annie, whose paternity was a little doubtful, was not.

'Now write down this telephone number and give it to the boys. Can you do that?'

The little girl who had not yet started school, said she could. Rosa was grateful, though saddened by the fact that Annie was so at home on the streets. She'd noticed that Annie was left alone to fend for herself and knew that she hung round the pub door to catch a glimpse of her mother.

So far she hadn't confronted Babs about her shortcomings. But things were coming to a head. Something had to be done.

Chapter Forty

The night after Grogan had confessed his sin to Allegra, whom he'd mistaken to be a nun, Tony Brooks was standing on his daughter's doorstep looking guilty as sin.

'I've got to tell you something,' he said haltingly.

'I thought you might.' She wasn't pleased with him and it showed in her voice. She jerked her head, signifying that he could enter.

It satisfied Marcie immensely when he stopped dead in the doorway to the living room.

'Mary!'

He hadn't got over meeting her on the last occasion when he'd been bundled into her car. He still couldn't quite believe who she was now. The girl he'd known was long gone. This woman was something harder and meaner than the innocent he'd known.

Mary eyed him with nothing short of disdain. At the same time she flicked cigarette ash into a tray from a long ebony holder.

'I keep telling you, Tony, I used to be Mary. I'm not now. I'm Sam. Sam Kendal.'

Marcie watched as her father sunk onto the sofa.

It was as though his legs had turned to jelly. They very likely had. Like most of those involved in the soft belly of the underworld, her father had heard of Sam Kendal, the gang boss who had taken over from her husband when he'd become ill. Not being privy to the higher echelons of crime, he'd never guessed that his former wife was that very person and he was having trouble getting used to it.

'I know what you did,' she said to him.

Tony's jaw hung slack. 'I didn't know where you were, Mary . . . sorry, Sam . . . I thought you'd shot off, so I filed for . . .'

'That's not what I mean,' she snapped. 'I'm talking about the drinks party you had with a group of Irishmen. Paddy Rafferty was out to take over the Blue Genie. Didn't it occur to you that they were working for him and ordered to set Michael up for murder?'

Tony stumbled over his words. 'I just thought . . . I mean . . . I'd had a drink . . .'

'That was always your problem,' said Marcie's mother. 'One drink follows another and you roll over and play dead.' She shook her head, her expression full of contempt. 'You're a selfish bastard, Tony Brooks. Always was. Always will be.'

Marcie wanted to intervene and say that her father wasn't entirely selfish. He did love his kids – in an offhand kind of fashion. And she wasn't really prepared to have her mother walk in here and take over after all these years.

She hadn't been so taken aback as she'd expected to be when confronted with her mother on the doorstep that morning. Marcie was still reticent about her mother's reappearance; they hadn't fallen into each other's arms. They hadn't burst out crying. It was as though the years had forged a huge chasm between them.

'Cut out the antagonism. I don't care what old wounds you two want to fight about. All I care about is getting my husband out of prison.'

'That should happen now,' said her mother.

Marcie knew she was right. Grogan, despite his protests, had spilled the beans; so had Paddy Rafferty. Sam Kendal had made sure of that. The girl had been killed by one of Paddy's gang on Paddy's orders.

Fearing he was about to be fitted with cement boots and left for the mud to drag him down and the tide to drown him, Paddy had sung like the proverbial canary. The girl had threatened to go and tell Michael Jones that the business about being pregnant was a lie and that Paddy had put her up to it. Paddy couldn't allow that to happen so he'd decided to kill two birds with one stone – almost literally.

'And after I warned you,' said Sam Kendal.

The police had everything they needed. Now all that Marcie wanted was for everyone to leave so she could make the house nice for when Michael came home and also make sure that everything was running well at the Blue Genie.

The phone rang just when she was about to suggest that they leave. It was one of her stepbrothers.

'Gran said could you come down right away. It's urgent.'

Marcie frowned. 'Shouldn't you be at school?'

'No. I don't like school. Neither does Arnold.'

'I'll tell Dad you're not at school. He'll go mad.'

Archie laughed. 'No he won't. He reckons we're just like he was when he was our age. We've got a nice little business going.'

Marcie frowned, alarm bells ringing in her head. 'Business? What sort of business?' As if I can't guess, she thought to herself.

'A bit of this and a bit of that. We've taken over Bully Price's territory. He's in borstal. Did you know that?'

'And you're going to end up . . .'

The pips sounded. Archie was gone.

She'd reined in her anger towards her father with regard to the gun incident telling herself he'd been duped. But this, to be aware that his sons were playing truant from school and up to no good fired it up again.

'Dad! That was Archie on the phone.'

'How is he?' her father said brightly, supposedly

unaware that anything was wrong even though he'd heard her end of the conversation.

'He's not in school! And from what I hear he's heading for borstal.'

Her father shrugged. 'I wouldn't know . . .'

'No,' Marcie shouted angrily. 'You bloody well wouldn't. Well, if you two old flames will excuse me, I'm off to see my grandmother. She needs my help and I'm giving it to her. In fact she's the only person in my life who deserves my attention!'

Luckily the children were at a very nice private nursery she'd found nearby. After Allegra joined holy orders it was the only thing she could think of doing – either that or sell the Blue Genie as Michael had ordered her to do.

Half in and half out of her coat, she stopped at the door and flung a question at her mother. 'How did you find all this out?'

Her mother got to her feet. 'I have friends in the right places.'

Marcie stood challengingly, one hand poised on her hip, her expression taut and impatient to hear the details.

'Sally got under the skin of one of Rafferty's associates. She was always good at that. You didn't know she used to be on the game?' she asked on seeing her daughter's amazed expression. 'So did I,' she added.

Marcie blinked.

Her mother nodded in the direction of her father.
'He knew.'

Marcie's mouth was dry. She felt uncomfortable
knowing her mother's past, but on the other hand
she couldn't condemn her. Women did what women
had to do. Career choices were minimal now let alone
nearly fifteen years ago.

Her mother didn't give her time to brood. 'Come
on. You'll get to Rosa a lot quicker if you come with
me.' She turned to Tony. 'By the sound of things you
should be going down there too – unless you've got
a previous appointment.'

Marcie caught the sarcasm in her mother's voice
when she addressed her father. Marcie guessed that
she too had once blocked out the truth that her
father liked women just as much as Babs, his second
wife, liked men. In effect he and Babs were made
for each other, she decided.

Sam opened the door. 'Come on. We'd better be
going.'

Chapter Forty-one

It was absolutely true that Barbara Brooks, Tony's second wife, was free and easy with her favours.

But this is true love, she thought, as she lay beside the man from the brewery, who after calling on the pub landlord, would pick Babs up from outside the cinema where she was supposed to be working that day.

Unbeknown to her mother-in-law, she only worked at the cinema three days a week. The other two weekdays were set aside for her meetings with Jim Baldock, the sales rep from the brewery.

He usually booked himself into a room above another pub at the other end of the high street from the one she worked in. It was no big deal to sneak her in when the landlord was supposedly not looking. In reality, he knew exactly what was going on. Boys being boys, they swapped stories of their sexual adventures over the bar after hours and with more than a few pints of ale beneath their belts.

Barbara was just another conquest on Jim Baldock's list, though she didn't see it that way. Barbara was in love. She'd read issue after issue of *True Romance* over the years so thought she knew what it meant.

She hadn't told Jim just yet. She was waiting for him to say it first. So far he'd only told her how much he looked forward to seeing her and how he reckoned their future was told in the stars.

'My mother-in-law sees things like that,' she'd told him with starry-eyed innocence, something she'd said goodbye to many years before.

He'd told her he was a widower, his wife having died some years before from scarlet fever.

'You remind me of her,' he'd said to her. 'Dorothy was the love of my life.'

She'd been sure she'd seen a tear in his eye and was deeply touched. He'd even shown her a photograph.

'And you've got no family?' she'd asked him. 'No kids?'

He'd shaken his head dolefully. 'Only wish I did. That's why I throw myself into my job, love. Don't get me wrong, I love my job and I'm very well paid, but there's nothing like having a curvy woman to cuddle up to at night.'

She told herself that he meant it because she wanted so much to believe it. And it was lovely being with him. He always smelled nice and wore a suit. He also drove a shiny Ford Zephyr. It was green and had tail fins that reminded her of an American Cadillac. She could never get involved with anyone unless they had a car. Even Tony, her old man, had a car.

Deep down Babs was in love with love. It had been this way when she'd first met Tony Brooks. He'd bowled her over with his Maltese looks, the way he flashed his money in the pub and his boasting about the 'heavies' he knew and the crimes he'd committed.

She knew now that his crimes were relatively minor. Besides that, she'd gone off blokes like him. Nowadays she liked businessmen, the sort who came into the bar and chatted her up over a gin and tonic. Now there was only Jim Baldock.

Barbara adored being chatted up and made love to with all the passion of a first encounter. Even better that she wasn't expected to wash the sheets afterwards. That was the joy of getting it together in a rented room paid for by the brewery.

It was on a Wednesday afternoon when the veil of ignorance fell from her face.

They'd just had something of a rushed session. His excuse had been that he had to get back to the brewery offices for an important meeting.

'Sorry about this, darling,' he said to her as he zipped up his flies. He gave her a peck on the cheek.

'Is that all I get?' she asked petulantly.

His smile was tight, impatient. He wanted to go, but he was good at being deceitful. 'What more can I give you?'

Smiling girlishly, she slid her hand down his chest and over the waistband of his trousers.

Judging by the sound he made – something between a sigh and a groan – he liked it a lot.

'Baby, I have to go. I have to get to this meeting.'

Perhaps nothing would have changed if she hadn't handed him his jacket. As she did so, his wallet fell to the floor scattering its contents. She bent down to pick them up at the same time as he did. A photograph of a six-month-old baby had landed on top of that of a smiling woman with dark hair and flashing eyes. There was some writing.

'To my beloved husband, Jimmy. Happy fortieth. Dorothy.'

Dorothy! It even gave the date! Only six months before. He'd told her himself that his fortieth birthday had been back then and how sad he'd been because Dorothy hadn't been around to share it with him.

This photograph declared him a liar!

It was like a stab to the heart. Dorothy's photograph she could cope with. Jim wouldn't be the first one to lie to her about having a wife. The one of his baby made her feel sick inside.

She glared at him. 'You bastard!'

His movements quickened. He was out of there as quickly as he could possibly go.

He didn't even try to pretend that it was all a mistake.

'You took me for a tart,' she shouted.

Shoving everything back into his wallet, he picked up his tie. 'I have to go, darling.'

'You said your wife was dead. You said you didn't have any kids. Is that baby yours?'

He didn't look at her but chose to busy himself throwing his things into his suitcase – even though he was booked in for tonight. Jim Baldock was out of there!

'No. It's my grandson.'

'What?'

Babs was only half dressed, but she didn't care. All her dreams of being in love were in tatters. Jim Baldock had dominated her life during the past six months. She'd neglected her home life because of him. She hadn't even bothered to seriously consider her and Tony getting back together. She'd thought she'd met Prince Charming but found he'd swiftly turned into a frog when the truth was out.

'How many kids have you got?'

'Five.' He regarded her with a smile, holding out his arms in a 'so what' kind of style. 'We had fun, Babs. Now it's time to go our separate ways.'

He looked full of himself, straight and confident with a mop of rust-coloured hair, surprisingly dark lashes and brilliantly blue eyes. A rugged rather than a handsome face had been the first thing that had attracted her; a physical man who knew how to handle himself.

His voice was deep and melodious like an opera singer trying to impress. Even now she thrilled to the sound of it.

'I'll be in touch. I'm sure I can fit in another time somehow – once you've calmed down that is.'

'Another time?'

Babs picked up one of her stilettos and sent it flying through the air. Jim ducked. The second shoe hit him fair and square on the forehead. After that he picked up all that he could and ran.

'Bastard!' shouted Babs running after him. 'You rotten, two-timing . . .'

People in the street outside watched the half-dressed woman chasing the smartly dressed man.

He made his car and drove away before she could get to him.

She stood there attracting the amused glances of passers-by.

'Ought to cover yourself up, a woman of your age.'

The speaker was a much older woman, probably of around the same age as her mother-in-law. Babs blinked when she looked at her. In the past she would have given her a mouthful plus a few well-chosen rude gestures. On this occasion she didn't. She was feeling devastated. The woman she'd thought she was – the good-looking blonde who all the blokes made a beeline for – had gone. The funny thing was she hadn't really seen her passing into history. She'd still thought she was that giggling girl with slim ankles and a twenty-four inch waist. Add another ten inches to that nowadays. When had the time of true romance disappeared? A tear came to her eye at the thought of her best years passing.

'Ma? Ma?'

She looked down into the confused little pixie face of her daughter.

The day before she would have told the child to shove off home and make herself a jam sandwich. There was always jam in the house. Today she didn't. To the child's great surprise, she scooped her up into her arms and hugged her.

'Annie. My lovely little Annie!'

At first Annie was confused. It wasn't often her mother hugged her. On finding she enjoyed the experience she wrapped her thin arms around her mother's neck.

'Can we go and buy some fish and chips?'

'If you like,' said Babs, giving her daughter another hug. 'Is that why you came looking for me?'

Annie shook her head. 'Gran's ran away.'

'What?'

'She's ran away in her wheelchair. Garth came round and she ran away with him.'

'Oh Christ!' She had to get the rest of her clothes. She had to find out where she'd gone before anyone found out about it.

'And Marcie's coming down.'

'Shit!'

'You shouldn't swear.'

'Who said that?'

'Gran.'

'Typical,' Babs muttered and quickened her footsteps.

Chapter Forty-two

The sleek black car belonging to Sam Kendal slid to a stop outside Rosa Brooks' cottage.

'It doesn't look as though anyone's here either,' Sam remarked.

There'd been nobody at home when they'd called round to the council house Babs lived in with the kids, which was very worrying. Marcie had been told that her grandmother was confined to a wheelchair. Basically she was now feeling guilty that she hadn't been there to collect her grandmother from the hospital. Her life at present was just too pressurised and too complicated.

Marcie grunted a remark to her mother and got out. Her parents, estranged but having made a lasting impression on her life, mostly by their absence, followed suit. They'd spoken little on the way down and Sam had insisted that Tony travel in the front seat beside the driver.

'I would like my daughter to myself for a while. You've had the pleasure of her company for years. I have not.' She could have added thanks to your friend Alan Taylor who you regarded as your best friend, but she did not. The accusation stayed unspoken.

Marcie's father was like a man struck dumb. He could not believe that his ex-wife was the boss of a famed crime empire. He kept glancing at her, a mixture of fear and marvel in his eyes. Women like her were a race apart, though if he really thought about it he would understand that he was drawn to strong women. OK, he wanted to control them, but in that was the fun. It was one hundred per cent certain that the Mary Brooks as was would never be under his thumb again. Sam Kendal terrified him.

Marcie's mother talked to her about the children and how she'd watched Marcie cross the road from her place above the sewing room to the shop opposite, holding Joanna in her arms.

'If there is anything those children should ever want, you have only to say.'

Marcie thanked her but told her Michael would always provide for them.

'Perhaps a private education,' Sam added. 'But anyway, I'd like to help you too. I know you're keen on fashion. I was at your age. I liked making my own clothes. I think you do too. If you want to open a proper shop or something, I've got the money and I'm willing to back you – you already know that.'

Marcie smiled. It was coming home to her now that her mother had been keeping an eye on her for some time, once she'd regained her memory. She couldn't help wondering at the contrast between the woman who had been named Mary Brooks and the woman known as Sam Kendal.

Her mother was endeavouring to make up for lost time. Marcie could understand and appreciate that. The only thing that jarred was her mother's involvement with the underworld. Marcie was troubled by it. OK, her husband owned a nightclub and his father was involved in crime, but she didn't want to be and Michael played things straight.

Owning a nightclub was not without its hazards, but being on the periphery of crime was one thing. Despite being a woman, her mother was a feared and respected head of a criminal empire. Even the Camilleris wouldn't dare cross her.

Her relationship with her mother was something she would have to deal with in time. For the moment her prime consideration was getting her husband out of prison. Jacob had assured her that it was all under control. Her mother had told her not to worry. Michael was about to come home.

The well-being of her grandmother was also worrying her. The woman who had brought her up should have been living in comfort with Babs. Babs had assured her it would be so when she'd said she couldn't get down there just yet.

Unable to do much else at the time, Marcie had convinced herself that Babs meant what she said. In hindsight she really should have known better.

The truth had been self-evident; the house was a mess and the room her grandmother shared with Annie was even worse. On checking the kitchen, Marcie had found little food in the larder besides a jar of jam and a loaf of bread. Dirty dishes had been left in the sink.

Marcie let herself in to the cosy cottage she'd shared with her grandmother and her father – when he wasn't in prison. She called out for Garth. There was no response.

She stood at the entrance to the kitchen taking in all the old familiar sights. A fire had been lit and the room was clean and tidy. Paper chains had been stuck together and hung around the place in readiness for Christmas.

Marcie smiled at the simplicity of the design; the ends attached to the light in the middle of the room and into each of the four corners.

She took a deep breath and breathed in the scent of lavender and beeswax.

'Polish,' said her mother who had come in behind her. 'I thought you said she'd been in hospital for weeks.'

'Garth did it,' said Marcie.

She opened the kitchen larder. It revealed a tin of beans, a tin of corned beef and the basics like sugar, tea, bread, milk and butter.

It was likely that Garth had gone shopping. There was nothing to do but sit down and wait.

There was the sound of water rushing from the kitchen tap.

'A cup of tea would be just the ticket,' said Tony, rubbing his hands.

His comment was met with total disdain from his ex-wife. 'Get the cups out. They're over there.'

In ordinary circumstances Marcie would have grinned to see her father meekly obeying his ex-wife. But she couldn't stop worrying about her grandmother and Garth.

'I'll go and ask the neighbours if they've seen Garth.'

The cold air pinched at her face. She'd left her coat inside so shivered and wrapped her arms around herself.

She got as far as the gate and looked up and down the road. What she saw made her catch her breath. 'Gran!'

Her grandmother was in her wheelchair being pushed along the road, a bundle of things wrapped in a cardigan sat on her lap. Garth was pushing the wheelchair. He waved. So did the little girl skipping along beside the wheelchair muffled up in a duffle coat, a bobble hat and a thick scarf that hid half her face.

'Garth! Annie!'

On seeing her half-sister, Annie tried to hurry. The duffle coat was too big for her, impeding her quickened steps. Marcie guessed it belonged to one of the boys but wasn't intending to ask questions. She was feeling relieved but also in need of hearing an explanation.

'Granny escaped,' Annie said excitedly.

'Marcie!'

Rosa Brooks sounded all in. She also looked tiny in the iron-framed chair.

'Annie found Garth waiting outside,' Rosa explained.

Marcie felt a lump come to her throat.

'Ma!' On hearing Marcie's shout, her father had come out to see what all the fuss was about. He ran to his mother, bending low over her so he could see into her face. 'What you doing here, Ma?'

'I want to go inside.'

'It's cold,' Marcie said to her father. 'Can you manage, Garth?'

Her father gave Garth a hand whilst Marcie caught hold of Annie's cold fingers.

As they entered the kitchen, Sam looked startled to see her old mother-in-law being wheeled in. No one had mentioned that she was there.

Rosa was fussed over. She explained how Garth had got her down the stairs all by himself.

'I couldn't stay there any longer.'

'You should have waited until I got here,' said Marcie. 'Isn't that why you phoned me?'

'No. It's about the boys.' She went on to explain that they were stealing from her purse.

'They're doing more than that,' said Marcie whilst throwing her father an accusing glance. 'Archie told me himself that he'd taken over from Bully Price and I know for a fact that he was a hood. He's not been going to school either.'

Tony Brooks snorted indignantly. 'I'll give him a right belting when I see him!'

'Would you, Dad?'

'Of course I would.'

'According to our Archie you likened him to how you were at that age and he didn't think you'd disapprove at all.'

'I can assure you . . .'

Sam Kendal had filled the cups standing on the table with tea. She'd done it silently.

Rosa Brooks was sitting just as quietly and, although her eyes were unseeing she looked like a dog that's sniffing the air, aware that something was there beyond her vision.

'Who's here?' she asked. Her voice was querulous as though afraid she had landed in a dream or even a nightmare.

Everyone looked at Sam Kendal.

'The lady who used to sit under the apple tree.'

It was Garth who spoke.

Marcie knelt beside her grandmother's chair. 'It's

my mother. She found me. She also found the real murderer of that girl that Michael was blamed for.' There was pleading in her voice. She didn't want her mother ordered from the house, but was certain her grandmother would do that.

'What are you doing here?' Rosa's misty eyes stayed focused on the woman who used to be her son's wife.

'I've come to wrong some rights.'

'It isn't the first time.'

Marcie was taken aback by what her grandmother was insinuating – that her mother had been back this way before.

Sam Kendal looked at her daughter. 'She's quite right. I've watched you a few times.' Sam smiled. 'You're my girl. Always will be.' Suddenly she seemed to become very self-conscious. 'Look. You have some time with Rosa here. I'll take this little girl home.'

'Shall I come?' Tony Brooks looked very hopeful.

'No.' Sam looked down at Annie. 'How about you introduce me to your brothers on the way?'

Annie nodded. 'I'll take you to their den.'

Marcie heard everything about her grandmother's ordeal of living with Babs. She held her hand as Rosa Brooks recounted how it had felt and was surprised to feel how birdlike her hands had become and how transparent her skin.

Her father stood by looking pensive as he heard all this. Suddenly he was also looking old.

'I should have been here,' he said softly.

Rosa shook her head. 'No. You should have been with your wife and children.'

He nodded then stopped abruptly as though a most terrible realisation had exploded in his mind. 'I've got to go. Be back in a mo.'

'I've made stew,' said Garth, after Tony had left.

Whatever it was smelled good.

After they'd eaten, Marcie, with Garth's help, got her grandmother to bed.

'I am so glad to be home,' whispered her grandmother as she snuggled down in her bed below a heavy satin eiderdown.

Marcie stroked her grandmother's head. 'Have a good sleep. You'll feel better in the morning.'

Her grandmother's smile was weak and wistful. For a moment she was certain that the jet-black eyes were seeing her as clearly as they'd used to. The moment passed.

'I will be very much better in the morning,' said her grandmother. 'Tomorrow I will be young again.'

Marcie heard Garth opening the front door to someone, then heavy footsteps walking along the passageway.

'Marcie! Marcie!'

Marcie gasped at the sound of Michael's voice.

'Now you will be young again too,' said her grandmother.

It was a strange comment to make but Marcie didn't ask her grandmother what she meant by it. She ran into her husband's waiting arms.

For her part Rosa Brooks was feeling incredibly happy. Her face was glowing and she didn't mind at all when Marcie dashed off, flying into Michael's arms, her face streaked with tears.

Rosa was happy because Cyril was here. Nobody else could see him of course, only her and he was here for her.

'You're wearing your white suit,' she said to him.

Beaming at her, again the young man she'd fallen in love with, he swept the familiar panama off his head and offered her his hand.

She took it, of course, whilst noticing that all her age spots, all her wrinkles were no more.

Her husband had come to take her home and home, she decided, was wherever he was, even in the hereafter.

Chapter Forty-three

The day had started grey and although rain had been forecast on the Home Service, it hadn't happened. In fact a weak sun was trying to force its way through the blanket of grey.

As though she'd ordered it, thought Marcie.

According to the doctors it was as though Rosa had switched herself off of her own accord.

'She would have lived,' reported the doctor.

'Without her sight and with one leg,' Marcie pointed out. She'd shaken her head. 'No. She'd decided the time was right.'

The words she'd spoken had taken her unawares. It was almost as though someone – most likely her grandmother – had whispered them in her ear. 'Don't worry about me. I'm joining Cyril on the other side.'

Before Michael had come marching down the garden path, her grandmother had told her how she'd met Marcie's grandfather, how they'd drifted, how they'd got back together again.

'This morning I am young again,' she'd said to Marcie.

Marcie hadn't understood what she'd meant, but

she did now. Her grandparents had been reunited after the Great War of 1914–18 and they were reunited now.

Marcie hoped they looked exactly as they had done then; in fact she was sure they did.

Christmas lights were glowing from windows and cheeks were pink in the icy air.

'Sad her dying just before Christmas,' someone said to her.

She shook her head. 'I don't think so.' Her grandmother having a funeral before Christmas was not a sad affair.

She exchanged a secretive smile with her husband. 'A death just before a birth.'

Everyone presumed she meant Christmas, but Michael knew and Marcie hoped, she just hoped, that the spirit of her grandmother would become the spirit of her daughter – the one growing in her womb.

People offered their condolences to both her and her father. She accepted them gracefully both for him and for herself. The hard man, who made a point of telling people that he rubbed shoulders with some of gangland's most noted felons, was crying like a baby, his shoulders shaking and tears streaming down his face.

Marcie looked at him clear eyed. I should be crying, she thought to herself, but I'm not.

It was a strange feeling; she would miss her grandmother very much indeed and yet she was not sad.

In fact she was glad for her. For some odd reason the words of Sydney Carton, the lawyer in Charles Dickens' A *Tale of Two Cities* kept running through her head; about him going to 'a far, far greater rest . . . than I have ever known'. She recalled her grandmother reading to her from Dickens when she was a child. Over time she'd forgotten that. How strange that she remembered now.

'Are you all right?' Michael's voice was gentle.

'I'm fine, Michael.'

He offered her his arm. She hugged it, glad of the warmth she felt through the fabric of his overcoat.

It was so good to have him back, so good to know that he'd never been unfaithful to her.

'I knew you'd be here. Home is where you run to when times are hard.'

Once he was safely home, she'd mentioned David Morgan to him, told him how he'd propositioned her, how she didn't turn up and that she'd been surprised at never seeing him again at the prison.

'Apparently he had an accident. He was on sick leave for a long time.'

If Michael knew any more than that, he didn't let on and she wouldn't press the point. They had a future to look forward to and that was all that mattered.

The church was barely a quarter full, but seeing as it held a great many people it didn't seem so bad.

Marcie felt her eyes being drawn upwards to the roseate window. At the very moment she looked at it a beam of light shone through each of its petal like portions, gleaming onto the coffin like a set of heavenly stairs.

Dust motes caught by sunlight danced like miniature stars falling onto the Christmas tree, dark green and multi-coloured to one side.

Marcie smiled. It was the same vision she'd seen in her dream after the one on the bridge, the man in the white suit and the glow on a young girl's cheeks. Her grandparents were together and young again.

Following the service the family divided themselves between two black limousines, following the hearse taking Rosa Brooks to her final resting place beside her late husband.

'I don't know what I'm going to do without her,' wailed Marcie's father whilst tightly grasping her hand.

In return Marcie patted his hand and murmured soothing words, the sort of words she might use to her children. Strangely enough she felt as though she were the parent and her father the child. Even Babs, dry-eyed beneath a candyfloss hairstyle, looked irritated by the way he was carrying on.

Not to be outdone, Babs gripped her husband's free hand, but only after giving Archie a clip around the ear.

Archie had asked his dad out loud when the cottage in Endeavour Terrace would be sold and how much would they get for it. And could he have a bike.

Strangely enough, Marcie was not offended by the question; neither was she offended that Babs was after the money. It was a certainty that Mrs Barbara Brooks would be reconciled to her husband at least until she'd spent some of what she considered her fair share of the money.

The sun was warm on Marcie's back as her grand-mother's coffin was lowered into the grave. As the first clod of earth fell on the coffin, she became aware that she hadn't heard a word the priest had said. And she still wasn't snivelling like her stepmother was pretending to do.

Archie, Arnold and her father were snivelling for real, blowing their noses into man-size handkerchiefs.

She sensed Michael eyeing her with a questioning look and realised he wanted some kind of explanation.

Marcie smiled. 'She doesn't want me to mourn. She wants me to get on with what has to be done. I have to care about everyone now just as she used to.'

He nodded as though he understood. The truth was of course that he couldn't understand. The bond that tied Marcie to her grandmother was very special. Marcie knew that now. She knew she'd inherited her gift and that, as far as she was concerned, was far more precious than money.

Epilogue

Marcie's third child, Rosa, was born very appropriately on a rosy morning.

From the moment her daughter blinked open her knowing blue eyes, Marcie had the feeling that her child had been here before.

Their lives had changed so much in a very short time. Following his arrest for murder, Michael lost his obsession to outdo his half-brother and prove something to his father. As a result of realising he had nothing to prove, he sold the nightclub, though kept his commercial properties.

The house in suburbia was swapped for one on the Isle of Sheppey. Big, square and white, it was surrounded by green fields and close to the sea and a long shingle beach. London was a train journey away. Michael also bought some shops in Sheerness, one of which Marcie turned into her own boutique with a sewing room above. Her dream had come true – if only in a small way, but who knows where it might go. The children could come to work with her when necessary and she had a ready trade. The girls of Sheerness were ready for what she had to offer and her fame was surely but slowly spreading.

They now had the best of both worlds. Whatever came they would cope with together. They would be a proper family.

Both Marcie and her mother realised that there were lots of bridges to build between them. It was never going to be easy to eradicate years of being apart and they were still learning about each other.

Sam Kendal – as Marcie's mother insisted on being called – was the kind of woman who could compartmentalise her life as Marcie never could. She could not forgo her London life whereas Marcie and Michael had found it easy to do. To both of them their family would always be everything.

Marcie's father's life had also changed after Babs had run off with a dog-food salesman. Desdemona had moved in to Rosa's old cottage with Tony and the kids. It was a little crowded but the atmosphere was good, the kids were being looked after. Tony Brooks would never be the ideal husband but with Desdemona he was better than he had been.

The boys also were sorted out. Archie had the promise of an apprenticeship in a local garage when he finished school. At present he was helping out there weekends and enjoying it. Arnold had taken a shine to the new woman in his father's life and enjoyed his father being there. Both boys were on a warning not to go back to the street gang they'd once led and neither were likely to, especially once they'd realised one of their number had robbed their own grandmother, Rosa Brooks.

Marcie was in no doubt that things in her family would not always run smoothly.

'They're far from perfect,' she said to Michael at twilight, as they sat and watched the sun go down. 'But I can't help loving them.'

He regarded her sidelong, a peculiar and particularly beautiful smile on his face. 'You love them despite their faults. That's how people should be loved.'

She realised he was right.

They linked hands, their love unspoken and their gaze fixed on their eldest two children.

Joanna was digging in a flowerbed with her little brother sat on a blanket watching her.

Rosa was asleep in her pram and being pushed around the garden by Garth, who lived in what had been an old stable. Michael had converted it for his use. Garth had festooned the walls with his paintings. To him it was sheer bliss.

Marcie and Michael caught snatches of Garth talking to the baby as he pushed the pram. He talked to her all the time as he walked, even though she was sound asleep. Anyone close by would be surprised at the familiar manner in which he spoke to her, almost as though he had known her before, a lifetime ago.

Some might think him mad, but Marcie didn't. Garth was looking after Rosa just as Rosa Brooks had once looked after him. He was telling her he hadn't forgotten her kindness.